Banished by Ancient wisdom, freed by modern spite, they come to make a living world wither....

When a mysterious substance starts jamming communications and a string of catastrophes brings the world to the brink, many thought it could get no worse. Some believed that God could not let people endure a fate so cruel, so terrifying.

They were all wrong. Because what's coming at Mankind from a brightening star in the constellation Aries is not his God, it's the opposite. Worse, these are demons from an ancient civilization known only to a select few. And one of those few has summoned them with a blood sacrifice.

Somehow, amid a collapsing society, three men and a woman must aim past the fuzz of confusion to strike at the heart of the very things that are feeding off the terror of a planet in order to grow stronger.

...But can they do it before the first demon lands to reclaim its Dread Empire on Earth?

COVENANT OF ARIES

JOHNNY S. GEDDES

COPYRIGHT 2012 DOUBLE BAY BOOKS

PRINTING HISTORY

FIRST DOUBLE BAY EDITION PUBLISHED APRIL 2012

WWW.DOUBLEBAY.CO.UK

9   8   7   6   5   4   3   2   1

FOR WAYNE TEFS, FOR HELPING TO KEEP MY GOALS IN FOCUS IN MY YOUTH.

ISBN: 978-0-578-10561-1

WWW.JOHNNYSGEDDES.COM

LIBER FATI

DURING THE ROMAN OCCUPATION OF THE NEAR EAST AND THE LEVANT TWO THOUSAND YEARS AGO, MANY GROUPS WERE OPPRESSED. WHEREVER PEOPLE COULD NOT SHAKE THEMSELVES FREE OF ROME'S YOKE, THEY HOPED THAT THEIR GOD OR GODS WOULD FREE THEM.

ONE GROUP TOOK THIS YEARNING FOR RELEASE FURTHER. REVOLTS AND UPRISINGS WERE FAILING – PERHAPS THINGS WOULD CHANGE IF THEY SUMMONED THEIR ANCIENT GODS TO AID IN VANQUISHING THE INVADER.

WHEREVER THEY FOUND THEM IN THESE LANDS, THE ROMAN ARMY HAD ORDERS TO CAPTURE AND DESTROY SUCH PRACTITIONERS OF BLACK MAGIC AND THEIR SPELLS. MANY ATTEMPTS SUCCEEDED.

THE COMPENDIUM OF ARCANE KNOWLEDGE AND INCANTATIONS OF SUMMONING WAS KEPT IN NUMEROUS FORMATS, ALTHOUGH TODAY NO COPIES OF THE 'LIBER FATI' EXIST. LIBER FATI MEANS 'THE BOOK OF DOOM'.

IT WAS APTLY NAMED....

FOREWORD

I'll always have a soft spot for this, my second novel and my third book. It's got quite a bit of history behind it, even if it's about the future... well, a few weeks after the week after next. Let's put it that way.

Once upon a time, there was a writer – yes, a younger version of myself – who'd been brewing up stories in his barrel for much of his quarter of a century of life. Just on the brink of seeing his first book released and having been making some notes for his next, he attended a writers' and artists' weekend in the wonderfully cozy Donegal countryside, in the village of Dunfanaghy. The Arnolds Hotel still runs those weekends, I think, and I was lucky to have landed in such a place to get my sophomore novel off to the start it had.

The course went very well and then, being 25 and avid for some hard writing, I did what I suppose other young writers might try – rent a cottage there and stay on for a week or two more to make a proper start on what felt like a great idea. It was November – out of season and then some! – and it was next to freezing, but I managed to keep warm. I had no car at the time. Firewood had to be moved over bicycle handlebars. The locals thought I was crazy, but we got on very well indeed and they were pillars of support.

This was the milieu into which the genesis of what would become 'The Aries Covenant' became a reality. I went back the next year and took another two weeks – some writing, mostly doing notes and research.

By 2001, I had got a first draft together. By then, I was doing my Masters Degree, becoming increasingly involved in short story writing in the sparse patches of spare time I could snatch. The short stories would eventually take over, the best of them turning up in *Séances with the Living*. Clare, my girlfriend at the time proofread 'Aries', as did her mother. They liked it... yet, I didn't feel it was quite ready somehow at the time.

Time marched on. Short stories, work, writing for magazines and E-zines and putting what I'd learnt in journalism school and in my MA in Biography to good use took over my writing regimen.

I went back to 'Aries' and, finally, it clicked. It's a novel with a big scope. It deals with an End of the World scenario that's happening on a much faster scale than the financial torture that's dragging on as I write this.

I'd been a bit unlucky when I'd gone back to look at it around 2006. I ended up being taken with another idea and got cracking with the first draft of that… that one's another story, though, but it will be coming out soon.

I've used the first-person pronoun quite a bit already. There are others whom I'd like to thank or re-thank here. Dr. Wayne Tefs, who helped me stay on track and feel hungry enough to graduate from high school whilst believing in my dream is the principal one. The Greenhalgh family certainly deserve a great deal of credit for their tireless work in helping this work in an earlier version. There are others, too, who have toiled since in that department. You know who you are.

The story you are about to have unfolded before you is about learning lessons. The most obvious one might be not to mess around with the occult and not to attack parts of a country that contain archaeological treasures. Yet, it runs deeper than that. The people in this book are about to learn lessons about themselves… and it will be the lesson of their lives.

In that respect, it's a book about revelations. I hope you enjoy whichever ones that might befall you as you read *Covenant of Aries*.

JOHNNY S. GEDDES,
NOVEMBER 2011

-1-
<u>June 28th</u>

Jurgen buried his face in the pillow and tried to stop thinking. Very soon the smell of breath-warmed, two-star hotel linen became unbearable.

'This is it. Really it now,' he assured his shadow, pushing himself up. 'No more bullshit. Good. Good.'

The cold air was beginning to get to him. It hit him full force when he went over to the window and knocked the air conditioner off.

Outside, the neon of the city skyline was more pronounced now, more angry.

What did *anybody* but he understand about anger? Jurgen closed his eyes and breathed in hard. The smell of pine needles had died off a little from earlier on. Only the naked night was there with its garbage-like aroma.

He shuddered. The shudder came again when he dared to want a final beer - something strong... a last screw-it-let-the-good-times-roll feeling before the next step.

No. No alcohol. It would diminish the effect of the ritual. His sacrifice had to be done with full intent - no Dutch courage. His eyes fell to the Tel Aviv streetscape below and stroked the crossed legs of a tourist girl at the café by his hotel. No...he couldn't masturbate, either. He'd have to go on to the next stage of things without anything spent from himself.

He touched the knife hilt in his pocket. As if charged by the contact, a hundred thoughts crackled through his mind. *Wait. No. Died? Death? No. No! Don't think of it that way. This won't be an end; it'll be the beginning of the truth coming out. Caterpillar-to-butterfly, not being-to-unbeing. You've been through this before, damn it; don't fuck me over now.*

It's all their fault, anyway. Yes - them. They're all damned, and 'The Damned will be made to account' is what they say in their stupid, church slave novel-manual. You'll show them. What do they know? Bet those professors all bought their dumb degrees, the crooks!

To Hell with the system that doesn't persecute them for it, too. All guilty: all of them. One or more of them knew your thesis dealt with a valid subject – the cowards had just covered it up!

Jurgen turned, looked at the case rack by the television stand where he'd laid out the pages of his thesis. The silent light from the television screen danced over the four stacks of printout leaves, making the top sheets look gaudy, worthless.

No respect.

Professor Arnott had shown no respect as well and he had had to pay - pay Big Time. His office had burned to a crisp nicely that night. Arnott would not be reading many papers for a while.

Jurgen grinned at the memory, at the contempt he'd shown before coming here with his four friends. No-one had been injured but the damage was immense. Jurgen hadn't seen anything on the news since leaving North Dakota – not at Minneapolis International nor at JFK but...

But there had been no fatalities, or even injuries. Even so, Jurgen had finished with North Dakota College and its overhyped archaeology program. And North Dakota would finish him if it or any of its sister states got him. A mature student should know better, they'd say before the book was thrown at him.

Knowing what he had done was an atrocity excited him even now. Atrocity was good; it would help pave the way.

Jurgen's eyes fixed on the topmost page of the stack furthest from him. He could read the word 'crackpotism' quite clearly at that distance. There was a lot of red ballpoint ink on that page. The dominant marks on the other three were 'lazy writing', 'research showing too much here' and 'we'd discussed this - *wrong again*'.

'Ruin my life, would you?' Jurgen smirked.

The smirk broadened when he replayed the memory of setting the blaze… the cans of gasoline sloshing about as he shook and sprayed.

Jurgen suddenly caught himself. 'Stop reveling,' he whispered. 'You might end up not going through with doing *this*. Get to the point of no return now - *do* something!'

The remote control of the hotel television was short and weighty. Jurgen smiled even harder as he flung it at the screen, transforming Lisa Simpson's pointy yellow head into same-sized shards of dark gray and sparks.

He drew the curtains and walked around the end of his bed. Ahead, the bathroom light hummed over everything that he had laid out on top of the toilet seat and the Formica counter above the sink.

Jurgen closed the door behind him, sniffing hard at the air after sensing something.

Burning. He'd seen the smoke source start moving from the TV to the floor back there. The smell of singed carpet fibers was nice but he didn't want to dwell on it.

His mind's voice was whirling and jabbing at him now. *If there's a fire, there's a fire. It'll make sure, at least. And it'll show the Mother of Hell you cared to impress. You'll be more welcome then.*

Jurgen kept his hand on the doorknob, thinking.

A good excuse for a last cigarette.

But this isn't an execution.

Have one anyway.

What if you're still around when the flames hit?

Chickenshit. Anyhow, you won't be. With these fibers, you'll be asphyxiated long before the yellow tongues come to sting your flesh.

Jurgen reopened the bathroom door and moved for the chair by the dresser where he'd slung his brown jeans.

The sparks from the smashed television had all died out now. He frowned, reaching into the pockets until he found the now shapeless carton of cigarettes.

Four stubby little Turkish ones were left. *Smoke them all at once.* He made a diamond formation with the butt ends and stuck them into the middle of his lips. His lighter was a two-week old disposable – it had to be close to full. It would do for this and the other task he was planning. He reached round to get his ponytail band.

Wait. His eyes shot up, scanning the ceiling for a smoke detector or sprinklers.

A straight run of plaster: the anti-fire stuff must only be in the corridors outside, although there did seem to be a vandalized-looking stump of what might have been a sprinkler above the air conditioner. It made sense for a dump like this hotel. *In the Mediterranean, everybody smokes - they expect it of guests here.*

But this is Israel. Aren't they strict about fire and things here?

Shaking, Jurgen lit his combo cigarette, choking on the first drag as he moved back into the bathroom to get the larger white towel nice and damp.

There was hardly any gap at the bottom of the door *to* block. He flicked off the light switch for the bedroom and stood back to look for yellow light lines at the other edges of the door.

Absolutely none were visible - almost like it was gasket sealed. That should give him an extra few minutes. He dropped the towel and kicked it up against the bottom, just to make sure.

Before he shut himself again in the bathroom, Jurgen checked the bedroom suite one last time from the doorway.

Curtains will burn first. They'll see that from the outside.

Then start the fire near the door.

He doubled up his ponytail band and slid it over the lighter's gas button. As he bent his neck, a huge strand of hair came round and fell in front of his combo cigarette's quadruple cherries. The stench made him smile but not too hard. His hair was greasy enough to be inflammable.

No. Immolation was for monks and martyrs; he was a High *Priest*.

He eased the flaming lighter sideways by the wall then closed the bathroom door, smiling. 'Accidents will happen,' he chuckled.

The bathroom light felt very warm now. No matter. Its heat would soon be assimilated.

After donning the decorated robe he'd modified from a pilfered bathrobe, Jurgen picked up the tumbler and slurped hard on the milky fluid.

The thirty-six sleeping tablets he'd pulverized earlier hadn't all been able to dissolve. His throat clenched and nipped in fiery stabs. He wheezed then refilled his glass from the cold tap, glugging it down until the burning became acceptable to his psychotic tastes.

Better hurry.

Jurgen flipped open the glass shower door and tossed a conditioner sachet so it covered the plughole halfway, just enough to create a mini-bath effect that could drain slowly.

He wrung the dial tap most of the way round. *No. No way: too hot. The steam'll make you pass out too quickly. You just want background noise - a constant to keep you undistracted.*

He placed the crown on his head and picked up the copper dagger from the top of the covered toilet seat.

He was proud of the dagger - he'd made it himself in his garage - but the crown was pure Chickburger City kiddy meal accompaniment.

When he got the temperature right, Jurgen lifted the dreaded pagan text from the Formica surface and smiled to himself in the mirror.

A few of the knife cuts he was making in his torso were oozing out heavy ruby threads. A couple spattered heavily onto his foot as he worked the book between some grooves on the soap dish and closed the shower door.

There was a humming sound in his ears that was too heavy to be from his dying mind.

When Jurgen reopened his eyes, there was a black oval churning in the space between his face and the water pipes.

A surge of joy rushed through him. He'd been right about the old gods, his Masters, all the time!

He could just make out some faces in the oval. He recognized one right away. Barry Nash, his room-mate from college.

The Masters were telling him about Nash now.

So Nash was to be the tool. The tool for *what*, though?

And these others…Four men and a woman. Why were his Masters showing him *them?*

A flash welled up from the lower part of the oval and, in a flash, he understood. *So Nash could be used as a weapon against one of them. Or more?*

Jurgen smiled weakly and leaned back against the tiles, satisfied now. His effort was not in vain. His Masters were watching…they had *seen.*

They were telling him to wait a moment before he started the ritual chants. The swirling oval was showing him an image overlying the faces now… A plane above the desert floor – a warplane. In some hazy corner of his brain, he remembered the war that had spilled over that nation's border last year and was raging at full swing now.

Of course! His Masters had once been venerated there in temples… venerated with sacrifices! Excited, he squinted to focus on the image past the numbness that was starting to take him.

The plane had markings - American or British. A flash glinted under its wing as it launched a missile at the gun post tracking it from the ground.

Jurgen's head was getting lighter with the loss of blood. He put his hands to his chest and belly to halt the bleeding a little…to buy some time.

Now! the Masters urged his mind. *Do it now, while our temples burn!*

'You're all dead,' Jurgen hissed at the faces of the five cursed ones his Masters were calling threats to their return to Earth. He put the knife tip to his forehead and gouged downward, to give his face as an offering to the faceless ones - his Masters. Grinning through the veil of blood, he began the invocations of the great black gateways. '*Iyur Setot.*'

Transcripts of items from BBC News 24, broadcasting from London, UK:

Sanatolian Chemical-Weapon Plant Destroyed

June 28th

Hassib Nembullah's encrypted arsenal was struck a serious blow today. Following a week of ultrasound monitoring during flyover surveillance runs, UN forces finally played their hand against what President Failey called 'a flagrant exercise in death mongering'. Overnight, a group of F-117 stealth bombers attacked and destroyed a bunker factory installation thirty-five miles north of Damascus where UN inspectors believe chemical and biological weapons were being manufactured. Sanatolia claims that a hundred and thirty people were killed when the missiles struck the plant, all allegedly civilians. The production of bio-chemical weapons violates terms initially laid down against neighboring Iraq in the 1990's and updated by the Failey administration's continuation of the War On Terror campaign to include all rogue states not seeking rapprochement with the US.

This is the first air-to-ground strike against Nembullah's forces in over a year and although the Security Council recognizes the need to keep a ban on biological warfare enforced, today's action is receiving vehement condemnation from China and the Russian Federation.

A further outcry has come from the academic world, which believes that the force of the air strikes would most certainly have damaged structures in the temple district of an ancient Sumerian city complex being excavated nearby.

This follows a tense two months of standoffs between the ailing Sanatolian dictator and the UN presence there that have so far culminated in the embargo on Sanatolian oil sales' being reinstated in full. Defense minister Omar al-Antakata has threatened to reactivate the nation's commitment to target Israel with SCUD missiles. Given Sanatolia's shattered economy and risk of military self-destruction, however, UN military experts deny the chances for any immediate reprisals.

(Gen. Oscar P. Kirschner - American Air Force)

'Nembullah will not strike back for this, provided we play him the way we always have played him in the wake of any disciplinary strikes we've had to take on him in the past. The key is to deliver the message that his behavior is unacceptable in a stark and firm manner but also in such a way that he can save face. Yes, there has been a missile strike on what must be one of his largest and most precious arms dumps, but I am confident he will find room to recoil from the blow without any risk of retaliation. The man is not stupid. We cannot afford to license him to play a Doomsday card from his death throes.'

-2-
<u>July 22nd</u>

Barry Nash was dozing on the floor in front of his suitcases and boxes when the two bangs hit his door. He awoke annoyed and just in time for the third and fourth thumps. They were official sounding - not another student's - and they had jolted his heart. Many joints on his right side cracked when he rose. 'Wait up! Be right there!'

Barry had not been expecting the campus police. Not really, anyway. 'Hi - can I help you with something?'

The campus cop spun his cap over a fingertip and asked if he could come inside.

'Sure. Sure.' Barry pulled the door back and welcomed with the other arm. His heart had stopped jerking now but a hot flush was beginning to emanate from his face. 'Erhm, I was just about to ship out for the summer.'

'You leaving today?'

'Tomorrow. Sorry to ask this this way but am I in, you know, *trouble*?'

'No. Not any trouble for you, Mr. Nash; but there's going to be a considerable bit of trouble for us. Your roommate - Jurgen Ganz: do you guys keep in contact at all?'

'He's not here. Israel: he's there on a travel thing. Archaeology dig.'

'We know that.'

Barry cocked his head back, squinting. 'Sorry, I don't underst-'

'*Have* you heard anything from him?'

'No. Nothing at all.'

'Know any of his friends round here?'

'Friends? No. I hardly ever saw him go out. Not even weekends.'

'Are you guys close or just sharing this room in the hall?'

Barry felt the truth rolling on his tongue, clenched his lips. *No, Mister Campus Policeman Loser - you don't make me say I hate the asshole now so you can tell me he's missing, presumed dead.*

The hot flush returned to Barry's head. He could feel his hair sweat coldly.

He'd just remembered the pot roaches he'd left in the beer can by his bed from last night after smoking behind the gym. He hadn't been outside since. The cop might smell them if he came in any further.

'We just share the room, that's all. We're not close or anything: friends with a very small "F" if you know what I mean.'

'Sure. So he wouldn't be the type to phone you then, would he?'

Barry heard the sound of Freshman laughter boom from the stairwell by the common kitchen. 'No. What's - what's happened?' he asked the cop, hoping it sounded just right for a loose acquaintance, not someone with an ax to grind.

Barry felt the jolt fill his high stomach and yank at his heart again as the cop perched himself on Ganz's bed, in full view of the dope-desecrated can. The cop scratched his temple but stayed silent. 'You guys don't think he's dead or anything, do you?' Barry asked, making sure he put some worry into his tone.

'He's been missing in Israel a month now,' the cop said plainly. He placed his cap by him on Ganz's top blanket, narrowly missing an antiquated cluster of questionable stains. 'Didn't even get to any of the digs they'd set up.'

Couldn't have happened to a nicer guy, Barry thought. 'Missing?'

'Yeah. Seems he vanished from the hostel the second day after he arrived in Tel Aviv.' The eye contact became heavier. 'Are you *sure* he hasn't been in touch? A postcard, maybe?'

'No. No - this's the first I've heard about Jurgen since before he left. I guess you guys have been busy with Professor Arnott's case.' *Moron*, he thought. *Why don't you just tell this cop you know Ganz did that, too?*

'You know anything about that?'

'Hell no.' Barry felt a paralyzing rush washing down him, freezing his mind, leaving only his hands and heart with feeling. The cop's eyes were cold and blue but they spoke volumes. 'Because, it so happens that both my department and others believe that we might need to speak with Mr. Ganz about just that very matter. We have done for a little while now. Now, that's a coincidence, isn't it?'

'I just meant that it's been a hard month for all of us here. Exams and stuff and - but *that* was awful; what happened to the professor's office and the building, I mean.' Barry tried to restore eye contact. 'You mean *Jurgen* did *that?*'

The cop rose, donned his cap, put his hands on his hips. 'We don't know right now, son. That's different from having a reason to believe something.' He moved for the door. 'Well, I guess if you say you haven't heard from Jurgen Ganz then that's all there is to it.'

'I haven't; honest to God. I don't think he'd ever figure on contacting me, ever.'

'Okay. Enjoy your summer, Mr. Nash. Still, if you do hear anything, be sure and contact us or your local police department. You live in San Diego?'

'Yeah. I hope they find Jurgen okay and soon.'

'Is that hope spelled with a capital "H"?' said the cop with a less than half a smile.

'Y-yeah, sure. Nobody deserves kidnapping or ... or whatever the hell's happened to him over there. Israel's a dangerous place, isn't it?'

'I guess; but then here's beginning to get a little dangerous recently, eh?'

Barry waited two minutes after the cop left before he walked to the window and stared hard through the red aspens at the big parking lot.

'You asshole, Ganz. You did that,' he whispered, wishing he'd never heard about North Dakota and its booming economy and good programs.

Another cold flush came over him then. He went to the door and opened it, surveying the corridor. Apart from subdued hip hop coming from Sharman's room on the floor below, it was a void out there. Barry closed the door, caught his reflection in the plastic fire procedure on the inside of the door. He looked as bad as he felt now.

Ganz had always looked bad.

'I hope you've totaled yourself, prick!' Barry spat at the image. He turned to look at beer can where his last stash of marijuana lay safe.

The sigh of relief never came to Barry Nash. As he stared at the black hole in the top of the empty can, he suddenly found that he could not break eye contact.

As he tried to remember why he wanted to break eye contact with the soothing blackness of the tiny void, the high, sweet laughter filled his ears.

*   *   *   *   *

Two Years Later

Transcripts of items from BBC *News 24*, broadcasting from London, UK:

<u>Aries Star brightens</u>
<u>November 16th</u>

Astronomers across the globe are astonished by the brightening of the star Hamal in the constellation Aries. The second-magnitude star has increased to a magnitude of -1.5 literally overnight, making it the second brightest star in the night sky. First noticed from observatories in Hawaii, the phenomenon is particularly worrying for astronomers and astrophysicists. Hamal, nowhere even near the end of its life, should not be capable of supernova.

British Astronomer Royale Sir Ronald Moulton said earlier today:

'This turns the tables on our understanding of how stars operate altogether. A century of understanding has been annihilated in just one morning. We have a jump in apparent brightness of whole units. That simply doesn't happen in the universe. I'm in shock. We all should be. If

this can happen in Aries, what about elsewhere: even our own sun? We've
been thrown back to the Middle Ages. It's a dark time for science.'

Yesterday's discovery follows in the wake of another phenomenon in
the world of star-watching. The Orionid meteor showers have been raining
material through our atmosphere for two weeks too many, or so said Dr.
Ludovic Praeger of Cornell University in Massachusetts last Friday:
[Re-run of archive footage]
'The Orionids are only supposed to last about two weeks, beginning
in mid-October which makes their peak to be about the twenty-first. What's
wrong with this year's batch is that they've outstayed their welcome grossly.
As we pass under fall-winter skies, we move through this meteoroid belt
every year, the radiant spot of which is the star at the base of the club in the
constellation Orion.

'This just shouldn't be happening. The only *surges* of matter are
supposed to occur about 25 to 10 years *before* Halley's Comet passes us.
Now, Halley departed us just a few decades *ago* so there's problem number
one there. The cause here is totally unknown.'

Massive Plague Strikes India

November 29th

Two months after the armistice between Pakistan and India, the
Asian subcontinent has been wracked by dangerously high levels of
septicemia. This has already taken the death toll from the conflict's aftermath
to over one million lives. When the rise in cases was first noticed late last
month, officials in the Indian health ministry failed to take preventative
measures, instead relying on the Red Cross for aid. Now, there are an
estimated five million cases of the disease in urban centers alone.

Senator Oliver P. Douglas, instrumental in seeing the Baltimore
Armistice Accord through said both nations illegally used biological and
chemical weapons in strikes along the Kashmiri border last March. UN
inspectors confirm chemical warfare was employed, but both countries refute
the claim and are demanding an official apology on threat of ambassadorial
withdrawal from Washington and London.

The epidemic is expected to mushroom out of control unless the Red Cross can set up enough emergency vaccination depots in time.'

Chinese drug crisis spirals out of control
December 4th

Three Triad leaders were executed in Tsientiang this morning after losing a joint appeal case. They were captured last month after Beijing began implementing emergency measures to crack down on the nation's opium crisis after usage reached a critical ten percent.

Louise Chow, our Chinese correspondent reports:

(F. correspondent footage)

'The executions have come at an especially hard time for China. With almost two hundred million heroin addicts to treat, the government has imposed martial law. This has been a very unkind year to the country. The failure of Beijing's decentralization moves coupled with floods in the Southeast have created an environment of desperation which the Triads have exploited mercilessly.

With the standoff worsening between China and the West over outsourcing recompense and bond commitments, unemployment has risen, driving legions of disenfranchised young people to heroin and crime. Beijing is turning back to the old methods. Human Rights violations will be inevitable. Purges of democratic reform groups are feared.'

Multi-Drug Resistant Bubonic Plague set to decimate sub-Saharan Africa
December 8th

Red Cross officials are exasperated at the overnight explosion of Multi-Drug Resistant Bubonic Plague (MDRB) Plague cases in Kenya, Tanzania and Uganda. Close to a third of Ugandans are infected, up from two percent just five weeks ago.

Unless serious anti-transmission programs are implemented by the governments of these poverty-stricken countries, millions of lives are set to be destroyed. MDRB is replacing AIDS many times over in its efficacy as a population decimator.

(Begin archive footage of Rwandan camp)

However, in some cases, the programs may be too severe. These

MDRB Plague infected people have been interned in what Human Rights observers term 'concentration camps'. And what's worse are the rumors of so-called 'mercy' killings: thinly veiled reprisal executions on non-plague infected rival tribe members for a defeat suffered twenty years ago.

Further south, in the relatively peaceful areas of Zimbabwe and northern South Africa, while there are no surges in multi-drug resistant plague cases being reported yet, political analysts are voicing their fears that the introduction of a pandemic during these unstable times could throw the whole southern part of the continent into a new Dark Age ...'

<u>Antarctic interior reports anomalous levels of contaminated precipitation</u>
<u>December 10th</u>

Meteorologists at the McMurdo base in Antarctica have released information that 28 mm of snowfall fell over a one hour period last night. The amount is alarming because it represents over half the annual mean precipitation for the desert-like interior of the continent. The Scott-Amundsen base at the South Pole has confirmed the phenomenon, citing a figure of its own at 20 mm. However, the anomaly doesn't end there. Our correspondent, Nicholas Dickinson, reports from McMurdo:

'Haggard and weary after a full night spent in front of monitors, both shifts of meteorologists at Antarctic station McMurdo are confronting an occurrence they are calling "impossible".'

A spattering of rust-colored material has been found in the snowfall. The actual extent of the contamination has been fixed at a radius of four hundred miles, with varying thickness. But if the actual quantity of precipitation wasn't enough to raise concerns among the meteorology teams, its chemical makeup certainly has:

(Interview)

We're still working this stuff through in the lab but so far we've been stumped by its properties. We don't have all the needed facilities down here so we're shipping out canisters right now. We're looking at either a compound so complex that we can't even separate any of its components for analysis or (shakes head, grins) *... it could be of alien origin. So far we've been working on twenty-six samples of the substance to establish uniformity and there doesn't seem to be anything in there that's a carrier for bacilli. I can* *say that it's non-radioactive, but we're exercising extreme caution in handling. We're stuck for clues as to how it managed to come through our atmosphere. Asteroid matter is definitely ruled out at this point. Once we get it Stateside, we're hoping more sophisticated tests will shed some light.*

Mysterious Red Rains strike Gulf of Mexico
December 20th

For the first time since its discovery at the South Pole over a week ago, the contaminated rainfall has reached US shores. Three inches of rain carrying what scientists from Cornell University have christened 'Agent 104' fell on Miami in the early hours of this morning. Worldwide, scientists are still trying to come up with a means of classifying the substance which, though so far believed to be harmless, has resisted every form of analysis yet attempted.

From *Time* Magazine's 'Year in Review'
(dated 29th December)

'When Humankind memorably began to embrace the Unknown, sci-fi fans and *futurephiles* were among the most hopeful. But they were also doomed to be the most disappointed. The same was true this year when the Unknown threw itself at our world, finding us even less able to find satisfying answers and results. Now it seems the results are all very negative. What sort of era will this year past herald? In the last month, the surface of this planet has borne witness to at least a century's worth of catastrophes - catastrophes for which no ... [irrelevant information]

'One thing does appear consistent: our resilience as a species. Where in earlier epochs humans cowered with superstitious terror, we at least possess a freshly drawn scientific heritage. By acting in concert against the harshness of these coincidences, the world's stronger nations are pledging an oath to not stop trying until the last answer comes. The emergency conference in Luxembourg between Security Council officials and the world's scientific community heads on January 15th will hopefully provide a consensus on the sheer importance that a year of total instability and emergency must now give way to one of resolution and confidence.'

From the *New York Times* - January 8th

<u>Scientific Community Desperate to find Breakthrough by 15<u>th</u> January</u>

'With just a week to the Luxembourg Emergency Conference, a spokesman for the Smithsonian Environmental Research Center in Maryland has said that scientists there are becoming frustrated by the lack of progress made in analyzing 'Agent 104' (named to show how the substance lies outside the classically defined Periodic Table of Elements). With world leaders set to tax the scientific community for answers, there are fears that none will be forthcoming:

There are over a thousand researchers working on trying to make sense of the exotic matter. The samples we're working with are taken from no less than sixty-seven sites. The proportion of exotic matter is constant to water at nine parts per thousand. But we've found no way to break it down so we're seriously considering it a totally new element in its own right. It doesn't actually have an atomic assignation of 104 - the name is just used to show it's outside our grasp. We don't know how it may be harmful yet - it's defeated our tests at every turn. We do know that the material can block wave frequencies when concentrated. If it worsens, we could be looking at communications systems being jammed worldwide. A disaster.

This stuff is still raining down, with equatorial locations curiously receiving less. Whatever this is, there's a danger the Industrialized World could be facing severe problems. As far as the summit in Luxembourg is concerned, we're in trouble.'

From the <u>*New York Times*, dated 16<u>th</u> January</u>

<u>The End of Hope</u>

'Talks in Luxembourg broke down at 3 a.m. local time with no decisive measures reached regarding the crises on the agenda. After spokespersons from the scientific community were unable to proffer any help over the matter of Agent-104, the Chinese representatives walked out of the summit chamber.

The failure to produce policies for handling the far-reaching dimensions of the emergencies means the international community is facing a crisis it cannot seem to resolve at all. The Security Council is on the verge of dissolution.

India's and Africa's epidemics were third on the agenda, after Agent-

104 and the continuous brightening of the Aries star Hamal. The scientific representatives failed to draw links between these phenomena and any of the disasters striking the world in the last sixty days, notwithstanding popular belief to the contrary.

The talks produced little except heightened tensions. India remains convinced Pakistan launched septicemia-plague impregnated missiles and is demanding massive reprisal measures from the UN or it will escalate the conflict to nuclear levels.

Pakistan did not appear at the convention.

The United States, Britain, France and Russia agreed that Agent-104 *must* be analyzable and pledge to form an emergency task force to handle its further study. 'Too much has happened for it not to be related,' said Francis Ronson, British UN official.

American ambassador to the UN Rudy Penrose stated that now the Security Council must fight a war on two fronts: scale down tensions in Asia and humanitarian disasters elsewhere while pooling academic resources in determining exactly what relationship exists between the events that have occurred outside the earth and those that have ravaged its surface.'

-3-

<u>16th April</u>

(FBI Central Crime Lab, San Diego)

'There?'

'You see it?' Nathan asked.

'I think so this time. I'll backtrack about eight or nine frames.'

Coleman's fingertip dug into the arrow key to take the still image back in time by one frame, then two, then three. He could hear Nathan's bad breath coming out in faster spurts, making his ear warmer. He was sick of Nathan now. He knew that Nathan had loathed him from the moment they'd met a few days ago. That was good - it felt more natural now, at least.

'C'mon,' Nathan said. 'Tap that thing faster.'

'Six.....seven.....eight,' Coleman whispered. His eyes were scouring the screen of the big Dell monitor for the slightest deviance in pixel formation. 'Nine.....ten.....el-'

'Jesus.'

Coleman didn't see it until a whole second had passed. He'd spent the last hour in the imaging lab with Nathan, picking through the securicam tape of Saturday's assassination and had until now been wanting so badly to get drunk on cheap rotgut. 'Wh-'

'Lower left,' Nathan blurted. He had a Bic in his fingers, tapped its cap against the display to point out the anomaly to Coleman.

'Now what in Hell's Teeth is that?'

'I don't... I don't-'

Coleman felt the coldness of Nathan's hand as it knocked his away from the keyboard. Nathan tapped once and the figure vanished, unveiling a few more faces in the crowd.

When Nathan went forward one frame, the anomaly reappeared.

It was tiny, perhaps sixty pixels long by fifty at its widest and laid on a diagonal plan. 'I don't understand,' Coleman finished. 'That wasn't there before.'

'No. It was,' Nathan said. 'It was....only it wasn't that strong.'

'You saw something there before? Why didn't you-'

'Thought it was a glitch - tape jizz. Let's enlarge this sonofabitch.' Nathan reached for the mouse. A few seconds later, Coleman was watching a yellow rectangle grow around the bottom left section of the screen.

'Go for two hundred per cent,' he whispered to Nathan.

At double size, the figure was just as indecipherable. It was shapeless, though to Coleman's eyes the figure could have passed for an upside-down wine bottle. Its color was black - not black black but more like the reddy hue of black that made Coleman think of looking through a glass of diet cola in strong sunlight.

'No go,' Coleman said. 'Try it at four hundred.'

Nathan's yellow rectangle encased a more localized patch this time before Coleman heard him tap the key. The figure now took up about a twentieth of the screen, hovering over the heads of the spectators that day. Its lower tip appeared to work its way into the mouth of a young brunette with perky mounds on her wool sweater. She was pale and had acne: maybe twenty years old - some college kid's eight out of ten.

'Keep going,' Coleman whispered.

'How the hell could we have passed this over?' Nathan sounded weaker now, scared. 'For Chrissakes, we've run the goddamn tape how many times?'

'But were we looking for something at the right *place?*'

At eight hundred percent, Coleman noticed that the figure had become shinier. 'How many frames 'til the bishop gets it?'

'From here; six,' Nathan said. 'Screw this. I'm taking it up to fifteen hundred.'

Within moments, the black anomaly had engulfed over a fifth of the display. Only the blackness was gone now. Coleman saw instead a hundred strands of deep red running together. He thought of blood in water and shivered.

'Let's try running it forward to next frame,' Nathan said. His breathing had become less intense, more frozen, Coleman noticed. 'This has to mean something.'

'No.' Coleman turned to look him in the eye. 'Let's get a hard copy here, at least.'

'Later. I think I got something with this.'

Prick, Coleman thought. *Yeah right, Mister I'm-FBI-and-you're-CIA (Certified Inferior Amateurs)-so-don't-you-forget-it Nathan; of course you'd figure that, wouldn't you?*

Unfortunately, the way things were now, it seemed like *anybody* could have figured that, Coleman thought bitterly. The CIA wasn't what it had been not even a year ago. A far cry from neutralizing Uncle Sam's offshore threats and undoing the screws of the machines these hostile powers played with, his guild had been drafted to help out with the internal security crises that were springing up faster than October mushrooms in Oregon.

The combining of intelligence agencies, the current administration had figured, was to be the alloy to cut through the mayhem. Coleman, like his superiors, had frowned on the marriage. Too much had vanished in the unholy union.

They'd gone and they'd emasculated the Central Intelligence Agency and given the FBI a downtrodden eunuch to play with. Coleman would have figured himself one of the sorest parts of the bleeding stump left behind. That was thanks largely to Nathan.

Nathan clicked on the tools icon at the top of the display, then the magnifier and took the screen back to two hundred percent. 'You watch the right side of the screen when I hit play.'

Coleman nodded. His eyes were sick of the show now. In half a second, his side-vision reminded him to watch the priest's skull explode in the bottom right corner of the screen. After so many plays, it still had not got any cleaner to his sight.

'Nothing; damn...Damn it all,' Nathan said. 'Okay, then; let's go back to the anomaly.'

The wall clock above the drinks machine read twenty-to-six. As Coleman made his way up to it, he shot a glance at the landing beyond the glass door. All told, that was eight and a half hours he'd wasted here with Nathan. Leah would be getting annoyed just about now. Leah never got worried.   She'd managed to channel self-hurting things like that into weapons long ago.   As he shot his second quarter through the slot, he pictured her surfing the Internet to get up some wallpaper of Christian Bale, just to piss him off.

He was already at the doorway when he heard Nathan yell. Nathan's head was blocking most of the display. 'What you-'

'Look at *this*.'

'What did you do?'

'Just look.'

Coleman leaned on the tabletop and tried making sense of the dark image on the VDU. Nathan sat rigid in the swivel chair, his head frozen. 'Are you *watching* this?'

'That's weird...that guy's black but his features don't go with it.' Coleman looked at Nathan's face, puzzled. 'What? You saw this guy in the crowd?'

'You'd think that, wouldn't you? Most folks would.'

Nathan's expression was leaden, worrying. 'C'mon, Nathan; spit it out. I got a home-'

'The fact that man is black without being a negroid isn't just it. Nor is that massive gash on his face.'

Coleman frowned. 'So you mean it's a white guy in the crowd with that crap covering him up a little.'

'No!' Nathan snapped. 'Coleman, that picture's at magnification three thousand. Unless someone's into shrinking heads down to the size of a dime, this is impossible. He's not in this crowd, this guy. It's something *else*.'

-4-

<u>16<u>th</u> April, Newport Beach, California</u>

Carl Becker kicked down with automatic foot strokes. All he thought was that the water off Newport Beach never got *this* cold. Okay, maybe in November or February; never in April. He'd been submerged for barely twenty seconds and could only just see the yellow twin tanks of his partner, Lopez.

Light smatterings of visible water shimmered about the murk in front of his facemask, reminding him of the fragility of life in this job. *God this is awful,* he thought again. He'd been a diving contractor for twenty-seven years and twelve of those were now used up on the public sector. There'd been a time when he'd wanted to boast at his thirtieth high school reunion that he recovered black boxes from downed airliners all the time, with the occasional military craft.

But that want had departed Becker's heart long ago. He couldn't remember exactly when or whenabouts he'd grown jaded, but it had happened all right.

Number eight for the big ones, this was. Becker had accustomed himself to christening each recovery dive with a number. His former running count made it twenty-six small civilian aircraft, four military and seven airbuses. And he knew when a black box wanted to be found and when it didn't. The water always did one of four things once you'd marked out the dive zone. If you weren't going to score a point, the water would let you know long before you got below ten feet down. It could be nice and clear and accommodating so you could look; it could be clear but cold or turbulent; it could murk over a little and want you out of it…

Or it could do its level best to screw you over the second you got in.

Lopez's yellow tanks had shrunk to the size of a distant buttercup. Becker dipped his head and kicked harder. He got jumpier every time he sensed that the black box *wasn't* going to come out and play. Adrenalin rushes and hope had always managed to keep his mind off the sharks before, but never when he felt this way.

Idiot, he thought. *Sonar never lies; that bastard's going to be within thirty feet of you when you hit bedrock. Just keep Lopez in sight and screw your hang-ups.*

Hang-ups…that was funny. The way the world was now with all its madness, how could he have any *faith* in the order of things anymore? No predictability these days… *What's to stop your air pipes from just ripping…*

Becker caught sight of the sand, eased his grip on the shaft of the blowgun. Two seconds later, he caught Lopez waving him over and he kicked toward her. He kicked quickly and heavily – faster than normal and it was because he had felt an old, old feeling.

He had to see it first. He'd only done a dozen proper dives with Lopez. If she found the target this time then that would make it the fifth time he'd lost to her on a discovery. Deep down, Becker liked getting frustrated that way with her. It made him fancy her more. Yet, the harder he thought about her, the guiltier he felt whenever his mind inevitably cast back to the family he'd once headed.

The box Lopez had found was cold to his touch. Once the cable was secured to it, he prodded her shoulder and signed 'OK' with his fingers and thumb.

Back on deck, Becker stayed close to the stern of the Newport Beach Police Department cutter and waited, passing up the chance to view his partner kick off her flippers and behold her succulent arches. Yolanda Lopez, aged twenty-eight; occupation - aquatic recovery contractor and non-aspiring muse of his life ninety percent of the time.

But now was one of those unchosen ten percent times. The winch motor ground in his ears as he watched the wire ascend all the way until the orange casket broke the surface. *How scared will they sound on this one?* he couldn't help but think. He'd never actually got to hear any of the voice recorder boxes he'd retrieved but he believed he had a gift for feeling the terror of every single pre-crash cockpit panic attack through his fingertips. And this one had been one of the worse ones.

The readings had gone off the scale this time around. When he saw the winch rotate and lower its payload down beside a fiberglass hold hatch, Becker waited for the dull thud with a dread he'd never got used to.

'Pay dirt,' he heard Lopez coo in her strained Agent Scully voice. Her feet were slapping up the deck towards him. He cast a glance across from the sight of the orange recorder to her pelvis and failed to make himself feel better.

'Pay dirt my ass; this one's pay *rock*. Whatever it is, it's got one hell of a lot of misery riding inside it.'

-5-
16th April, San Diego, California

Dave Reynolds was tired but he'd forgotten about that now. He'd been tired all weekend but today had drained him extra because of Billy. Billy was twenty, living with his and their parents and going nowhere with a sociology major.

Yesterday, Reynolds had also been forced to forget that he'd threatened to kill his little brother if he ever downloaded porn again. Billy had put up a lame defense during his faked breakdown at yesterday's confrontation not even an hour after their dad had returned from La Jolla with the Compaq tower unit as good as new.

Sure, one of your friends uploaded it on a shitload of e-mails. Then why do the sites show up on the history roster as well as the temp file list, Einstein?

Kill. As he took the exit ramp from the post-rush hour freeway, Reynolds suddenly remembered that he'd applied that word to Billy and felt like weeping for it now. How many people had been shown dead or dying on CNN this weekend? But then, how many had died since the start of the Crisis: that Agent 104 bullshit?

He got thinking now. Thinking how anything felt better than this. Even the anger from yesterday hadn't gnawed at his innards like this was doing now. The phone call had ruined everything this afternoon. Anline was just his present job, the same way he'd worked systems at Delos in L.A. for a while and had gotten out the other end when he felt he'd run too far ahead of anybody else for them to see what he was doing anymore.

Great, he thought. *Now you're trapped in San Diego and sided up with the great crusade.* That cause now was not to help knock off consumer ISP competition as it had once been. Now it was all about *survival.* Agent 104 was making every comms device fitted with a copper terminal go <*Fzzzt*> and he was one of the only realists he knew who was lying to himself that he still had a future in this job.

A pang of dread took his heart when he thought about that again. He slowed to twenty mph and prepared a vapid expression for Charlie the ancient security man at the compound gate.

'Hi, Mister Reynolds.'

'Hi, Charlie. I'm expected on the Eighteenth Floor.'

The bar lifted as Charlie flashed approval with a Polygrip-fitted smile.

That kind of looks like an emergency meeting alright, Reynolds figured as he added his Jetta to the right end of the long row of cars parked right in front of the building. They called meetings like that as good as every other week just to dredge the think tanks for ammunition to be used in the war against collapse.

But the trademark lackluster tones of Parker, the overlord of Anline in south Southern California, had been absent on the cell phone. This time Parker had sounded really, *really* anxious.

The elevator doors fell away to present Reynolds with the sight of bonsai palms and the only floor apart from the first not to be cursed with light blue industrial cord on the floor. He saw Hank Jarvis ahead up the center corridor, running from the men's and pulling up his fly. 'Hank!'

Jarvis looked almost jaundiced. Jarvis made sixty-nine G's a year as the team leader of technical support on the fifth floor. In the collapsing economy, he'd be needed no matter what. He had no right to look that ill.

'Hank, what the *hell* is going on today?'

'Parker,' Jarvis said, pointing at the open white blinds on the inside window of the eighteenth floor's informal conference room. 'Parker's been on some kind of paranoia trip. He's been waiting for you, Dave. He's kept the rest of us in there stewing for half an hour now.'

'He's kept you guys back on my account? Christ, man; good job I was long gone from my folks when he called.' Reynolds let Jarvis go through the double doors first and noticed that Parker had pulled out all the stops.

Twenty plus faces fixed on Reynolds and accused him of mass

mental cruelty. 'Take a seat, David,' Parker rumbled while trying to raise his blubbery behind off the Durafoam surface.

Reynolds clasped the chair back nearest the door and saw Parker's disapproval. He moved up two seats, sat down and started rubbing his thumb tips. Something was very, very wrong indeed for Parker not to have any papers in front of him, he thought.

'You've all heard about it on the news. I thought we could have been safe from it in our cyber fortress but it seems I was wrong.'

Reynolds pulled a fist on the table top. Yes, he'd heard about how the whole planet was being rocketed to Hell in a hand basket, piece by piece in less than a year. Who hadn't heard yet?

'Those of you who came in here suspecting a virus then you're right.'

Reynolds' fist tightened until its knuckles went white. 'A *virus*? That's *it*?'

'Yes and no,' Frank Gill said on behalf of Parker. 'Yes it's a virus, and no it ... it doesn't appear to be acting like any that could be devised. It behaves ostensibly like the old Melissa virus from '99. Users get e-mails with download attachments that wipe their "C" drives clean.'

'I know what Melissa does, Frank,' Reynolds said. His knuckles were aching so he unclenched his hand. 'That's Stone Age stuff.'

'If you'll just let me finish,' Gill replied. Gill had soft features and wore horn-rims to mould himself on a retro-fetish of the retro-Seventies fad. Now the corners of his puffy mouth were upturned with menace. 'This one does something else ... something we don't yet understand. *This* virus cleans out your hard drive of everything except your boot up files.

'When you boot up the next time, you get this,' Parker added, pulling a Presario laptop up from the floor.

Reynolds waited, tried to keep his gaze from returning to Frank Gill and thinking of well-earned violence. His loose fist fell onto his thigh.

'Reynolds, come up here first. I gave the others a sample of this before you got here.'

Reynolds rose and fixed Parker with a stare. 'Alright; let's see this thing.' He passed Gill from behind, resisted the urge to pretend that Gill had put the porn on his father's computer.

Gill was ugly and had a hot wife who wore leather skirts and worked out like Richard Simmons had died and possessed her.

'Now what do you make of that?'

'What - wallpaper and no files; start menu icon. I don't know, Nick. Looks to me like a classic case of data loss. Lets you into windows and-'

'And if you were Joe Public and knew damn all about doing up SCSI cards and the like, what would you do?'

A heavy atmosphere of stale but good cologne and sweat lay about Parker's neck as Reynolds leant closer to view the liquid crystal display of the laptop. 'Stick the red CD-Rom in the tray and hope for the best?' Parker asked.

'What, Quick Restore disk? No. At least, not until-'

'You're Joe Public remember. No expertise.'

'Yeah, but remember - they know what Quick Restore will do from the manual.'

'Alright, so we go to the manual; excellent.'

'Okay, now I'd tinker with the available options,' Reynolds said. 'If I was your average idiot, I'd run and get the troubleshooting section. From this kind of problem, I'd assume it'd be a matter of restoring the registry.'

'Okay,' Parker said, reclining hard into his chair. Reynolds noticed him run his index finger over the side of his nose and prop it under his chin to help with the weight of stress. 'Okay.'

'Look - what is this?'

'Just continue,' Parker attempted to disarm. 'Please, Dave. Indulge me; it's all part of what I'm trying to show you here.'

Reynolds reached for the keypad and depressed the grey power button, waited for the Compaq to restart and hit 'F8' when he saw the 'Starting Windows' cue. 'Alright; now I prompt it with the "attrib-h-r" commands.'

'And then the "copy system" and "copy user" ones,' Gill cut in.

'I think I know that, Frank.'

'Then what?' Parker asked. His cologne was starting to irritate Reynolds' eyes. 'Restart?'

Reynolds guided the arrow to the start menu and clicked for a restart. 'If this doesn't do it then I guess I'm one unhappy camper,' Reynolds whispered. 'And if I'm to represent your typical moron in the street, I guess I'd have to take it in for repairs if it doesn't - now ... now what in f-'

'Same problem all over again,' Gill said, sounding ecstatic at Reynolds' failure. 'Why don't you go for the works and do what your average moron would do. Go on, Dave. Why not press your palms all over the keypad and pretend you've just lost a best-selling novel on the hard disk and have no backups.'

'Okay, Frank,' Parker cut in. 'I think Dave knows that much.'

'What?' Reynolds issued when he saw the change in the display. 'It's just a line.'

'Green line on black display?' asked the unknown middle-aged man near the back of the huge, leafed table. 'But it's not a line, is it? Not a straight one.'

'No,' Reynolds said weakly. 'It's little hills and valleys.'

'If it wasn't a laptop, I'd have said it was CRT related at first,' said Eddie Binks, also from technical support and with three bachelor's degrees worth of hobbies crammed into his thirty years of life. 'But it's nothing to do with the screen.'

'Where's the sound gone on that thing?' Gill asked Parker. 'Did you turn it off?'

Parker sprang to life, nearly clipping Reynolds' chin with his crown when he moved forward to shoot a fingertip to the plus key on the speaker control. 'Sorry, Dave; I guess you were wondering about the noise. Or lack thereof. It's not the soundcard.'

Reynolds heard the whine gather volume until 'stop' fell from his mouth and Parker let go of the console. 'This has to be preprogrammed.'

'It's not.' That was Hank Jarvis this time. 'I've had the HDUs of half a dozen units sent out to the repair shop and they can't find anything to account on the disk itself. All there is is corrupted boot files and rudimentary data.'

'So the folders are gone for good then,' Reynolds said.

'Of course they are.' That was Gill again. 'Otherwise Mister Parker wouldn't have coined the "Melissa" reference.'

'Then what the hell is doing that?'

'You got no ideas at all?' Hank offered, waited for Reynolds to shake his long bangs from side to side. 'It's an anomalous signal.'

'Wait; you said you sent some drives to the shop before? When was that?'

'A couple of hours ago,' Parker levered in. 'Your day off and there wasn't time to call.'

'Okay, so it's anomalous - that thing. Tell me something I don't know about it, Hank.'

'From what they've got out of all six specimens, each one is carrying a code. The sequence activates the second the customer trips four or more keys at once. Same thing happens with the "Alt", "Ctrl" and delete cue.'

Reynolds felt his blood drain. 'A signal? You mean there's actually info inside that waffle?'

'Could be,' Parker said, raising his palm to let Hank Jarvis off the hook. 'All we know is that it's a code of some sort. Repeats in twenty-one second loops and it isn't encoded in binary or base three.'

'Which puts us where, Nick?'

'It puts us in the shits as far as customer service goes.' Parker blew out a hard stream of breath and cradled his nose with interlocked fingers. 'This thing started Friday night for us. Carrier files coming in with emails. New York, L.A. and Chicago hubs got their proof just before midnight.'

'This is crazy.' Reynolds scratched six o'clock shadow on his bottom lip. 'Kills all your files, let's you get wallpaper and then hits with that crap. Now what kind of thing can do that?'

'That's why you're our systems chief, Dave,' Parker said flatly. 'I need you to get this bastard as soon as you can. Screw Y2K-sized problems; this thing is poised to kill the whole goddamn internet and us with it. As if things weren't already bad enough with Agent 104!'

-6-

<u>16<u>th</u> April, Newport Beach, California</u>

'God Almighty,' Becker murmured, driving the froth of his value-but-strong lager back into the bottleneck. He'd just switched the set on CNN's Headline News with the intent to unwind and get away from lurid thoughts of Lopez, lycra-lining and water sports.

He'd caught much of the news that way recently. In the past month, coming across snippets had made it all the more insane for him to take in what was going down in the world.

INDONESIAN PLANE OVER CALIFORNIA – DEATH TOLL: 382..

Jesus.....how many plane crashes have I seen now?

He'd seen nearly all of them on Headline news: eleven plane crashes containing eleven V.I.P.'s and political emissaries; eight assassinations - two with shootings and six with plastique; and then there was the Bermuda Triangle deal they'd just set up in that weird part of Russia.

'You're not missing much, sweetheart,' he promised the portrait in the Wal-Mart silver frame atop the drinks cabinet of the sideboard and instantly felt worse for it. 'Sweetheart' was Ida, his pride and joy. She'd been the product of his and his ex's love for thirteen years and had now been dead for twelve of those.

Becker tried to keep himself from pulling his gaze back to the TV screen but found it too painful. 'Death's selling like goddamn hotcakes these days,' he murmured into his bottle.

Skin cancer had killed her. Cancer had wasted a few lives in his family history but...

But he'd denied the connection in her case and chosen to take the pain instead. Abbie had chosen to take off instead. Three months after Ida's tiny white coffin had been laid to rest in the Southside's Lutheran plot, her role as his wife had ended with a new-found penchant for solo bar-hopping, valium popping and private sessioneering as *consort officiale* to Captain Morgan.

'Morons.... can't they even fly a plane straight?' Becker squeezed the bottleneck, played back in his mind the time when he'd been with the merchant marines and Gary Lister and he had been arrested in Jakarta for playing craps in public while intoxicated.

Gary Lister had been hanged in Bangladesh over ten years back for stuffing two freezer bags of China White between the back wall lining and the back inside cover of his case.

Luckily, he'd already fallen out with Gary.

Becker straightened his back and belched as hard as he could.

The phone was bleeping away by the time the shockwave cleared from his stomach. Becker struggled to his feet. He always found himself running anytime somebody was calling.

Abbie calling? Abbie finally getting the guts together to report that she wanted to save this thing called their marriage. The divorce had never come about - there was hope, yet.

'Yep?'

'Mister Becker?'

(Damnation!) 'Uh-huh?'

'Are you alone in your residence, sir?'

'Ehmmm, just me. Yeah.'

'You led the dive on the Indonesian charter jet today, didn't you?'

Becker felt more gas building up in his stomach, tried to stifle it. The woman on the line sounded like a definite pencil-pusher. *'Might* have. You a journalist?'

'No, sir; I'm with the FBI.'

Becker knew it was true: the line was too clear for it not to be. Normal phone calls had been poisoned with static now from that shit they'd found in the rain.

'Yeah? I thought you guys only made house calls.'

'I have to ask you something about today's dive, Mr. Becker. I realize it's late but it's vital you tell me all you remember about the location where you found the flight data recorder.'

'Grid refs? I - the Coast Guard would be the ones to tell you that.'

'No, sir. I mean the physical location. *Where about* on the sea bed did you and your associate discover the data recorder?'

'Just on your run of the mill bed. Well, what - do you mean *terrain type* or-'

'Yes.' The woman's voice was colder than Abbie's the first time he got speaking to her after she'd taken off. Becker felt the rumblings of his aborted, second belch stretch his stomach and grimaced. 'It's very important that you remember if you retrieved the recorder from plain seafloor sand or-'

'Rocks? No. It was lying flat on the dirt. Why do you ask?'

'You're absolutely sure there were no hard objects under it or in the immediate vicinity?'

'Sure. Nothing. Just a straight run of sand down there.'

'And how clear was visibility under the surface?'

'Awful. Now, look; I don't mean to sound rude but you're talking to a guy who's been in the business for twenty years, lady. I have good radar for rocks - you have to if you're going to be a diver or one day you'll crack your brains open.'

'Thanks, Mister Becker. That's all I needed to know.'

'*Wait* a second; what's this all about?'

'Don't worry about what it's about. You'll find out what's going on from any press release we give in the near future. You yourself are bound to silence by contract.'

'*Hey!* Now you just wait! Look, I've made coffee for more FBI men than anybody else I've ever had round here; now I figure that makes me-'

'We're obviously at a misunderstanding. You were contracted to recover an item for forensic analysis. You've fulfilled your role; please accept that and leave us to handle the rest.'

'What *rest?*' Becker could feel his gears changing now. 'Hey now; what's so wrong with that flight recorder that you had to ask me that?'

'Sorry, Mr. Becker. I'm not at liberty to discuss this any further. Thanks for your co-operation and good evening to you.'

'Wait!'

Plink

Becker squeezed the handset, thumped the space in front of the phone console with the heel of his other hand. 'Bitch!' He hung up, rubbed both palms up his face and squeezed at his scalp, catching his reflection in the darkening window. He looked like he was a hundred years old in it. 'What the Hell is going on?' he asked it, hoping somehow it could answer with the wisdom of an even older man.

-7-
<u>17th April, Western Siberia (Loyalist Zone)</u>

Major Vladimir Olentiev was having another bad day. Siberia had not been kind to him nor to 100,000 other Russian heroes. He'd been here for both wars and the first time was easier.

As he flew above the parched tundra, that thought nagged. But now there was this – a hole in the sky, a plague of skin cancer cases from the ultraviolet death rays and radiation levels that went off the scale. Olentiev didn't see how the Siberian rebels could tout that as an excuse to break away from Russia. Moscow wasn't 'into' stripping ozone away above parts of the country that annoyed it. As a boy, he'd heard about the 1908 meteor blast near where the cancer cases were now at their highest. He sometimes wondered if there might have been a connection, some smaller hole that had begun like a cavity in a rotting molar... Fat chance of ever learning the truth.

He'd just been briefed yesterday about today's reconnaissance run. Two days before, he'd led a detachment of SukHois on a surgical strike against rebel guerrillas who'd spilled over into the loyalist, western Siberian frontier towns. His planes had left very little alive down there.

An LED flashed on the console. Olentiev tapped the stick switch beneath it. 'What is it?'

'Sir, I'm getting above normal levels of static on my base receiver.'

Olentiev pulled a frown, hesitated long after even registering his wing man's complaint.

Askenskaya... Askenskaya was the sort who would do things by the book even if it meant death.

'Sir? Are you reading me?'

'Wait,' Olentiev allowed. 'Adjusting now... Calm yourself there.' The static was hard – far crueler than the despondent fizz Olentiev was used to on long distance recon or strike runs.

'I can't fine tune to base, sir. Didn't you notice when we lost contact?'

'Hold on.' Olentiev's fingers thrummed the communications channel selector. The LED that illuminated when the strongest signal was attained was now flashing crazily. 'Askenskaya, how far back did you notice we were out of comms with base?'

'Just in the last minute there. Didn't you hear it, sir?'

'Hear what?'

'A clicking sound. I thought it was on my system only, so I took some time… to verify that.'

Olentiev grimaced at the other instruments on the middlemost control panel. Askenskaya's sweat was silent but thick in his helmet speakers. They were closing on the last thirty kilometers of the recon run. The glare from Lake Baykal was insufferable to Olentiev's visored eyes. It was conspiring now to join forces with the giant, dipping sun and melt his irises.

'I don't know what this is,' he said. 'Could be anything. See how close we are to the Baykal coast now, Askenskaya. Drop your altitude to two and a half thousand meters ... now.'

Olentiev's gloved palm eased up on the joystick. 'Askenskaya?'

'Complying, sir; but do you think it's an insurgent jamming signal?'

'If so, we'll be free once we clear their radar,' he said then followed Askenskaya's dip.

The water on Lake Baykal had lost its sheen now. As he fidgeted with his channel selector, Olentiev saw the hard waves breaking and the lighter shades of rippled, purple water, forming patterns that reminded him of a huge fly swatter. The shoreline outlying the abandoned town of Khurkutsk was more visible now. Olentiev spied the black sands of a far-off beach and recalled with horror the state news reports from just a week ago. The skies running from the southern coast of that lake all the way up to north of Strelka had been raped of *all* ozone and God knew what else. Space had leaked in, destroying life beneath the hole and in the surrounding hundred miles or more.

'We're nearly there, Askenskaya, so we still play according to the briefing.'

The briefing… Bits of that were starting to trickle back into Olentiev's mind now with cinematic precision. General Alexiev had been uncommonly jumpy during it. 'You'll encounter instrument trouble,' is what he'd said, but Olentiev hadn't expected today's problems. Putin may have tried to leave the cream of the crop in the cutbacks, but Alexiev had been a missed dud.

The fizz was getting hypnotic. 'Two minutes until we hit the shore,' Olentiev whispered.

That's right, he thought; you hit the shoreline and you'll find that you've entered a ghost country with no capabilities for defense. He'd learned that from watching the news, not from Alexiev. Most of the population of central Siberia had escaped - refugees of the first future war.

'Still nothing on our base frequency, sir.'

'Concentrate on the terrain ahead.' They were looking for ... *what* had Alexiev said? A small impact crater eight kilometers from the coast and some wreckage. Alexiev had tried to assure them by saying that the piecemeal Siberian rebel defense systems didn't include auto-trip surface-to-air missiles. There was just the UV to worry about... and very high radiation levels.

Olentiev saw the blip. He let it flash again before speaking. 'Check you scanner there.'

'I see it, sir. I have it clocked at about eighteen kilometers.'

'That rules out the meteor theory. Whatever it is it has an electronic makeup. Stand by to prime your weapons; I'll run a scan on it.' Olentiev thumbed a switch, trying to ignore the deviant LED flashes. 'Strange.' The crackling in his helmet was getting bad now. 'Askenskaya?'

'Sir?'

'Fall back one kilometer, drop five hundred meters and cut comms for thirty seconds.'

Olentiev waited for his scanner to clear of his wingman's signal. Now all that remained was the anomaly ahead, just under twelve kilometers due east. The blip was flashing faster now.

Olentiev locked on and ran the scan. Precious seconds brought no results. He flicked over the comms selector and found the static clearing on one channel. 'Channel sixteen.'

'Sir? Did you say sixteen?' Askenskaya's voice came back, but very faint and crackly.

'Hold your space there. Can you hear that, Askenskaya?'

'Negative, sir.'

'Are you on sixteen yet?'

'Yes. Static has cleared a little but that's it.'

Olentiev glanced over his instruments: fuel gauge, altimeter, peripheral weapons gauge, laser target tracker, chaff canister level, oil pressure, autocruise. 'Hang tight a moment,' he said as they passed over a giant black beach. 'Askenskaya?'

Nothing. 'Askenskaya?... *Askenskaya?!*' Olentiev thumbed the comms dial, calling, noticing how it was like all power had gone altogether. He eased his flight stick. The airspeed needle fell to three hundred and fifty. If Askenskaya was there, he should be roaring past any second....

Now? The drab hues of earth and evening sandstone told Olentiev all he needed to know. He felt the sweaty underarm of his jumpsuit freeze him when he jerked the stick to the right. Yawing, the SukHoi's canopy showed a reddening sky and a shimmering seaboard.

The scanner blip wasn't flashing anymore when Olentiev managed to restore his flight path and summon enough of himself to look for it. In fact, it wasn't a blip anymore... it was a steady dot in the middle of the top scanner quadrant, two thousand meters and closing. Olentiev saw the billow of smoke at the bottom of his canopy. 'Askenskaya?'

He dropped speed to 280.

What caught Olentiev's eye first were the Doppler dirt rings lying outside the blast area. The table land had taken a direct hit and now bore a black indentation. In the middle of the hole was something metallic, something...

Olentiev's blood froze. How could it still be *burning?* Nothing had those kinds of fuel reserves.

He caught the solar sail out of the corner of his eye. It was charred, corrupted but he recognized the structure, barely a kilometer below him. He barely noticed the crackling sound while he watched. In fact, he would have totally overlooked that had the Geiger counter not been switched on and pumping a hundred vibrations a second into his chest.

Lethal radiation if you were standing on the dirt by that thing, Major.

...Wait... who was that walking around down there? 'Askenskaya?'

The figure continued trouncing toward the pit and its silvery payload. It was a pilot all right, wearing a standard Russian Air Force helmet and stepping lazily but with intent. 'Askenskaya?'

Olentiev pulled up a little on his stick, tried to yaw right. From the corner of his canopy, he saw that the figure had now made it into the pit and was touching the side of the silver craft.

Five hundred meters above, Olentiev tried easing back on the stick but found himself straining to look down, pooling bootfuls of sweat chilling his feet.

The figure was looking up at him, the sun flashing in its helmet visor. 'Askenskaya?'

Olentiev couldn't catch the angle of his descent. He *did* notice the skeletal complexion of the figure when it drew up its visor and hissed 'Dead Voyager' into his helmet speakers before the thunderflash came.

And then came the fizz before Olentiev knew only blackness.

-8-

17ᵗʰ April, San Diego, California

Coleman rolled over and came to a grateful rest on his side of the mattress. 'Rick,' Leah whispered to the ceiling. 'Don't go. Stay for a bit.'

'I can't.'

'What time is it?'

'Seven-fifteen; I gotta motor.'

'Don't go.'

'Must.' Coleman shot a leg out from under the comforter. He thumbed the TV remote.

A colorful dinosaur was skipping around like a Haight Ashbury homo. Coleman yawned, sent a charge of his thick, milky breath over his wife. Her hair was a massive tangle of black kelp over the pillow, her head woozy, motionless after the rapture of only minutes before.

'Let's see who's died today,' Coleman mused. The novelty of the world's slow death process had waned on him in the last week. Nathan of the FBI had seen to that at any rate.

'That's not funny. Don't put it on the news.'

'Tough.' Coleman's thumb pressed down and annihilated the prehistoric fun.

The reception was awful. Coleman knew the cable companies would be toast soon if they didn't come up with a cure for the cosmic, rain-borne poison that had come from nowhere.

The screen's fizz allowed an unfamiliar landscape. The correspondent was English.

"*Authorities in Russia are citing the incident as a phenomenon. Unconfirmed reports have cited the object as the Voyager One space probe which NASA had recently lost communication with. The craft had been venturing further into deep space since departing Saturn in December 1980. Now, it had somehow entered the ozone hole in Siberia on its trajectory earthward. An impossible journey, considering many factors, not least its programming and heretofore understood distance from the Earth.*

Scientists from around the world have been expressing exasperation by rumors of this development. The guidance systems on board the probe could never have caused a complete turnabout. It appears that this will be yet another entry in a bizarre and lethal chain of international events to mar this year further still."

The picture changed to show the spacecraft's wrecked hull on display in a hangar. 'Jesus, look at that,' said Coleman. 'Why the hell did it do that?'

"The fallen spacecraft was recovered earlier by Russian army logistics personnel in protective clothing and using heavy transport. While the crash location is too suspicious to put down to coincidence, Russian scientists are showing more alarm at the excessive levels of radioactivity in the immediate area. The landscape has already been heavily poisoned by radiation from the Tunguska ozone cavity."

A goateed Russian astronomer appeared and was dubbed two seconds after speaking.

'Honey, listen up to this stuff.'

Leah grunted, jabbed her big toenail into his buttock.

"<Nothing like this. No. There is absolutely nothing to account for the levels of radiation the wreckage is emitting. Even with the parting of the atmospheric layers in that region, it should not have survived re-entry in as good a condition as it is. Even after capture and transportation to Novgorod, it continues to bombard its surroundings with more than enough rads to kill an unprotected human within minutes.>"

The picture shifted back to the correspondent, microphone in hand, speaking from the security entrance of the Novgorod labs.

"Of course, the recent destruction of the central Siberian landscape by the so-called 'Hole in the Sky' is adding to the problem. In a month that political analysts have called the most precarious and significant ever experienced by the world, there is much room for speculation as to what may happen next."

'What's going to happen next is I'm getting some damn black coffee,' Coleman muttered before reaching for his pants, slung by the nightstand. 'You want?'

'No. You better get yourself in gear for today.'

Leah's words cut a swath through the cobwebs in Coleman's mind. He shot her a wry smile and slid the wool shag rug over the hardwood floor as he lumbered off downstairs into needed wakefulness.

7:28

The phone never rang around that time: morning calls were rare occurrences that the voicemail ended up taking. Both he and Leah worked and had to negotiate rush-hour traffic at only slightly differing times. Coleman had his fingers clasped around his Doctor Who mug, came close to dropping it as he moved it to his non-handset friendly hand.

'Hello?'

'Coleman; Nathan. I need you to come to the lab now. Can you leave right away?'

'Nathan, what is this?' Nathan's breathing was shallow and fast. Something *was* up.

'Just, can you leave right away?'

'Look; just tell what it is. C'mon, Nathan, I'm not just some technician at Crime Lab.'

'That's why I need to consult your expertise. You were in surveillance for a few years. You're the only one I can share this with for the moment.'

'For the moment?' Coleman felt hairs bristle up on his nape, only half from feeling cold.

'Please. You're senior personnel; you can get in before working hours.'

'Nathan, is this about yesterday?'

'Yes. This is all about yesterday.'

'You've found out something?'

'You know I can't talk here, Coleman.'

Screw your FBI protocol, jerk, Coleman thought. 'If you're sure it's not an error, why d-'

'Just get over here. I can expect you in vid analysis in twenty-five minutes, then?'

Coleman felt a lump forming in his throat, tried to check the beginnings of a panic feeling. 'Make it thirty and I'll meet you in the foyer. This had better be good.'

'Right. And Coleman, better bring your wits with you. We'll need them.'

-9-
<u>17th April, Newport Beach, California</u>

Becker awoke sometime after eight in a half-stupor. When his foot swept to the left, it knocked over what sounded like six spent beer bottles.

But there was another sound there, too. A buzzing coming from the other way.

He looked over the armrest and felt a charge of vomit sear upward when he caught sight of the additional quintet of emptied pilsners. 'Going to be a hard night's day, this.'

It was cold in his basement. Even the light coming in from his high double panes was a frigid, unforgiving lemonade tone.

Somehow the TV was on, spewing out images of his favorite talk-show fight baiter and a panel of penitent-looking transsexuals. 'Shit,' Becker spluttered, shoving his elbows back on the rests while he tried to rise. 'Don't know who's crazier - me or the world these days.'

Nak-nak-nak

Becker bolted upright, overbalanced and took the impact with his DVD stand painfully.

Nak-nak-nak

'Just hold your horses!'

The doorbell chimed as well this time, as Becker thrumped up the staircase. He struggled to walk straight, the cramps in his thighs failing miserably to confuse his hangover.

The beige-white-black silhouettes in the bubble glass of the front door told him there were two visitors in neatly pressed suits… the type who *knew* he was in.

'Hang on.'

The gap revealed two black-suited Shaun Bean clones. 'Mr. Becker, may we come in?'

Becker felt his scrotum retract into his intestines. 'Uhh, sure; I guess.'

Shaun Bean Doppelganger One moved through the doorway while his twin cased his sunglasses and made a sweeping scan of Becker's car-less cul-de-sac.

'Which branch of Uncle Sam's extended family are you?' Becker chanced on the way round the corner from the hall and into the dining room he hadn't used since he'd had a family.

Shaun Bean Doppelganger One waited for number two to close the front door. 'C.I.A., Mister Becker.'

'Yeah? Well, I thought you were too, well, *different* looking from the F.B.I. They're not as Church of Jesus Christ of Latter Day Sainty looking, if you get me.'

Shaun Bean Doppelganger Two moved into Becker's living room and selected the middle of the beige loveseat Abbie had selected years ago. 'Sorry for the trouble we're putting you to, Mr. Becker,' he said, actually succeeding in sounding sorry, Becker thought.

'It's Carl. When you're under the roof, it's first names… Unless I say otherwise.'

'We have to have about half an hour of your time now, sir,' Shaun Bean Doppelganger One cut in. 'Are you contracted for any work today?'

'Not this morning.' Becker noticed the sharpness of number two's pupils and felt his insides sinking further down on the way to meeting his genitals. 'Look, can I get you guys drinks - coffee?'

'No thanks,' number two said and kept his stare on Becker. 'We're here on business and it won't take long.'

'This about the black box yesterday?'

'No,' number one said. 'We know the FBI has already contacted you about that. There's no more you can help with on that.'

Becker grimaced. 'What? This is something else entirely?'

'Yes. You haven't been watching the news this morning?'

Becker pressed his thumb tip against an eyelid, tried to hold down a laugh. *Yeah, right. I was up all night with the TV,* his mind's voice jabbed. *Ask me when I'm asleep again and let my subconscious tell you what I saw.* 'No, no … I've actually only woken up.'

Shaun Bean Doppelganger One assured: 'No problem. That's fine.'

The other commented: 'If you'd seen it, you would've found that one of NASA's Voyager craft crashed straight into the southeastern Tungus Basin, Russia.'

Becker shrugged. 'The *Ozone Zone?* God. As if they need any more grief out there.'

'But that's not what we're here to talk to you about.'

'Hey, well; I'm not into space stations anyway.' Becker drew his lower lip in hard over his incisors, bit down when he saw that neither Bean Doppelganger had been amused.

'You were in Operation Desert Storm,' Shaun Bean Doppelganger Two declared.

The other followed with: 'You sub-directed de-mining runs about the Kuwaiti coast. Your first military contract was Grenada during the overthrow of the Bishop government. Prior to that, you'd founded your diving business purely on a touch-and-go basis, relied on word of mouth and yellow pages ads in San Diego. You've been contracted to work on submarine hulls for the Japanese and Venezuelan governments.'

Becker's eyes dropped to scrutinize the cigar burn he'd deposited on the supposedly non-burnable mock Turkish rug the night after the night of his daughter's funeral. 'Thanks, but if I'd wanted this I'd have asked Jack Perkins to cover me on A and E's "Biography".'

Shaun Bean Doppelganger One perched himself on the armrest of the loveseat's single companion, folded his arms and looked apologetic. 'I'm sorry, Mister Becker. What we're driving at is that your name is as good as being at the top of our shortlist.'

'Shortlist? What, you mean you want me for another dive?'

'Yes. We've been asked to interest you in a highly classified project which the State Department has designed in the South Atlantic.'

'South Atlantic? Never been there!'

'That's okay for the moment. It's just that there's a situation there which no-one else on our database can handle with as much care as we believe you can give,' Shaun Bean Doppelganger One continued.

'*Situation?* What're you talking about? I thought it was Russia that was having the sh-'

'At oh four hundred hours, the seafront residential and business zones in Montevideo, Uruguay were shelled by high-caliber artillery.'

'Sea-based artillery?'

'Do you know anything about Montevideo's history, Mister Becker?'

'Sure.' Becker's guts had eased now. The intrigue that was making his eyebrows go higher was as pleasant as a tenth shot glass of gin with an old friend in a sports bar on the strip. 'Every seafarer with half a brain from my generation knows that that's where the Brits axed the *Graf Spee* back in 1939 or '40. Is that it?'

'Alright; what we're going to say next may upset you, Mister Becker sir. Upset your sense of reason, that is,' commented Shaun Bean Doppelganger Two.

'Upset my sense of reason.' Becker laughed, cut it short when he caught number two's gaze. 'The world's been flushed so fast you can't see the peanut chips and you're worried about-'

'The Uruguayan army and navy reacted speedily. They incapacitated the aggressor craft with heavy arms fire. The craft appeared to make no escape attempt when navy gunboats closed on its position.' Shaun Bean Doppelganger One interlocked his fingers as he finished speaking.

Shaun Bean Doppelganger Two took the cue. 'At dawn, reconnaissance planes from the Uruguayan Air Force tracked debris to the point of submersion of the craft. Cutter crews did the salvage work. Just two hours ago, we were briefed on the affair. The Uruguayan analysis points to something that is impossible for us to make sense of.' The second Bean lookalike was sounding blunt now.

'Which is where you come in,' his twin lookalike conjoined. Pressure from them both, Becker thought… just like a rehearsed scene or a segment of somebody's else's life in a movie.

'What? You mean they think the *Graf Spee* came up from the depths and tried to blow the seaboard to Kingdom Come?!'

'Analysis on the wreckage has shown it to be about eighty years old, well rusted and barnacle ridden. It's a battleship all right, regardless of the fact there's no Nazi livery in evidence.'

Shaun Bean Doppelganger Two added: 'And the Uruguayans are already conducting a sweep of the shelf-bed where the *Graf Spee* sank. If its hull isn't anywhere inside those co-ordinate parameters....'

Becker had his cigs out now. Shaun Bean Doppelganger One guided him to his lighter on the lower shelf of the coffee table. 'If that hulk doesn't show up where it went down,' the other agent continued, 'That means it was dragged up from the floor by something that then made it sail.'

Becker lit up then pressed a cheek against the knuckles of his other hand. 'You guys realize that what you're saying would get you put away if you weren't on the putter away side.'

Shaun Bean Doppelganger One made an abortive try at a smile.

'Now you want me to dive down to the wreckage of this thing and confirm it as-'

'As whatever it is. We can't know for sure what we - what *you'll* find down there. We know the new wreck lies in the shallows off the mouth of the River Plate. A submersible won't be needed.'

Shaun Bean Doppelganger Two made a cradle with his fingers and pulled a praying position. 'But we need your consent to go there this morning. And you're bound to secrecy on this. Protocol *two-six-eight-one-four-stroke-cee.*'

'I've been there before,' Becker said. 'I got nobody to tell, anyhow. Except my associates if this - if this'll take more than one or two d-'

'You have three people under you: Paul Clay, Mark Davidson and Yolanda Lopez.' Shaun Bean Doppelganger Two raised his palms, shook his head gently. 'They've got to go on ice for a while.'

'But they can't go freelance. I'm the job hub; they're subcontracted under me!'

'Then you'll have to call in sick,' Shaun Bean Doppelganger One said. 'You'll be gone for maybe as long as a week or so ... That's if you decide to accept the arrangement.'

'There's going to be a generous commission on this: close to twelve thou for this dive whether the wreck's German or not.' Shaun Bean Doppelganger Two rubbed his chin at that, prepping himself for optimum persuasive delivery. 'If you have a conscience about your people here, you can pass the inconvenience benefits on to them.'

Becker took a hard drag and pondered. In a flash he'd fused a new jeep with being scared witless with Yolanda Lopez smiling on the hide-a-bed in his basement, bathed in red light.

'It's your call, but you're subject to secrecy provisions now whether you say yes or no.'

Becker stared into the glowing orange cherry of his cig and saw the world. 'What can I say? I might as well just do it then.'

-10-
17ᵗʰ April, San Diego, California

'His name's Jurgen Hiram Ganz.'

Nathan was unshaven, carried the stench of an hour's sleep on his skin. For a man of forty-five, which is where Coleman would have placed him, he seemed headed for a hospice.

Coleman tried breaking eye contact with the magnified, blackened face on the VDU and found he could not. 'Okay. So what's this guy's story?'

The booth in the video analysis lab was wide enough for Nathan and Coleman to sit side by side with a comfortable striking distance. Coleman watched bewildered as Nathan pulled up the tab on the legal-sized, bubble-wrapped envelope.

'This is what we were able to get on him.' Nathan laid a set of mug shots out on the ply veneer and reached back inside. 'Age 29, anthropology major at North Dakota College.'

'North Dakota? That's quite a way away.'

Nathan smirked. 'I know. California's problems get shown up by these little league states. Apparently their economy up there was hot shit enough for them to attract some serious brains and money. They're like the third best state to live in or something crazy like that.'

'So what'd he do up there to get arrested?'

'The mug shot is for an assault charge back in '12. Seems Mr. Ganz was upset at the results of a midterm he did for an elective course during his undergrad.'

Coleman held the square photograph close to his face. Ganz looked Bohemian: delicate features, dark hair, twinkling gray eyes but with gigantic pupils. 'This guy for real?'

Nathan didn't answer. 'Arrested November 2012 for assaulting his earth sciences professor with a hardcover textbook; suspended from North Dakota College. Prosecuted and missed the year.'

'What happened to him?'

'Fine options: five hundred hours community service paid in full by

April 2013. Sued by victim for ten grand; looks like his parents settled out of court.' Nathan produced the 8 mm video cartridge. 'But here's the real treat.'

Coleman watched the cartridge roll into the older vid machine. 'What's this then?'

'No; just watch it. This is from over two years ago,' Nathan whispered. The screen shot from matt black to show a newsroom with a blonde thirty-something lady reading an item:

"The family of Fargo man Jurgen Ganz is tonight appealing for help from Israeli authorities over the disappearance of the 29 year-old postgraduate student. Ganz had been on a travel course to Israel to conduct archaeological digs in the ancient city of Joppa."

The footage showed the central administration building of the University of Tel Aviv.

"Ganz went missing just a day before his study group was to head to Joppa to continue work on the site begun two years ago by Dr. Gunther Kresge."

The camera returned to the news desk.

"His parents and Fargo police fear that he may have been abducted in Tel Aviv, possibly by a terror cell in the area. Mr. Ganz was exhibiting no signs of uncharacteristic behavior before departing for Israel, according to acquaintances at N.D.C."

Nathan switched her off. 'So what d'you reckon? It took me until two-forty this morning to get this up on this guy.' Nathan's pride was more than evident – another victory for his kind.

'How'd you get his face paired up to a database match with that black crap in the way?'

'It wasn't easy. Had to take the saved thumbnail and use an enhancer to handle the monochromatic anomaly.' Nathan smiled wryly, bared more urine-colored enamel to Coleman. 'And then there was the scale problem.'

'Because it was only a few pixels by a few pixels?'

'Exactly. The main trouble was the image enhancer. Had to use really low resolution just to take away the blocks and square edges.'

Coleman breathed out hard and tried to empty his mind as Nathan explained himself the rest of the way. 'This is why I had to call you in early.'

'And nobody knows about this guy showing up in the film ten thousand times too small.'

'Got it in one. The only problem now is where we go next with this.'

'What do you mean?' Coleman's voice was strained. He felt ice forming in his chest.

'What I mean is how we present this at a press conference.'

'*Press* conference! They'll never allow it. Red tape – we've got red *rope* on this thing!'

'Coleman, do you realize what's at stake here? We're talking about ghosts here!'

'But you have to submit a report on your findings before that happens.'

'Precisely why I called you in here early... Before anyone thinks about shutting us down with this, I want you to understand what we really have... what we really had here before anyone else does.'

'Well. It'll be risky. But Carmichael and the Pentagon will have to take notice. No?'

'Coleman, in twenty-five minutes I'm due to fax base here in San Diego with the results of yesterday's work.' Nathan rose, ejected the tiny video. 'If I just say "anomaly", they'll turn up the heat on you guys here to break it down more. But if I start in about all *this*, it'll be another Roswell. At least a bogus we'll-let-you-know story will keep everyone off our backs.'

Coleman grinned drily. 'But the whole world's unraveling. Nobody in high government is going to try going covert with this. Too much to lose by cutting down researcher numbers.'

'They won't want research from the likes of you or me. It'll all be boffins and they're gonna run this round in circles until they're blue in the face.'

'Nathan, we're sitting in the top place in the country for processing this stuff.'

'The top place that we *know about*, Coleman. Remember that.'

Coleman shook his head and shrugged. 'Think we'd really get pulled off it after all we-'

'Yes; I do think that. Who was FBI here, Coleman, you or me?'

-11-
18<u>th</u> April,
Undisclosed Location, Russian Federation

Olentiev tried moving his leg and banged his knee into the sheeted cage above it. A scream welled up behind his lips but he couldn't bear letting it go. A dirty, creamy white room did little to soothe him. 'Where... *why* am I here?!' he spat at the ceiling. 'My plane: Askenskaya?'

'You're in Irkutsk, Major Olentiev. You crashed four kilometers southeast of the target in the burn zone. Neither you nor Lieutenant Askenskaya made a successful reconnaissance.'

Olentiev's eyes fell to his left, tried to peer around the edge of the sheet cage to put a face to the voice. He'd already put a career-type to it: military, but not the down-to-earth military he knew so well. 'You are special forces, aren't you?'

'Yes; but don't let that put you off from speaking freely.' The owner of the voice got to his feet and moved up to Olentiev's field of vision. 'We've all been through an ordeal with this.'

Olentiev felt a pang of dread enter him then. There was something in the man's gaunt features, something satanic about the sunkeness of his eyes. Yet, he couldn't have been much older than Askenskaya, not outwardly. 'Askenskaya. Where is Askenskaya?!'

The visitor reached into the lapel underside of his coat for a moment then entrusted his hands to the care of his trouser pockets. Olentiev had heard the soft click of the Mp3 recorder.

'Yes. Let's both talk about what happened to Lieutenant Askenskaya, shall we?'

'He's dead? That's what you mean.'

'His craft has not been recovered. Maybe *you* can shed some light on its and his fate.'

Olentiev found he could feel his legs burning. 'Please. I'm going to need to smoke.'

'Here.' The visitor flipped an unfiltered Sophy at him. 'You also wonder about yourself, no? Nothing that'll kill you. Remarkable, as you only ejected about four hundred meters above ground.'

Olentiev's gullet rose in protest from the first puff. 'I - I wasn't burned by my SukHoi?'

'Your flying suit was damaged by a bad landing. The burns you're feeling on your thighs and shins are from sun exposure in the Sky Damage Zone.'

'Askenskaya *didn't* crash ... then he must have *returned.*'

'He didn't return. It is unlikely for him to have crashed without due cause, either. You both left base with enough fuel for the round trip.' The visitor lifted his eyebrows, allowed the cold hospital light to trickle under his brow. Olentiev saw that his eyes were very bright and very blue.

'You've checked around for his wreck?'

'With the aid of crack detachments from the Kazakh Airforce, we've scoured the route you took yesterday. Unless it was in Lake Baykal, we can virtually rule out his having crashed.'

'Still a big area.' Olentiev sighed. He'd never figured before that he had known Askenskaya for what felt like a long time yet was still a short time.

'Unless he disintegrated on impact with the lake, dead-center, we'd've heard something by now. You don't vanish with hardware like that for long, not with the type of tracking you know we have.'

Olentiev's cigarette was half spent. The rising smoke from the cherry was thick, toxic; it added an even unholier dimension to the special forces man's face. 'I can't remember anything about Askenskaya. All there was was this great silver thing in a crater and... and I panicked.'

'Why did you panic, Olentiev? A man with your years' experience, your background?'

'That thing ... that fuselage: that was like an old western spacecraft!'

The visitor's face froze. 'You went into a state of shock from *believing* what you saw?'

'N-no.' Olentiev bit his lip. 'I mean it was that and the r-'

'Radiation?' The face smiled. 'Come now, Major; you were flying very low over the crash area. At your speed you would have felt the first effects of sickness much later, if at all.'

Olentiev checked a surge of rage. 'I don't know. All I know is that when I flew lower to get a visual on the... on the craft, I became ill very fast. I- I must have blacked out.'

'But you ejected. There's no way to activate that without your knowing it.'

'I'm sorry, but that's all I can tell you. All I'm *able* to tell you.'

'But Lieutenant Askenskaya? Surely you kept in contact with him until your problem got the better of you.' The visitor scraped a chair to the bedside and sat. 'You were patched into his cabin: your comms selector dial was still on a plane-to-plane frequency when you were found.'

'Lieutenant Askenskaya and I were having comms problems.'

'And when did these problems begin, Major?'

'About... about the same time we cleared the Baykal shoreline.' Olentiev had to strain himself from looking for where the microphone was. 'We had some other difficulties long before that, though.'

'You lost base contact twenty kilometers from Lake Baykal: what do you make of that?'

'At first... at first I thought it was a scrambling device. An enemy installation.'

'But you know that no remote device could operate at that range, given the absence of rebel units in the area.' The visitor leaned forward, looking very much like he was enjoying this.

And why wouldn't you, you bastard? Olentiev thought. *Years of pathetic paychecks and now you get a shot at something hot.* 'Look,' Olentiev said, 'General Alexiev warned us of-'

'But you continue to think your insurgent Siberian radio scrambling installation was responsible for the lapse in communications?'

'That's all I *can* think. Your bureau must have known about the problems with central Siberia since the occurrence.' *Occurrence!*, Olentiev thought. How could he call this sort of thing just an "occurrence"?

He looked the special forces man dead in the eye. 'Their aerospace must have had many anomalies after what happened... no atmosphere to speak of... and now that thing crashing from space.'

'It does, Olentiev. It's just that planes have been flown around there many times in the last month. Even the high ambient radiation and the smattering of that alien elemental precipitation isn't enough to block communications *completely*.'

Olentiev broke eye contact. 'I can't understand it. Look, I'm in shock still: no condition to be interviewed over this.'

Special forces man restored his grin, bowed his head, raising his palms upward. 'Very well... Yes. Perhaps later, though. You'll have time yet to remember. We can be sure of it, in fact, eh, Major Olentiev?'

-12-
18ᵗʰ April, San Diego, California

'Christ, it's cold in here!'

'Sorry; air con's always messed up in this part of the building.'

Reynolds grimaced but kept staring into the monitor Hank Jarvis was seated in front of. 'I say it's time we had a coffee break.'

Jarvis reached for the thermos. 'No, Hank. Let's walk to the machine: help me to think.'

'Hey, we've cut through a lot today,' Jarvis said when they got their drinks.

Reynolds sipped his decaf, sighed. 'Yeah, but we haven't exactly narrowed things down. We just know the guy's ISP, that he's based in the U.S. and that he's good at this shit.'

'The knot's tightening on him at least.'

'Okay. But you know how many people are registered with us now?'

Jarvis slowed his pace in the corridor, frowning. 'I'd say we're about a third of the way there now, Dave. From here, it's a matter of tracing and rooting: a ton more research, okay, but let's look at what we've got on this guy. He's a big-time nerd and he's got a big-time ego crisis.'

'So you reckon he's one of those losers who's out to do heavy duty damage just so he can get snatched up by his ideal firm once he's out of the can?'

'Yep. Seems to fit the profile.'

Reynolds pulled a chair from the centermost desk of the office and flopped down on it. 'No; that's too thin. If it was any other kind of virus then yeah - fine, but *this* thing can't be the work of a college boy. Not that I can see. I mean, the way he's got that line thing to trigger on its own after a while on the reboot - what we'd missed at first?'

Jarvis hit a function key and the screen filled with machine language. The program that was executing now was their best machine's best attempt at simulating the virus. 'I'm not so sure. I mean, to look at it freestanding and all, it could pass for a more basic kind of I.T. poison.'

'Until it executes, Hank. It's like this guy wanted to mask his baby with something generic - something that could've been whipped up by any geek with a gripe and a keyboard.'

Jarvis kept scrolling down the file. 'Wait,' Reynolds said. 'I s- I see something in there.'

'What? Where?'

'Hang on; keep your finger on there until I say. Steady; wait....wait.'

'What you g-'

'*There*. Those blocks keep showing – see… there's another clump. Get a fix on that line and measure it back to the last time.'

'Fifty-eight,' Jarvis said when he was done. 'Every fifty-eighth line they come up.'

'Doesn't that strike you as weird?'

'Patterns happen, even in complex executable files such as viruses.'

Reynolds shot the rest of his drink straight down the hatch, shook his head. 'But how many have you seen that include squares and blocks that way?'

'Viruses are like fingerprints, Dave. Each one a unique set of hieroglyphs and wingdings that can equal a lot of misery once you've downloaded them.'

'Or in this case, *not* downloaded them. I don't know; I'm not buying its viability as a basic one from its code structure.'

'But the code is what makes the virus.'

'No. Too much has been going on with all this for it to be that easy.'

'What're you saying here, Dave?'

'I'm saying this is engineered with *self defense* in mind. Whoever did this does not want anyone to see inside his bag of tricks. He knows he's on to something with this new formula and he wants the ace to stay up his sleeve.'

'But that's imp- look, no way can it be done without a core code.'

'Fuck that. You mean to tell me what happened in Russia would have been considered *possible* at one time? What's beating the stuffing out of the Third World right now, *possible*?'

'The program dictates the virus's function. It's as simple as th-'

'Then we're screwed, Hank. You know that?' Reynolds rose, paced over to the wall. 'This thing's wiping out businesses all over and by all appearances we should have been able to cook up a neutralizer already.'

'Okay; that's why we need to trace the problem to the root.'

'Pretty soon there'll be no equipment left to trace anything with. God, Hank, this guy must have realized that his PC would get hit from the ricochet effect.'

'Unless he's shielded himself. Anyone smart enough to do this must be smart enough to have either an antidote or-'

'Or a firewall way thicker than any file transfer protocol safeguard that we know of.'

'Which means the only way is to take this jerk alive.'

Reynolds retook his seat, gawped at the screen. 'How in Hell could something like this be *designed*: something that turns your hard drive to shit *the second* you log into your ISP and only tap the fresh email icon?'

'And then there's the line sequence that comes on the display. Now that has to be a secondary program being injected via the virus. But I still say it's down to codes,' Jarvis said.

'And yet there's no evidence of that in the code *structure*.'

'Well, we know it's not a logic-inspired screen fault. That goes without saying.'

Reynolds let his fist drop to the desk top before he got to his feet. 'Well that cuts it, Hank. We're stumped on this one. Let the domestic C.I.A. play with it all they want.'

'Where are you off to?'

'Gotta pick Raina up from my folks.'

'You not coming back, then.'

'No.'

'What about Parker?'

'To Hell with Parker. Something this serious needs government attention. I just hope my little girl still gets to have a world to grow up in.'

-13-
<u>18<u>th</u> April, San Diego, California</u>

'Daddy no good!'

Reynolds crossed his eyes, frowned and looked over at his daughter.

'Please, Daddy!'

'Oh, alright. But no McDonnies now for the rest of the month.'

'That's okay,' Raina cooed, jumping in her seat. 'Not long 'til May.'

'Still in the weeks. You can't wait that long, can you?'

'There's always Kentucky Fried, Daddy!'

Reynolds pulled up to the speaker in the drive thru and ordered two highly contented burger meals and sundaes. 'Why, you little schemer. At least it's only May coming up; remember what *October* is, little girl?'

'No?'

'Scary-wary month!'

'Barry's scary, Daddy.'

Reynolds pulled up to the service window too slowly for Raina. 'What's wrong, Daddy?'

'Nothing, sweetheart; Barry's someone from TV?'

'Nnnnnawh!'

'Then who?'

'A friend of Billy's'

Reynolds suddenly felt a surge of rage coming on. Billy's friends were usually potheads; potheads had to be kept away from Raina at all costs.

But can you keep her safe from the news about this self-destructing planet?

'When did you hear about him, Raina?'

'Daddy, is something wrong?'

Plenty was wrong when it came to Billy's friends. Scary? They were bad. Although that was bad as in 'trouble', not 'evil', it was too much. 'No. Just, how do you know about Barry?'

'Oh... he came round to granny's house today.'

'He what?' Reynolds felt relieved when he saw the light go red at the intersection ahead. 'When did he come round?'

'About an hour before you came. Billy left with him.'

'Did you answer the door?'

'Yyyyes?'

'Wasn't very smart, sweetie, was it?'

Raina stopped munching on her fries, hung her head in silence.

'Where were Gramma and Granpa?'

'In the gazebo.'

'And Billy?'

'He was downstairs. Had his MP3 music on.'

'He should've answered; why were you inside, away from Gramma?'

'Toilet, Daddy.'

'How long did you talk to Barry before Billy came up?'

Reynolds heard her sniffle then.

No, I am not an asshole: please don't let me come across as one to her.

'I'm sorry, pet. It's just you forgot what your mom and I told you about front doors. Opening *any* doors.'

'Oh, Daddy!'

More sniffles came as Raina repeated that with a break in her voice.

Yes, you are an asshole, David.

'Because... Because, I was...I was...I was only there for a few seconds. Honest. Uncle Billy was on his way up from his room when I opened... When I opened the door.'

'It's okay, sweetie. I'm not angry with you. I just want you to remember the door rule.'

'S-sorry, Daddy. I won't do it again; I promise.'

'Here, give me a French fry.'

Reynolds pulled into the gas station four blocks shy of his street.

What are you doing? The tank's two thirds full.

Screw off. Can't let Raina get home still sniffling.

Reynolds did self-serve, paid with his card and slid behind the wheel feeling a little bit better. 'We friends again, sweetie?'

'Only if we can do burger drive-thru once more this week.'

'Why you little monkey!'

'I mean it, Daddy!'

'Alright then!'

Reynolds' Jetta was nearing the drive when Raina finished her last French fry and asked: 'Daddy? What's suicide?'

-14-
18th April, San Diego, California

Coleman had totally forgotten about his other cell phone. He'd turned off his work cell when he was on the way back from the lab. The other's factory set screech was what woke him, jarring against his ears as he had to stretch out his legs and bend his back to reach for it.

Leah moaned when he slid out from the covers to answer it.

'Coleman... you there, Rick?'

It was Carmichael, the closest thing he had to a boss in an organization that could not afford to reveal too much structure now that its framework had been chopped and changed.

'Yeah?'

'Red dove, Rick. Red dove.'

Click

'Damn it.'

He heard Leah rustling the comforter behind him. 'I better go. Sorry, hun.'

Damn thing would be military classification for sure, he thought as he got ready. So much for Nathan's talk about keeping it out of the underground bunkers now.

Leah exhaled her disapproval but stayed comment-less. Coleman could see the pain in her eyes by the subdued, curtain-filtered power of the streetlight outside.

How many times in the past had he had to tell her she'd asked enough questions for her own good? She had learned well over the years, though.

'You just take care out there, Mister No-say.'

Coleman kissed her forehead then reached for his pants. 'Anything for you.'

'How about a week away in Paris?'

'You might have a week away *from me* if you're lucky.'

Leah straightened up, grasped his shoulder. 'Rick, no!'

'Can't help it. Pretty heavy stuff flying about now.' He saw the full darkness of the night in her eyes. 'So I need you to be strong for me.'

'Alr- alright...'

'We'll hit Paris Christmas-time, maybe.'

'We better. I'll take that "maybe" as a "yes", Rick.'

'I love you.'

'I love you, too.'

'Paris it is, then. I swear it, Leah.'

Coleman gunned his Grand-Am hard through the night streets, trying to dilute the pain of fatigue with fantasies of solving Nathan's proposed Ganz case.

The harbor's north entrance gate glinted back a warning to him.

Red dove. Red dove was the location codeword for S.S. Nimrod 3. Red Dove was also second from the top of the list in code priority.

Carmichael was waiting at the gate of the docking tower, smoking a stubby cigarette.

In silence, the two men made their way to the mess hall. When Coleman followed him into the brightness, he found five other agents.

He knew only one of them.

'Durning.'

'Coleman.'

'What you got for us, sir?' Coleman asked as he took a seat at the corner of the centermost table.

'Gentlemen, we have something of a development, I'm afraid.'

Coleman felt his blood run colder than December dew. 'Development' from Carmichael's lips meant bad news. No need for 'afraid'.

'Late last night, we received word from our FBI liaison. It seems there's a tentative link between the anomaly that appeared on the surveillance footage Mister Coleman was analyzing and one other tape.'

'Which one was that?' Coleman asked.

'I'll let Mister Allinson answer that,' Carmichael answered, extended his arm at the blond-haired agent furthest away from Coleman.

The agent rose from his chair and moved past Carmichael to the laptop, securicam monitor and digital camera setup at the back of the hall.

'Gentlemen, please come closer,' he said after he'd switched everything on. Coleman's gaze was greeted with a split screen as he moved closer.

'The image on the left is from the Tierney ecclesiastical assassination you were investigating, Mr. Coleman. The other's a still taken from outside the World Health Organization's headquarters two months ago.'

Allinson took up the control cord, thumbed its button. The pictures magnified to include only the central thirds of the original images on the liquid crystal screen. 'Both images are stills from CCTV tapes taken from the incident scenes. Mr. Coleman's assassination footage on the one hand and Mr. Jessup's fire at the W.H.O. building on the other.'

Coleman searched, found the girl in the red boots he had given a bored moment's lust to then scanned the other picture just as Allinson clicked his thumb once... twice. His eyes fell on a bearded Jesus lookalike before they moved up a little, seeking to make sense of the tableau. The girl above the lookalike could have passed for Leah, minus the perm.

'Note the dark discolorations in the center of each image,' Allinson continued. 'Right now, they don't look like much until I ...'

Click-click-click-click-click-click-click-click-click-click-click-click

'Now we have the blotches at a magnification of sixteen hundred. Notice the similarities between the tinting.'

Coleman couldn't feel his stomach anymore. Allison's tone had the clinical detachment of a coroner. *Click-click-click-click-click...* 'Resolution two thousand, high mag, low zoom.'

Coleman's eyes juiced the picture on the right for something with meaning, but there was nothing human-looking left there. The browny black blotches were taking up more than a fiftieth of the screen now.

Coleman could see no internal markings in the one on the right.

Click-click-click-click-click

The images expanded, engulfed an area three times their original diameter. The one on the right was still amorphous, opaque to Coleman's eyes.

He shifted his gaze back to the other still for a comparison check. The face was present on that one – his one. The definition in its cheeks was eerie. Evil. 'So it's the same color,' he said. 'But, what else about it?'

'Just a minute,' Allinson said. 'Note the formation on the left discoloration now. If we-'

'Do you know if they're tape faults?'

That had been Durning. 'Sorry?'

'Grains on the tape or system itself? They are both different *shapes*, aren't they?'

Allinson fell quiet for a moment. Coleman felt his stomach return to him when he saw the profoundness of the blond agent's uncertainty. Perhaps Nathan had been spoon-feeding him so much story now that Allinson couldn't find a decent answer. Or was it something deeper – something that needed to be restricted even from their ears? Coleman wondered.

'No,' Allinson replied at length. 'Our process scoured the source medium for physical abnormalities hundreds of times over.'

'On the original?' Coleman tried, hoping.

'Yes, and all digital transfer copies.'

'And didn't you find *anything*?' Durning again.

'As far as our laboratory was able to take it, *no*.'

'What about static discharge?' Coleman asked.

'We're sure it couldn't have been that or any other kind of *direct* camera interference.'

'How sure?' Coleman jabbed. He'd caught Carmichael's dirty look too late. *Christ, don't say that sounds like I don't want the case solved*, he thought.

'As good as a hundred per cent, Mr. Coleman. There's just too much data for there not to be a parallel here.'

'You mean these glitches happen at the same point in both incidents?' Durning asked.

'Yes. Both less than one quarter of one second before each occurrence. As you know, the fire in the W.H.O. building began *explosively*,' Allinson said, moving back to take up the control cord. 'Once I'm done with this, I'll run the Mpeg versions concurrently and at high magnification so you can see.'

'Let's return to the markings themselves, please, Allinson.'

Coleman dropped his stare to watch Carmichael hard at work stubble scratching, fishing for words that could mete out facts economically.

'We better get that bit straight quickly so I can brief you all on where we go with this,' Carmichael added.

'Sure.'

'That's if Mister Coleman and Mister Durning are happy with that.'

'I'm fine,' Durning said. 'It's just that I never realized the fire at the W.H.O. building had been determined as *bona fide* arson.'

'It hasn't. Not yet,' one of the agents unknown to Coleman - the black-haired one - said. 'It's still in our top five at the moment.'

'Let's get *on* with it,' Carmichael blurted, his eyes fixed on Coleman's.

Coleman felt the jolt of an argument brewing on the tip of his tongue before a pang of guilt froze it away. The World Health Organization headquarters had almost been *deleted* that day. He remembered the Reuters images: the girl with the puss-puffed red face and the clear mask filled with ointment overlying it; the ice rink that had been closed to act as an overflow morgue, and the Nobel Prize winner who'd lost both legs to hideous incendiary wounds.

Chalk up another one for the powers of Chaos that prevail in the world, he thought.

'Okay,' Allinson said. 'Gentlemen, we have two dark patches that were recorded onto the digicam footage from both incidents.'

'I see something in the left image,' the black-haired agent said. 'I know this sounds crazy but is that a *head* in there?'

'*My* head,' Coleman whispered. 'The one we found.'

'It's the likeness of a college graduate who went missing abroad a couple of years ago,' Allinson afforded.

'Jurgen Ganz,' the second unknown agent to Coleman said.

'Okay, so where are we going with this?' Durning threw in.

'You've seen this image before?'

'Yes; Coleman and I worked on it at the same lab here in town once the FBI let us be.'

'In that case,' Allinson said as he moved for the laptop keyboard, rolled a yellow rectangle around the outside of the right half of the screen, and prepared to thumb the control cord some more. 'In that case I better get to the point with this.'

Click-click-click-click

'Is that it?' Coleman asked.

He didn't like the look of Allinson at all now. He looked too much like Hutch from *Starsky and Hutch*, only minus the altruistic, pally-pally demeanor and soft jokes.

Coleman could hear his mind's voice praying there would be no...

Connection?

'You guys see just a dark blob on the W.H.O. screen now, right?'

'Let's get on with it,' Carmichael said. 'We've got to move fast on this.'

'Sorry, sir. As I was saying, there's no definition right now inside the discoloration.' Allinson typed in a sequence of function keys and one involving a three fingered command.

The deep brown mark warmed, brightened into a beige pool: a pool with dark features.

'My God,' Durning issued in a weak breath.

'Now that's with light enhancement of twenty-two candela equivalent to this screen.'

'My Lord,' Coleman joined. 'They're the same face. It's him.'

-15-
<u>18th April, San Diego, California</u>

'Billy!'

'Yeah?'

'Get your ass out here right now!'

The stream of metal music continued running unabated.

Dave Reynolds hammered the heel of his fist against the door. *'Billy?!'*

The door fell in by a thirty degree arc. The gap left by its passing brought Reynolds face to face with his kid brother. 'Yeah, Dave?'

Was that pot on his breath?

'What do you mean by letting delinquents into the house when Raina's about?'

'What you talkin' about?'

'Barry. You're pals with a freak called that?'

'*Aw*, he's not a freak, Dave!'

'Well what would you call him then?'

Billy fell in from the doorway, turned the volume dial counter-clockwise on his PC.

'He's not that bad, Dave.'

'Why was he talking about *suicide*?'

'How'd you know that?'

'Because Raina asked *me* about suicide.'

'She *what*?'

Billy looked stoned to Reynolds. His tailfin mustache was all curled up in bewilderment.

'Why was your friend carrying on about offing himself with my little girl in earshot?'

Billy drew back his shoulders, raised his palms in the air. 'Hey, no way; he wasn't joking about it.'

'What was he talking about it for, then?'

'He thinks his roommate up at NDC totaled himself.'

'Oh, right. And just who is this Barry guy anyway, Billy?'

'He, he was in high school with me.'

'I don't recall any friends of yours called that.'

'You never met him, Dave. This dude turned up for grade twelve only. His dad got a job transfer here from up north.'

Reynolds backed away from the door, shot a sheepish look at the carpet of the corridor. 'Well… Sorry. I guess I'm just stressed out from work.'

Billy was silent. Reynolds could feel his younger brother's quiescence spin like a drill bit in front of his head.

'It's just that I'm trying to keep Raina safe from that sort of shit. Things are bad enough in the world without-'

'Sorry. I headed out for lunch with him just a minute or two after he turned up. I didn't know Raina was still in the house; thought she was out back with mom and dad.'

'So was this guy a friend of your pal?'

'Uhmm?'

You have *been blazing up on weed, you* little *asshole*, Dave thought. 'The suicide guy.'

'No. They just dormed together. Barry's not broken up over it at all. Happened a long time ago, anyway.'

'Oh, right.'

'He hated the dude from what I heard. Strange creep: into Satanism and that kinda shit. Weird thing is, Barry says he's been getting calls from some lady who says she's this dead guy's mom.'

Dave Reynolds' belly turned to vapor. 'You mean he doesn't know if she is or not?'

'She sounds like she's eighty years old is what he says. Been calling him two, three times a day just to ask him crap like how his dorm looked when he left it.'

Don't tell me this, you little prick; I've got enough on my plate without more. 'What?'

'Not only that; he says she knows he's alive and well and that he wants to get in touch with him. Weird, huh?'

'Yeah, I guess. Look, I got to be at work in twenty minutes.'

'Big emergency meeting or something?'

'Yeah. Look, I gotta motor now. Tell Mom I said hi when she gets back from the mall.'

Reynolds opened the front door of his parents' house, cast a pained look back at his younger brother. 'And Billy; I'd stay away from that fella.'

'Why?'

'Because things are bad enough right now without you going out and finding more trouble for yourself.'

'Barry's okay, though.'

'He may not be for much longer. Sounds like someone's out to get him.'

'Then he needs help - protection, right?'

'Wrong. You keep away. Don't cause us any grief by walking into a trap.'

-16-

<u>18th April, Uruguay, South America</u>

Becker's jet kissed the redness in the sky above Montevideo just as he was coming out of a mini-coma. He hated military planes. The netting within the fuselage had been spurring him into binges of sour recollection; the stench of so much exposed metal conjured train tracks in his mind, and train tracks smelled identical to blood. Gallons of it; gallons upon gallons of blood oozing from the cancer sores and malignant moles of untold numbers of people in Siberia.

And your daughter, Becker: remember her? The bright, rosy red apple of your eye plucked and stamped to pulp in front you by the Evil Big Cee?

Becker squirmed at that thought. He wanted Bourbon. A fingernail would have to do instead. Across the aisle was Graham Hartley, the nanny Uncle Sam had sent and behind them both were eleven of the navy's finest aquanauts, all short-listed under Becker and all under thirty-five.

As Becker prepped his stomach for touchdown, he couldn't help playing back snippets of the conversation he'd had with Hartley just after boarding in San Diego:

'This stuff is all crazy. Personally, Becker, I believe it's Divine Intervention. Of course that sounds crazy, too, but nobody has any answers to this.'

'*Yet*, you mean.'

'No.' Hartley had hesitated, seemed to be searching for words. 'Ever. I don't think *ever*. I mean, how does a hole the size of France get knocked in the sky like that without years and years of environmental abuse times a hundred? Do you know how under-industrialized that part of Russia is... was?'

'Can't say I do,' Becker had shrugged. 'But I guess the Commies never gave a rat's ass for sprucing it up with goodies in the good old days. Just maybe with warheads and a few silos.'

'You're thinking of Kazakhstan with the nukes. Know what the weird thing is about Siberia? It's where a meteor hit like a nuclear missile over a hundred years ago. Weird, eh?'

'Well, I guess if there is a God, he sure as hell hates Siberia for whatever reason,' he had told Hartley.

Now Hartley was just waking up. A dark patch lay just under his collar from his sleep spittle. Becker could have pegged him as a used car dealer if he hadn't known otherwise. Hartley exuded that kind of commercialist odor. He looked like he'd enjoyed talking shit all his life.

'We're here,' Hartley told his Rolex. The watch had bothered Becker ten hours ago when he'd first caught sight of it in the airport. Not jealousy; just plain bothered that he'd been sent out with a prick like Hartley.

The ride out to the Marine Base was quiet in the darkness. The cabin of the transport had strong lights that turned Becker's window into a black mirror all the way there. His inner voice wouldn't shut up on him. *Just think - whatever the hell that was is out there still, not even a hundred feet down. A lot can happen a hundred feet down, Becker. Remember the four the minesweeper missed altogether and you and Jerry Kane had to track their paths?*

Kane had died in Hawaii of natural causes, but even so....

'When's the first dive?' Becker asked Hartley.

'Tomorrow after your briefing.' Hartley's tone was coarser, more direct now.

You gearing to show off for the brass, are you, Hartley? Prick. Becker pressed his face against the tempered glass, tried to gaze through the smoky night haze. 'If we find enough of this thing to write home about, what then?'

'You'll find out tomorrow. Please, just get a good rest tonight. We have one hell of a big day laid out for us tomorrow, believe you me.'

Becker felt like death warmed over when he grabbed his hold-all from the back of the transport and followed the others up to the glass double doors of the compound entrance.

He wasn't ready to meet a three-star general - not the way he felt.

'Becker? You got a military record?'

'US navy, nineteen eighty to eighty-three, sir.'

General Nesmith shot Hartley a smirk. 'So this quitter's the best there is, is he?'

Becker was unaware of his fingers curling up until he felt their jagged, nailed tips complaining into his palm. General Nesmith was boarding a fast train to Yellsville.

Hartley's laugh resounded around the foyer and mess hall before it threatened to spill into Becker's empty, scrunched-up stomach bag. 'Just pulling your chain, Becker,' Nesmith said. 'Lighten up. You'd better get fed before you hit the sack; you look like you've been chewed up and spat out.'

Becker slammed his bag onto the lower bunk and mounted the frame. They'd given him his own quarters with Hartley next door. He hated Hartley now. Becker could not understand how a man balanced that way could function. Sure, these people happened in the White House but a Pentagon rep with that kind of mentality? He hated Hartley with one more stab of a thought and fell asleep.

Dark gray ceiling greeted his eyes. Then it was a lighter gray with a hint of yellow and with...

Boom

Becker very nearly fell out of bed when he swung round for his watch. 'What the fu-'

Boom-bah

The siren in the corridor burst into life a couple of seconds later.

'Becker? Becker?!'

<Dumnch - dumnch – dumnch>

'You in there, Becker?!'

'*Yeah!*' Becker snapped. 'Yeah! What-What the holy hell is that out there?!'

Hartley's wiry T-shirted form lit up before the next explosion rocked the night outside. 'I- I don't know! Hey... We better assemble!'

'Where do we do that?!!'

In the dimness, Becker could make out the sheen of Hartley's eye whites, his quaking jaw. 'Just follow the others! I dunno... Just follow 'em!'

Becker was reaching for his pants when he heard the longer break in the flashes and booms. Hartley was still at the door when he realized that the interval had developed into a lull.

The lull held for over a minute before Becker looked up and said:

'We might as well go home now, you know that? That ship won't be down there anymore.'

Hartley managed just a panicky 'what's that?' before he let go of the doorframe.

'Those had to be shells hitting out there,' Becker said.

Hartley balked. 'But- but we're right by the water here. Just the city on the other side.'

Becker bit his lip. 'It's them again. I know it's *them*. From that old battleship.'

-17-
<u>19<u>th</u> April, Montevideo, Uruguay, South America</u>

'Gas mains explosion?'

'My ass it was.' Nesmith was upright in his chair now, each pupil stuck on Hartley and Becker like a laser-target finder. 'If that was gas blowing off by itself then why did the damn locals come running to *me*? I had six different reps in here earlier.'

'Maybe they wanted to see how things had gone on at the base last night as well.'

'Yeah, right; we're not a detective agency, Hartley. That kind of crap lands on your doorstep, not mine.'

'Then the gas lines are going to be the *official* story.' That came from Hartley. 'I think these locals must have thought it was unexploded shells from the ghost ship.' Becker cast a nervous look at Hartley. 'It was a long firefight *before they nailed her* that other night, wasn't it?'

'I'm not cleared by the Pentagon to speak about that.'

'You do know what he means, though, General?' Becker asked.

'Suppose,' Nesmith said, 'A few heads land and they're duds, at first. And we're talking large caliber shells here. Just how many do you suppose would have delayed detonation, considering that for a naval artillery head *not to* explode on impact after being fired – *not* lying as an unexploded bomb for years - is on the same level of odds as a comet smashing up the earth?'

'So it *was* gas, then,' Becker said. 'Obviously brought on by the attack on the city the first time round with that phantom ship. Either *one* of these old rusty shells went off or somebody accidentally ran across a damaged line and *kboom*.'

'And I think it's more the latter scenario there, Becker. But I'm no authority. Just the same way that I'm no authority on this part of the world yet here I am. You'll be relying on representatives from the Uruguayan navy and coast guard to handle this once you're briefed.'

Hartley sprang into life: 'Which we should handle right now. I'll get the squad together.' He tipped his cap at Nesmith before moving for the door.

A shadow of worry moved across Becker's insides. He had to ask.

'General, is it alright if I ask you why the Uruguayans are giving us all this to do? I mean, we're talking about a not-so-poor Latin nation... should be able to afford this kind of maneuver on its own.'

Nesmith tossed a gum stick into his mouth and cracked a smile. 'I can tell you some of the answer to that, Becker. I can tell you that you're right with your assumption that this place *should have done* their own dirty work. I can even tell you that we made base here just hours before you and your diving troupe arrived and that we're *just as* confused as you are. But I can't tell you why our government has agreed to try and prize the lid off somebody else's problem because I just don't *know*.'

'The country is coming apart,' Hartley cut in from the doorway. 'Uruguay is actually facing a massive crisis brought on by the onset of MDRB Plague and the depletion of petroleum deposits in the rest of South America. The government's putting a lot of energy into prepping the army for civil unrest. Doomsday cults are drawing in recruits at record rates. You've seen what happened in India over this.'

The briefing took just ten minutes and a third of that was left aside for questions. Questions had indeed been asked - about a third of them by Becker. Now he felt disgusted: disgusted that a so-called democratic government could lie so easily to its people. Was that a naïve feeling? He didn't care. He was even more disgusted that over twenty people had died the night before and that Nesmith and the top brass knew the real reasons why; disgusted that...

Disgusted that he'd ever taken up diving. He headed for the big van at the compound entrance. It was coming up to ten and the morning sky was fully overcast, threatening rain.

Christ, Becker thought. A hundred feet down under light this bad.

He felt a little better when he caught sight of the charter cutter.

'Alright, people,' Hartley microphoned from the front. 'Your equipment's already on board. Mr Becker, as leader of the *squad*, you're to meet with the government people now.'

Hartley handled the introductions, reading from a picture card. Hernandez, the graying Uruguayan minister of internal affairs, introduced himself with a bear's grip of a handshake to Becker. 'I hope you were not too shaken from last night's explosions.'

'No,' Becker replied. 'But I'm eager to know what did it.'

'My people are still investigating but we suspect retardation in some of the shells that may have landed before; from the attack by the assault ship.'

'Retardation.' Becker's stomach sank in guilt as he pictured how gladdened he would have been if his daughter had never had cancer but had merely been a little special.

'Yes. Two more unexploded shells were found earlier this morning by our men in the southern suburbs.' Hernandez shrugged. 'I have no understanding of the reasons behind this.'

'A lot of things have happened that don't make sense,' Becker said. 'But this is the first time I've ever actually been scared to go in the water.'

'The wreck appears to have remained virtually intact according to our sonar survey of the submersion point,' Hernandez explained before turning to show Becker and Hartley two uniformed, mustachioed officials.

'Admiral Vitolini of the naval high command, Commissioner Bejas from the coastguard.' Vitolini gave a cursory nod, allowed Bejas to move forward with a handshake. 'Mr. Becker will be leading the recovery team on the project; Mr Hartley is our liaison with the American government.' Hernandez turned to face Becker, nodded. 'I understand you've been briefed already on what you may find down there.'

'Or what we mightn't find,' Becker said. 'None of this should've –

could have happened. This is the first time I've ever dived after ghosts.'

The ride out to the submersion spot was short. Becker had been studying the underwater rock formations and then the darkening hues of purple all the way out from the dock. The water where they'd stopped was a deep, space-like purple, two notches shy of being black.

Shallow? That was easily more than a hundred feet of water with that color, Becker thought before he headed for the hold to don his gear. On the way down, he thought of what Hernandez had said about the mission: how Uruguayan divers could have done the job, but these special circumstances demanded *sophisticated* aid, especially with lab work afterward.

The water itself was deathlike. Becker had felt two dozen types of salted H_2O against his face and hands over the years, but never anything as thick and as frigid as this sheeted iron. The dullness of the splash shocks made by the squad as they followed quivered his shoulder blades.

But the wreck was there, lying blacker than black over a mess of kelp strands and dark sand. Becker's heartbeat thudded hard in his ears when he noticed the frayed edges of the stern.

His grip tightened on the big flashlight. He was about halfway down there now, the slain Nazi hulk getting huger with every kick.

It wasn't nearly so black anymore. Instead, Becker's eyes were rewarded with a color more faithful to the decay of oxidation and a more sprawling, unship-like form. *Looks like a turd*, he thought and felt warmth from the idea. *A huge one that was too big to make it into the bowl.*

But how does eighty year-old turdage just rise up one night and blow the hell out of a city?

Twenty feet to go before you touch its rotted carcass... Above, Becker could hear the whirr of the cutter's pulley motor and remembered the submersible propulsion modules.

Okay, he thought: *you're really gonna get that inside those jaggedy corridors.* He could feel pressure on his temples now. His fingers skimmed a shredded flap of stern hull and welcomed a brown mist. The pale circle from his flashlight beam was wasted for a long moment.

Just as he saw the first three divers move above him and make for the deck, Becker shuddered, nearly dropping his flashlight. *No*, he thought.

This is too cold. Water never gets that cold at these latitudes. He tapped the flap of stern metal again and rubbed his fingertips together.

What was that? He shone his beam to the right and caught a pillar-shaped object leering over the end of the stern. He swam for it, didn't recognize it as one of the rear cannons until his palm rubbed over the limpet-encrusted breach lever. Ice cold… No, even colder than ice. This felt like it could rip a few layers of skin off you if you pulled away from it too quickly.

Better stay in eyeshot of the team, he thought before releasing himself from the cannon base slowly, turning around in the water and casting an arc through the murk with his lamp beam.

No-one was in sight further up the length of the light battleship. No air bubbles were in evidence, either. Becker turned his head, tried to make an analysis of the rest of the stern of the *Graf Spee*. Everywhere his beam went, the sight of mangled, super-oxidized steel came back to his eyes in many shades of brown. The rear deck was barely recognizable as a place where men had once rushed about or paced with binoculars.

His beam passed over something then shot back.

Was that a…….?

It took Becker's legs several seconds to respond. The kicks were light, carried him slowly over the oxidized desert to the lone cream-colored object. His beam wraithed down its length when he was a few feet from it then arced back.

A thigh bone: human, all right. It even had some cartilage left at the knee. *Twenty years' bad luck to touch it.* He froze, planted his flipper tips under a ridge in the artillery platform and looked round. Apart from about a hundred square feet of stern space, the rest of the *Graf Spee* was blocked from view by what Becker took to be the collapsed rear section of the control mast.

He checked his meters: Depth: 103 feet… Pressure: 3.1 atmospheres.

The mast tower was gigantic this close up. To Becker, it looked like a big gun, pointing right at him as he scanned it. It looked long dead: totally incapable of being in that recent attack.

Better get back to the group. Nothing else here. Becker shifted his weight, bent his knees to spring up and out.

No movement; pressure on his insteps.

His big yellow flashlight was spiraling in the water by his pelvis. He grabbed it and turned its beam through the bubbles at his locked flippers.

Idiot. Keep that up and you'll really lose it... your mind.

A shadow came to the extreme top of his field of vision. It was moving. Becker saw the diver make an '*O*' sign with his fingers before he let go of the out-turned ship rail and swam back to where he'd come from. Becker kicked his flippers from the lip of the ridge and swam after him.

The rest of the *Graf Spee* looked flat, empty to Becker when he made his way over to the cluster of four divers who'd accumulated on top of the control deck. He came up to the hole and joined his beam to the combined ones of the other divers. A fifth diver was inside the compartment below, just visible at the corner. Becker's eyes fell to the two pits in the floor. A bent cage structure where he knew a console must have once been leaned over in the far one, threatening to tip over at any minute and wrench the fragile floor rivets out of their fastenings.

The diver on his left tapped Becker's shoulder and pointed to the compartment. Becker nodded, held his flashlight in both hands and leaned every pound of himself forward.

Even colder down here. Becker was surprised at how he hadn't got used to the cold yet. This water was unholy and it was starting to make him...

Scared? Yes; more scared than the time he had dived amongst mines in the waters off Kuwait and scareder than when he'd been in Grenada with Cuban gunboats skimming over the surface above him.

The compartment was the size of his living-room and more empty than mangled-looking. Near the starboard side, a ladder protruded from a service shaft at an odd, looped inclination. Becker moved forward a couple of feet to see the extent of the damage to it. Twisted: perhaps by as much as 720 degrees.

Christ, he thought; *even fish would have a hard time getting through there.*

The stream of carbon dioxide bubbles was getting weaker from the bow-ward doorway. Before he moved to follow the other diver through it, Becker noticed the speaker grille by the telephone handset on the side wall.

He couldn't shut out the cries of the crew that sprang to mind.

The Germans scuttled her themselves, you prick. Stop that and get moving.

Darkness... The darkness in the passageway was so intense it made his light beam cut just a tiny conic swathe through the murk. The murk allowed Becker only a haphazard glimpse of brown serrated protrusions from blast holes and the occasional stretch of ten foot visibility. Becker was positive he could smell the murk through the rubber and salt in his mask. The tang made him think of a bottle of New Year's Eve champagne he'd found lying open in a cupboard in February once.

The other diver's light up ahead was shimmering back in phantom ebbs. Becker kicked harder to keep up with it.

His hip screamed at him to stop. When he looked round, he saw the nick on his exposed waist and the belt band of his jockey shorts through the rip in his suit.

You're bleeding. You bleed harder down at this depth. No way to save yourself.

Becker reached for his waist, rubbed it to search for a gill of lacerated skin.

No; that was sea borne oxidized residue floating there. *You're okay.* He started to kick again but slowed to negotiate a ladder in the corridor. He was trying to gather thoughts, work back some kind of mental map from his journey when he saw the darker brown circle above.

There was a hatch at the top of the ladder. He went up to find it hopelessly sealed.

Sealed... Like your fate if anything goes wrong. Anything else, that is.

The pressure was beginning to make his cheekbones ache.

How many feet had he traveled since the control room? Had to be more than forty or fifty. Arcing his beam about him, Becker found a sealed door on either side and two more further up near the end of the corridor where the other diver's light was strongest.

Scuttled? Why would they do that and then go and seal the compartments?

Becker tried one of the big lever door handles and couldn't make it budge.

Maybe some of them never made it out, he thought. *Either that, or...*

The light from the other diver was faltering again. Becker moved his finned feet back against the crusty surface of the ladder, palming the water to reverse, and then pushed off from it.

The corridor ended, opened out into a large stairwell flanked by two new passageways. He picked out right away that only the left one was passable.

A diagram of the ship Nesmith had shown him in the briefing lit up in his mind. *Must have been a different ship altogether back in those days. Nesmith's diagram is worthless in this mess,* Becker told himself. He resurveyed the doors.

No; there's just bare deck out there at this level. Let the others handle it.

A ghosted green cone of bubbles was streaming up from the compartment at the bottom of the stairs, one level down. Becker did a fetal rotation, raised his feet high behind him and kicked down, found the other diver over in the left corner behind the stairs, struggling with a service hatch. Becker noticed the Farallon propulsion device nestled between his elbow and ribs, switched off - useless now in these confines.

Becker felt the smile that came to his lips threaten his grip on his mouthpiece. *Serves you right for relying on that thing so much, you moron. No wonder you can't open doors, you're so weak.* Stuffing the butt of his flashlight into his armpit, Becker closed his fingers above the diver's hands on the top of the lever. The metal was cold but not as cold as what he'd felt before.

They tried forcing it round clockwise once.

No go. Try again.

Twice. Becker felt it sink by about one degree to the right.

Three times and the handle went down all the way. The hinges of the hatch seal weren't stiff at all when Becker pried at the gap with his forearm.

The compartment behind was large and desolate with only one other doorway. Becker could tell that right away because there was a gaping hole right in the side of the wall, letting in bluer light.

He shook double fingers at the doorway for the other diver to see. The diver nodded, activating his Farallon and edged forward and away from Becker. Becker kicked after him, his belly taxiing precariously close to serrated flaps, shards and diamond-shaped rips that jutted upward from the sheet metal flooring.

The water was warmer here. The door in the far wall gave without complaint. Once through, Becker's flashlight illuminated a large room with intact tables.

Mess hall. Where these boys had their last supper. Casting an arc with his own light, he saw that some of the tables had managed to retain the gray metal look. No crockery, no knives or forks... just tables flanked by the odd, mangled frame of a chair.

The other diver was already at the far end of the hall. Becker kicked his way over, ignoring the brown-encrusted side door to the right, glued to its frame by a blanket of limpets.

A larger door came into view. Becker moved past the other diver and gripped the lever handle, pulling hard. It was jagged with growth, and stubborn. It took five tugs to move halfway.

Black corridor space greeted them when they got it down. The other diver's nodding beam seemed to apologize to the gloom for the disturbance. The corridor looked in better condition, less brown than anything before it.

Becker noticed the stairs going down at the far left. He tried to squeeze in a memory of Nesmith's floor plan. No...no use. It was too hard to think that way at that depth...at that pressure.

The dorms are down there. How'd you like to go down and sleep for a while?

Yes. Sleep forever and forget this madness. Who wants to live in a world where ancient battleships like this can come back to life and blow the bejesus out of things?

There were three doors in the corridor. Becker zoomed in ahead of the other diver and tried the first one on the left.

Sealed... A smaller door than the other two... Probably a closet of some sort.

The next door was far up on the right. When Becker tried the lever he found it went down right away, startling him. His beam lit up a near empty, garage-sized compartment at the end of a short corridor. He felt the wake of the other diver behind him, making for either the last door or the stairs down to the bunk dorms.

Becker moved further inside the compartment. He had his light trained on the racks by the far wall and the countertop just in front of them.

The galley and bakery. *You can't find any clues here, Becky Boy: get out.*

You're running out of air anyway. Remember your consumption depth.

But he was at the far wall now, still scanning... looking for anything that might just be out of order.

In the galley, though? His mind's voice began mocking him.

There was everything in here, even the long baking spatulas and the crushed remains of tin loaf pans. Becker edged his way behind the counter to inspect the short corridor that led off from the bakery.

...Nothing: nothing, except for dancing black shadows on rusted steel and the odd barnacle-encased kelp chandelier that had once been a humble, caged light bulb.

The silence between his exhalations was unsettling him now. Through the empty shelving, he surveyed the extreme right of the kitchens and caught only locked cupboards and locked memories of the kitchen crew.

Ghosts can come from memories… Wrong: ghosts *are* memories.

He felt really uneasy now, began kicking back from the tiny passageway. On the way, he shot a look at his watch and grimaced.

Thirty minutes' oxygen for practical purposes, the rest for decompression.

Becker's eyes suddenly fell on his light beam, blinked, then opened again and saw that its sharpness was increasing a little in relation to.....

The matt black rectangle of the doorway he'd come in from had turned jet…

You're trapped!

The lamp fell out of his hands as he shot for the door, leaving his mind to sprawl and reel with it. Stuck…stuck…*stuck!* The lever was vertical and jammed in position. Becker's wrist was quick to overheat from the strain. He tried harder with both hands… harder… harder still.

The flashlight was still rolling about on the floor, sending smatterings of diffused, weak illumination at his feet. Becker heard how clear the bumbling of his screamed words was through the veil of globules when he stopped jerking the handle.

And then he found he could hear the faint, gloating hiss of laughter.

Air. You use up more air when you get that way.

He pounded the heels of his hands against the door, ignoring the discomfort of the spiky brown scales, trying to block thinking of the inevitable.

Yes. Remember that 'Veils of Fate' video you rented before you went to Grenada. You, Bob Meier and Tony Shrimpton; remember how you called the guy who'd got stuck under the electric swimming pool cover and drowned a loser?

And now here you are. You're going to die, Becker, and after you're dead you'll have to explain to the dead sailors why you were screwing around with their ship. They'll be blue and rotten and they're going to chase you forever.

He heard the laughter start up once more… He screamed again, eyes panning crazily. About him, the light was too weak to see anything by except the cold gray of spent, useless air.

The other diver. Had to be. He had to have done this. Nobody else knew where he was. *I'm going to kill you, you bearded asshole!* he mind-shrieked.

Yes, Becker thought when his throat started hurting; *you came back here and locked me in. So it's a government ploy to get rid of me, is it? The black box from that plane I fished out was too much for them, was it?*

Becker's fingers tore back the strap at his ankle and wrenched up the knife. He started bashing the hilt against the door.

How many minutes of air left?

Who cares, anyway? You'll either die or get the bends so bad you'll want to die.

Do something for yourself and do it NOW, fool. He stopped pounding, turned and darted for his flashlight. Within two seconds, he'd begun the process of scouring every surface of the compartment with its beam.

Has to be another way out. This is a galley: service hatches... Think!

His heartbeat was thundering in his neck, deafening him. *Oxygen level?*

Stop that! This is a galley... a lot of rushing about with food. You think they'd only have had one tiny little shit of a door for all that activity? Navy sails on its belly... no food, no sailors.

But YOU can't live without oxygen, Becker. To hell with food!

Nothing. The walls were awash with brown and gray streaks... No openings.

Becker arced his beam high above his head to scan the ceiling and was rewarded with a straight run of steel sheeting dripping with thousands of miniature, brown stalactites.

You're going to die.

Now he could feel his brain thumping against the back corners of his skull. As he kicked back across to the other side of the kitchens, he didn't notice that his air bubbles had got smaller and less numerous from his gibbering.

You're going to die down here, for sure. Ha ha ha - 'Faces of Doom'; who's laughing now, though? Welcome to the Flying Deutschman, jerk!

He was back at the short corridor now, twisting and turning his light at every square inch on all surfaces, piercing black water and making it greeny-gray.

...Nothing... blank; just a small blast-hole by the ovens behind him and that was too small to be of use. Not even a dog could get through-

You're going to die, Becker. It starts with a sore pressure in your breathing tract, then a bad headache, then the pain as your lungs scream for air and you have none to give so you give them water instead. And you don't pass out too quickly either. No sirree. Life flashes in your face.

You could get it out of the way now. Your knife?

Becker felt his fingers closing harder around the hilt of his forgotten knife. He looked down at the silhouette of its blade and tried to think.

Could I do that? Should I cut my air hose or my wrists?

Either....It'd be less depressing if you did it now.

He shuddered, let the knife fall out of his hand. No. No; the others were already scouring the wreck for him right now. They had charges on the cutter; they could blow the door with those, couldn't they?

He checked the gauges on his stab jacket. His single oxygen tank was at fifty-five percent capacity: just under half an hour left.

Minus decompression time, though.

You'll get out, don't worry. A lot can happen in twenty minutes... Twenty-five, maybe.

Becker kicked his way up to the wall behind him. The bakery oven doors were all lying fully open, as if they'd been set that way before the *Graf Spee* had been scuttled. *Give the sea this day its daily bread...*

He already knew the flues would be too narrow, but he had to see for himself. He entered the middle oven and rotated himself once inside.

The flue was a quintet of holes around a solid core, each one the size of a fist.

He swam into each of the other three and found the same. In the last one, he pictured someone closing the oven door behind him and firing it up to regulo 10. A nightmare's nightmare to burn the shadow of a mortal.

When he came out of the last oven, Becker shook his beam straight ahead at the far wall and just made out the roller blind pattern dead in the center of it. It was camouflaged well into the rest of the wall with spatterings of brown rot and the remains of shell creatures.

He kicked toward it like a mad thing and felt his way to the bottom of the slats. He didn't have to tug at it even once to know it wasn't going to budge, no matter what. Turning, he surveyed the counter that stemmed off from the adjacent wall for a crowbar substitute.

The drawers were full of utensils. Within an hour of a minute, he'd found a thick rotisserie skewer, unspoiled by the exposure to the depths.

He stuck it in the gap between the bottom slat of the blinds and the ridge of the service counter, praying. The gap was uneven with calcified gunge. He jammed the skewer harder into the gap and butted the ringed back of it with his flashlight.

A puff of taupe dust billowed away from the join and he felt the skewer move in a few precious millimeters. He dinked it again until he reckoned it had gone in by two inches or so.

Becker shoved down on the handle with all his might. The skewer jerked then dipped and bent, its tip slipping back out of the gap, costing him precious seconds, making it all useless.

His light beam displayed the brown rot that had welded the bottom slat to the sill of the service counter.

Becker shuddered for seconds. *You'll need a blowtorch to get through that, not jerking it with this crappy little tool.*

Fifteen minutes of air left now.

You ARE going to die whether you DO anything or NOT.

No. Calm down; you'll use less air if you just… just calm down.

Becker shone his beam all over the roller curtain, praying in staccato, jagged gibbers. He felt the cold current on the back of his torch hand before he saw it. A hole the size of a thumb tack head had been punched into the other side of the curtain, just over halfway down.

God, will I have the leverage for this?

Becker tried easing a fresh skewer into it. It took four attempts before he'd pushed the gap's lining of rust and gunk away so he could insert the huge needle all the way to the hilt.

Please let me have enough leverage to take it up from here.

I can't die here…. not now…..not like this.

He wrenched the skewer once, yakked out a stream of bubbles when it slipped his grip.

The laughter was back again in his ears, intensifying now.

Fifteen minutes was nothing. In his crackling mind, Becker recalled the lightning speed of coffee breaks in his pre-diving jobs and grimaced.

He jerked the skewer into the space and tugged once... twice... three times... four!

The roller curtain gave on maybe the tenth tug. The brown clouds coming off it and the wall joins of the curtain now were swelling in front of his flashlight. He reached into them to push the curtain the rest of the way up, hoping with each inch until he knew his body could clear it.

Beyond the gap he had just created was the way back. Two chambers down, he found the other diver who was shaking his head profusely now to indicate his lack of a find. Becker could read his eyes even in the bad light. He was innocent, totally oblivious of what had happened back there. And yet, no way could it have been an accident.

It was time to think about starting to head back up. Both men ascended one level to make their way back. Becker found he had forgotten even the basic layout of this deck.

A little further ahead, a blast hole loomed, the water around its mouth looking much lighter and filled with green streams and tiny bubbles.

That's it for this ship, Becker thought. *Certify it as a mystery if you like.*

Then he recalled the large door at the rear of the control room. He checked his watch. *Eleven minutes' oxygen left. You need time for decompression so consider it five.*

Becker raised his flashlight, shot a look at the other diver and indicated that he was going back the way they'd come. The other diver nodded, moving for the hole in the hull.

At the top of the stairwell, Becker felt the coldness return through his suit. The pressure on his cheekbones was starting to make his top molars hurt. The champagne smell came back to his nose somehow, made him think of being in his lounge with friends and Abbie.

He kicked harder, forgetting the danger of the sharp protrusions on the corridor's walls until his flashlight beam fell on a large one. *Slow down, fool. You want to get cut up some more?*

Becker's right hand reached for the lever of the nearest door. Stuck fast... He didn't need to point his beam to see the warped frame and the brown residue at the lever's base.

No way through that except with a remote charge.

He turned to survey the other sealed doors, tried the first to find the lever turning but not activating the door. He swam past the ladder in the corridor for the last door on the left.

Ten minutes left in the tank, four max for practical purposes. Count yourself lucky you aren't any deeper and using that helium mix. You'd have died long ago.

The door fell in as soon as Becker depressed the lever. His light beam showed a compartment the size of his bedroom, filled with rows of empty racks.

Small arms armory, he thought. His hand moved forward to pull the door closed again. The lever was freezing to the touch: that frostbite cold he'd felt before.

Three minutes' oxygen left if you don't want to bubble your blood.

He swam down the last twenty-odd feet of the corridor and emerged in the control room. Cold - the water all around him was very, very cold now. Becker could feel the shocks of energy being taken from him as he kicked to get to the door behind the far console space.

The door was sealed with a wheel-lock the size of the steering wheel in his Cavalier. Before his fingers made contact with it, Becker braced his arms for serious resistance.

Christ! He retracted his hands, punching himself in the nipple with one. His flashlight fell from his armpit and bounced away from him on the floor sheeting.

Reaching to retrieve it, Becker's fingers stung against the sheeting surface. *Cold. What was it: liquid nitrogen?* Shaking his head, he felt the strain of exertion and the awkward atmosphere wringing his lungs. He tried to force measured gasps and found himself failing.

The wheel gave slowly after two hard jerks clockwise, a near century of putrefaction and dirt whooshing from the seals and edges as he tugged the door out.

The twisting jolt came to Becker's chest after just a couple of seconds then, only this time it was his heart, not his lungs, that was the root. His light, still on the floor, illuminated the huge message etched into the rusted, shallow opposite wall of the safe locker.

'TYUR SETOT' the graffiti screamed.

From his knowledge of saltwater effects on metal, Becker knew the cuts could only be a few hours old.

-18-

19<u>th</u> April, Undisclosed Location, Russian Federation

Olentiev awoke to greet another day in the private ward with an ache in his chest. It was an ache he knew well now. He'd nurtured it like a baby since the visit he'd had with the Special Forces man.

His arm was itching under the cast that was now moist and stinking. He had it resting on his breastbone. He'd had to keep it there all through last night and when he'd dozed after lunch because of the aching in his heart and his stomach.

The Speznaz crack intelligence unit would be coming for him today, no question. He'd been sure they would come yesterday, a couple of hours after their lesser counterparts in the regular special forces had called, but he had heard the orderlies talking outside his door about no more visits then.

No-one is going to come in here and make me say I saw something else down there that day, he determined. *Same goes for making me deny anything out of the ordinary happened.*

Olentiev was halfway through a yawn when he first heard the footsteps welling up from the corridor beyond his door. The hospital staff all wore softer footwear, he realized, grimacing.

The door swung in silently. The lone Speznaz man turned to close the door.

'What are you here for?' Olentiev asked.

'A moment of your time, Major Olentiev, sir. And an oath.'

'An oath?'

The Speznaz man grabbed a chair, parted his coat and parked

himself. 'Yes, an oath. You've got a service record solid enough for me - us - to *trust* any oath that you might make.'

'That depends on what the oath is about.'

'Twenty-two years in the air force; fourteen successful surgical strike runs in Siberia. Your father helped co-ordinate ground force movements in Czechoslovakia during the invasion. That makes your word good enough; trustable.'

Olentiev beheld the decay of the ceiling paintwork. 'What else do you know about me?'

'Maybe you wouldn't like me to tell you all that.'

'Why did you come here only today?'

'Maybe I think you've had enough time to think things over now.'

'Like what?'

The Speznaz man eased himself forward, smiled at the floor space under the bed then reached into his breast pocket for a cigarette. 'About central Siberia, your lieutenant, your claims about what you thought you saw.'

'What I *did* see.'

The Speznaz man's smile broadened. He took his first drag on the smoke, began shaking his head. 'No. You're not playing the game here, Major.'

'There's no game I can see.'

'Look, Olentiev, you're leaving this hospital tomorrow. When your arm heals you'll be reassigned. They tell me you have barely even a fracture. It could be Siberia again... If you want.'

'What are you threatening me with?'

'That brings me back to the issue of the oath I think you'll make to me today.' The Speznaz man clasped his hands together, revived his ageless grin. 'It seems you haven't grasped the gist of what others were talking to you about on their visit with you.'

The pain in Olentiev's breastbone grew sharper. The face facing him was incorrigible. The Speznaz were the worst, but they were the best at being the worst and Olentiev knew that.

'You witnessed the impact crater of a large meteor that hit the area near Lake Baykal.'

'No. No, I didn't. That's untr-'

'Let me finish, Olentiev. The radiation present in the aerospace there was sufficient to poison you, hence your passing out and summary delirium.'

'I'm not - wasn't - delirious.'

'And your wingman experienced a similar change in state. Except he lacked the instincts you exhibited: very poor self-preservation technique on his part.'

'You've found Askenskaya's plane?'

'No. We never will because Askenskaya's aircraft slammed into the tableland at high speed and the debris has been dissolved by the harsh elements present in central Siberia.'

'Don't hand me that! I *know* what I saw that day.'

'Major Olentiev, let me remind you you're subject to the State Security Protocol as defined in the 1977 provision and renewed in 1993. *Any* breach of that could and *will* mean your liability for trial as a traitor.'

Olentiev clenched his eyelids, wished he knew how to pray to a god of truth and not the one that allowed a man to disappear very easily in Russia. 'Please. I'm not trying to be difficult.'

'What are you *trying to be* then?' The Speznaz man stubbed his forbidden smoke against the side of the chair, let the crumpled butt fall to the rotten lino.

'But I saw machinery below me that day: a piece of *spacecraft.*'

'You mean you saw the remains of your comrade's SukHoi, unrecognizably mangled.'

'That was no plane.' Olentiev replayed that in his mind, bit his lip to stop saying more.

'The Voyager probe is still in interstellar space. We have facts there, not propaganda.'

'No! That had to be it I saw! Same struct-'

'You want me to prove myself on that?'

'But...sails: there were *sails* on that thing.'

'Or what you took to be objects that *appeared* as sails, Major.'

Olentiev remembered he was being recorded now. 'Please. I was on the verge of blacking out when I saw them. It's hard to remember everything about them, but they *were* sails.'

Speznaz shook his head. 'So you'll agree to giving your formal statement saying that you saw the wreckage of your lieutenant's SukHoi in the vicinity of the meteor's crash site?'

Olentiev closed his eyes. 'Whatever... Whatever you like.'

'And there was no other manmade material in that area.'

'Yes; yes, I agree. Please...let's just be *done* with this.'

The Speznaz man dropped his smile entirely. 'We can't be done with this until we're sure that *you* are done with it.'

'How... What do you mean by that?' The pain in Olentiev's breast made him think of a jackhammer on concrete flagstones at a construction site.

'Without being unnecessarily grim, Major, I'll refresh your memory about our procedures. Just a little over two decades ago, the words you've just spoken would have earned you, at best, three years in a labor camp and, at worst....' The Speznaz man slapped his breast pocket, reanimated his smile. 'Do I need to say it?'

'So... so you want me to issue a statement to the press secretariat?'

'Yes. Today. You'll appreciate our need to speed things along as best we can. There have been a lot of admirers of yours wanting to speak to you in here since you arrived, you know.'

Olentiev raised himself upright on his elbows, fixed the Speznaz man with as penitent a look as he could but found only soulless, black windows in his eyes. 'May I ask you something?'

'Yes, Olentiev?'

'Why so frank with me? Why the directness? You thought I didn't know you guys are big on what gets said?'

The smile grew wider as another cigarette popped out from the carton. 'Because, my friend,' said the smile. 'Your wife and two sons have already been notified of your presumed death. Whether or not we tell them otherwise is up to you.'

-19-

CNN Headline News Broadcast transcript, April 19ᵗʰ

'Scientists at MIT in Boston have found a link between the exotic substance dubbed Agent 104 and the blocking of virtually all types of transmittable wave radiation. So far, over a hundred and fifty tests in labs there have uncovered fresh properties of the elemental body which have alarming implications for the global economy and state of world affairs.'

Shift to Dr. Richard Paulin, MIT chemical engineering head.

'Certainly the analyses we've been conducting in the past weeks have proved critical. We've put the chemical through experiments which the Department of Health had overlooked. Agent 104 is a very real threat to all of us in that, as far as we've been able to test its properties, it has the characteristics of all the things that could seriously harm our collective wellbeing...

...We already know that given a large supply of it in any precipitation, say a seeding proportion of 50 parts-per-million or higher, and radio, television and cellular telephone devices are rendered useless for the duration of the rainfall, snowfall, storm or what have you.

But at higher rates, such as 100 up to 250 PPM, we've discovered that the wave blocking effect will continue indefinitely after the initial host precipitation has fallen for everything other than light and heat. Luckily, the substance hasn't turned up at such high levels, but...

... Essentially, this substance has the potential to knock all human communications, no matter how refined, out of commission for good. Couple that with the decimation of internet users due to the proliferation of the 'Bogeyman' super-virus and we'll be facing a pre-1900 style of existence. The best we can do is search for a counter-agent that could reduce the impact of Agent 104 on global tele-information transmissions. We're a long way off finding an antidote. This is like a Cure for Cancer quest, except there aren't even any precautions we can suggest...'

-20-
19th April, San Diego, California

Billy Reynolds' basement line caught him entirely off guard. He'd just cleared the third level of 'Bloodrangers 2 ' when he paused his PC, reached back for it. 'Yep?'

'Hey man.'

'Hey; what you up to?'

'Weird shit again, Bill.'

Billy paused, spun his mind round in a circle to suss out what might have happened to Barry Nash now. 'Oh yeah: that crazy woman.'

'Right first time.'

'What she do now? Call you again about that dead guy?'

'Way worse. Damn well came round to my folks' at noon, banging on the door for me.'

'Freaky.'

'Freaky for her. Old bitch threatened me.'

'Threaten as in take you to court or coming to *get* you threaten?'

The silence in the earpiece stuck in Billy Reynolds' brain like a huge air bubble trapped inside a water pipe. 'Hey.'

'She threatened to *kill* me if I went back to NDC for my last year.'

'Huh – and you've gone and registered already.'

'This ain't funny. Old hag. I'll tell you, there just wasn't something right about this lady. Ganz's mother…I swear.'

'Sounds like it.'

'No. I mean the way she *looked*. Ganz was dark and this woman had *white* hair; eyes really light blue. But she was way too old to be his mom.'

'Maybe he takes after his dad.'

'No; there just was something really unnatural looking about her. *Albino*, is it?'

'Sounds like she really screwed you up; she pull out a knife or something?'

'No. She just said her piece and walked off. That's what made it scary for me.'

'You just opened the door to her and she said she'll kill ya if you go back to school?'

'Yeah. Wasn't on the doorstep more than ten seconds.'

'Christ,' Billy Reynolds said, setting himself down on the end of his bed. Nash was a liar when it came to girls and when it came to money. But Barry Nash never lied about any more than he thought he had to, as far as Billy knew. 'How many times is that?'

'Huh?'

'How many times she contacted you? 'Cause you were well messed up yesterday with it. You had five beers and it wasn't even three p.m.'

'Who cares; I'm calling you for a favor.' Nash's voice had lost its gentle shakiness now.

'Make it good 'cause you're wrecking a good game for me here.'

'To Hell with that. See, I followed this bitch some ways after she walked off.'

'So you know where she lives?'

'Yeah. Tiny bungalow on *Jasmine Street*. East of Gaslamp quarter.'

'That's some way out. You walk it?'

'Yeah. No-one but *no-one* says they'll off me then walks off.'

'What's the scoop?'

'The scoop is we give her a scare.'

Billy Reynolds sensed an anvil on his heart.

'What do you say, Bill?'

'Uhmm. I dunno. Let me think.' Billy thought. His mom would be hit the hardest if it went wrong.

'Just bang on her door and scare the shit out of her with a mask on.'

Raina's face popped into his mind then. Dave would kill him if - when they got busted. 'No. Not this time.' Raina's face smiled in his mind's eye then. 'I'm not doing it.'

'C'mon. No-one'll see. We'll do it at four-something in the morning if you're scared.'

'No way, man. I don't do that kind of thing.' A feigned giggle came out of him then. 'Serious, Barry. Just let it go. Get back to your life.'

The five-second silence that followed was good. It nearly NEUTRALIZED his dread at Barry Nash's suggestion. Billy broke the quiet to try gaining some more ground. 'Yeah, man. No way. I've got too much to do tonight, anyway.'

Barry was silent for several seconds more and then sneered: 'Yeah, right y'have.'

'Hey. I got a date with Kelly at *The Sunfish.*'

'Yeah? Kind of hard seeing how Kelly's in Acapulco.'

'She got back two nights ago.'

'Don't lie. Jenny Pinder told me she was out there still.'

Billy felt a hot flush coming. 'Look, man, I'm not in the mood.'

'Chill, Reynolds. I'll do the driving even: my car, my plates, my risk. Anything happens, I'll take the rap. Full deal or no deal.'

'I said no.'

'Shit, Bill. This bitch threatened to off me!'

'So why not go threaten her back yourself?'

'Reynolds, you know I know enough to get you in serious shit with a lot of people.'

'Look, I'm gonna hang up.'

'All I have to do is talk and you're history.'

'Leave me alone, you prick.'

'Let's see, slander, theft of park property, vandalism of a perfectly defenseless cigarette dispenser to name *some.*'

'Why don't you grow up.' Billy's eyes were burning a hole in the CD case at his feet. The quartet of heavy metal heroes pictured were sneering back, as if demanding him to stand up harder for himself.

The strain on his heart was getting sharper now. 'Nash. No-one will believe you, number one. Number two, I've got more than enough dirt on you to-'

'Mutually assured destruction is fine by me, Reynolds; but you know I'm crazy enough to go first. I don't think my exam results will get me work anytime soon: what have *I* got to lose?'

The silence dragged just long enough for Billy to analyze. He found himself more confused when he thought he was done analyzing. 'You really think I'm going to scare the shit out of someone in a ski-mask. What if she has a heart attack? Then we get done for murder?!'

'Then you can drive me in my car. Okay? We'll head out after the bar closes.'

-21-

<u>19<u>th</u> April, Newport Beach, California</u>

Becker watched his laptop boot up with his fingers crossed. A fingertip hovered above the power button at the top left side. That virus they were all talking about in the news at least had the decency to be called something weird in the unread email folder, after all. It would be noticeable.

Granules of sleep nicked his eyelids when he squinted at the brightness of his screen's wallpaper of turquoise ovals of water ruptured by orange breaks: the Great Barrier Reef.

Becker blinked, clicked on his internet icon the second it appeared, and noted the blueness of the screen wallpaper. Miraculously, he wasn't too jetlagged after returning from Uruguay... Water...he'd grown up with water. He'd been born around, had learned to swim in water from the age of four.

Bremen. As the connection processes started up and Becker waited, he leaned back fully in his cheap office reclinable. The water off Bremen had been the first he'd ever loved. How many times before they'd come to America had he leapt off the rocks and stayed swimming in, diving in or just treading the stuff for longer than one hour on most days?

Too many. The connection to the server was abnormally slow. No - *abortive* this time, giving him time to puzzle at what had happened in Uruguay.

'Just let me on, you bastard,' he hissed with jetlagged temper.

Nesmith had debriefed him in Montevideo then shoved him back on a plane. What the Hell had that been about? He was an experienced diver; he deserved to know more than the hush they'd forced on him.

Becker closed his eyes as his computer continued its battle to get online and a new screen to appear over his turquoise water and coral ridges desktop wallpaper. How many generations of seafaring Beckers had been now? The ones he'd heard about were Granddad and *his* father. The ones he knew were his own dad and himself.

Great-grandfather had shipped Norwegian ore home so enough steel could be smelted to feed the Kaiser's hunger for the proto U-boats. And Granddad had given his life to the sea aboard the later, more efficient versions. Granddad was thirty-four, had volunteered and had been rough-and-ready for the demands of the eastern North Atlantic theater when he joined up.

But Granddad had only been second in command on the U-28 that night and all the other nights he'd spent running through those service hatches in the mayhem. They must have shit their pants when they heard the English engines penetrate the murk, Becker considered. Did death by depth-charge mean you copped it from being knocked about in the sub or from getting your head hit by blunt, rivet-stamped steel plates? Or did it entail getting crushed to death by the frothing, murderously cold jets that ripped through the hull?

Becker shut his eyes as the log-in program attained the link and presented him with the latest news of the world. What was it now? he thought. Any more long-dead wrecks come up overnight to take a potshot at people, shopping malls, libraries?

What if the U-28 was to rise and go shoot the hell out of the seafronts of the Azores, near where it went down when the English pummeled it?

Becker let that thought run for a second more before reopening his eyes. A skeletal version of the red-haired, bearded guy with the white wool turtleneck he'd seen holding his dad on his shoulders in the mantelpiece picture had drifted in there.

It was unacceptable to think a wreck could rise to fight. It was...

... It was obscene to drag the past into the hell of the present.

Frowning, he clicked the email inbox, finding there was a lot of stuff waiting for him in there. The hourglass turned to an arrowhead, revealing twenty-four emails.

Becker ran his eye down the list at lightning speed, checking each address, each title against the blank in his mind. He'd actually forgotten the name of that new super-virus but from the lack of noise or motion on his hard disk, he intuited safety, immunity for the present.

But his blood was freezing now. Four of the emails were from the same source - Kurt, his brother. Three were together at the top, the last one - the earliest - separated by junk and business mail. All bore the message: 'Get to Bremen A.S.A.P. - Dad ill.'

The phone line rang only once before Kurt picked up.

'Carl. Thank God.'

'What's happened?'

'Dad had a stroke the other night. We couldn't get hold of you.'

Carl Becker's heart raced a jolt up the side of his neck and into his brain as he recalled where he would have been at the time his father would have been suffering… So uselessly far away for him to be able to help.

'I went to see him right away,' his brother continued. 'I didn't know where you'd got to.'

'Gov- government. Special contract in South America. Oh Jesus, how *is* he?'

'Not good. Not good, Carl. He needs neurosurgery. It's a clot or … it's a clot.'

Becker heard his brother take a long sniffle. 'They told Mom and me his brain is all filled up with blood and they have to cut into his head. God damn it, Carl. I tried to call you! But the phone lines are on the blink all the time!'

'Wait. It's okay, Kurt. I'm flying out now. Hang … just hang tight; I'll call you back right after I book.' Becker lowered the handset, tried making his mind push through some tears.

But his mind was busy and refused to permit him the luxury of an outlet. It played him a notion instead and Becker saw his father drowning in a sea of salted, bilge green-tinted blood.

It was a war now: a war with the unknown. Somehow, that unknown which involved the *water* was winning it already.

-22-
19th April, San Diego, California

Barry Nash's '78 El Camino droned as it ate up the route to the target zone. There were two blocks left to go and Billy Reynolds was sweating moisturizer-seeded droplets into his tee/grunge plaid shirt combination.

There had only been one cop car and that had passed broadside at the lights less than a mile back. Billy was scanning the side-streets and back lanes like a G.I. in Helmand Province.

He'd let Nash drive: a concession he'd been allowed in the Deal.

'Okay, we're in business,' Nash said. 'Bomb bays open!'

Billy's knuckles brushed against something cold and smooth as he squeezed the edge of his seat. He looked at the floor space just in front of the mid part of the bench and found Nash's .44 Magnum Automag replica Cruzman air pistol.

He shivered. 'What the Hell is this?'

'What's your problem, Bill? You actually *scared* here?'

Billy took a hard look at Nash. He'd known him three years: a short time by some measures but long enough to perhaps be able to get inside much of his head.

The streetlights passed by, lathering Nash's face in slow streaks with craziness just before he slowed, pulled in at the curb.

'Nothin'. Just thinking.'

'Don't think, dummy; that air gun's just there for my peace of mind. Grab a sense of humor, why don't you!'

Billy panned the street one last time then thought about the dangers of waiting in Nash's vehicle while he did a ski-masked intimidation job. It's okay to do this, he told himself. The cops have too much else to do to be pissed off about a practical joke on a ...

...On a defenseless elderly woman.

Wait. She'd threatened Barry.

That's Barry Nash you're talking about.

The prosecution would eat him alive for -

'Okay,' Nash said as he parked and donned his black ski-mask and woolly gloves. 'See? I'm even leaving you the damn keys, dickwad!'

The makeshift, uneven eyeholes Billy would have found funny in another universe, another situation. After Nash's door slammed, he squeezed his eyelids shut and saw Raina's face weeping at him in the gray of the curtain backs of the lightless house across the street.

The door re-opened. 'Oh yeah, I'm takin' this,' Nash said.

Before Billy could stop him, he'd seized the Cruzman. 'No!'

'Shaddup, wuss.'

Slam.

Shaking, Billy slunk low in the cabin and tried to think about walking home now and calling the cops. It would be easy... would it? Could he think up some way of...

He heard the *pathok* and cringed, his heartbeat skipping. It wasn't fair. No... He couldn't have known that Nash would be getting up to *this*.

Another two minutes had already passed when the door opened and slammed again, accompanied by the tune of a breathless Nash.

'Nailed that bitch good!' Nash mused as he ground the key round in the ignition and screeched it.

'For f-!' Billy wheezed then felt something hard hit his shin when the car lurched forward. He grabbed the object and grimaced hard then threw the Cruzman onto the floor space.

His fingerprints were ON it now. His fingerprints were ON a lot of Nash's interior. God, he thought. Could they tell how old prints were, down to the hour? He saw little Raina sitting in the backseat, crying that Uncle Billy could be so bad to somebody.

'What did you *do* to her?'

'Oh, it was a classic, that!' Nash boasted. 'She won't trouble us again!'

'What the hell did you do, Nash?!'

Nash turned his head, issued a grin. 'Just you wait 'til you hear about it, pard!'

'I'm not your partner!'

'Not how they'll see it.'

Billy could feel his system starting to heave, the tears forming, too.

But he hadn't done anything! They'd find some way of fixing that: accessory of some sort. He turned round to monitor the road.

They were almost at the lights to Carter Street when Nash said: 'She would've killed me, man! Rotten old hag.'

The silence dragged like the anchor of an aircraft carrier on the seabed. 'What's eating you?' Nash jabbed.

'Nothing. It'll hold.' Billy stared at the dash and tried to think through icicled veins.

What if the old woman had had heart failure? If she was dead, that would be twenty-five in the can for Nash and maybe as many for him for being there...

Nash would run out on him. Nash would even try and turn it round so he'd been taken hostage by mad Billy.... Billy the Kid. And someone would've seen them for sure. No; someone had definitely already witnessed it, had seen him sit in the cab, an accessory, while his pal had done the dirty deed. Nash's Camino had been too loud. There'd been two gas stations on the way... CCTV cameras.

'We have to go back,' Billy said after they'd cleared the main intersection.

'You what?'

'Christ, man - let's just go back.'

'You crazy? The cops! We'll be toast.'

'I don't care: we... we gotta go back, see if she's not dead.'

'Fuck off.'

'I mean it, man! God damn it - I won't sleep tonight if I don't know!'

Nash shook his head, scowled at the emptiness of the road. They were closing on the exit to the Freeway now. 'No,' he said at length. 'And that's that. Don't be a pussy.'

Billy could have started crying when he heard his mind start at him, armed with the info it had been fed from Chapter Eight in his course textbook.

Yes; sociologically speaking, he was now a societal DEVIANT.

-23-
19ᵗʰ April, US Navy Harbor, San Diego

'Okay, so now we *know* it's Ganz in both images, what do we *do?*' Coleman asked as Allinson folded the laptop's screen down and everyone else got ready to leave and greet the pre-dawn hours outside. 'How do we go after a target like him?'

'We go to a code red two with it is what we do,' Carmichael said. 'That's all for now.'

-24-
20ᵗʰ April, Undisclosed Location, Russian Federation

Sergei and Rosalina, Olentiev's kids: his job wasn't fair on them. Valentina, his wife of fourteen years, had always hated it but she had loved him enough to understand how useless hating was when it came to a reliable income for a reliable man in unreliable times.

'Here; something to read before you go,' one of the Speznaz men said, throwing him last Friday's paper.

Olentiev caught the headlines as the BMW left the hospital gates. The Friendship Cup was being postponed. Eleven of the teams' heads of state had expressed concern at the 'prevailing climate of dread and suspicion in the cities throughout the globe'.

Olentiev stared out his window at the blackness of the road, the grayness of the sodden grassbank at its side as spring battled to melt the last of winter's kingdom.

'Your papers, Major,' the Speznaz in the front passenger seat said, handing him a wallet of yellow documents. 'Report to Marshal Bucharin upon arrival. Enjoy your freedom there.'

Olentiev took the wallet, shoved it into his fatigue jacket pocket. From the back of his mind, the cliché about Russia's freedom involving one's freedom to suffer crackled at him.

Death is the only real Freedom; select yours with dignity.

The drive took over an hour. Olentiev was deposited with foreboding ceremony at the compound. Marshal Bucharin, veteran of Afghanistan and the first Chechen adventure, was standing behind his desk in his office - a camo-colored portacabin.

'Major Olentiev, sir,' Olentiev said as dutifully as he could. 'My papers are here.'

Bucharin ran his eye down the first page, stopped, eyeing him cautiously. *Malevolently.* 'We have been awaiting you, Major. The injuries you sustained from your accident have healed?'

Olentiev managed half a nod.

'Good. We need you to spearhead a surgical strike on the rebels in the Southeast. None of our men have the qualifications to substitute themselves in your place.'

'Permission to speak freely, sir?'

'Yes – what is it?'

'Surely, sir, I am one of many that could lead a squadron into the heartland for a missile strike.'

Bucharin turned to face the portacabin's sole window, spinning silence.

'I mean only that I've been wounded, sir. Have any operations been launched since?'

'None that were as successful as we had hoped. You are wondering, perhaps, what became of Marshal Timushenko, my predecessor and your old over-commander?'

'Yes; with respect, sir, I had wondered.'

'He was relieved of his duties due to poor health two days ago. Since then, two air strikes have occurred: one long range and one short one to support ground forces in the northwest. Both fell short of their goals, one being absolutely disastrous.'

Timushenko ill? Olentiev couldn't accept that. Timushenko was ten years younger than this new man. He was a realist. Next to experience, a realist was a pilot's best friend here.

'You'll be briefed in full tomorrow morning.' Bucharin turned from the window, smiling. 'Since your incident, the rebels have recovered much hill country. They are maybe two thousand up there in dug-outs and existing installations.'

You're trying to kill me, you bastard, aren't you? Olentiev thought, but not with his eyes.

'Yesterday, two of our MiG Fulcrums were shot down by rockets there. We hit the rebels back hard to clear the northwest, a sector we'd secured for weeks when you were last active here, Major.'

'You managed to knock them *all* back from there?' Olentiev noticed the glint in Bucharin's eyes matt over just before the latter turned back to the comfort his window.

'Yes, but only just. These dogs are running wild everywhere from the central country down round to the south and the east. It seems even the killer radiation is not deterring them.'

'And I'm to lead an air strike on them there?'

'Everything will be explained to you in your briefing, Major… Tomorrow.'

Bucharin turned back from the glass. Olentiev could see his eyes had been recharged. They fixed on his own like drill bits, whirring away, gouging his spirit, daring him to give any hint that he suspected why he had been selected for it all. 'Find your billet, Major. It's getting late.'

-25-

<u>20<u>th</u> April, San Diego, California</u>

Dave Reynolds sped into work early that morning and double parked.

Parker and Hank Jarvis were waiting for him when the elevator doors shot back. Parker looked like he'd been chain smoking through the night. 'We've got big problems.'

'What kind of problems, Hank?'

'Shareholders,' Parker informed like a boss. 'This is what we'd been fearing the most from day one.'

Reynolds made a move for his office, ignored Jarvis's signal to stop.

'Don't go, Dave.'

'Why not?'

'Because the FBI will be here any minute. We have to be careful where we go today.' The look on Jarvis's face was pathetic, even for someone as wet as he.

'So? It's about time they got involved with this.'

'They've been hard at it since the virus first struck,' Parker said. 'Only now their labs have finally turned something up.'

'What exactly?'

Jarvis gestured for the water cooler and the trio began walking.

'The source?' Reynolds asked. 'They're onto the infector guy yet?'

'No,' Parker growled. 'Nothing about that.'

'Well, it's more to do with the screen distortion,' Jarvis said.

'What about it?'

'We'll find out exactly when they get here at nine,' Parker ordered.

'But you must have heard something?'

'I know what you know, Reynolds; leave it alone. Everybody on every floor of the building is going to hear what the deal is,' Parker said as he filled one cup from the dispenser, shot it back then refilled. 'Just wait 'til the damn FBI people get here.'

'We've got a camera link for everyone,' Jarvis said. 'Team leaders from accounts, technical support and sales will all be patched into this.'

Reynolds couldn't drink. 'Well Mr. Parker, sir, do you really think we'll get totaled by this super-virus?'

Parker remained silent, sipped his water like the cup was an ashtray. 'The virus hasn't spread far enough yet,' Jarvis said, studying Parker for the slightest hint of objection. 'But that's mostly because a lot of our and other server users just aren't going online due to all this.'

'Right,' Reynolds said. 'That's heavy.'

'That's close on ninety-five percent of private users not playing ball with us.'

'And businesses?' Reynolds asked, knowing full well the corporative elements constituted just the periphery of Anline's clientele.

The elevator buzzer stabbed a fist through the silence that rammed Reynolds right in the guts. 'Right. Check out Mulder and Scully,' he whispered when the doors parted.

'Mr. Reynolds?' the female agent called as they moved up the corridor.

Reynolds noted that each agent carried two laptop cases. 'Yes?'

'FBI, sir; agents Fenton and Lippmann.'

'You can have my office,' Parker said. 'You'll need some space for those.'

'Thanks,' the woman said.

She looks like Cher, Reynolds thought before he extended his hand to each. The man looked nondescript enough to possibly be very important. She wore a power business suit with above-the-knee, coal-colored skirt and low-heeled pumps; he wore a crisp opal-colored suit. They looked the part.

'I'll put the meeting on standby, Reynolds,' Parker said when the agents moved past.

No sooner were they inside Parker's enclosure than both laptops were whipped out of their cases and booted up. Reynolds noticed the linking wire that Fenton, the male, was running between his and Lippmann's computer and wondered. Could the F.B.I. have devised a shield?

'The hard disk on agent Lippmann's computer here has already been infected by the super-virus,' Fenton began as he started poking keys on his board.

The screen on Lippmann's laptop brightened to a light matt black rectangle. Reynolds leaned against his boss's main desk, watched spellbound as Fenton mashed his 'Alt', 'Ctrl' and 'Del' keys to reveal....

The green line started running, cultivating a jaggedy horizon midway down the screen.

'As you can see, my computer is now useless,' Lippmann said.

'You got your wallpaper only when it *first* got infected – before powering off, right?'

'Yes,' Lippmann told Hank Jarvis. 'But we can't replicate that now it's happened.'

Fenton hunted for a chair; Reynolds obliged with the one from Parker's smaller desk. 'So the disk is now wiped on her computer,' he half informed but half asked, too.

'Yes. On every test case we ended up taking out the infected disk and trying to boot up on other hardware.' Fenton replied.

'Every time, we only ever got a few spins and then a black screen,' Lippmann commented. 'Did that green line turn up on the other equipment that we linked it to?'

'Oddly enough, no,' Fenton nearly whispered. 'Doesn't carry over at all.'

Reynolds felt some intrigue at that. 'But that's a file in itself,' he said.

'Yes; it is. In theory, it is a program that's giving the screen activity,' Lippmann stated.

'The only problem is that there's nothing to account for it in the drive.' Fenton offered.

Reynolds perked up. 'Then it's got to be in the ROM...coming from in there.'

'That's what we had thought, but no,' Fenton responded.

'But it *has* to be there.'

'One hundred and fifty-five tests with as many wiped chips might say otherwise.'

'Are you telling me that a motherboard can't hold enough memory to keep a little line like that running on a loop?' Reynolds asked and noted a rebuking grunt from Parker.

Lippmann started looking edgy. 'That's what we want to show you.'

'What?'

Fenton took over. 'It's not a short loop program. It's fluid, linear.'

'No way; there's no way it could be,' Reynolds said, shaking his head. 'It's illogical.'

Fenton leaned in behind the screen. 'Watch,' he said as he removed the power cable.

In the space of the next minute, both agents had unscrewed the base of the machine. Reynolds felt his sickness return when Lippmann pulled the socket to the motherboard.

She held it up in front of him. 'See? There is now no connection at all between this unit's logic and the VDU. And we still have our friend running free and easy over the screen.'

Reynolds moved away from Parker's desk, took the motherboard in his hands. The ROM chip looked immaculate, the processor also. 'This is impossible,' he said.

'Yes. Impossible,' Fenton confirmed as he lifted the laptop's severed part and rotated it all the way round, as if to satisfy kids of all ages at a magic show that no wires were in evidence.

'There is no way by all the laws of electronics for this display to be doing what it's doing right now,' Lippmann said. 'But it's running on with its program as if everything was A-1.'

'Nobody's at home, but the lights are still on,' Fenton said.

Reynolds put the motherboard on Fenton's chair and touched the screen. 'Holy shit.'

'You've got quite a background in computers, haven't you?'

Reynolds peered over the top of the screen, fixed Lippmann with a stare. 'I - I was a systems engineer for Compaq for a couple years.'

'February 2003 to October 2006,' Fenton said.

'And before that?' Lippmann asked.

Reynolds couldn't answer. The blips and troughs of the green line were running into his fingertips, threatening him with brail hate messages.

'We'll tell you?' Lippmann answered and asked. 'Nice little hacking jobs in 2001.'

'First CompuServ then Microsoft.'

'And then us,' Fenton finished.

Dave Reynolds raised his eyes from the green line and spent the prayer he'd been saving on the tip of his tongue. 'God, you people are for *real.*'

-26-
20ᵗʰ April, San Diego, California

Billy Reynolds awoke to a strange setting. Worse still, he found he'd awoken to stranger thoughts. *Detectophobia* - the fear of being caught or discovered.

In the deep gray of Nash's basement ceiling he saw his niece, his brother and his parents staring down at him with tear-stained, dour expressions.

'I'm sorry,' Billy told them then tried replaying last night in his head.

No. That hadn't been last night. It had only been this morning that you'd gone out and done that. You risked everything today.

He rolled over, came nostril to fiber with Nash's smoke-seeded sofa cover.

You are a DEVIANT. 'No,' he pleaded, rolling back until he was belly down. 'No.'

Non-psychopathic DEVIANTS are created in the decay of post-postmodernism's social systems.

Billy Reynolds punched the sofa once, twice, then kicked it. He could not stop the flow in his head. *Oh yes, the old woman had had a heart attack. She must have had one. The old woman had had a heart attack, and she had died because she was too poor and decrepit to enjoy the protection of a family.*

...Too DEFENSELESS... And all because of you.

Billy shot upright and pictured it: pictured the cops hauling her out under a blanket with the straps at either end, leaving their boiler-suited friends behind to dust down the evidence.

Billy kicked the sofa again, watched the tiny stream of spittle fall out of his mouth while he tried to shut out the sound of his heartbeat.

No. Maybe it was alright. Maybe Nash had just fired the air gun randomly into the air without even going up to her door.

Get real.

No; *wait...*

No *'buts'. They have you by the -*

'No, wait....*wait,*' Billy whispered, his voice a spilled crate of broken glass. He could dust down the gun now, and the bench of the car and its cabin. He could take a plastic sandwich bag and pick out his long brown hairs, just to be sure... Eradicate any of himself from in there.

Very good, Billy. But how about your ALIBI for last night?

Billy started pacing the room. He was dressed from the waist down when he tip-toed away from the sofa and entertainment center to check the stairs. The morning's semi-darkness and silence frowned back upon him from Barry Nash's back hall and kitchen.

Barry hadn't mentioned his parents. Perhaps they were....

Up. Billy started making his way up the steps, shifting his weight from threadbare lip to threadbare lip. *God helps those who help themselves,* he thought and felt a little warmed by that.

The landing was tiled. When Billy looked round to his left and through the window there, he found Nash's lemon yellow El Camino lying in the drive.

It as good as had a sign slung over its tailgate saying 'Crime in progress, please overtake,' he thought.

You murdered that old woman, his mind jabbed then. Third degree they'd call it... life in prison. Billy thumbed the latch of Nash's back door, moved the screen door a few inches away from its frame. It creaked at first, then gave, but with no guarantee of not creaking again.

He let his fingers ride with the handle until it was wide enough to get through, the yellow of Nash's El Camino scowling at him. He let the screen door go back very, very carefully.

Nash's door was locked. Had he pushed the button in on his one? He moved to look. Nash's jean jacket was resting right up against the passenger window, covering the door button.

'Please,' he whispered, pulling up on the black handle.

Locked. 'No,' Billy gasped. 'Jesus, *no!*'

He stood like that for half a minute, forgetting about neighbors at windows or Nash's parents at windows, before he tried to see if Nash's Cruzman pistol actually lay inside. He'd forgotten.

The darkness of the jean jacket in the window allowed him a very clear reflection of himself. His eyes were identical to his brother's, Raina's and his mom's.

It was no use. He'd have to leave it; wait for Nash to give him a ride home and do it in the car. That was *if* Nash *would* drive him home.

Billy scanned the visible stretch of bench space within the cabin: blank CDs, old, dirty store-bought CDs, empty ciggie packs, scrunched up T-shirt, and miscellaneous wrapper trash.

...And that damned black jean jacket. Billy peered harder through the glass, moved a little to the right to see away in under the dash. He really didn't remember Nash taking the gun out of the car last night.

'Hey; what you doing down there, man?'

'N-nothin'.'

Nash pushed the window further outward, leant his top half over the sill. 'You still scared about the gun, *ainchya*?'

'Not so loud!' Billy moved towards Nash's back door.

They met on the staircase, Barry Nash smirking like hell, shaking his head. 'You are one sorry sonofabitch, Reynolds.'

'Look, man; I think something bad's happened. I just wanna see the pistol - that's all.'

'Do you now?'

Billy tried to pass Nash on the stairs, failed. 'Get out of the way, Barry!'

'No. My house. You're intruding.'

Billy tried brushing past again. Nash's freezing hands clasped his forearm. 'I said, no.'

'You asshole!'

'You really are a chickenshit, aren't you?'

'Just let me see that gun, then I'll go,' Billy said then shook his arm free. 'You won't see me again after that.'

'Oh, but I will. In court.' Nash smiled a punchable, tobacco-sallowed grin with that.

Billy took a swing, not caring if parents might emerge from doors above. Nash moved his head back just in time to take only a glancing strike from the tops of his knuckles and shoved.

Billy fell back three steps, nicking the back of his right hand on the rail. 'Just let... just let me get at the gun. Please.'

'No. Forget it.'

'Barry, don't screw me over like this!'

'Did it to yourself. You're the one who shot it. I wore gloves. You're *my* stooge now.'

'This'll be the last you ever see of me.'

Nash scratched his stubble, fixed him with a squint. 'How much is it worth to you?'

Billy felt something sink in his gut. 'What?'

'No; let me put it another way: what will you *do* to get your hands on my gun?'

'Don't be a cunt, Barry.'

'Flattery will get you nowhere.' Nash sat down on a stair and shook his head.

Billy saw his chance, rushed at the wider path to the right of Nash.

Nash was quick; he blocked him, pinned him against the wallpapered stairwell. Billy groaned as the sill of the small stairwell window thudded into the ball of his nape. He lashed out at Nash with a right hook, catching him squarely in the temple.

'Wanna play games, eh?!' Nash yelled, thudding him back, dully slamming the same part of Billy's neck into the sill. 'Think I'd go an' leave it up here?' he said and squeezed his neck.

Billy Reynolds thrashed about when the first pins and needles crackled in his brain. Something was badly wrong. Nash wasn't supposed to be stronger than he. Nash had failed hockey tryouts two years in a row because he couldn't take hip checks and slams on the boards.

Billy kneed Nash in the balls and the pressure at his throat decreased.

'You prick!' Nash cried before he let go of Billy's neck. Billy ran down the stairs.

'Wait, chickenshit!'

Billy turned from the hall. Nash's face had gone a gray purple, but he wasn't panting. 'I've got a little deal to strike up with you, Billy.'

'*What?!*'

Nash clutched the banister with one hand, pressed the wall with the other to barricade.

The look on his face was INSANE, Billy thought. 'What deal, you dick?!'

'Option A or B, just like a parking ticket, Billy.'

'What are you talk-'

'Option A is you give me a thousand bucks and I let you take my gun and do whatever.'

Billy's heart sank. He did not like OPTION A one little bit.

'Or there's option B,' Nash said, his grin restored, undamaged by his ex-friend's assault on its suburbs. 'You'll like Option B, Billy. You go over to that old bitch's place and say hello.'

'You're crazy.'

Nash's grin intensified. 'No, seriously, Billy. You get to go check her out. Just think, you could dress up and sell her some God while you're at it. Kill two birds with one stone, huh?'

Billy didn't feel his heart sink again until he thought about it.

He was now AFRAID that OPTION B sounded better than the first one. *You'll see if she's okay,* he thought.

'How about it, Billy? Think you could pass yourself off as a Jehovah's Witness?'

Nash's grin fell in a little but his eyes were full on.

'Let's end this right now,' Billy said. OPTION B pleaded with him not to continue until he snarled at it. 'Option C. "C" says I get the hell out right now and never see you again, Barry.'

'But you won't,' Nash said. 'You won't leave it that way.'

'Why not?'

'Because number one, you ain't got the balls to walk away from yourself.'

'Whatchya mean "*yourself*"?'

'I mean, you'll go home, walk circles all over that nice carpet in your basement, hoping to God nothing shows up on the midday news about what we - sorry - *you* did to her last night.'

'It - it's eleven-twenty right now.' Billy had heard the jitteriness in his own voice. 'That's only... just another forty minutes.'

'That's just today, though, Billy. What if she didn't report the gunman to the cops or if the shock from that kills her in the next couple of days? What then?'

Billy felt Option B tug at the bottom of his heart. He'd heard about legal culpability in slow death cases before. He'd seen it on Twenty Twenty. And it wasn't always manslaughter...

Shit.

'You won't get much sleep with Option C, pal,' Nash said. 'Number two, if you do want it that way, I'll tell everybody it was you that did that before I head back next semester. Hmmm... how long would it take for word to...?'

Billy started to tremble. 'Everyone' by Nash's description meant all their old high school friends as well as some of the new college ones Billy knew hung out at the Perkins near the Marriott and the marina.

'Think about it; think about how it'll feel when you see them all again in September and they rip you up behind your back. Or when Kelly calls you up in the next week or two to ask you if it's true and you don't sound secure enough so she tells you it's over.'

Billy tried to stop his jaw quivering but couldn't. Kelly might well be his wife some day.

Nash's grin, stare and the calmness of his posture were agonizing. 'Why,' he continued with relish, 'a friend of a friend might even do the decent thing and call the cops.'

'I'll drag you into it,' Billy said. 'Your car, your action - you were *all* of it.'

The grin survived. 'But *you* were the one that fired. That's all they'd really care about.'

'This is the end of us as friends, Nash; you know that, don't you?'

'I couldn't give a shit. You're a loser, anyway.'

'Fuck you, you prick.'

Nash's grin fell away but his eyes kept their strength. 'So, then. You just gonna turn tail and walk outta here like nothing happened last night? You can't walk away from this now.'

'Option B,' Billy said, at length. 'I go round, see if she's okay and that'll be the end of it.'

Nash nodded once. 'There's just one other thing.'

Billy's heart dangled again on fresh cheese wire. He wanted to KILL Nash now.

'You have to spend one hour or longer inside her place.'

'No.'

'That's the deal, amigo.'

'I'm not your friend.'

'Neither will anybody else be if I blab about why you asked me to take you up there.'

Billy thought hard. He had a good suit, could get his hands on a bible all right. An hour equaled one episode of 'Battlestar Galactica'. That wouldn't be all that long, would it?

'Okay, Nash; but for one hour, I get to keep the gun just like I'd paid for it.'

'Yeah, we can arrange that.'

Billy turned to leave. 'Today?'

'Yeah,' Nash said. 'You go home, get changed and I pick you up at about two, drop you off at the end of her street. You go in, do your business with her, come out… End of story.'

'Wait; don't use *your* car. Someone may've seen it last night.'

'Okay; there's my mom's if you wanna keep on being a pussy.'

'Wh - where your folks at, anyhow?'

'I don't give out family secrets to non-friends, Reynolds.'

Billy started walking for the back door, stopped when he had his hand on the lever. 'Why are you being such an asshole over this, Nash?' he called.

Nash smirked from the staircase. 'Because I *can be*, Reynolds. Now outta my house.'

-27-
20ᵗʰ April, San Diego, California

Leah Coleman was glued to CNN's breaking news bulletin when her husband came through the side doorway, cigarette in mouth. 'God, Rick; what've they been doing to you?'

Coleman reciprocated with a weaker embrace, ditched his butt into the ashtray on the kitchen countertop. Leah's hair smelled sweetly of evening primrose and looked like she should be in a commercial shot on location in an Alpine meadow. He looked like Death warmed over.

'Sorry, hun; it's all being shoveled into the fan right now.'

His wife released him and stood back. After so many years, she still had difficulty in accepting the vagueness of his answers sometimes. 'It's this Agent one-oh-four thing, isn't it?'

'Something like that.'

She let him go. 'Rick!'

'I can't tell you, baby. You know the game now.'

'No I *don't!*'

Coleman grimaced and shot a look at his plasma screen mounted above the fridge. The woman was finishing up talking about the tests the French had been doing on the substance:

'*....Say the high melting point suggests a metallic makeup. Dr. Jules Bertrand of the institute claims that de-statifying equipment has so far proven ineffective against the chemical.'*

(Camera on Dr. Bertrand)

'*Certainly these discoveries are disturbing to come across for us. There is no precedent by which we can measure the far-reachingness of this, eh, problem. At present rates where we find the agent, it is very worrying for global communications. In liquid precipitation, it has the power to knock out everything from satellite receivers to even the strongest radio signals.*

In the tests conducted here, we have so far learned that the agent dubbed "104" will throw more than enough static into the air to completely diffuse the signals of all types of radio - long, medium and short waves, and block satellite signals. So in the context of global communications, this is a very serious difficulty.

The problem is made worse by the potency of the substance long after it has settled on the ground. The chemical is absorbed by the terrain which in turn becomes a producer of static. Depending on the material used to cover the contaminated surface, we have found that for every micrometer of penetration about one meter of soil coverage is needed to reduce the effect of static. But, given the scope of it all, how can such burials be carried out with effectiveness?'

(Shrugs shoulders, flashes ironic smirk)

'As you can imagine, it is impossible for people to be out always patching over the contamination. Even if that was to be a reality, there is too much land to treat. No region, no climate is immune, although the high snowfall rates to be found at more northerly latitudes in this hemisphere increase the destructiveness of the agent to transmitters and receivers both.

Put shortly, if the proportion of Agent One Hundred Four remains constant then we will go on experiencing static-poisoned communications. Should that level or the frequency of rainfall increase, however, we must be prepared for the collapse of every mode of, ehm, telecommunications we have at our disposal.

Essentially, it will be the start of a new Dark Age.'

'Turn it off,' Coleman said, eyes darting over counter Formica to find the remote. He could hear the crackles bleeding out from behind the mild fuzziness in the screen. 'That's what that bastard's doing to us,' he said when he hit the red button.

'What bastard?'

He gave Leah a hard look, saw little in her face that he recognized from before....

From before that night and the meeting with the Doom Crew.

'Rick? What've they been telling you?'

'I can't talk about it; you know that.'

'Then just tell me if it's going to affect us.'

'Honey, just back off for today, okay?' He reached out, squeezed her wrist, cradled his brow and nose in the other. 'This is all beginning to get to me. I'm sorry... I'm so sorry.'

'You know what's doing this, don't you?'

Coleman nodded. To Hell with Carmichael, he thought in a flash of anger... Family first. As long as he didn't *really* talk, they'd be okay.

'All I'll say is that we're one step closer to the source, baby,' he said, re-squeezed her wrist then wiped the grit from his eyes. 'But things are getting heavy with it now.'

Leah shivered. 'Do you have to go anywhere?' she asked.

His job had been a hard pill for her over the years. She had that glassy look in her eyes now, reminding him of Mina Harker clutching her husband, urging him not to venture to Transylvania in *'Nosferatu'*, a very, very old but still a scary movie. 'So far as I can tell, no.'

'You *would* tell me if something - if - if something was going to happen, wouldn't you?'

'Of course.'

'Rick, I-'

'Look,' he said, wiping the side of her face with the flats of his nails. 'We're onto something now. Let's just accept that. But nothing's going to happen to me, you or anyone.'

'Can you promise me that, Rick?'

'I am now. As soon as we've nailed this…'

Coleman's veins ran cold, clenching, too. *Lesson number one in the CIA - you keep EVERYTHING to yourself*, he thought. 'When it's over, we *are going* on a second honeymoon.'

Coleman caught the figure in the window, let go of his wife.

'What's wrong now?'

'Who's that?' he asked.

She moved behind him, looked over his shoulder. 'Mailman. I'll get it.'

'Doesn't our mail guy have a moustache and a beer gut?'

'So maybe he's sick today.'

Coleman watched him open his mailbox and deposit some manila envelopes. Coleman also felt something in his gut twitch. 'No. I'll go get it.'

There were four letters: two bills, one junk and one….

Coleman felt his heart fall toward his scrotum. He tried walking back for the side door to his house but could barely manage.

The mailman had looked back on his way to two doors down, nervously.

'Rick, what is it?'

Coleman pressed the envelope to check for wires. It could be a lightweight explosive. His department had used a few in the past... most recently on a Colombian cocaine kingpin.

No wiring, Coleman's fingertips told him. *Safe, right?* his mind dared to ask.

Wrong. The connections could be monofilament. He moved to the lights above the stove, held the manila up, catching only the shadow of what felt like he thought was inside.

A thick card or a thin plastic plate.

'You don't know anybody in Israel, do you?' Leah asked.

'No. I don't.' Coleman tried prying up the back 'V' seal with his nail and couldn't.

The filleting knife begged him to lift it from the salmon-shaped knife block.

Knives are useless against a thing like Ganz, his mind scolded... *What could it be?*

As he jabbed at the top corner and started slitting, Coleman felt his heart going haywire. *When they run the film of this back, they'll find Ganz's head laughing, snickering at your death. That's assuming the camera survives the...*

Explosion?

'Rick? What d'you think it is?'

Coleman didn't answer. He stuck the knife tip into the gash he'd made, twisted it to get it broadside. The gap widened and he noticed a fuzzy-edged card shape.

'What is that?' asked Leah.

'Get back,' he replied. 'Stand well back from me.' He shot her a freezer of a stare, compelling her to take shelter in the corner of the kitchen.

'For the *love of God*, Rick! What have you got ther-'

'Shut up! Let me get it out, will ya?!'

Coleman inverted the envelope, tried to coax the object out onto the counter top with jerks, shakes and tugs upward. *Come on; come on,* his mind dared as his fingers deftly plucked.

The thing clacked edgeways then plopped flat, face down... A business card.

Sent by a sympathizer of Ganz: the dangerous unknown quantity that he was? Coleman turned the card as the very nasty revelation that he and Leah were in their third house in four years twanged a new worry about having to move again.

'Maybe Anthrax?' read the sole word on the other side of the card. 'Get back,' he ordered. Leah retreated to the hallway, covering her mouth while he drenched his palms with alcohol cleanser then reached for the yellow rubber gloves left slung over the sink. He slipped his plain white Tee undershirt up to cover his nose and mouth, donned the gloves and picked up the card. Turning it, he read: 'Gotcha… But it could've been! Keep looking.'

'How the *Hell?!*' Coleman gasped. 'That was *blank* before!' he said before realizing that the writing had been paintbrushed on in a clear veneer which he could only see if he tilted the card.

'Now what the Hell is *that?*' he asked when he noticed the tiny corner of another piece of card poking from the open envelope. He sensed Leah approaching. 'Baby, stay back.'

Coleman pulled the other card out gently, hardly breathing through his 'mask'. It was a photograph. The picture was terrible, though. Its emulsion had run at the edges and its finish had breathed bubbles down from its surface.

'What's that of?' Leah asked from the corridor.

'I don't know,' Coleman said. 'I don't understand. For God's sake, keep your nose and mouth covered…' He swiped a trace of fine white powder and dared to lower his shirt mask. 'Thank God – it's talc. But this - this other thing looks like it's a hundred years old, but… but the picture's modern.'

'Are you sure that's not anthrax?' Leah gasped.

'Next to certain. It's a spook… someone trying to put the frighteners on us. This photocard thing is the main feature here.'

He stared hard into the center of the image, finding he could pick out some faces. The picture quality was abysmal - so soft that many of the men on either end of it seemed to merge into each other as Siamese twins, triplets or quadruplets.

Coleman trained his eyes on the faces and heads in the middle. Multi-ethnic: African blacks, Arabs, South Americans and a myriad of European heads were there. The bodies below them were all wearing suits and ties and stood outside some building more than five stories high.

It was like someone had snapped the shot at a range of fifty feet.

But why was it here?

'This is big,' he told her. 'I've got to call base in a minute. You stay just there and get some alcohol cleanser from the bathroom.' Before he put the card down, he noted that the color was all wrong, the saturation, too. That sort of gray wasn't photo-like. It was a smoky gray that let some of the subdued constituents bleed through in places like a packet of mixed up Play-Doh.

Setting the image card down, he felt the fluffiness of its edge and it reminded him of ancient photographs he had seen of his great-grandparents' childhoods. A piece of card in that condition had to either be from 1910 or it had to have been fished out of the sea and dried out.

He was about to back away to where Leah stood when he took up the envelope once more. He turned it over, the hunch that there might be a return address too strong to leave.

'Jesus,' Coleman said when he saw the black flame marks at both top corners of the manila envelope. 'Jesus H. Christ. *They weren't there* before.'

He dropped it, backed up until he was standing level with his wife, rubbing the last of the drying alcohol up and over his fingertips. 'We're going to have to get out of here.'

'Rick, I'm scared,' Leah said as the first tears came and they made for the front of the house and the downstairs bathroom with its half bottle of germ cleanser. 'I'm so scared. What if that's real... that anthrax?!'

Coleman balked as he fired cleanser into her hands. He'd forgotten about the anthrax. As he rubbed his hands, a puff of white powder wafted up from his wrist. He recognized the brand from many years ago.

'No, we're okay – that's definitely only talc. Our boy's playing hardball mind games now.'

-28-
<u>20th April, Bremen, Germany</u>

'Carl.'

Becker took the full force of his brother's hug before he let himself cry. He'd been meaning to cry since leaving JFK... having resolved to reach his father before the Reaper did.

'Thank God you got here; the way planes are now with all the static, I didn't think.'

'It cost a bomb at that notice, but I did it okay. Somebody canceled. How's Dad?'

'Mom's in there with him now.'

Carl Becker moved past his brother, gazed at the outside of the door... The door to the last room he knew his father would ever occupy alive. 'You said he's conscious.'

'Yes, but Carl, he's in and out. Doctors say he's got a 20-80 chance.'

'It happened when he was at home, you told me.'

His brother nodded, gulped. Carl Becker moved inside the room, found his mother perched on a padded chair, clutching his father's hand, fingers rubbing, looking just as frail as he.

'I'm here, Mother. Dad.'

She turned her head, greeted him with tear-flooded, red eyes. 'Heinrich, Carl has come,' she whispered, rubbed the old man's wrist harder. His father was propped up on three fat pillows, eyes open but unable to move.

Becker moved up to him, kissed a patch just below his hairline.

'He's been asking for you,' she said, taking Becker's hand. 'Heinrich, look who's here.'

His father's eyes yawed rightward, scanned his chest then his face weakly.

'H-how did it happen?'

'We were sitting at home,' his mother told him. 'The lottery numbers were coming up.' Her voice and grip on his wrist broke.

'Easy. Easy, now.'

'There was... There was a knock at the door.'

Becker sensed a pang of rage brewing. 'What?'

'An old... An old woman with white...with white hair. Like wire.'

'You answered the door, mother?'

'No, your father did. But...but I saw. Was at the window and I looked round.'

His father's eyes were flickering now. Becker could see new vigor in there. He'd seen that look many times when the face had been younger, its mustache darker: his dad's angry look.

'What did she do to him?'

'I - she... She was only there for a few seconds. I - I only heard things.'

'What did you hear?'

His mother sniffled. A torrential downpour was imminent from that sniffle. Becker grasped her shoulder. 'Easy, Mama. Don't strain yourself. It doesn't matter – really, it doesn't.'

'Yak... *Yak* something. That's what I heard her say to your father.'

'Yak?'

'Y - yes. Yak, like one of those Chinese... Yak.'

The glare in his father's eyes boiled over. Becker heard his breathing quicken.

His mother cupped the old man's hand. 'Heinrich, please don't. Just get well. Please.'

But Becker had read the eyes; he had to accept their invitation. 'He's trying to say…'

'Carl, don't make him do this to himself... Oh, Dear Lord, please!'

'Easy, Mama. He's trying to speak.'

'No,' she said, shooting a hand at Becker's arm, pinching it. 'Leave him be!'

'Yyyyyyut....yyy-'

'Heinrich, don't. Don't try to say anything! Carl, *let him alone!*'

Becker leaned closer to his father, thinking: *If he dies, it'll be all your fault, you bastard.*

'*Carl!* Heinrich, don't!'

'I have to know, mother.'

He saw his dad's lips purse, widen to make a 'Y' again.

'Eyyyyut Set!'

Becker's blood stopped dead.

'Eyutt *Settot!*'

'No,' Becker whispered. 'Oh Christ, no!'

'Please...please, get out,' his mother gibbered. 'Can't you just leave the poor man be?!'

Becker wanted to move back from the bed, found he could not. He'd only managed to cry out a couple of drops from each eye. 'This is... this is insane,' he managed to whisper.

'Oh, Carl. Go out, talk...talk to your brother. He knows... Kurt knows all of it.'

Becker kissed his father on the forehead, tried to swear him a vengeance with his eyes, squinting every ounce of it, wanting him to feel the frozen field of newly seeded anger within him.

Outside, his brother had just returned from a smoke. 'You know.' Kurt's tone was sour.

'Why the hell didn't you tell me?'

'I didn't want you to know 'til you were here. I'm sorry.'

'Who *was that bitch* who came to their door?'

'We don't know. Dad collapsed as soon as he opened it to her.'

'Those words, though.'

'I know. That's all he's been say- that's all he's been *able to* say since.'

'You don't understand. I - I do.'

Kurt threw him a pained stare. 'Understand what?'

'I've heard - seen them before; those words.'

'What you mean *seen them before?*'

'They're bad news, Kurt: really bad.'

'For fuck's sake, man, how can that have anything to do w-'

'You don't get it. They've got something to do with-'

'That's crazy, Carl. Are you listening to yourself?'

'Listen. There's been things, stuff that's been happening.'

'What kind of *stuff?!*'

Carl Becker glanced up at the corridor ceiling then back down, somehow hoping that God could see his pain through the Plasti-foam panels and lights and do something helpful.

'You're out of your mind.'

'Try me.'

'How can *words* do… You're talking about this Agent one-oh-four shit, aren't you?'

'No. Kurt, I don't know about that, but there've been other things.'

Kurt shook his head, took a seat on the low courtesy couch. 'You're really gone.'

Becker grabbed his brother's shoulder, seized the windup punch with the other hand. 'Don't…Kurt, *don't!*'

'Get your goddamn hands off me!'

Becker shook him hard, not caring if every security guard in the building came. 'Kurt, I've been working for the C.I.A. for the past three days. I'm telling you, those words *mean* something.'

'Oh, this is *rich.*' Kurt pushed him back then. The force was enough. Carl Becker toppled, nicking the back of his head on the lever of the fire extinguisher near the door.

On the floor, he caught the camera out of the corner of his eye. They'd have security up there any minute now.

'I hate you!' Kurt gasped. He was standing over him now, his fist curled back on his forearm, waiting to strike. 'If Dad dies, I'll never forgive you for this!'

Carl Becker shot to his feet, raised his arms, his hands surrender-style. He was thinking at a speed he'd never had to deal with in his life. They'd find out if he told his brother the truth: a hundred Shaun Bean doppelgangers after him, with dogs lapping at his reservoir of blood.

Becker heard the footsteps coming from far up the corridor. 'You wanna know, Kurt?'

Kurt was sobbing on the edge of the couch now. Carl Becker heard his mother crying. 'Kurt?' He touched Kurt's shoulder. 'I'll be at your apartment in an hour. I'll tell you all I know.'

Carl Becker caught the pair of shadows moving across the curve in the wall.

He did not have to force the tears to make it look good.

Tears were made of water. He never wanted to see water again, he thought as he explained the situation to a couple of fossilized hospital security guards.

-29-
20<u>th</u> April, San Diego, California

'Where's Daddy?'

Helen Reynolds dipped the dinner plate back into the sink. 'At work, pet.'

'He's always at work!'

'I know. But he'll be in soon, alright?'

'I'm sick of him being at work all the time! Can you say that to him?'

Raina's mother stared into the bubbles - all that remained of lunch. Two plates, two cups, two sets of cutlery where there should have been three.

She was sick of Dave being at work, too. This was supposed to have been the start of a week off and a car trip to Sacramento but...

But Parker and the heavies had yanked the chain. She pictured the calendar Dave had hung in the basement back in their house. Oh, how she'd cheered him on when he'd marked out nine notches in April the same night they'd had that fight.

And now it had come to this. This was quickly becoming intolerable, never mind the state of the rest of the world. She saw his family more than him these days. Sure, Dave's folks were undemanding and they doted on Raina, but they weren't in her inner-circle view of the world.

'Look; Uncle Billy!'

And then there was Dave's kid brother. Helen Reynolds only caught the back half of her brother-in-law. Billy was a punk and punks were in her distant past now.

'Hi,' she said when she heard the door swing back.

'Oh, hi, Helen,' Billy returned as he moved through the kitchen doorway.

'Hi, Uncle Billy!'

'Hey, how's it hanging, Lala.'

'You promised you wouldn't call me that!'

Billy ignored that, headed for the door to the basement. 'Where's Mom and Dad at?'

'La Jolla, shopping.'

'No Dave today?'

'No,' Helen said, not even trying to take the edge out of her voice.

'He at work or at play?'

'Work. He's stuck in that place again.'

'I thought you guys were thinking of heading out Sacramento way sometime soon.'

'Well, things didn't pan out the way we wanted, Billy; *okay?*'

Raina jumped off her chair, backed into the hall. 'Don't shout at Uncle Billy, Mommy!'

Helen cast one final look at him before he vanished down the back stairs. 'There's a crisis on or hadn't you noticed?!'

'Mommy! Please!'

She used to like Billy, not for Dave's sake, but because he'd been fun to be around, back in the early days. But he'd changed after high school.

And the porn had got to her, too. She knew he'd always had a girlfriend since before it had mattered to her. Why he needed the amount of trash she knew he had had always got to her.

Not your *Playboy/Penthouse/Club/Hustler/Swank* variety of stuff, either. No. She knew that her daughter's Uncle Billy's porn was all hardcore. Gangbangs, blowjobs, penetration into three holes or more at the same time.

And hadn't Dave been forced to get liquored up the night he'd found the shit on his dad's server? Whips, chains and rubber leggings.

She'd confronted Billy with it in a joking way some days ago, when she'd left Raina over with her grandparents. He'd stumbled into that same kitchen stinking of musk-masked weed and that's when she'd cracked it. Nothing direct because Raina had been milling about in the back garden and the slide door had been open. Just: 'I'm sure you'd like to put handcuffs on a prettier girl than that,' with the 'that' being the mascara-smothered Kelly he was after.

He'd just laughed it off at first. But then he'd opened on her with: 'I'd let you play with them… if your wrists could fit, that was,' and: 'Give me a break; you can't even wear over-the-knee boots without getting alterations.'

It cut her to play it back in her memory. *You're not fat.* No, but Raina had heard the last bit and hadn't stopped talking about Julia Roberts and the cover of 'Pretty Woman' for hours.

Helen Reynolds moved to the ElectroLux combo, reached down two cans of soda, opened one for Raina and handed her it.

Raina was going to be a beautiful woman some day, she thought. It chilled her... *Imagine some goateed punk pulling himself senseless while thinking of her.*

She took a sip of drink, did not feel refreshed. In an instant, she had wished Billy Reynolds into oblivion.

-30-

20ᵗʰ April, San Diego, California

Billy pulled his good charcoal jacket out from his closet corner, unzipped it from its bag. The coat hanger was heavy, made him wonder until his fingertips found the prong of a belt inside.

It was all straight from Draytons department store, bought by his mom for him four years back. He could have counted on the fingers of one hand the number of occasions in which it had left its protective membrane.

Once, the first time, had been in court for that minor disorder he'd taken part in at the shopping mall's parking lot that summer. It hadn't been the intention behind his mom's getting it for him. As he took it out of its bag, a pang of something like guilt twanged on his heart strings.

He threw everything on in the space of two minutes, checked himself out in the mirror by his CD stack. 'Looking pretty bad there, dude,' he rewarded the image. 'Pretty bad for sure.'

Now came the hard part, he knew. Helen would see him whether he left through the front or not because the kitchen was open plan. Raina would see him too.

No, don't think that, he forced himself to think. *Don't mix the two in the same picture.* Raina was sacred but Helen was ruthless, critical, overly conservative. Like she'd been born at the age of twenty-seven, married, and became looked after like a carefully cultivated flower, and so very, very easy to shock and distress.

Billy checked the digital display on his DVD player, tried to suppress the temptation to superimpose Helen's head among the other victims-in-waiting on the cover of his 'Final Destination' poster. That head of hers had thought many thoughts against him, had it not?

Billy's heart started thumping when he came out of that reverie to prepare himself. His wallet was lying in his jeans pocket, flaccid and old. Did he dare to identify himself?

Those evangelists always did, didn't they? Assuming a homeowner was sad enough to press them hard for ID on the doorstep, they would always produce it, right?

He paused, staring at the rough, card and paper-stuffed mess of his money pouch.

If she asks you to prove yourself, you could flash your license.

No, too risky. You'd sweat, she'd see it and make the connection with your name, all ready for the cops to listen.

How about your DVD club membership card?

No. No good. No picture equals no credibility.

The thoughts crackled painfully. Billy picked his wallet out from his jeans, started rifling through the occupied slits and the booklet of clear card sheathes at the side.

'Right on,' he said when he found his fake ID. Well, Francis Reilly's ID it was in actual fact. Billy had sometimes led the life of Reilly in his – well, both his and Francis Reilly's - past. Reilly had been a big help to him when it was time to go to the bar for ages now. Reilly, you see, had been born in the wonderful year of 1990, apparently in the far-off kingdom of Billings, Montana. His usefulness would be at an end in June, but Billy was more grateful now than ever.

The lamination was peeling at all four corners. You could even see the ink bleeds.

She's an old woman with bad eyes, you dork.

He buttoned the card into his breast pocket then checked himself once more. After dampening and gel-combing his hair, he checked the time: 13:39.

Twenty minutes to kill before Barry Nash came for him.

Helen might be wondering about the silence down here.

Billy moved to his midi Hi-Fi system and hit the 'play' bar below the LCD strip. The speakers spat out the first bars of nu-metal, warming him as he turned, stared at the parting between his closet doors. In the murk caused by his pulled, tawny curtains, he could see the spent CO_2 cartridge.

He'd used that in his own air pistol in antiquity. But then, he'd bought those propellant cartridges by the caseload back in those heady days of valor... target practicing on books in his room and just feeling good that, given his slightish build, he actually had a means of defense if it came to it.

Billy drew back the doors, reached for his leather jacket at the end of the rail. His own Cruzman pistol was still in the pocket, wrapped up in plastic, its handle protruding.

It was calling to him now.

Billy checked for ammo in the other pocket and then dug his hand down the inside of the breast pocket. The bottom was ripped; he stuck his hand down way inside the lining and felt the top of the tiny cylinder carton of ball bearings.

They'd been in there since the payback on Lance Kudrow's bike for beating the living stuffing out of him in the locker room. Billy had emptied as many shots as would go into the hole on the underside of the barrel. It hadn't been anything life-threatening – he'd just written 'FUCK U' in pellets into Kudrow's leather saddle.

Seventeen shots - more than enough if push came to shove. There was already a year-old gas cartridge inside when he lifted the panel on the handle... *No good: get a fresh one.*

He squatted, raking the fingers of his free hand in under the debris lying over the closet floor. He knew the carton of cylinders was away in there, lying dormant during now calmer times.

A pack of novelty condoms toppled out from the back pocket of his old brown pair of Wrangle jeans at the apex of the mound. As his fingertips discovered the CO_2 cartridge box, he noticed the tear in the top of the pack and the long-passed expiry date. It made him feel...

Bad? But then he'd bought them just because of the girl on the cover… and in case he found himself in that situation at the age of 15… and because he'd wanted to try one on then.

He smarted at the sound of footsteps on the stairs.

…The footsteps were at the bottom of the stairs now, too heavy, slow to be Raina's.

Billy shot to his feet tossed the gun into his bed sheets, removed his jacket, threw it on top and kicked the box of condoms back into his closet.

'Billy?'

Helen. What did she want?

'Yeah? Hang on.'

'Don't bother to open up: your mom just called from La Jolla.'

Please don't say car trouble and I have to go pick them up, he thought. *Not now.* He turned the volume down all the way. 'Anything wrong?'

'No. She and your dad are at the exhibition all evening now. Says you're to get pizza or something tonight. Okay?'

'Yeah. No problem. I'm out with friends tonight, anyway.'

'Okay. I'm taking Raina home now. If Dave calls round and you're in, tell him I left some calzone for him in the microwave, alright?'

'Sure. Can you guys let yourselves out?'

'We're okay. See you later.'

'Later, Helen.'

Billy waited until her footsteps had ended on the stairs before he turned the volume back up and finished off readying himself for the mission. He was smiling now. *How jammy is this?!*

He took his Cruzman out from the mash of his comforter and pillows, donned his good black jacket again and fished for a tie.

The CO_2 cartridge hissed when he connected the neck to the pin-valve.

'We're back in the bully-busting business, girl,' he said, waiting for the slam of the doors in Helen's Bonneville and the engine to start.

He caught himself in the blank screen of his TV just then. *God, I look good*, he thought.

But I don't feel good at all.

Nash was going to be very, very sorry he'd treated him that way earlier.

Billy waited until he saw the shadow of his sister-in-law's car lift from his high windows before he selected a target and squeezed the trigger.

Pathok

'Haven't lost our touch, have we, girl?' he said when he saw the silver circle twinkling in the binding of *Huck Finn*, right between 'Twain' and the publisher's insignia.

He'd read that book back when he was eleven: back when he was innocent.

No. He'd just been LESS GUILTY back then.

Billy checked his DVD clock: 13:53. *Better get upstairs, just in case Nash pulls in early.* He pushed in the plastic peg that safety-catched his air pistol then eased it into his inside pocket.

The ammo reserve marker caught on the lining on the way in, slid forward when he jerked it, released two, three, four precious shots into the void below.

Billy took the rubber band from the BB carton, reloaded his weapon, tied the marker pin to the sight then round to the mock hammer. 'Try getting out of that,' he said when he'd got his gun all the way inside his jacket.

On his way out, his eyes drifted over the racks in the alcove behind his door that represented his DVD collection. Half pirated, half bought at the store; half horror, one quarter sci-fi, one eighth miscellaneous and the rest of it porn.

The sight of 'Freeway Warrior' made him pause before he moved through the doorway.

What had he heard Helen say upstairs? *Crisis*, was it?

The notion amused him. Even with all the poisoned rain, all the computer breakdowns and that part of Russia that had no atmosphere, it was still nothing compared to the apocalyptic dystopia portrayed in 'Freeway Warrior'.

Billy went upstairs, locked the sliding door to the back and took his house key from the table by the back door, thinking.

If this was 'Freeway Warrior', he would've gunned Nash down by now. If Nash tried to change the deal or do anymore, Billy promised himself he'd pull his own pistol on him and let rip.

-31-
20ᵗʰ April, San Diego, California

By two o'clock, Dave Reynolds had had enough screen squinting to wreck his eyes. Parker's office had got colder, somehow, and that had sharpened him up for other pains.

He was feeling every second of every minute now.

The detached laptop screen lay discarded on top of Parker's cabinets by the window, its connecting wire dangling like the severed windpipe of a guillotine victim.

Decapitated heads could live for up to a minute, he had read long ago, somewhere. This one, though, had lasted fifty-two minutes, as timed by Fenton.

Fenton and Lippmann were seated at Parker's second, smaller desk at the other end of the room, sifting through the notes he and Hank Jarvis had made. Parker had gone home about half-an-hour after he'd ended the building-wide emergency meeting.

Reynolds closed his eyes, rubbed hard at them. What exactly did his new pay structure mean? he wondered. Parker had gone through the deal once only: no diagrams, no explications beyond answering the repetitive questions of a dozen terrified office folk.

He'd suspended everybody's contract, effective next Monday; everybody, that was, except Reynolds', Jarvis's and Piper's, the whiz kid from technical support.

Together with the elite short-listed from Anline's New York body and the handful of other offices across the country, the three of them were on *special assignment.*

Special assignment meant being loaned to the Secret Sector, or what Parker had honestly called 'The Men in Black'. No pay changes. *A job is a job,* he'd had to remind himself.

Reynolds checked the spreadsheet, acknowledged each scrap of data he needed with a squint. 'Yes,' he said at length, 'I've got the point of entry.'

Fenton and Lippmann looked up in unison. 'Where?'

'Norfolk, Virginia.'

'Infection date of?'

'April fifth,' Reynolds replied, frowning. 'No... no – wait... That would have been far too early. But... but it *does say the fifth here!*'

'That means it was into your users' emails by the second or third day. So most likely April 2nd.'

Reynolds looked up. Lippmann was glaring, having lost all of her former charm.

'Anline is pretty big, you know,' he told her. '*Was* pretty big.'

'Let's look at things the way they were back then,' Fenton said with an energy that Reynolds did not find helpful. 'Our source logs onto his Forserver account on the first or second of April, uploads the super-virus to Forserver's customer service department.'

'Which only accepts uploaded files via file transfer protocol,' Lippmann said.

'You forget - they didn't have to download the file,' Reynolds scolded. 'The virus would've cut into Forserver's entire user directory and *kkbamm*, Forserver's out of business and so's one huge chunk of the nation.'

'And we can't root out the source's email address or anything about him?' Fenton asked. 'He had some kind of self-deleting mechanism put into his address?'

'As far as Jarvis, I and the New York heavies now understand it, yep.' Reynolds thought about Jarvis and little Kenny Piper trying to figure out where to start with the virus shield Parker had proposed at the meeting. If he'd had the strength, he might've laughed at the futility of it all.

'So to find this individual,' Fenton drilled, 'we'd have to -'

'You'd have work his address back from the telephone company and know exactly what time his account was activated that day.'

'Or night,' Lippmann said.

'Or night. And seeing as how Forserver lost all of its account data in the space of a couple of hours, the only way to do it would be to get onto the phone companies and work back every single access number worldwide.'

'You think he...she could have done this from outside the US?'

Reynolds caught the sincerity in Fenton's eyes, felt a little stamina return to his own mind to do it justice with an answer. 'It's unlikely but there's that possibility.'

'But you and Jarvis wrote on here that it came from the States.'

'We based that on the timing of the first documented non-Forserver cases.'

'Offshore companies?'

'Yeah. But look at where they are: Japan, Australia, Philippines. Give it an hour to clear the Forserver boundaries and I say this guy was either working by day over there or in the wee hours here on April 1st or so. Also, our friend could have activated an American account from any cyber cafe in the world. I hope you realize how big your dragnet has to be in this case.'

Fenton nodded. 'Interpol's on it, too, Mr. Reynolds; don't worry about our resources.'

'And the F.B.I. have been working with all the domestic and Canadian phone companies since last week,' Lippmann joined.

'My, the phone companies *are* doing well out of this super-virus, aren't they?'

'That's not funny. Reynolds,' Fenton said.

Of course it was funny, Reynolds thought. The whole world had been knocked back to the 1970s overnight. The whole world had learnt that too much faith had been put in technology.

'Okay,' Reynolds said. 'Suppose they *do* try for a roundup of Forserver users from that day. When they're done, they'll have a list of names that'll take months to go to to get interviews.'

'If that's what it takes to get him then we've no choice.'

'That's a lot of lie detector tests. Your resources going to stretch over such numbers?'

'You haven't been contracted to worry about that,' Fenton said. His stare was icy now. 'You're a virus expert; you're familiar with the ins and outs of them. Just do your job, please.'

'No-one can be an *expert* with this,' Reynolds said. 'I just happened to study them as a core subject because I knew there'd be a job in it. These things and the software we develop to respond to them change faster than that.' He clicked his fingers, hoping it would give them a jolt.

'But you can tell us what category this one falls into,' Fenton returned, unblinking.

'I can't. This one's a new breed entirely. On the surface, it looks way different from anything we've ever had in the past.'

'It's not a Trojan Horse, a worm or a logic bomb, you mean?' Lippmann fished.

'Right. To the semi-trained eye, it's something that could pass for a multi-partite. I know better, though... Most people would just balk at it.'

'That's incorporating characteristics of bootstrap and-'

'The whole shebang minus companion and data-file,' Reynolds cut Fenton off with.

'They're the ones that self-replicate and trick you; make you think you're accessing the files whose names they've adopted,' Lippmann offered.

Reynolds nodded and upturned his palms. 'What I'm saying here is, this virus acts like any other in its general methodology and purpose. But free-standing, it's impossible to define it.'

'Hence the badge "super-virus"?'

'You saw what it did to that monitor screen,' he answered her. 'We're talking about something that simply *can't* or at least *shouldn't* exist. Something that's been told how to use power when there's no battery or mains. Can't you see how crazy this is?'

Fenton turned his eyes back to the notes Reynolds had co-authored, looking defeated.

'You people don't know what I know about the *logos* behind a computer virus. You deal with the cleanup after one strikes but you can't see what I can here.'

Fenton looked up hungrily. 'I don't understand you.'

'A virus is supposed to incapacitate a system, the more malignant ones being those that total the files - clean out your PC so you can then run crying that you've been hit.'

'And this one?' Fenton asked. 'What's this one about, do you think?'

'Hard disk wise, it's the same deal as the most severe of conventional infections. You guys have seen those victim disks we've been examining. You lose all your files in the long run. Everything you may have had on that drive gets zapped. Kaput... Dead. Understand?'

Lippmann waited for Fenton, issued a nod when he didn't. 'I think I do,' she said.

'But if you see how fast it saps your bytes away, you'd understand what I'm getting at here. I mean from the second you hit your email recovery link once you've accessed your ISP, you're toast. This thing devours information about a *million times* faster than your disk *can rotate*. It's too fast to be possible.'

'But it leaves your screen intact,' Lippmann said. 'Even if you waited for your drive to empty, shouldn't your last screen be affected? Either frozen or blacked out?'

'That's another anomaly I can't explain,' Reynolds allowed, shrugging.

'Why not?'

'Because I've got no precedent to compare it to. Most viruses activate after you consciously come across the file they're parasited into,' he replied.

Lippmann perked up a little at that. Reynolds could tell she was following his thread of argument now. 'And the screen? Why does it only go that way *after* you've attempted a restart?'

'You can't restart a wiped out hard drive when there's no boot program,' Fenton offered in a stronger tone. 'But there is something *encoded on there* to bring up the green line?'

'And I can't explain that,' Reynolds said. 'You saw the look on my face when you ripped out the ROM, didn't you? And somehow, without any direct or residual data or power to run it, the monitor was able to stay active and show us that.'

Lippmann eased herself back on Parker's seat, shaking her head. Her frown might have made her attractive to Reynolds; in a parallel universe, of course.

'Okay, let's talk about the monitor's role in this,' Fenton said. 'Anomaly number one is that it can stay powered on for so long after the supply was terminated. Anomaly number two is that the flat line is perpetuated at all given the fact that there's nothing governing its execution.'

Dave Reynolds nodded.

'Then it has to be the monitor itself that we examine.'

'That's nuts, though,' Reynolds nearly snapped. 'Unless there's a drive inside it!'

'What *isn't* crazy about this?' Lippmann threw in. 'You've been using that word a lot yourself recently, haven't you?'

'A monitor is nothing but a display, okay? You can't make it do or show much of anything unless you connect it to a data source.'

Fenton pointed at the laptop screen on top of the cabinet. 'We can't say we've hit a dead end until we exhaust every possibility, Mr. Reynolds.'

'Fine. Let's look at it. But I'm telling you, it's a no-go.'

'Remember that as you're now contracted by the F.B.I., you're subject to our authority,' Lippmann said. Reynolds eyed her hard, bleeding the sincerity in her expression for his memory. Was that frustration he felt toward her now? Or was it a muddied attraction to her? 'Okay. Let's go do that then,' he allowed. 'But I'm telling you, we won't-'

Parker's phone rang in his face.

'Don't answer that!' Fenton said as Reynolds leaned over the desk. Reynolds watched him pick up the receiver, wondered if it was Parker checking up on their progress.

But Parker had looked close to a nervous breakdown this morning. He said he was taking sick leave when Marcy Andrews, Jarvis's secretary jabbed him with the issue of the suspension of his own contract.

'Be right up,' Fenton said, replaced the handset.

'What is it?' Reynolds asked before his mind's voice shouted at him: *'Never ask the Feds questions like that. They only tell you THINGS, not answers.'*

Lippmann nodded after Fenton whispered in her ear. She rose from her chair.

Reynolds saw the tiny silver Mp3 box in her hand. 'You've been recording me?'

'You better come upstairs with us,' she replied. 'There's been a development.'

-32-
20th April, Bremen, Germany

The sky was violet and the air cold when Carl Becker heard the key of his brother's apartment turn in the lock from the living room. He mashed his half-spent cigarette into the ashtray, stood up, trying to remember which part of the speech he'd rehearsed came first.

Kurt was silent until he made it into the short corridor that segregated the kitchen from the bathroom.

'You've been out there for hours,' Carl Becker said. 'How are they?'

'No... no change. Dad wouldn't stop muttering that.'

'You heard it, then?'

Kurt gave him a harsh but agonized look. 'Yeah, I heard it.'

'Kurt, I don't know what to-'

'Mother wouldn't stop *crying*, Carl.' The fire his brother had had in his voice at the hospital was there again. 'Why'd you have to go and do that?'

'I had to know, Kurt. Please, don't get upset at me for th-'

'She's still there with him. They're putting her up for the night again.'

Carl Becker moved to the large window that was the sole giver of sun and street light to his brother's home. 'You should have told me everything before I got here, you know, Kurt.'

Kurt didn't answer him. Carl Becker watched him sit on the armrest of the sofa, his head slung so low his chin was jammed into his collar bone.

'Kurt?'

Silence prevailed. Becker thought about seizing him, shaking him so hard by the lapels of his thick flocked jacket that he'd have to break down the rest of the way. And then at least that bit would be over, out of the way and Kurt might really start to listen. 'Kurt... That old woman...'

Silence again.

'The words she said. I told you, I've seen them before.'

Kurt looked up. In the dimness, the glassy non-focus in his eyes made him look drunk.

'Just before I flew over here, I was in Uruguay. I told you I was on a job with the American government. Do you remember?'

Kurt nodded, closed his jaw halfway.

'Now what I'm going to tell you is classified. It's illegal for me to have even told you this much. Do you understand?'

'What do you have to tell me?'

'Have you been keeping up with things over there? The news?'

'I - I heard something from that way.'

'They said a foreign ship sailed right up to the harbor in Montevideo and started shelling the hell out of it.'

'Yes… Yeah. I heard that.'

'And they said it was *destroyed*. An unmarked vessel with large gauge guns just sailed in, heading straight for the mouth of the River Plate, acting like it was in the middle of a battle.'

'Pirates; I heard it was a bunch of pirates. Russians, North Koreans or something like that. Mutineers of some kind.'

'And you think a ship that had been taken over by angry sailors would have just sailed for a foreign port and attacked it – firing willy nilly into it?'

'I don't know what to think anymore, Carl. There's just too much happening nowadays.'

'Kurt, what you heard about that thing in Uruguay is bullshit. It's a cover-up; you know: *censorship*. They don't want the truth getting out on this.'

Kurt glanced up from his coffee table, looking even more confused now. 'What *truth*?'

'The *Graf Spee*, Kurt. Have you ever heard of the *Graf Spee*?' Carl Becker asked without reckoning on the question. *Your brother was in the West German equivalent of grade ten when you moved, moron…Of course he's heard of it.*

Kurt's look intensified to a stare on Becker's eyes.

'I was flown down to Montevideo from California to dive after the *Graf Spee!*'

'No… no, I can't- *Why?*'

'Because it was that ship you heard about!'

'You're crazy, Carl.'

'Don't say that! After what happened to Dad? I'm not bullshitting so don't you say that!'

'You're lying. You have to be.'

'Would I be lying over something this big?!'

'Why don't you just get the hell out of my apartment now!'

'Don't do this to me, Kurt.'

'Get out, *now!*'

Carl Becker jumped then; he jumped and then pushed his brother's rising form backwards until they were both on the floor. *'I was inside it, Kurt! I saw the markings!'*

The first fist caught Carl Becker on the cheekbone; the second came to his nose. Dazed, he pinned Kurt down, knees and shins over the shoulders until the struggling stopped.

The spit glob caught Carl Becker in the eye before it ran down his nose, reeking of anger. *'Listen to me!* I was aboard that ship *two days after it came alive and attacked the coast* with shells. *Goddamned seventy year-old shells!'*

Kurt was silent now, his head lying sideways, deflated. 'My dive team went inside the hulk of that thing, Kurt. You know what we found down there? Eh?! Not a single soul. Nothing. It looked the way it should have looked.'

Carl Becker grabbed his brother's head, turned it to face his. 'Bent rails! Rusted-over sheet metal with the same barnacles they'd had all these years! But something else, too... *Shell holes in the hull, deck and towers.* Recent fighting, Kurt!'

Becker jerked his knees together, made Kurt's eyes narrow. 'The shell holes the Uruguayan military shot into it! To sink it so it'd stop its attack on their goddamned capital city!'

'L-leave me alone. Just leave me-'

'That's not all, Kurt! Do you know what I found when I dove all the way to the base of the command tower? Do you *know* what I found in that little room down there? After the damn *ship* tried to *kill* me by shutting me inside one of its rooms... *Do you?!'*

Kurt had stopped baring his teeth now. His eyes had taken over to beseech a stop.

'I saw *two word*s carved right into the wall there.' Carl Becker found that he was near to tears as he spoke. 'Ee-ee-*ey-eey yuh-yuhr-yure... Iyur Setot... Eey-yur set-oh*, Kurt!'

The next half hour passed in silence. Each brother stayed sitting or crouched at his station: Carl at the window and Kurt by the coffee table. Carl Becker had managed to calm himself. Like a disease, he felt he'd transferred it to his brother, who was now battling it in spurts.

Kurt was the first to speak. 'I never planned it this way, you know? Never thought I'd come back here after finishing school, college in the States and bring them back with me.'

'They wanted to move back, Kurt. Mom and Dad were going to move-'

'You were the one. You were the one who was always talking about being German. I thought *you* would come back, not me!'

'Leave that, Kurt. Don't think about it.'

'Dad loved it here. I wanted him to get back, to settle again. Oh Jesus!'

'Kurt.'

'All he ever talked about was here. Remember? In Bremen, you can smell the bread all day long. In Bremen, the salt in the air is like an old friend welcoming you-'

'Kurt; don't.'

'Welcoming you back home. *Oh God!*'

Carl Becker could see the life force drip out of his brother. Kurt - the tough guy; the one who always got yelled at; the one who got the beatings when it was really bad.

Don't think of that word, Becker; not with your father sick like he is, his mind's voice snarled. *Your father is dying.*

'I - I'd trade places with him in a second, Carl! I always try... Always try to see them every evening. *I should have been there when it happened!*'

'You work nights a lot, Kurt. There's no way you could have got-'

'That creature! *That creature!* I bet she was a *Gypsy!*'

'Don't do this to yourself. Please, for Dad's sake if not your own.'

'But I work boats for the *immigration service*. We get... We get *them* all the time!'

'No - you couldn't have stopped it, Kurt.'

'Turks, Bosnians, Albanians - all the *dregs* from that part of the world turn up in their stupid little *boxes* and *vans*!'

'There's nothing you could have done, okay? That old hag probably came in overland.' Carl Becker felt the jolt as he said 'hag'. *That old hag nearly killed your father. Will kill him.*

He went over to his brother, gave his shoulder a gentle shake. 'Kurt.'

... The hag has already done it – she did kill him. She's given him a bad stroke. 'Kurt. None of this is your fault. Not yours, not mine.'

Kurt's sobbing died away a little. His fingers came up in front of Becker, curled into their palm, mashed into the floor beside him.

'Easy there,' Becker said. 'Know what I say? I say we get outta here and go for a drink before we drown ourselves in tears.'

He got to his feet, took his coat from the sofa back. 'C'mon. We stay here any longer, we're gonna end up basket cases. We have to be strong for Mom and Dad or we'll all lose.'

'Y-yeah,' Kurt said as he tried to stand. 'Okay.'

'Alright then, let's go get some beer. No more to be done here.'

Carl Becker moved to the window to... he suddenly wasn't sure why – perhaps it had been to close the curtains.

The jolt that nailed his heart knocked his head back. 'My God!'

'Wh-what?'

The figure below the window gave Carl Becker one last sneer before it turned, walking stick dangling from its hand, and started hobbling leftward.

'Kurt!'

'What's wrong?!'

Carl Becker pointed a quivering finger. 'L-look...*look!*'

Kurt made the five-foot journey at breakneck speed, knocking one of his armchairs halfway round on its wheels as he passed it. *'What?!'*

Carl Becker pressed his face against the window, trying to cop a sign of-

'*What?!* I don't see anything!'

'It's that bitch! That bitch... the old hag watching us here!'

'Carl?'

Becker ran for his brother's front door, threw it back and sprinted for the landing.

He jumped when he was less than halfway down, his mind pumping hosed, lava-like wrath through clenching veins, screaming, too. *I'm going to kill you, whoever you are!*

The glass double doors resisted when he yanked them. 'You're dead when I get you!'

He pulled the right-side one back the rest of the way and thrust himself out into the dank night air. The stretch of street to his left was straight, long and flanked on his side by three, four, five huge apartment buildings.

Becker restarted his sprint then slowed to a jog.

What if she had double-backed on his way down?

He turned, scanning the street west of his brother's block for the scuttling, hunched form. People, perhaps a dozen, perhaps twenty, were walking about in their own easy worlds.

'Carl?!'

Kurt was coming out of the main entrance now. 'What's wrong with-'

The side-streets… The old witch was hiding down one of those.

Carl Becker sped up to a full run again, feeling the buzz of thunder powering his legs now, milling the hatred in his mind. *I'm going to get you and when I get you, I'm going to kill you!*

The first side-street wasn't even street width. It was just a lane with a 'Stop' sign that fed the parking lots of Kurt's and the adjacent apartment block…. It was a dead end as well.

Becker stared at the stretch of sidewalk ahead of him, panning his field of vision round ninety degrees rightward. The next break in the pavement was over a hundred feet away. His stare lashed the front of the next apartment block.

Solid, post-1970s glass and concrete assured him there was no way on earth it was going to harbor a fugitive.

Becker heard the frantic, slapping footfalls getting louder behind him. His fist was reeled, ready to strike when he wheeled round.

He saw his brother's eyes blink as he reached, grabbed his hand.

'*Carl!* Carl, what's wrong with you?! Where *is* this woman?!'

'Keep your eyes on that block!' Carl Becker yelled before he broke free, started down the alley to the lots. 'I've got you!' he hissed to his unseen quarry. 'Got you now! I've *got* you!'

His eyes were panning over cars, shadows, graffiti, scanning between the diamond-shape spaces in the green wire mesh that cordoned the lots off from each side of the alleyway.

'You're going to die! *I'll rip your head off your goddamn body for what you did to him!*

He picked the lot on the left first, passing his brother's Saab, a Jetta and a Skoda before he stopped, rotated, mining every bit, every detail of the lot with his swirling pupils.

The lighting was poor: two lamps per lot only. Carl Becker was already most of the way down the front aisle when he heard the shuffling start then stop.

He froze, feeling the pressure of fear return to the backs of his shoulders. From where he stood, nothing could move down the alley from the street he'd come off without his knowing.

...No shadows, no movement was evident up there, anyway.

A twitch came to his neck. No: a premonition...

A BLADE coming for the back of his neck! He spun on one foot, drinking up the tableau from his closest surroundings, feeling the buzz all the more because nothing was there.

The pressure on his shoulder backs had spread to his heart now, as he tiptoed.

Parked less than ten feet off to his left was a white pickup truck. Becker's tread slowed when he dared to think again. The height of the wall surrounding the exposed flat back of the truck was easily two and a half feet.

She could be crouching in there now, all the way up at the end, by the tailgate... An ambush with her hardwood walking stick, all sharpened at the end and ready to ram through his eye the instant he poked his head over the rim.

Becker crouched until he dropped a foot from his five-eleven build then started bringing his feet forward at a slug's pace.

He refroze when the shuffling started again: hollower, more tinny this time. It had sounded closer now... From the flatbed of the pickup truck. Yes, the thumping: he was sure now.

A surge of adrenalin welled up from Becker's feet at that moment. It almost succeeded in making him yell a war cry and leap for a bloody victory at the back of the pickup truck, a mere four feet away from him.

The red mist within him was too much now. He burst into a sprint and leapt, his hands and elbows slamming and scrabbling at the side of the pickup, ready to flail blows at the hag.

He pounded at a folded up tarpaulin lying against the back of the cabin. Only that and an overturned toolbox with some large tools lay atop the embossed molding of the floor.

Taking the crossbones wheel wrench nearest him, Becker dropped back down to the parking lot, crouched and kicked a sweeping leg out under the truck,

She wasn't under there, either. He tiptoed past the cabin, looking in.

Nothing. He was just a few paces away when he heard the shuffling again. And there was laughter this time…very faint, but he could hear a high pitch in the cackling coming from…

The other parking lot.

Becker ran for his life to get to it. He'd just made the alley when the side arm of the wrench caught him high up on his thigh and he overbalanced over it, tumbling.

The stinging of pitted concrete against his cheek and arm and the chime of the wrench against the ground came at once. Steeled from the pain by his nerves but now quite dazed, he threw himself up into a kneeling position and instantly caught something in his peripheral vision.

Becker had seen the feet this time, their movement synchronized with the shuffling, away up among the far line of cars, right up against the wall of the other apartment block.

He lifted himself up, ignoring the gore and grit on his skin, feeling energized by the weight of the wrench in his hand.

There is no escape for you, witch, he seethed. *No escape.*

He was speed walking now, was almost across the full span of the first row of cars that led off from the lot entrance.

As he moved down the lot's central lane, Becker started slowing his gait.

The back aisle of cars was fuller. *More hiding places.*

For her or you?

You. The picture of the crone's sneer came to Becker's mind's eye just then, her eyes empty and skeletal.

He beheld the vista before him. The lot had just one operational light on a crooked lamppost. The illumination it gave was poor compared to the working pair in Kurt's lot.

Kurt's apartment was also partially whitewashed. The concrete of the other one that lay at the end of this other lot was blackened by grime at ground level.

Becker started advancing in half-steps, gripping his wrench, aware that he was praying to gods of luck and vengeance.

The hag's eye sockets taunted him from the corners of his eyes like satanic shadow mirages.

Pray, Becker.

Prey, Becker. Her eyes had been so deeply set, he had noticed, in that glimpse he had snatched of her. Deep... just like the sea, the ocean, and the room in the *Graf Spee.*

Where *she* had locked him in.

Becker shuddered, stopped dead, stunned by the connection.

The laughter restarted as soon as he realized he was standing in the narrowest part of the lot, right between a VW van and an ancient Volvo 760 estate.

'Show yourself!' he commanded.

The silence seemed fatal to him. 'I'm ready for you!' he cried. 'Take me, not my dad!'

There was a twenty-five foot run to the end of the lot: four car widths or so. Becker tried to walk further, couldn't. Instead, he crouched low again, swept his eyes under the wheels, finding only tire outlines, concrete, dimness and the perpetual shadows.

That was when the laughter started up again.

Becker stood fully upright before he turned round.

'Iyur Setot; *IYUR SETOT!*'

The figure opened its mouth all the way, blew a freezing stream at his face from it, from its nostrils, from the black caves of its eye orbits and then it vanished.

Becker stood still, heard his wrench clunk onto the ground and urinated.

When he fell to join it, he knew no more.

-33-
<u>20th April, San Diego, California</u>

'Ready there, bud?'

'What do you think?' Billy Reynolds was not ready. His guts were bubbling away in spasms. He hadn't eaten at all that day and he knew he couldn't if he tried.

That was smart, he thought as he got into Nash's car. He would need all the strength he could muster to hold a straight face in front of the old bat whose house they were headed to.

Or to start running from the cops and the neighborhood watch program when she would recognize him from the window and call them.

She never saw me, his mind taunted him. *Oh yes she did.*

'You better not run out on me,' he said and managed to sound stern.

Nash looked over, restored the grin he'd worn during their fight on the stairs.

'I mean it. I get into trouble here and you take off, I'll drop you in it. I knew nothing and it was all you.'

Nash's mother's ageing sedan turned onto the street and sped up a little. Its muffler growled unhappily into Reynolds' heart. 'Not so fast! Damn it, you want her to go to the window?'

'That's your problem, William Reynolds - not mine.'

The house was coming up on the right, the seventh one along.

'Slow down!'

'Why?'

'Because she'll see us! What kind of evangelist gets driven in a heap like this?'

Nash slammed the brakes, thirty-five to zero in a second. Billy saw the couple in the oncoming Pontiac stare in at them. Stare in at him.

They were level with the old woman's house now. 'What you *doing?!* Move on!'

'Now you walk, Mister Bond!'

'No! Let me out at the end of the street!'

'You paying a fare here?'

Sweating, Billy opened the door, swung his feet into a small dog turd on the unkempt green grass partition. 'For God's sake… Where'll you be?'

'Parked a few houses up there,' Nash replied. 'Eventually.'

Billy swung his door, hoped the shutting sound wouldn't stir the occupant of the house.

'Wait!' Nash said. 'You forgot your books, little boy!'

Billy reached in through the open space, removed the Book of Mormon and the mini, onion-skinned Gideon Bible from the cloth bench cover.

As he started walking, he heard Nash gun the engine, the muffler droning mockingly.

Boards on the windows, Billy thought. He noticed they were plywood and wondered how long they had been on there. For a terrible second he wondered if they could have been as a result of Nash. No, they looked ancient – like they'd been put up a year or more before.

Billy felt a harder jolt hit him when he started to move up the cement path. Maybe the old dear *was* staying with relatives, he thought. *And the cops are watching you right now!*

As he closed on the front doorstep, he fought the urge to look up for cameras or turn to see if the neighbor behind him might have a telescope or binoculars trained on him. *You're a Christian missionary*, he ministered to himself. *And you can cite the dreadful state of her house as the focal point of your visit… a welfare call.*

Are you sure you'll be able to hold a straight face through this, though?

Yes, he snarled to his inner voice. *Tell her you saw the boards in the windows and then ask her if she knows why bad things sometimes happen to good people.*

Billy stood on the cement flagstone in front of the mosquito mesh outer door and raised his knuckles to the glass plate in its upper half. As he gave a few light knocks, he considered the situation. The old lady had allegedly threatened to kill Barry Nash. Billy wanted to kill Nash now, also... well, maybe not kill... just get him out of his life. What sort of person really meant to kill?

It occurred to him then that this was not your average granny. Billy's stomach whined, telling his heart to come down from his throat.

Ten seconds, was that now? He rapped the upper window of the mosquito door again and stepped back from the step, waiting... Counting: three heartbeats to a second. From there, he could see in through the crack between the board and the window edge.

He waited, staring into that gap... seeing only blackness. There was no sign of movement: no vibrations, no shuffling sounds coming from the hallway, behind the door.

Nobody home; bet's off, he thought and felt better.

Wait; didn't they sometimes put boards in behind busted windows, too?

Billy turned to survey the other, smaller window to his left and thought about that. It was April and the nights could still get chilly.

The smaller one on that side had the same kind of plywood covering a presumably broken window. He noticed that its gap was a little wider between the board and the darkness of the cavity it overlay.

It had been twenty seconds since his last knock now. His inner voice was going into overdrive. *She's not there for sure.*

Or maybe she died last night? You forgot to check the local news, moron.

Or maybe it happened this morning, in hospital?

And now you've been seen at her door. Maybe one of her neighbors had seen your face in the car last night and now here you are.

At that time in the early morning? No.

Yes, Billy. Not too many people round here are likely to be employed... Lots of late-night television and ears listening out for street sounds...

And wrongdoers always return to the scene of their crime.

A prison term, Billy. Nash can out-bullshit you. Your brother got done for being a hacker and soon you'll be a captured harasser.

Billy tried to turn, tried even harder to fight the urge he had to run. He couldn't move. His eyes were stuck on the dark triangle at the bottom corner of the smaller of the two windows.

There was air coming out of it at him. It was four feet from his cheeks and he could feel the sharpness of the damp in the current.

Fifty seconds, maybe a minute since you knocked last time; you had better leave it before it starts to look really SUSPICIOUS.

The triangle of darkness wouldn't let him leave, though. His eyes had found that it wasn't total darkness. They had now grown accustomed to the black, dispelling it into a few shades of deep, dark gray.

Was that spotted wallpaper in there?

No, he thought as he dared to lean over a little to peer. No, the pattern was too irregular... *Mold*, more likely. That was a lot of mold for one patch of a wall, though. No way an elderly person could survive in that at night. Not with the risk of pneumonia, pleurisy, death?

It's only a short walk round to the back, Billy. Go find out.

No. Maybe Nash was wrong. Maybe Nash had made all this up just to screw with his mind. He hadn't seen Barry Nash in ages prior to this – anything could have happened to his brain to make it sicker. And this house he now found himself at could have lain derelict for ages.

Anyway, how could Nash have been so positive he'd get paranoid about the air gun?

Billy found himself looking through the moldy wall at these scarier thoughts, not at it, when the darkness came back to the gap.

He froze solid, except his book-clutching right arm, which jerked upward like -

Like it was a GUN recoiling. Billy had forgotten he had his air gun in his inside pocket now. The darkness in the triangular gap had stolen his memory.

He dared to blink, taking a butterfly in the heart when he saw no change.

The air current that had been feeding his skin grew far colder. Freezing cold. 'He-hell....hello?' he essayed.

The darkness held, unmoving, uncaring for his greeting.

'Is...is anyone there?'

Either that old lady was wearing all black or...

No, he thought. That was the darkness of space in there, not the blackness of an obscuring object with a physical base.

The air was so cold against his face and neck now that Billy found that he couldn't smell the mold anymore. He backed off by a pace or two, failed to notice the height of the grass blades on the tiny lawn.

'Sorry....sorry for disturbing....sorry I disturbed you,' he said weakly. 'You need....you won't be needing our ministry, today.'

He didn't know when his legs started moving in as close to a normal walking mode as he could make them. By the time Billy Reynolds had nearly got to the sidewalk, he'd even forgotten that he'd been driven there that afternoon.

The coldness in his face was still there. At the end of the path, Billy looked back at the ply-board on the smaller window. He could see it shaking, vibrating just at that bottom corner. Impossible!

No. It *was* moving. The grains and cracks in the wood were moving by maybe hundredths of an inch.

Impossible! his mind jeered. The board had eight or more huge nail heads sticking out of it, joining it to whatever was under there – the window frame, he assumed.

He could hear the air rushing through from behind that gap, calling him. *Inviting him.*

Billy turned his head then, imagined Nash's mom's car parked somewhere in eyeshot of him. Nash would know if he went back now. Nash would not let him sleep at night worrying about what had really happened out there and if his prints were on the gun. Nash was psychotic.

Billy checked the windows of the house directly across the way, shuddering.

Was he hoping someone was living, maybe *watching* from, there or not?

Five windows and no sign of life. Billy sensed the dark air from the old lady's house brushing against his nape now.

He wheeled around and stared at the ply-board over the smaller window. It had stopped moving, but he could *hear* the whispers now - more invitations to venture inside.

The air was cold, not only from the mystery wind but somehow the sky seemed darker now. Billy looked up, found the rays of the sun scattered far and wide over the tops and edges of a city-sized cloud complex.

'I'm coming now,' he said as he dropped his books into the forest of grass. His hand, freed now, reached into his inside pocket, its fingers wiggling.

The diamond grip of his pistol was wet from his armpit stains. He walked back up to the mesh outer-door and drew his gun out all the way but kept it close to his chest so no-one could see from the street if they should pass by.

The gap between the ply-board and the window cavity was still black when he gazed at it, its wind rushing out in hard, frenetic spurts now.

The sweetness of the whispers he'd been hearing was still there… it was a feeling of invitation, of supreme welcome he couldn't describe.

Without looking away, Billy removed the elastic band from the ammunition level flag and started nodding his head to the sweet voices that were ushering him inside the house.

'Yes. Round the back. I'm coming in; coming in now,' he agreed before he stepped off the cement of the path.

-34-

20ᵗʰ April, San Diego FBI Lab, California

Dave Reynolds wasn't expecting to find three men in the twenty-first floor software lab. Worse, he wasn't expecting the software lab to look the way it did when he arrived.

Twenty or more monitors lay open, some still powered on, fluke meters latched to their logic boards… an even larger number of base units and laptops sprawled in varying states of vivisection and dissection.

Hank Jarvis and Kenny Piper were sitting side by side in front of a group of objects, some familiar to Reynolds, some not. What were they doing with a DAT tape recorder? he wondered.

The third man, a plump, forty-something, intense-featured Federal type, looked up from the bench and then approached Fenton. 'We've got something big,' he told him.

'How big is "big"?' Lippmann asked on her way over to the bench.

'Big enough,' he replied.

'What's with the tape recorder?' Reynolds asked.

'It was a lucky shot,' Hank Jarvis said. 'We'd totally overlooked the sonics.'

'Mr. Reynolds; Detective Nathan, F.B.I.,' Fenton said.

Nathan eyed Reynolds for a moment then nodded. 'You're the virus expert.'

'I am, that,' Reynolds replied. 'But we won't get anywhere 'til we get a hold of this guy.'

'Which is going to prove very difficult, it seems,' Lippmann said. 'Even then, I don't think we'll be able to get things back to the way they were.'

Reynolds noticed the wild glaze in Nathan's eyes as the latter shrugged his shoulders.

'Well, it seems the rules have changed in this ball game,' Nathan said, then extended his finger and depressed the 'PLAY' button on the DAT player.

Reynolds listened to the playback with his eyes on a nervouser-than-usual Jarvis.

'But this is gibberish,' Reynolds said after the first minute: 'Absolute nonsense.'

Nathan allowed the tape to run on. 'We thought that on the first run through.'

'What? Is this from the green line on the screen?'

Nathan nodded. 'Just try to think about what *sort* of sounds they are,' he said.

The sounds were of human vocal origin: words, phrases – none of them in English, even though Reynolds could make out the syllabic structures in every utterance on the tape.

But the voice, the accent seemed – no, it *was* – non-human to his ears. It sounded like one of those electronic voice boxes that throat and lung disease sufferers ended up with.

'That's Indian or something, right?' Fenton asked the two, seated Anline workers.

'I'd shoot for Arabic,' little Kenny Piper answered. 'Heavy "ach"s and "wa"s.'

'We can't be sure until we submit this to a linguist for proper analysis,' Nathan said. 'But it's something.'

'We had to enhance it digitally to remove the anomalous material,' Hank Jarvis said. 'And then transfer it to tape.'

'Why?' Reynolds asked. 'Why a tape?'

'Because the sampling rate on our highest res disk reader just couldn't cope with the detail,' Jarvis said weakly. 'You were elsewhere when we did it.'

'Plus the fact we had to invert the direction of data flow,' Piper said.

'Running the thing backwards?'

'Yes.'

'How'd you know to do that?'

'We didn't,' Jarvis said. 'Trial and error. This way sounds more coherent than the other one we had. The syllables in this version are more natural sounding.'

'How did you guys work it out as a sound recording?'

'The blips and troughs on the green line made me think of a vocal pattern.'

Reynolds shook his head at Jarvis. 'But that line never cracked much above a pixel or two in deviance,' he said. ' A vocal pattern?'

'I know that,' said Jarvis. 'That's why I only brought it up after we'd exhausted every other possibility.'

'Binary, base three, base four,' Kenny Piper offered. 'It looked like it would have a numeric grounding.'

'But it didn't hold,' Hank said. 'In its natural state, the line just wasn't giving us much above the appearance of a simple monitor fault... something like a collapsed screen.'

Reynolds looked at one of the screens that was still going far to his right on the work bench. 'How much did you have to enhance it before you thought it was a voice graph?'

'We had to save the image as a picture file,' Hank replied. 'Once we had it as that, we could enlarge the imprint; what was one pixel deep we got to show up as ten sub-pixels deep. And that's nuts because there's no such thing as a sub-pixel... somehow we managed to break down the basic pixel!'

'But most of that line is straight,' Reynolds said, eyes still on the monitor. 'An enlargement would just give you an even chunkier flat line.'

'That's where we had to rely on the digi-enhancer program,' Hank said.

'I don't follow you.'

'Show him,' Nathan said. Hank Jarvis rose, gestured for Reynolds to follow, walked on until they were close to the other end of the lab and a forty-two inch Eidzo screen.

Jarvis tapped a key and the display brightened, presented Reynolds with a black Dos shell display. 'Watch the top parts of the line especially, Dave,' he said then typed 'RUN' and hit 'ENTER'.

The green line came up, swallowed an easy eighth of the screen height.

Reynolds noticed the first lumps blipping past a couple of seconds afterward.

'The enlargement enabled us to find data in the image we couldn't on a normal scale,' Jarvis explained. 'See the single, double and triple pixel heights on the top?'

'Yeah?'

'They never showed before.'

Reynolds couldn't blink. This was crazy, he was thinking. Analogue tape players and graphic enlargement into sub-pixels! Jesus – how the Hell could a pixel be split? It wasn't like an atom!

'The ones we did see the first time now vary in pixel height from six up.'

'It's still too flat, Hank,' Reynolds said. 'I can't buy the voice graph theory. Real speech vacillates on a graph, doesn't it? This is hardly wavering at a-'

'Okay. You're seeing the data in its rawest form, Dave. The way we were given it,' Jarvis advised as he reached for the keyboard.

Reynolds didn't, couldn't follow Jarvis's fingertip to see what key it pressed. 'Now this is it with the enhancer on.'

'Holy shit.'

Jarvis waited, gave Reynolds almost ten seconds to get used to the flow. 'See it now?'

'What kind of enhancer program is that?'

'Mongoose.'

'What's that?'

'It's a Linear extrapolator, Dave. Somehow we had one copy in the drawers.'

'What's it used for?'

'That's an F.B.I. toy,' Nathan called over from the far end of the lab. 'We gave you it. It's chiefly used for comparing voice graphs for authenticity in criminal cases. Unless it's being worked on a voice recording from a damaged or deteriorated file, it's supposed to go the other way round. Take somebody's voice, file it down a bit and work back the likelihood of it and another recording having come from the same individual.'

Reynolds' eyes were beginning to tire, but he couldn't break his gaze off the green.

Green was an earth color, a *safe* color. It was supposed to indicate fertility, nurturing, leafy, living... all things to do with life. But now green was allied with destruction, chaos.

'What's it keying off, Hank? The lines are too tall for the pixel blips they came from.'

'They're cutting through the pixels on a mean average then carrying through.'

'And how'd they know when to stop?'

'Based on the strength of the signal, Dave. It's to do with the actual pixel height stroke depth plus whether or not a peak or crest is capped or runs on a straight hump.'

'How long does this thing run for?'

'Like this, fifty-six minutes, thirty-two seconds.'

'Fifty-six?'

'Yeah,' Jarvis said. 'We tested it on four, five different base units.'

'Fenton, we had fifty-*two*, right?' Nathan asked his underling.

Agent Fenton looked up from the papers Nathan had handed him. 'Fifty-two minutes on the unpowered laptop; yes.'

'That's close to what we had,' Kenny Piper offered, turning in his seat. 'Well, fifty-two minutes and ten seconds before termination.'

'How d'you account for the difference?' Reynolds asked anyone in earshot.

'We only ended up with a longer message once we saved the data as a disk-based file, Dave,' Hank said. 'We don't know why.'

Reynolds peered into the screen, eyes devouring the green-fimbriated black mountain range scrolling across it. 'Did you save any blank data onto the end of this, Hank?'

'N-no. No.'

Reynolds grabbed his shoulder. 'Are you *sure?*'

'S-sure I'm sure! There were three of us there to see it.'

'Then somehow it got elongated. You think…?'

'No,' Kenny piper said. 'The crude and treated versions run at the same speed.'

'I didn't realize you guys had had the time to do all this while I wasn't here.'

'Multi-tasking,' Piper said, flashing his best Harvard graduation portrait smile.

Reynolds did not smile back. The kid did not understand death and the dependence his species were supposed to have placed on logic, on order in the world.

'But that *end* bit,' Reynolds said at length. 'How could you have saved that if the original stopped over four minutes short?'

'It probably was the enhancer, Dave,' Hank replied.

'So a stretch occurred via transcription. Yeah?'

'No. Not necessarily. Remember that we're dealing with two types of data here, two formats and the end results being played out on two types of media.'

'Yet the tape's still longer than the visual version,' Nathan said.

'So that's down to *what?*' Reynolds demanded.

'It's got to be down to the enhancer protracting the pulses and troughs in order for the extrapolator to follow through and define the sonic equivalent,' Jarvis finished. 'It *has* to be that.'

Reynolds fixed Nathan with a freezer of a gaze. 'When are you guys gonna get this analyzed for the actual language being heard?'

'It's being done now,' Nathan answered. 'Before you got up here, we sent the WAV file to our department via FTP.'

'So they'll be analyzing a voice file transcribed onto a tape, run backwards.'

'That's right. That's all we have to go on right now.'

Reynolds gave the big screen another long stare. 'This thing's flickering.'

'I'd noticed that,' Kenny Piper said. 'It does that on all the screens.'

'Powered up?'

'Powered up, powered down: screens that have been disconnected.'

Lippmann was the only one left reading when Reynolds sat down next to Piper.

'What you got there?'

She looked up from the Duo-tang with an irritated expression. 'It's a list of Anline users with virus-related offences.'

Reynolds had to smirk. There *was* no more Anline Internet Service Provider left now. The shareholders would see to that. There would soon be no more Internet left at all, either.

'I thought we'd worked the source out as being a Forserver user.'

'The service we belong to never rules anyone out until the end of the game,' she said. 'This is going to be the biggest manhunt in American history. Forget the usual suspect enemies.'

'I think we should be hunting for technical *reasons* first,' Reynolds said. 'Like why a screen that has no power in it can still keep itself going regardless.'

'The CRT or flat-screen equivalent stays energized by some phantom source,' Jarvis said, coming over to them. 'There's an answer, only we don't have it yet.'

'Use your head, Hank. In the real world, there's no accounting for those screens doing what they're doing!' Reynolds snapped. 'Don't kid yourself into thinking outside of the box here!'

'Well what do you suggest, then?' Jarvis answered, sounding as flat as morning water.

Reynolds tried to think. Lippmann would have her Mp3 recorder going; he knew that much. 'This super-virus wipes your disk, dupes you into thinking that you're restarting if you *do* pull the plug when the infection hits and then plays that signal,' he said at length. 'Somehow.'

'Or plays it anyway if you wait for total blankage,' Fenton said.

'Could part of the program be that it reduces the power usage in the screen itself?' Lippmann asked. 'There are tiny batteries on logic boards, I mean.'

'And the screen is much dimmer,' Kenny Piper said. 'It flickers, too.'

'It's unlikely,' Hank Jarvis offered once the silence began to drag. 'Dave's right in denying this. I mean, we *are* talking about an unpowered screen having to last for up to an hour.'

'We need monitor experts here,' Kenny Piper said, looking proud of that declaration.

'We've already got them on the case,' Nathan rewarded. 'That's priority two.'

Reynolds rose from his chair. He needed coffee to awaken him from this nightmare.

'They might be able to tell you the nitty gritty,' he said as he started walking. 'But I've already told you the theoreticals.'

'It's got to be the CRT or the digital equivalent, Dave,' Jarvis said as Reynolds passed behind him. 'This old monitor's CRT gun inside it is still firing. We just have to isolate the cause.'

'Just?'

Reynolds did not notice his shoelace had come undone until he was well on his way down onto the workbench.

'Dave!'

Reynolds blinked before and after his eyes had told him his hand had met the anode cap of the live monitor whose plastic casing had been removed. It plinked out from the inside of the screen, its forked tongue ready to spit venom onto his wrist.

Hank Jarvis was already helping him up off the floor when Reynolds felt something worse grip his heart.

The anode cap swung back and forth from the live monitor, its twin prongs waiting to bite doom into the next taker.

'Hank,' Reynolds gasped. 'Something.... something's wrong here!'

'You almost killed yourself, Dave! If you'd touched the metal you-'

'I did.'

'But that thing's *live!* Twenty thousand volts are in that anode cap!'

Dave Reynolds watched Jarvis grimacing up at the screen. He heard his jaw drop when he saw the green line alive and well on the display.

'Fifteen thousand volts, Hank. Fifteen thousand. I *should* be dead by now. But so should that old screen with its anode cap removed like that.'

Jarvis did not answer. His grip under Reynolds' arm started to weaken.

'Screw the CRT or image gun, Hank,' Reynolds gasped as the others leant over it to see for themselves. 'This is way beyond anything that either we or the monitor people can ever even hope to work out.'

-35-

20<u>th</u> April, CIA Headquarters, San Diego

Coleman was ten minutes in reception before Carmichael let him come up. Ten minutes to try and come to grips with the newest installment of madness in his life.

Their life. Leah was in it, too now.

Coleman had chosen to try pacing in the lobby of the C.I.A. building, uncaring how he'd look on the cameras.

He'd fallen in love with her when he was thirty-two and she twenty-seven. Her looks, mannerisms, brain, heart had seemed to him to be too good to be true. Wedding bells had clanged happy peals soon after because they had both seen magic in one another.

Coleman raised his eyes to the portrait of Harry Truman high on the *faux* marble wall and tried to remember back to the time when he'd been able to see magic in his job.

Once you said you were C.I.A., his uncle had told him when he was in high school, 'they'll never ever dare call you a cop'.

Generally, people knew the difference and respected it. But did he, anymore?

No, probably not. The danger in his work had never let up and had, in fact, only gotten worse. To make it even worse, Coleman had never let himself get desensitized to the perils.

But Leah had never been able to sleep properly at night because of his job.

That's why the phone had had to be moved out to the landing and then the downstairs landing a long time before...

Before all this heavy stuff had begun. Coleman bit his lip, took the polythene freezer bag from his jacket.

Now, there was this new shit... where someone was striking out at him in his home. What was Leah making of that?

Jurgen Ganz. He saw the face from the film footage in his mind and squeezed the envelope so hard he could almost hear the fibers of the card inside getting sheared, mangled.

'Don't you start on my life!' he whispered to the card, to the face in his mind. 'Or my wife. You don't have the right.'

If Leah ever got hurt, he'd travel to Israel himself and find Ganz.

You can't unless you're assigned. They have the Mossad, anyway.

Fuck that, he thought. *I'll go freelance and waste this little shit.*

If Leah ever got hurt by him, he'd go buy the plane ticket right away.

It's okay, his mind cut in: *Ganz is only hurting the world.*

Or was it someone trying to frame Ganz? Some psychic with a big time grudge?

No, it was Ganz. It had to be. Coleman squeezed the envelope one last time before he heard the receptionist call him over. Leah was the biggest part of his world… no - *all* of it, he thought as the receptionist buzzed his clearance and he boarded the elevator.

Carmichael was waiting for him on the top floor. 'Sorry I kept you dangling, Coleman.'

Something was wrong. Carmichael had NEVER been SORRY in his life.

Durning was sitting in the middlemost of Carmichael's five interviewee chairs, looking plenty dour.

Or was that sour? Durning's on your side, remember.

'I think I had better do the talking first here, Coleman,' Carmichael said. 'Take a seat. This one's going to be a hard pill.'

Coleman eased himself down with a frown. Carmichael's hard pills, he knew, always had hard suppositories lying at the bottom of the pack.

'I've been briefing Durning so I may as well include you now. Headquarters have been doing some digging on our boy - Jurgen Ganz. Seems that before he went over to Israel on his college dig, he decided to settle a score with his Anthropology department head at North Dakota College. Burnt out his office and a few others around it. Arson. Apparently, the course co-coordinator for the trip never picked up on the fact that his failed thesis disqualified him from the dig.'

'That was sloppy,' Coleman said.

'Ganz had had a month's worth of extensions. Only got his paper back two days before he was due to go.'

'Nice prof,' Coleman said and instantly felt guilty when the image of a benevolent academic clutching his chest at the sight of a career's worth of annihilated notes and books flashed in his mind. 'This Ganz guy is pure badness.'

'He's still classified as a missing person. Tel Aviv police had that in mind when they re-opened their investigation on the Bel-Shalom hotel fire that happened when Ganz and his group arrived. Three dead with confirmed identities: problem is, no forensic evidence for him.'

'They know if he escaped the fire?'

Carmichael shook his head. 'No. Late at night. Roll call only started long after the fire crews went back.'

'You're sure he started it?'

'Sure, no; believe, oh yes. Fingerprints on a pen the clerk stated Ganz had left at reception match his prints on file. A little over two years ago, they were on a four-week archaeology project out there. We're near interviewing the last of the people who went on that dig now. Everyone so far says Ganz was acting funny on the way over. Obsessive.'

'Obsessive over *what*, though?' Coleman asked.

'He didn't say much to anyone, but we've got five eyewitness accounts of him reading through that thesis of his.'

'Couldn't take that "F"?'

'Sure seems that way. He jumped the gate at the hostel soon after arriving and, until you found his face on that tape, he hasn't been seen. Two years – missing, presumed dead. This side of the Atlantic, anyway.'

'Hmm... Either botched suicide or a deliberate vanishing: I'd call it a bit of both.'

Carmichael frowned. 'If it was botched, Coleman, he would've *surfaced* by now. The Israelis are the tightest asses about getting people they want to get.'

'And yet he's turning up on film, all right.'

'Coleman – on a different subject here, I just want to see what you know of the occult.'

'Yes, sir?'

'Do you know anything about a book called *The Liber Fati*?'

'About as much as the average idiot. Those demon possession movies; maybe more.'

Carmichael kept the intensity of his stare trained on him. 'Which is *what?*'

'Some bunch of mumbo-jumbo cooked up by a so-called historian way back.'

'That was what Ganz did his thesis on.'

'What? The origins of the book?'

'Yeah. His Teaching Assistant from his course said he kept showing up every other day to talk it over with her. Says he had an *unhealthy fixation* with it.'

'Wait, we're talking about horror movies here,' Coleman said. 'That stuff isn't real.' He looked around the room and wondered why Durning wasn't joining his side of the argument.

Carmichael shook his head. 'Ganz apparently wrote a thirty *thousand* word paper arguing just the opposite. His T.A. got reading the bits of it he brought her as he worked on it.'

'What – I mean, what *kind* of stuff was he saying in it?' Coleman could feel two cold patches on his body now: his heart, and by his left hip. Something was very cold in his pocket.

'Mr. Ganz claimed that the so-called Ancient Kings did exist.'

'H-hang on. These Ancient Kings were who?'

Carmichael unclasped his hands, sifted through the pile of papers on his left and slid a paperback out from underneath. 'Here, have a look.'

Coleman did not enjoy the tug he could feel in his chest when he began flicking through it. The foreword caught his attention – how this book had been contrived from scraps of tablets found when the Romans had occupied southern Anatolia and the Levant. He forgot the icy stab at his hip as he examined the heavily stylized pictures and small blocks of text. He'd seen this book years ago at a frathouse party: many, many years ago – a novelty.

His fingertips stopped rifling midway through and began turning the pages more slowly. Spirals, lines, hieroglyphs stacked on the pages, leaf after leaf.

Too sinister to pass as the squiggles of a child, he thought. Yet it was too authentic-looking to be the contrivance of some introverted professor in a Cambridge back office.

'Christ,' Coleman said at length. 'Looks different to the way I remember it.'

'Mr. Ganz was very taken with it right from the start,' Carmichael offered. 'By every account that's got back to me, sounds like that little book changed his life.'

'After his 2012 arrest, that was?' Coleman asked.

Carmichael nodded once, took up the papers to his left and began to sift through them, scanning. 'Our boy had three additional arrests as a juvenile, Coleman: major school trouble.'

'Three?'

'Three. Nathan didn't tell you: he hadn't *dug* the way we did. We did the F.B.I.'s job.'

'Any family history of disorders. Schizophrenia, say?'

'None that we've been able to establish. His family's Swiss; moved to North Dakota 1991; father went straight into Wells Fargo. Mother fell in with Hertz as a domestic analyst.'

'Stable home background then. What went wrong with Ganz?'

'Expelled Bismarck Junior High, November '99… burning a human effigy stuffed full of insects in a ritualistic sacrifice. The fire destroyed the outside of a public restroom.'

'So he'd been brewing for a while,' Coleman issued. He'd heard about these type of kids on Geraldo, back before most talk shows had traded even onstage bust-ups between cheating partners in favor of the new topics… Agent 104-tainted drinking water hypochondria… People going mad from the brightening of the stars… Women made infertile by the shit reception on their television sets. 'And is *that* what we're dealing with in the pictures on the surveillance footage?'

'Tell him the rest,' Durning said. 'There's more than that - way more. Right, Mr. Carmichael?'

'Oh yes. After that, we don't hear from him 'til Grade Eleven. Assaulted Phys. Ed. teacher with a hockey stick and then urinated on him.'

Carmichael took the printout out from behind his heap of ring binders.

'And the jewel in the crown: graduation night.'

Coleman could have felt surprise at hearing 'graduation' applied to Ganz had he not been so scared now. 'What did he do?'

'Bit a classmate's date in the calf for making fun of him going stag.'

'Wasn't he put away for that?' Durning asked.

'No. Judge deemed mitigating circumstances and Ganz got two hundred hours community service.'

'I can't believe we're sitting here talking about a *student*,' Coleman said when his chest allowed him the breath. 'No way.'

'Well that's the profile of our bunny.' Carmichael pulled out a pack of menthol cigs, withdrew two and handed Durning one. 'You think I'm treating this just like any old case, right?'

Neither underling answered Carmichael. Their eyes fell to the floor.

'Well this kind of thing isn't something you *can* get used to,' Carmichael explained. 'Nothing I was ever trained up with could've prepared me for this case. Hell, the second I hear the word 'psychics' I get the willies more than I ever got 'em as a kid.'

Coleman could not imagine Carmichael as a child but allowed him that.

'But this's what the training's for. An emergency's an emergency.' Carmichael leaned forward, pausing for effect and tapped some ash into the tray. 'I'd given up smoking two years ago. Now here I am smoking indoors in California... I'm *that* scared I just don't care.'

Coleman could see his own fear mirrored in Carmichael's pupils now. 'These aren't normal times, sir,' he allowed.

'Except something like this just doesn't happen, *ever*, not in our world,' Carmichael continued. 'No textbook or instructor ever told *you guys* you'd get hauled into weirdness like this.'

'Just how involved *are* the psychics now?' Durning asked.

'They're in it up to their necks.'

'No results yet? Nothing to say if it *is* Ganz or some rogue psychic?' Coleman asked.

'No. We won't know on a day-to-day basis, anyway. The psychic bodies we have working for us, plus the independents are too numerous for us to keep immediate tabs on anything barring a consensual report on Ganz. These people have their own lunatic fringe, too.'

Coleman thought about the pain he'd felt at his hip and remembered something. 'I have to talk to you about my problem now, sir,' he said. 'It's directly related.'

'Fire away; you're among friends here.'

'I got something in the mail today… a letter from Israel.'

Carmichael broke off halfway through a drag and spluttered. 'What is it?'

Coleman pulled the bagged envelope from his pocket. 'Here; look,' he said as he offered it. The look on Carmichael's face would have been priceless under other circumstances.

'A photograph?' Carmichael said as he clutched the contents, using the freezer bag side as a kind of glove.

'Just take a look at the envelope first. Ignore the card – whoever it was put talcum powder in and joked about anthrax… just to soften up my head a bit more, I'll bet.'

'Anthrax? Christ, why'd you bring it –'

'Seriously, sir. If that's anthrax, I'll eat my pants and yours. Whoever sent that was setting up a sucker punch – which you'll see. Just have a look at this.'

Carmichael gingerly obeyed. He scanned the manila, his brow furrowing. 'Burnt. But how?'

'That didn't happen until *after* I'd opened it, sir.'

'You saying *you* took a flame to the top corners of this?'

'No; *shit no.*'

'Then how'd it get that way?' Carmichael scowled at him.

'I only had the contents out for a minute. When I checked the envelope, it was fried.'

'Just in the bits where the stamp and the return address would be – like it is now?'

Coleman nodded fast.

'I can't make out anything on this stamp. You sure it said "Israel"?'

'Yeah. I don't recall how many shekels it was marked on there.'

'And this picture inside: that's all there was?'

'Y-yeah. No – there was that little card that joked about anthrax but that's all it was. You can get me tested if you want but I'd've been sick already if they weren't fucking about. I think they wanted me scared enough to take the other thing seriously.'

Carmichael turned the card over and over a few times, rubbing the surfaces with his fingertips, rifling through the fluffy layers in the edges. 'The photo: you get it in this condition?'

'Yes.'

'What's the picture of?'

'I don't know.'

'This doesn't even look like a *proper* photograph, Coleman.'

'Let me see,' Durning said, reaching.

'So for you to have been sent this, this person would have to know your job.'

'I - I think it's a fear tactic from someone,' Coleman said, more to Durning.

'Who, though? Who knows we're dealing with a case where our chief suspect has a link with Israel?' There was a hint of threat in Carmichael's tone – a reminder of the secrecy oath.

'I don't know. I just don't-'

'This is Milan,' Durning cut in.

'How can you tell?'

'That's the UEFA building.'

'What's *yoo-ay-fah*?' Carmichael asked.

'Soccer,' Durning replied.

'I didn't know you followed that,' Carmichael retorted.

'I don't. Just, it's kind of hard not to come across that stuff when you've got a big dish and a gold account with your TV provider.'

Carmichael reached forward, took the photograph back and stared hard at the image. 'I say we get the lab to run this over with *all they have got.*'

'You're right. It doesn't look like an actual photo,' Durning offered. '*Not* with that color.'

'We won't be able to say that until we get some hard results, Mr. Durning.' Carmichael turned to address Coleman then. 'You say those burn marks only happened on the *outside?*'

Coleman felt the jolt pump him twice. He rose to inspect what Carmichael's thumbnail was pointing to on the photo – a dark blemish that he hadn't seen before.

'Good God,' was all he could manage when he noticed that the dark mark was of a different consistency than the eerie substance around it. 'It – that can't be a burn mark,' he said weakly. 'Can it?' he asked the silence.

-36-

20<u>th</u> April, San Diego, California

Billy heard Nash honk his horn just as he stepped out onto the sidewalk from the path and the house.

The house with the black breeze.

His air pistol's butt jabbed his ribs as he cleared the last few feet to Nash's mother's white sedan and opened the door.

'You do it?'

'What'd *you* think.'

'You *didn't do it*, did you?'

'Course I did. Only I had to go round the back.'

'Alright, Reynolds, get in.'

Billy climbed in with a smile on his face. The gun felt so warm in his inside pocket now.

Nash started the engine, pulled out and sped off to the intersection, hung a left. 'You hungry?' he asked.

'Sure.'

'Burger Shack. We'll go there.'

'Whatever you say. Your car, you're driving.'

Once seated in the mid-size restaurant, Billy looked up from his quarter-pounder to find Nash picking at his fries, watching him, about to pounce with a question. 'What, you not hungry?'

'Oh yeah, I'm hungry all right.'

'So eat up.'

'Just I ain't used to eating in the company of liars.'

Billy kept chewing and kept his expression so he didn't look fazed.

'If you went in there, what did this hag look like?'

Billy kept chewing. He *was* not fazed. But he wanted to pistol whip Nash for that.

'You're a liar, Reynolds. You busted the deal.'

'I never bust the deal. I *did* get in her house, Barry.'

'The hell you did.'

'I left my books there, didn't I?'

'Then tell me what you saw when you were inside.'

'That old lady… About eighty or so, I'd say. Far too old to be-'

'What'd she look like *exactly*?'

'White hair, long nose, hunched over a bit… bad breath.'

'What color eyes?'

'Blue. Light bl-'

'No they weren't.'

'It was dark in there, Barry. She never turned on the lights.'

'What was her voice like?' Nash was squinting now – perhaps he could be convinced.

'Foreign. European...Eastern European, I think.'

Nash started shaking his head, looking at other tables.

'You still think I'm lyin' over this?'

'Yeah.'

'Well that's too bad, then, isn't it?' Billy said and shrugged his smart-suited shoulders.

'Too bad for *you*. I've just changed the deal to suit a lying lowdown skunk like you.'

'You wanna drive back there and ask her yourself if she-'

'No. How about this; I drive *you* back there to *spend the fucking night*.'

'Now, you just look here,' Billy hissed and noted the frowns of the young family two tables down.

'I mean it, Billy. If you don't do it, I'm gonna frame your ass with my gun.'

'You wouldn't be able to.'

'Try me, Billy.'

'Your prints are on it, *too*. You'd get implicated.'

'There's something I never told you about my lil' ol' Cruzman, Billy. I only got it last year and I've worn gloves *every single time* I've ever touched it.'

'Bullshit you have.'

'Your prints are on file for that nice little nickel bag of weed you sold on campus in 2012.'

'No they're not.'

'Yes they are. Go where you like and do *what* you like, but you can't change the fact you dealt in weed!'

'You're not scaring me, Nash. You can't blackmail-'

Nash smirked. 'And after they get you for harassing this old dear, I'm gonna make sure all your little college pals and gals know everything about how screwed up you really are.'

Billy tried to finish his quarter-pounder but the quivering in his jaw wouldn't permit it.

'That's what they'll say about you, Billy. Porn, drugs, scaring grannies... *Some* future!'

'You can't prove a thing.'

'Oh, but I can. And links can be drawn. Kudrow's motorcycle that got vandalized, hm?'

'That was nothing to do with me. Shut up.'

'Meanwhile I'm onto my chemical engineering degree. People respect jobs like that.'

Billy Reynolds gave his ex-friend a look that he wasn't sure was carrying a plea or a threat. 'What's in this for you, Barry? I mean really what's in it? Why the push to screw me up?'

Nash sneered. 'Because I don't like yellow bellies!'

'For Christ's sake, we're both twenty-somethings; grow up!'

'All the more reason for you not to be a scared little kid.'

'I'm not scared, Barry.'

'Think which scares you more: meeting a witch who you pulled an air gun on one dark night or meeting a cop on your doorstep maybe a week from now... or maybe a month or more?'

Billy Reynolds lowered his voice to a bare whisper. 'You wouldn't sleep at night, Nash. Cops aren't dumb; I'd turn it back on you sooner or later and they'd-'

'Oh, but I will sleep - sleep *very well* at night. You see, Billy, *Kelly's* going to be coming round my place a lot once I tell her how disgusting a pervert you were. We'll start out as friends.'

'I told you; I *saw* that old lady today,' Billy said. 'She was at the back of her house.'

'Sorry, that's the deal. Take it or leave it, Bill.'

'Hey, I'm outta here.' Billy mashed his fist into his small bag of French fries and got up.

'And that,' Nash said, pointing at his jacket, his voice a whisper for 'and' and a near bellow for 'that'. 'You want me to yell out right now you're walking round with a loaded air pis…?'

Billy froze, his heart squeezing itself into a tighter mess.

'You try walking away from this or me, I'll smoke you,' Nash said. 'That's a promise.'

Billy's eyes ran an arc about the restaurant. Oh God, he thought. Two tables, plus another one way back at the far window had their eyes on him and the back of Nash. How much had they heard, even with the radio on? He smiled, sat down and stared at his half-drunk soda.

'Can I take that as a yes, Billy?'

'Why can't you just be a friend?'

'Uh, wait; we've been here before with that subject, haven't we?'

'No, I mean it. Why the sudden drive to do all this?'

Nash reached for a French fry from the crushed bag, his smile sustained. Billy could feel his fingers beginning to curl round into a fist. Nash had a minute left to smarten up, or else…

Or else 'what'? What are you going to do when he doesn't? Billy's inner voice jabbed.

Nash was continuing to eat his fries in nonchalance. 'Good fries here,' Nash said.

'What say we quit this now? I get up, get out and we never talk, email, contact again?'

'No,' Nash said. 'No good. That won't give me the closure I'm lookin' for.'

Billy's guts sank into arctic waters. 'What *closure*? You never cared about getting that old lady for threatening you! *If* she ever did! You just dragged me into it so you could do all *this!*

Nash kept eating. 'Really good fries,' he smiled back, at length.

'Yeah, I bet you made the whole thing up just so you could pull this on me now!'

'Yeah? Is that what you think?'

'Yeah. That's what I think! I bet nobody lives there for real!'

'Fine. Think that then. It'll make it easier for you tonight.'

Billy began squeezing his drink cup when he saw the mother of the toddlers moving her head past her husband's to get a good look at him. Had he been raising his voice? he worried.

'I'll finish you for this, Nash. No-one messes me over this way and laughs.'

Nash started wiping his fingers in his serviette. 'Whatever.'

'I mean it, man. You're *toast* after this. No-one does this to me. I don't care if the whole world's ending right now.'

'But Billy,' Nash said as he got up. 'You're doing it *to yourself*, too.'

-37-
21ˢᵗ April, Western Siberia, Loyalist Zone

Olentiev had been breakfasting on sausage, black bread and coffee in the pilots' mess tent when the loudspeaker crackled on and summoned them all for the briefing.

He had been picking at his food and was in no mood to wolf down the balance now.

What's wrong here? he kept thinking. *Why can't I recognize any of the pilots?*

It was too weird. He had been gone for not even a week and they'd changed the entire base company? Twenty-eight pilots and he didn't recognize one.

But their insignias all seemed so familiar. Not his division but....

Had all the men in his division been discharged with Timushenko? Or been *killed?*

Olentiev filed out with the others, made his way to the larger, corrugated-iron, reinforced briefing cabin and found a seat at the front.

Marshal Bucharin and an unknown colonel both seemed to be staring him down, searching for heretical expressions on his face.

'Gentlemen, this will be short but intense,' Bucharin said, at some length. 'Colonel Krasov will lead you through the intricacies of the mission after I've given you the background.'

Olentiev sensed himself starting to shiver. 6 a.m.: the air was so cold at that time.

No. He felt cold from the *inside*. He was thinking of Askenskaya and what might have become of Askenskaya now.

'Your objective is straightforward,' woke Olentiev from his reverie. Bucharin tapped his pointer stick upon the grid map of Lake Baykal's southern shores and hinterland. 'As you know, the rebels are dug in well into these hills and passes. So far they've been successful at retarding our ground units and they've proved themselves capable enough to resist air bombardment.

'Air reconnaissance and the small bits of intelligence we've been able to get shows them as numbering just over three hundred. Small, admittedly, but quite fluid and well armed. These guerrillas are so adept at using their terrain to their benefit that, should ground forces be deployed without air support, our casualties could run quite high.

'It is absolutely *essential* that we cut them out from there before another week is out. Every day they hold their positions means more time for their supply lines from the south and east to run unhindered behind them. What is worse is the issue of *morale*. The *longer* they stay, the *braver* they will become.

'Now you can forget about the danger zone north of Lake Baykal. *They* certainly have.'

The red dots on the chart were upsetting Olentiev now. He'd flown the skies over there how many times in the last couple of months?

Eighteen, was it? Twenty, even?

Bucharin was pointing the tip of his stick at the middle of a crescent of them.

No way, Olentiev thought. There was no way the rebels could have popped back that fast since his last strike mission. As for their having pushed back up that far northwest – *impossible!* Who was Bucharin trying to fool? All the land out there was toxic, anyway! They'd need radiation suits.

'Fourteen planes should finish them. Your mission co-coordinator will speak. Colonel?'

For the next half-hour, Olentiev found himself trying not to think and actually trying to listen. There was too much about this that seemed unreal.

Had Putin truly given in to the Sergeyev camp and pledged himself anew to injecting so much into Siberia? There was no way to know. In the ever-evolving 'New Russian' military, truth was a luxury beyond affordability.

When Colonel Krasov – one of the few clean cut and *un*shiftiest-looking officers Olentiev had ever seen - was done, Olentiev left the briefing tent last, wanting so much to ask questions, but they were questions he couldn't safely put into words.

Outside, the young sky was being warmed by only the apex of the sun. On his way to the MiG pen, Olentiev saw his children's faces in the clouds. What sort of Russia would they have when they grew up? What sort of world? Would he ever get to *see* them grown up?

The colonel had said the rebels had a handful of Surface to Air Missiles. Olentiev imagined their impact as he walked, picturing the flashes of flame, the deafening *whoompffs.*

The MiG-29's looked ill, reluctant to him as he found his and his co-pilot, Gorov, made for the mounting ladders. Budgets had let these Fulcrums rust quite a bit through neglect.

Once the canopy locked around him, Olentiev heard his heart thumping away. He flicked the control panel levers, watched the red, green and yellow LED's glow dully from casings.

This is your last flight, major.

He shuddered at that thought and shuddered again when Gorov spoke in his helmet speaker. The last time he'd heard someone's voice in his helmet, it had been....

They taxied on the runway seventh in line, Olentiev gripping the flight stick for dear life.

The sun was halfway up when they got into the air. Olentiev could feel it warning him through his visor, urging him to throw in the military and find something else. But in the new Russia, there was nothing else left for a man like him and he knew it. The military had always provided a helping hand, the grip of which he'd felt slip so far after the collapse of the old regime.

'Unstable times call for strong actions from strong men', his father-in-law had told him through his long smoking pipe.

Now, as Olentiev looked down, he could see only the same sun-baked dryness between the wisps of cloud as he had seen the last time he had been out this way. Back when…

Damn it. His mind was firing him memories, images now. *Askenskaya was still alive.*

No, you fool; of course he's dead.

But he was walking around down there - his voice had sounded strong.

Think of the rads he would've been subjected to out there.

The ones coming into your cockpit would have been enough to kill you if you'd been flying longer than six hours.

One blue LED flickered on on the armaments display, then another, then two more. Gorov was priming the four small missiles. 'Now, Gorov?'

'Yes; we had better. Just in case.'

In case of what? Olentiev thought. They were only a few miles into No Man's Airspace.

'Sir, we better be prepared for rebel activity *anywhere* here.'

Olentiev remained silent. The sun's oblique rays were beginning to cast a glare on the inside of the cockpit canopy. He could see the portrait of his family in the haze, taken only two years back and wondered how long it would be before he'd see Valentina again.

Maybe he really could promise her a new life. Ditch this sick joke of a job and use her family connections, get something good like dealing in cellular phone apps software.

Olentiev heard the front man call through the static: 'Drop to four kilometers.'

He reached forward, powered up his target grid, tailed the flotilla down past the wispy clouds and suddenly heard: 'Targets expected in T-minus three minutes! Prime small missiles.'

They were in a half-arrow formation now. Olentiev could see the detail on the ground: hill ridges, dead forests, the odd grays and browns of now-deserted hamlets.

So easy to hit from the air. *So easy for them to shoot up at us.*

He felt the shiver in his tailbone now. The hills were rising into low mountains - the enemy's chosen home.

'Rebel positions sighted,' another pilot called out a few seconds later.

The front man dipped his nose, embraced the thicker, deadlier air of two thousand meters' altitude.

Olentiev saw the dugouts when he followed: empty holes ringed by sandbags with....

His heart hit his ribs, pumped hard at them when he saw the logs - dislocated telephone poles stuck out of them to look like heavy guns.

'That's a trap!' he shouted into his mic. 'That's a decoy. Recon's all wrong on this!'

The front man and planes ahead broke starboard. Olentiev yawed with them, staring down at the sandbag rings over the sill of the canopy. They looked like eye sockets in a skull.

'Leader to reds at rear; you make anything of that?' the front man called through static.

'Negative. Count five abandoned or dummy enemy encampments,' one of the rear pilots confirmed.

They swept low. As Olentiev followed, he could make out the bodies lying on the rocks, in the grasses and weeds. 'That has to be a deception,' he said.

'Agreed,' the front man replied. 'We'd better push on.'

'Wait!' one of the rear pilots yelled. 'We have movement at three o'clock.'

Olentiev jerked his head back, caught the figures on the ground.

'We're at the target center,' another pilot continued. 'That's them there!'

'Affirmative,' the front man called out. 'Back and downsweep, get ready.'

Now, at just under one thousand meters' altitude, Olentiev followed the loop back and caught sight of the cement block buildings.

Were those children?

'We have armed rebels dead ahead,' the front man said. 'Lock on and fire.'

'They're children,' Olentiev whispered, disbelieving. 'Children.'

'Locked on,' Gorov declared.

Olentiev could see them all taking up their positions in the clearing… out in the open and not even using the felled tree trunks at the edges for cover… tactically suicidal positions. Kids, running with carbines, Kalashnikovs in hand. They couldn't have been more than ten, eleven years old. *What were they doing running around with no radiation suits on?!*

And another figure standing in the center: an old woman with long white hair.

Olentiev's fingers squeezed the flight stick as he watched two of the Fulcrums near him release a missile each. 'Gorov, no - *wait!*'

Too late. The single smoke stream whooshed ahead of Olentiev, slammed into the ground just a little to the right of the two black-flamed fireballs. He saw the bodies flying forward before the flames shot up from below.

...Bright, yellow flames. They couldn't have come from his small warhead.

Olentiev pulled his flight stick hard left and checked his monitor. 'God, we must have hit an *ammo dump!*'

His eyes dropped to the scanner. The thirteen dots on his screen that had been the other Fulcrums were now only nine.

'We have an emergency!' one of the pilots behind him screamed. 'Pull out!'

The heat coming into the fuselage of Olentiev's Fulcrum was intense now. As he yawed round and straightened, he saw the remnants of the squadron at the back, felt his heart thud harder.

And then he looked down at the earth below.

Fire: an expanse of flame running outward from their missile strikes, burning harder, higher than a parched forest conflagration... Burning almost white hot against the early morning gloom about its edges.

'Climb higher!' Olentiev screamed as he pulled up on his flight stick.

'Abort!' the front man yelled. 'Abort! Abort!'

Olentiev heard him scream like a dying dog and checked the monitor.

Eight blips left now. Excruciating static was rushing into his helmet.

'What *is* that?!' Gorov shouted.

'Olentiev?!' another pilot cut in on the channel. 'You're in command; what do we do?'

'We head back. Mission aborted!'

At five thousand meters, Olentiev touched the clouds, fingertips scrabbling crazily over the channel selector, his heart palpitating as he readied himself to speak to mission command.

Krasov's voice was intense when it greeted him. Did Krasov know already?

'Mission aborted, colonel. We had to abort!'

'Why?!'

'Unexpected...emergency! Emergency!'

The static intensified in the clouds. Olentiev remembered the warning from the briefing and climbed until he was back in the open blue of the stratosphere.

'What was that, Olentiev? Repeat... Repeat!'

'Fires, fires everywhere down there, sir!'

'I don't read you; over?'

'Located a rebel outpost and struck it with missiles, sir. Fire erupted after that!'

Olentiev gazed into his grid monitor, saw that the blips for the other MiGs were pulsating at a lower rate than his heart. 'Sir?'

'Negative, Major. We don't read you.'

'Major Olentiev?'

Gorov, his voice dry and crackling even in the static-free line: 'Check your display, sir. Looks like another one of ours made it out.'

Olentiev caught the blip at the bottom of his screen, a finger's length away from the cluster that represented the survivors: the known survivors.

'Sir? Do you see that?'

'Affirmative, Gorov. Hailing now.' Olentiev frisked the channel selector after failing on the main frequency. Something was wrong with the way that blip looked. 'Rear loner, identify.'

Olentiev flicked the communications dial on the panel round to the last notch and repeated himself. The static in his helmet was snowballing with every second.

Wait. What was that?

Olentiev isolated the static then trained his hearing on the voice.

'Rear loner, identify yourself, over!'

The voice was weak, its words only coming over in broken syllables.

'Identify! Identify!'

'-entiev.....lentiev....'

Olentiev froze when he saw the rear blip vanish, reappear further up the monitor then vanish again. He couldn't speak now. Gorov was talking; asking him for info.

The blip reappeared just a couple of millimeters away from the two stragglers in the MiG formation. 'Rear reds,' Olentiev called. 'Do you see the loner?'

The static grew as Olentiev listened for a reply.

'Repeat! Do you see the loner?!! Level with you now! Portside!'

'....lentiev.....Olentiev,' bled through the distortion. It was not

Kukolev's – the mission front man's voice.

Olentiev *knew* that voice. The blip had come up past the rear pilots now, was close to being level with his own Fulcrum.

It took Olentiev twenty seconds or more to turn his head to greet the nose of the aircraft flying alongside his.

When he saw the occupants, he screamed.

·

-38-

20ᵗʰ April, San Diego, California

Regret.

That was a feeling Billy Reynolds had rarely experienced in his short life. Not the true kind, like this. But now it was there in his heart, pressing in on him as he made his way up the street to the house with the boarded up windows.

Nash had parked a little further down than last time. Billy could feel his eyes burning into his back as he walked.

But he could feel other eyes burning into him from other places in the street.

Billy's own eyes were panning, scanning and feeding him the information you only get when crazy with fear. Low income housing in San Diego was a sight he'd never really taken in before. But he knew the low income areas were supposed to mean something safer, cleaner here than they did in L.A. or in San Fran. In San Diego, the poor and near-poor folk had always seemed to keep more or less in step with Reagan's vision for success.

But this, this was not part of that. Everywhere he looked, he saw the dilapidation.

He was a couple of houses away from hers now. Bungalows on that side - all decrepit, all with unkempt lawns and grotty paintwork. *Why weren't there any cars in the drives?*

Billy came to the top of the path and paused, turning to look back at Nash.

Nash was sitting behind his wheel, smoking, grinning.

That grin. Billy moved onto the path, feeling regret anew. The boards on the windows he could feel searching him for that regret, some hint of repentance for this whole affair.

He got to the end of the path and started to cut round the side. The back of the house looked different in the evening light. Billy turned, saw the dying rays warning him from between the holes in the fence slats.

He would make Barry Nash *very* sorry for this tomorrow.

His knuckles rapped the glass diamond plate in the back door. He waited a couple of seconds then knocked again, just to be sure.

A new worry shot into his chest. If she came and opened up, he'd have to draw her out to the sidewalk as proof.

A paralyzed minute passed, allowed Billy to check for movement in the sole window to the right of the door. Its glass was ribbed - the bathroom.

No movement there, either. Billy pushed in on the door.

He was not expecting it to be open. When it swung inward, he waited a few seconds.

The smell... The smell was nothing like the sweetness he'd sensed in the breeze coming from the window on the other side. The air now coming out at him from the dimness of the back hallway was the smell of an old woman: stale perfume masking elderly inconvenience.

He moved through the doorway, listening. A partition wall shut off most of what he knew must be the kitchen from him.

He suddenly braced his arms against his chest and face.

What are you afraid of? She's too old, too weak to swing an axe!

Yes, but what about a kitchen knife? Or scalding water from a pot?

Billy reached the corner, caught the deeper blackness of a doorway on his left.

Two fronts to cover now. Great.

'Hello?' he tried. 'Ma'am? Are you in?'

Don't be stupid. She'll come for you now.

Billy stood, deadly frozen like that for half a minute, thinking... listening... trying to combat some thoughts with others and losing.

She'll be calling the cops. Break and enter on an old lady.

I didn't break in!

Billy jerked his head back to survey the inside of the back door, saw the lock hanging on by one hinge and bent. His eyes flashed over to the door frame and found the lock's counterpart there hanging out, its screws about three threads shy of plummeting.

Yep - that's break and enter.

'Ma'am?' he called. 'I'm from the Church of Art Science.'

Your books, you idiot! You left them....

Billy could not remember. He fixed his eyes on the grilles of the old gas stove immediately to his right, pleading for some sound - anything to break the awfulness of the silence.

It was getting cold now. All the sweat his good clothes had absorbed was not helping. He could spend the night *outside*. Nash had never said anything about not doing that.

...Or he could jump the fence and be done with it all now. There was an industrial railroad behind there; Billy had seen its tracks at the top of the street.

No. Nash wasn't stupid. He'd be in through the night to try and scare the hell out of him. *If he can't find you then....*

Billy peered around the edge of the partition and found a squalid, windowless kitchen-dining room.

Blackness. He wheeled round to check the doorway of the other side...

It was still but pregnant with menace. His fingertips rolled the flint of his lighter just in time to see that the darkness there ran for less than five feet. A cord from the ceiling was swinging in a gentle arc above pile after pile of newspapers and magazines. A thought was happening in his head when -

Billy turned round fast just then, killing his flame.

Something had broken the quiet. Whistling?

He relit his lighter, took careful note of his surroundings. The flame cast enough light to show him the rest of the kitchen.

'God,' he whispered to the ripped linoleum. 'This is nuts.'

It didn't look like anyone had been in here for years. He wasn't thinking that from the dust coverage on the floor and on the table, counter and shelves. No: the cold of the room, the look of the soup tins and cereal packages. Ancient. 1970's style food packaging.

Two doors taunted him: one straight on, the other, mold-peppered one to his left.

Billy searched for a light switch or cord and was unrewarded. His thumb was starting to burn from the flame of the lighter.

He made for the door dead ahead, not breathing. The bathroom: that one had to be the bathroom.

He touched the lever handle, found he couldn't seize it.

Freezing - hideously cold. It made the heat at his other thumb all the hotter.

He pressed his ear to the door… Nothing but the rushing, muffled seashell noise of amplified silence.

Maybe she was in there, cringing in a corner: in the bath tub.

She afraid of him? But she'd threatened to kill Nash, hadn't she?

Billy released the gas plate on his lighter to stop the stinging on his skin.

Maybe she had a gun trained on the door right now, ready to plug him.

Billy backed away as far as the stove. 'Ma'am, you in here?'

Ten, maybe twenty seconds later, he'd made it to the light cord in the tiny adjoining pantry – more an alcove or a slot for a large fridge than a room. Yanking it produced no light. He looked up and could just make out soot lying at the base of the bulb. 'Shit.'

Before he moved back up to the bathroom door, Billy relit his lighter, held it close to the kitchen counter in search of a better weapon than his Cruzman.

He found a knife when he pulled out the second drawer by the sink. It took him a few seconds to pick it up.

Fingerprints. How many sets of prints had he left already?

What if the old hag was lying dead in the bath and someone - a son or daughter - came round right now?

Billy squeezed the hilt, listened to his heartbeat thundering away in the mad silence.

When he sensed his leg muscles thawing, he tiptoed straight up to the bathroom door, knocked on it with the flat back of his hand.

Ten seconds ground past. 'Ma'am?'... Thirty seconds? When he'd had enough, he pushed the handle down, kicked the door and ran back as far as the back hallway.

The creaking in the hinges lasted too long for his liking. Before it stopped, Billy found he could smell the stink from where he was at the gas stove, could see the thickness of the stench in the new, less-black light coming in from the window in there.

It wasn't feces. He was sure of it: not even the feces of a chronic penicillin user or whatever medication she was on.

Rotting flesh? Could it be that? Billy had never smelled that before, although he'd heard it was like....

No. He couldn't know unless he....

Okay, then. Go up, have a look and if it's that woman lying in there, you damn well grab a bit of cloth and dust down everything you touched.

The smell was changing in his nostrils now: sweeter.

And then you go get a brush cut, bleach your hair and try for a proper mustache rather than that peachy fuzz when you get home.

They'd reactivated the death penalty last year... To show how chaos could only be tolerated to a point.

Holding his breath, he moved back to the doorway and peered inside.

In the forlorn light coming in through the window, Billy could see that the tub was deep, high-walled and rounded... totally ancient looking. It lay amid ripped-up tiles, rags, browned towels and balls of pantyhose.

When he felt safer, Billy tried for a light switch and found one.

Nothing in there, he thought when the sallow beam warmed up.

That thing's too deep: you can't see all of what might be in there from here.

The air flow suddenly felt different in the room.

Behind you!

Billy wheeled round, braced for the old woman standing poised with her gun, eyes and teeth searing hatred.

The image vanished from his mind but the jolt remained.

He felt the cold again, only stronger around his pelvis and legs this time.

Shut the door. For God's sake, shut the door.

He closed it most of the way over and turned back to the deep, old tub, about eight feet distant.

The smell was putrid, fetid now. Billy covered his nose with his lapel as he moved up to it. His Cruzman tapped his collarbone with each step, impotent and mocking.

Hair: he saw the white hair first and his blood froze.

Wait…that was too thick to be human.

The big stuffed toy sheepdog stared back with plaintive blue irises… Was it a trick?

Billy dropped his gaze to the floor just in time to see the mouse carcasses by the stem of the toilet bowl receive their dues from huge, fat-bellied spiders.

Shaking quite badly now, Billy backed up against the towel rack, catching his reflection in the mirror. In the bad light, he could see the glossiness in his eyes.

He wanted to cry so badly now. He had to cry for his stupidity, for risking himself like this - for trading the comforts of home and the joys of college for something as worthless as silly, teen honor.

You're not a teenager anymore. Did 'honor' even have to do with why he'd come to this Hellhole?

He saw Raina's face appear over his own in the mirror, starting from his eyes… he saw his mother in his eyes; he saw a pain he no longer had a right to have in those eyes. 'I'm sorry,' he gasped. 'Just let me out of this; I'll throw away that gun…please.'

'Where's Uncle Billy?' he could hear Raina ask his mother. His mother would be hospitalized for days if…. 'Oh Jesus, I'm not a bad person!!'

Billy Reynolds fell to his haunches on the floor and cried some more into the stink of the air. His sobs were loud, hard throat wrenchers. They didn't let him hear that the air he'd felt earlier in the front room with the smaller window was singing a different tune now.

-39-

20ᵗʰ April, San Diego, California

Dave Reynolds was gazing *through* the display screen that he'd fallen against, *not into* it.

He was thinking. Thinking hard about the - *his* - future.

It was okay to think now; Lippmann, Nathan and Fenton had vanished to go back to Parker's office down below.

8:25... It was almost a completely violet sky out there. Under the hum of the fluorescent tubes in the tech lab, Reynolds could hear a premonition brewing.

In the matt black of the screen, he could see how haggard he looked.

Defeated, too. Of course he was defeated. His company was totaled now. Suspended contracts were total garbage: he'd never see the others from the office or any of the tech support people again.

And he and Raina would have to rely on Helen for money: her with her skimpy little job at the crystal craft shop down in the sea village by the marina.

You've failed your family, boy.

I'll get another job; systems engineer. I'll fix up PCs.

No internet means fewer PC problems.

I'll load software onto servers; that's what I'll do. Firmware and stuff.

You haven't done that in close to a decade, though. Ever heard of changes?

Reynolds looked down the bench at Kenny Piper, then further down at Hank.

Kenny Piper was making it look like he was analyzing the interior of the monitor after he'd removed the CRT and the anode cap. Hank Jarvis was sitting with his face buried in his hands. Weeping?

That was the funny thing about Hank. In all the time Reynolds had known him, he had always seemed on the ball, almost confident, in that wettish way of his: as long as things were going right and Parker was happy with the numbers.

When things went wrong, though, Reynolds knew - had seen firsthand - that Jarvis had all the strength of character of a chocolate teapot.

Reynolds popped a cig in his mouth, instantly thought better of it and tugged it out. 'You getting anywhere, Kenny?' he asked.

Kenny looked over with his hands on a fluke meter. 'It's tough.'

'You actually know what you're doing?'

'I think so. Mr. Jarvis said check for continuity between the diodes and the LOPTY. If.... if there's any sustained bleeps then it means a logic board fault.'

'Has nothing to do with the logic board, Kenny.'

'But...but Mr. Jarvis said it did.'

'Mr. Jarvis tells you the moon's made of green cheese, you'd believe him?'

Jarvis reanimated himself in a flash, fixing Reynolds with a pained glare. 'Have you got any better ideas, Dave?'

'I know it can't be the logic in the screen, that's for sure.'

'Well we're screwed then, aren't we?!'

'Maybe so.'

'So now what?! You think we're gonna be kept on payroll? This is a brick wall we're stuck at!'

'I agree,' Reynolds said. 'That's why I don't think we should be doing things that we know won't get us anywhere. Way I see it, we have to look at this in a new way.'

'Awwh...How d'you mean?' Jarvis asked in a sigh.

'We take this at face value; we end up breaking it down into *two different* problems, right? The instant you hit on your email container and that thing's in there, your disk is toast. That's problem number one, right?'

Kenny Piper waited for Jarvis to nod before he contributed his head.

'Problem number two comes later when your monitor comes up with this - what you guys are calling a message.'

'It *is* a message, Dave,' Hank said.

'Whatever it is, forget it for a second; look what's happening. Your screen essentially goes haywire, is able to run a display without the gun firing from the tube and there's no way to switch it off once it's running until the message concludes… that's unless you bust up your screen.'

Jarvis's face paled like a wheel of Monterrey Jack cheese. 'Where are you taking this?'

'I say we stand back for a second and look at the logic going on in this; correction, sorry - the *lack* of logic going on. Put the two problems together and see how impossible they are. I mean something that wipes your disk *totally*, without a prompt and something that makes a theoretically dead screen alive… *come on.*'

'You have any hypotheses for the screen, Mr. Reynolds?' Kenny asked.

'No. Unless it's some weirdo source the screen is tapping into like bioelectricity or static, there's no way I can see for it to work.'

'Agent one-oh-four produces static, Dave,' Hank said. 'Could it be that-'

'I don't know, Hank. Could be; judging by the weakness of the display and the fact it's flickering, and the fact you can't adjust the brightness or contrast or degauss.'

'You were saying about how we should be approaching this, Dave.'

'I'm saying we tackle an impossible situation with an impossible solution.'

Jarvis's face screwed up. 'No, Hank - think about it. You were in the trenches here how long before you became head of tech support?'

'Four years.'

'Okay. Take this laptop. Say someone had his just over a year, the warranty's run out and he tries booting up only to find his wallpaper and nothing else. He's an Anline client and he thinks it was something he downloaded. He's savvy enough to know it's not just a registry error – something he might be able to fix. What'd you say to him when he called for support?'

'I'd tell him to take it in to get the hard drive looked at.'

'Pretend that's not an option. What then?'

'How could it not be an option, Dave?'

'Just humor me.'

'I'd recommend formatting his disk, but *no-one's* gonna sacrifice their data just like that! Not just like that.'

'Let's say this guy doesn't have that much to lose. Let's say he follows through with that restore disk in the CD drive, right? Just like Parker suggested that time?'

'Yes, but I don't see how-'

'*Think*, Hank: we're using one extreme on another here. Remember, what we're dealing with now isn't *supposed* to happen.'

'Fighting fire with fire,' Kenny Piper said. 'Kind of?'

Reynolds nodded, pointed at the software drawers. 'Let's try it. That laptop you have beside you, Hank, it a fresh hit? Hasn't run the green line yet?'

'Uh, yeah. I think so.'

'Good. Let's try powering it up with a restore disk in the drive.'

Reynolds nibbled some skin from his dry lips while he watched the laptop's corporate insignia appear. The restore disk engaged seconds later, feeding the option on the screen.

'Hit "yes", Hank.'

Jarvis clicked the icon and the program executed. Ten seconds passed before Reynolds saw the blue bars start to build on the horizontal gray fields.

'You know what this is doing, Dave. It's just killing what little was left befor-'

'Quiet; wait for it to finish. If I'm right then we're in business.'

Ten minutes passed. A new dryness rasped in Reynolds' throat.

'It's done,' Hank said when the screen reverted to black.

'Good. Reboot,' Reynolds said.

'Look,' Jarvis gasped when the screen came up, offering him the full complement of folders. 'This isn't the original configuration, Dave!'

'Bingo. If that's old customer data then it means....'

'We formatted the virus?' Kenny Piper extended.

'Or what we *thought was a virus*. We just negated the thing that had negated the original files... *without wiping the good information, too!*'

'Simple as that?' Hank gasped. 'God...why didn't we see this before?'

'Because we're not meant to, Hank. No-one in his right mind is going to do to his computer what we just did; not as the first option *before* the virus appears to be causing trouble. All that time we were just watching the symptoms... not the big picture.'

'But that means the purpose of the virus is what?'

A grinding sound droned through the double doors just then. The elevator was bearing the F.B.I. up from the depths.

Reynolds shot his finger forward, pressing the silver oval at the top left of the keyboard with all his might.

'What'd you do that for?'

'Hank, don't let them know about this. Okay?'

'But what if-'

'Just don't!'

Jarvis's jaw dropped, his eyes falling from Reynolds to the screen to the floor.

'You guys find out any more on the monitor?' Nathan, first through the door, asked.

Reynolds shook his head. 'No. This is definitely going to take some figuring out before we can even start on a counter-virus strategy.'

'Well, we can shed a little more light on the source of the problem,' Lippmann said as she took a seat at the corner bench. 'We've got a fix on the language on the tape taken from the screen message.'

'What's that? Is that even a real language?' Reynolds asked with something darker than intrigue. 'Arabic?'

'Sumerian.'

'What's that?'

Fenton lifted the fax out of his inside jacket pocket. 'An ancient Semitic tongue that vanished three thousand years ago. Babylonian grew out of it.'

'We had to pull a lot of teeth for this,' Lippmann said. 'Only a handful of experts can speak – *write* it, worldwide. Luckily our eastern links could find some at Cornell University.'

'The message itself is still partly undeciphered,' Nathan cut in. 'But our source has been able to certify that it's a list of names of Sumerian deities plus worshipping or hailing chants. Salutes...That sort of thing.'

Reynolds felt a jolt take him right in the heart. 'God; this is straight off Channel Weird.'

'There's something else in there,' Nathan said. 'The four minutes at the end that only appeared when you saved the anomaly to disk; from what Cornell made of it, we think it may be a warning of some kind. The tone of the vocal at the end of the file became much more energetic.'

'What kind of warning?' Reynolds asked. His jolt was harder now: much harder.

'Do any of you *know anything* about the Sumerians?' Lippmann asked. 'Their belief systems, mythology?'

'Just from horror movies,' Reynolds said, watching Jarvis shake a little nearby. 'Are you saying we're seeing a message written by *demons?*'

Nathan's eyes washed over Fenton then over Lippmann. 'We can't say anything at this point except the givens,' Lippmann said. 'We're looking at a message coming up on every computer that's been hit, and it seems to be a threat.'

'But you don't know that for sure,' Reynolds said, partly to console the trembling Jarvis.

'Whatever it is, we know it certainly *isn't friendly*,' Lippmann continued. She crossed her legs, displaying lower thighs, calves and size sevens squeezed into kid pumps for them all.

'So that *message* was programmed into it to appear onscreen as intentionally as it destroys data on the user's hard disk,' Reynolds said weakly. 'So then it's not a byproduct.'

Nathan moved round to Reynolds' right side, leaned against the bench by Kenny Piper. 'On that premise, it looks like a different ballgame now,' he said. 'Are you positive that you haven't been able to make anything of it? The PCs or the screens?'

Reynolds shook his head.

'We've got something else,' Fenton said from the back. 'That first user of yours to get hit - the email address in Virginia.'

'What about it?' Reynolds asked Fenton.

'It's - it could be a coincidence, but we just don't know. That address belonged to the International Generalist Assembly of Spiritualists, Norfolk. On the surface it's not too much, but what tickles us is the link to the occult nature of the screen message.'

'With these bizarre happenings, we don't know what to make of it,'

Nathan contributed. 'You guys say there's *no way you can think of* to combat the technical side of this?'

'No way at all,' Reynolds said.

'Tell them, Dave,' Jarvis gibbered. 'Just tell them please, before this thing gets worse.'

'Well,' Lippmann said. 'You've found something.'

'I wouldn't say that,' Reynolds replied. He could see himself working for beans at his parents' art gallery in La Jolla for the next ten years.

'The disk, Dave,' Hank said. 'J-just tell them about the formatting.'

'That was just chasing shadows, Hank. It came to nothing, remember?'

Nathan scowled. 'Reynolds, I'll remind you you're working for the US Government here. Tell us *now* or-'

'Okay. Okay. I thought that the best way we could fight this would be to look at the psychology of it.'

'How'd you mean?' Nathan asked. 'Psychology?'

'We only tested this once, you know,' Reynolds replied. 'Well, the virus doesn't appear to hold as a virus. All I did was stick a formatting CD in the drive and started it up.'

'The drive of an afflicted computer?'

'Yes… in that the virus was on board; it just hadn't been able to execute yet. As I was saying, I started it up and it somehow managed to recover the files, folders, all the data that looked lost at first.'

'This disk wasn't supposed to do that?' Nathan asked.

'Hell no. Those things are only ever used as a last resort; for when you think your system's so hopelessly messed up that the only way out is to restore the original config. *Eye-eee*, it brings your hard disk right back to the way it was the day you bought your computer. At least, it looks that way.'

'So you're saying this virus isn't a virus at all?' Lippmann asked. Her legs uncrossed and recrossed the other way as if to coax a response quicker.

'It is in the sense it infects, it gives the impression of destroying data and it renders the PC useless in the long term. But the laptop we tried this on had been turned off at the instant of the email transfer. Joe Public wouldn't have been that quick on the uptake. Well, if someone *has* stumbled on what we've just done, they sure haven't called in about it as a fixer.'

'You intended to do that?' Nathan asked.

'No. This is something we just stumbled over in the last little while before you three came back from Parker's office.'

'Why did you want to withhold this information?' Lippmann asked.

Reynolds saw the tiny bulge in her light gray jacket by her left breast, remembered the Mp3 recorder. 'Because it was *so experimental* we didn't know if it was just a one off. If anyone else has done it, maybe they've got reasons for not sharing it... something other than being scared of others finding porn on their disk!' Reynolds grimaced. 'We need to think about how to use this now where it'll matter most - a PC that's been powered up *after infection* with its monitor giving that junk,' he finished, half glaring at the throttleable Hank Jarvis now. 'But how to get it to recognize a boot disk when it's like that?'

'Let's go back to the *psychology* of this,' Nathan said. 'You said you thought of this because you knew it was an illogical step to take.'

'Not so illogical as *unlikely*. How many people would think of using a formatter as clearing the first hurdle? The other issue is the volume of *totally* infected PCs.'

'But the creator of this super-virus...wouldn't they have seen the faults?'

'That's what's stumping me right now. I mean, he seems to be bright in that he's duping the user into believing he's just latched onto a virus and the rest plays out the way a severe parasitic virus, say, would play out.'

'And the screen message?'

'Who in America can understand Sumerian, though, let alone work it back like you did?'

'But the fact that it continues to play even with the power off...' Lippmann threw in.

'I don't know. Maybe it's a shock tactic.'

'How'd you mean that?' Fenton asked. Every member of the F.B.I. trio was leaning forward, forming an arena around Reynolds.

Think carefully, Reynolds; remember you're being recorded. 'Well, what's the first thing you'd feel if you saw your beloved computer dying in front of you? You'd be scared witless, right? I mean, people with years' worth of data stored on their 'C' drive would be terrified if they saw the screen black out, their guts twisting like crazy. And trying to remember what's kept on their backups. When they try powering on afterward, they get that string of shit on their screen.'

'And the purpose of that "string of shit" you think is a scare tactic?' Lippmann offered. 'Like this guy programmed it in there just to drive his point home?'

'Fear is the key, isn't it?' Reynolds replied. 'If I came across this at home, lost all my work, my personal files and addresses and then all I got at the end of it was this long green string, *I'd* be mighty scared.'

'It's unknown,' Jarvis said in a more confident tone. 'This thing stays on your screen without power; it looks strange; we *fear* what we don't understand. I think that's what's in here.'

'Someone trying to a pull a big viral prank,' Reynolds said without thinking. 'He knows the world's upside down with the Third World crisis and the Agent one-oh-four problem. I think it's sabotage being played by some very smart but very sick high school nerd or college geek.'

'The trouble is, Mister Reynolds, *this* prankster is responsible for abetting the mass paralysis of the Internet and knock-on effects that go all the way to manslaughter. Retarding business and commerce as well as damaging essential communications for a lot of governmental agencies, ourselves included. When we find this individual, he's going to be charged with the attempted assassination of the *country.*'

'Fear *is* the unknown,' Reynolds whispered, more to himself than to his audience. 'The Unknown is the absence of knowledge. Mr. Jarvis is right on the money with that.'

'What're you saying?' Lippmann asked.

'What's the Internet if it's not an information superhighway? It's like our friend behind all this wants information - knowledge - to be stamped on like a queen ant.'

The phone by the ID card swipe in the door rang just then. Fenton went, picked it up.

'Hello? Yes, Mr. Carmichael?'

The ten second silence could have been excruciating until Fenton nodded, almost with a smile. 'I see, Mr Carmichael. Thank you.'

-40-
<u>20th April, San Diego, California</u>

Blackness. Pitch blackness. Billy could feel revulsion for the dark more than he could for the parodied carcass of the dog in the bathroom.

He was sitting with his arms hugging his shins behind the partition wall in the kitchen now, wondering how he'd let himself get dragged into this madness. The darkness was making him wish he could scrunch himself into a tighter, invisible ball on the ripped linoleum.

Funny, he was thinking. He'd loved the darkness once, not so long ago. In high school, he'd actually retreated into darkness to enjoy the glory of gothicness, heavy metal, weirdness... everything that was cool about death except death itself. Funny that, and so incongruous with the family orientedness of his brother.

Dave was the one who'd embraced everything he hadn't in high school. Dave had been in the soccer team, in the hockey team and, even with his relatively unimpressive size, the basketball team.

Mr. Yasgur, the Phys. Ed. teacher *cum* coach of the hockey and soccer teams had loved his brother, but had hated Billy for his rebellion, for his deliberate effort to deny the significance of sports in his life. For trying, as Yasgur saw it, to *desecrate* everything Dave had been from Grade Ten on, when really Billy had only thought he was being himself.

As he stared into the wall of blackness, Billy tried to imagine how it might have worked out if he'd *tried* sports in high school... if he'd *tried* to be less of a nihilistic little upstart, or maybe that would have been asking too much of his personality.

Going on to college, he'd actually *tried* to turn it around, to break his old way, to *try* not to seek to *shock* people with his manner. But it had only held for a while. Billy had not been able to forsake the wiles of the dark ways he had enjoyed in the old days. His music had been too hard to give up, same with his dress sense, his attitude....

And his friends.

Why was Nash being such a prick to him now? He hadn't seen him since New Year's, but Nash had shown no signs of having changed, of having even attempted to leave the mocking fetishistic faith of darkness Billy had known he'd shared.

Now, Barry Nash *was* the darkness. And he'd probably been the one who'd *driven* that college roomie of his up north to suicide and all the other shit they suspected this Ganz guy of doing.

Billy tried to train his eyes on the bathroom door, locating it only by the single, purple line that ran under it, and thought of the new self he'd present to the world once tonight was over, done with. No more metal T-shirts or thrash guitars blaring out of his car's old Alpines. No more renting *Faces of Doom* flicks or any of their equivalents from the Video Shack just outside the mall.

No more of the old Billy Reynolds. No; he'd start anew. Tomorrow morning, he'd come out of there, pick up Nash's air pistol from his house, maybe have a Corona or two in the kitchen just to talk things over with and call it quits.

There would be a lot to *talk over*, though. Billy cringed when he thought of how easily Nash could go ahead and do it anyway - tell on him.

But might Nash get drawn into doing that at some point? Would he be that suicidal?

You can always deny. Just like your mother told you when you told her you were scared about Frank Jennings coming after you when he got back from his year off in England because you told Sally, his then-girlfriend, that he'd been messing around with a Grade Ten fling.

Billy clasped his hands around his knees and thought hard about his mother. How she'd stood by him, how she'd made his dad lay off every time they'd come home from a PTE meeting and Yasgur and Mister Richards, the vice principal, had fed his dad and her the same line one more time. How he'd stuck a knife in her back by going out, risking himself with a devil-may-care attitude. She'd been an angel to him and he'd bit her in the back of the neck.

'I'm sorry,' he said to the darkness. 'It's going to be different now - promise.'

Different... There was something *definitely* different about his surroundings now.

The other door - the one up there by the bathroom... Her bedroom. She: the old woman who had threatened death to Nash and he now was sorry that she hadn't just killed the fucker.

His mother would be an old woman some day. Could he bear it if someone else - some little punk like him - the old him: the him that would be *neutralized* come morning - was to go out, break into her house and be ready to do violence unto her? Could he justify that now?

Don't be stupid, he thought. *People are different. Old women take many shapes.*

Rustling?...yes. Billy definitely could hear a rustling sound coming from up there. He waited, stopped his breath just to monitor it.

Fifteen seconds and it was still going. Billy reached for his wristwatch, pushed in the light button. 21:20... Under nine hours to go. That was if Nash took 6am as a fair finishing time.

Billy kept his watch button depressed and crawled on the kitchen floor to investigate the sound. Five, six huge cockroaches, their shining backs coming back in the weakness of his light in sick ambers, oranges and browns scuttled barely ahead of him. Billy stood up halfway and moved his foot in to squash them all dead before he squat-walked back to the partition wall.

He was there only a few seconds more when he heard the rustling again, stronger this time and at a different pace, rhythm. Not insect movement but...was that *curtains* rocking to and fro in the draft in the bathroom?

No. He'd seen no curtains there. That room had been *burned* into his memory. He closed his eyes, tried to think of anything, everything except for that glimpse of something he'd caught in the front room earlier. Earlier there had been daylight and the assurance of an easy escape. It was no use – it glimmered in his head now.

Remember when you were looking in through the gap between the board and the windowsill, Bill? Remember the dark that suddenly came in and...

Curtains. Black curtains those had been... nothing else.

Are you sure? He thought hard about that. The curtains would have to be *very* black to have achieved that shade…

Billy squeezed the hilt of the kitchen knife and tapped his fingertips over the undulations on the edge, tried to imagine how they'd look in the light of day.

A good weapon, Billy; but could you kill… Actually, really stab someone?

Please don't make me think that way! Not now!

Seriously, though; do you have the balls to defend yourself if it actually comes to a kill-or-be-killed situation? Could you neutralize the life of someone who'd only be protecting their house in a court case, thereby neutralizing yourself and your freedom?

Billy moved leftward a little to be closer to the metal trash can he knew sat between him and a guaranteed exit through the back door.

Oscar the Grouch lives in a trash can like that. You will, too, when you get let outta jail. Let's see, forty-five, no job skills, criminal record and homeless.

How will mommy view that? Little Raina will be big and her kids will never hear of Great Uncle Billy, the slayer of old women in their little homes.

Billy froze, sweating icicles. The rustling sound from the door by the bathroom was easing off a little now… But he could feel the air current now in place of the noise.

He checked his watch, saw that it was 21:23 and then registered the thought screaming in his mind. The air had no right to be blowing at him from that direction. If there were gale force winds outside, would he not have heard them already?

He moved around the corner of the partition wall to test the air coming in through the half-open back doorway, first with his face then with a licked finger.

Nothing - not even the gentlest breeze rewarded him. The night was only a little less black out there. A solitary, faraway street light shone back at him from way beyond the railroad track behind the fence.

This is what you get for going into a house that lies near the city limits.

That thought stabbed Billy's mind like a barbed trident. He moved up to the back door, pulled it back so it was ninety degrees to the frame and stepped out onto the cement block step, panning his eyes. The dampness out here was colder than indoors. He looked to his right, up at the corner of the house, started thinking how easy it would be if he jumped ship now.

Go on, be done with it. The lighting on the street is just as pathetic. Or you could jump the fence, head up the train tracks 'til you hit a store, or that noodle bar away way up at the top.

No. Nash could see you and that would be it.

Wait - was Barry Nash really hung up on wrecking his life?

Don't risk it. Remember, the last day - night - of your old life. This is Ground Zero, Billy boy. Only eight hours and some left - a day's work.

Billy moved out into the back garden, wished he had a smoke. Wait; maybe he did. He jammed his hand into all his pockets. Lighter, cig papers, tissues, air pistol - fully loaded and awaiting firing instructions.

Shit. You forgot gloves. Again…

What was that sound?!

Billy froze, listened harder. Nothing else came after ten or so seconds, but he knew that sound had come from the front - up at the top of the path…Someone treading on a rock or concrete.

…Could it be Nash, coming to make sure he was there?

…Could it be the cops, acting on a tipoff from Nash?

Billy thought about that for a second or two more before the crunching noise threatened him once again. He ran on his tiptoes for the back door, quite able to hear the animal gibbering his sinuses were making him sound out. He pushed it closed as far as it would go while lifting so the hinges wouldn't nark on his presence.

From the back of the partition wall he listened harder, placing his fingertips above the kitchen knife atop the trash can, in case.....

In case of what? *If that's Nash, you won't stab him. He'll just start bawling with laughter the instant his flashlight beam blinds you to death and that'll be the end of this shit.*

And if it was a cop or cops? *Knife at the ready, air pistol ready and waiting in your pocket, Mr. Reynolds. How many hundred feet a second do those pellets travel?*

You'll be in jail before you know it with a charge list as long as a weekly grocery shop receipt that you will have given the judge yourself.

Billy moved back toward the bathroom door, his ears tuned for sound, his eyes peeled for the slightest change in the density of the darkness coming from the tiny corridor beyond the partition wall.

He was right by the other door up there when he heard the crunching sound again, only lighter textured this time…like a foot mashing some dried weeds or sticks round the back.

His right hand told him it was being chilled by an air current. The keyhole.

Where's your knife, dickwad?

He'd left it back down again over there, on top of the plastic cover of the trash can.

The crunching sound broke the silence one more time just then, closer. That would be either Nash, the cops or... or *her.*

If it was the cops, they'd be in with flashlights for sure. They might not check the rooms at the front, especially not the smaller one if they'd already shone a light through that gap between the board and the sill.

Billy's fingers curled around the doorknob then rotated it a few degrees clockwise, trying not to think what he'd find.

Wait.... she could be in there, waiting for you with a weapon and a telephone.

No. She'd have come out to inspect long ago.

Maybe she's hard of hearing - deaf even... Did you make enough noise for that?

Wait... what's that over there? Back there!

The blackness at the wall beside the door to the small room and the stove had changed, darkened and solidified from a purplish matt to a jet opal... the shadow of a person?

Call out to it? If it's Nash, at least get it over with. Don't do this to yourself!

Billy felt the catch disengage in the door. He pushed it in a few inches, pulling up a little on the knob, praying that the hinges wouldn't creak or whine regardless.

The last he saw of it, the blackness by the gas stove was still very black.

Someone was standing there, poised, listening, waiting, pondering for sure.

Before he knew anything, Billy had squeezed around the edge of the door and replaced it into its frame. His heartbeats were starting to explode in his neck and inner ears now.

The air in here was freezing, mustier smelling. Nothing like the sweetness he'd breathed in earlier from outside the front.

And the floor felt less solid, too. Billy moved a foot or two down it, his arms probing about like he was a sightless mime earning his pay on the streets of La Jolla, near his folks' shop.

Two surfaces walled on either side of him. He was in a corridor.

Where's my lighter? Oh God! He dug a damp hand into his pants pocket for it, wrenched it up then thumbed the flint to find himself in exactly what he'd pictured.

Green mold caverned in around him, at its thickest up near the ceiling. Three doors challenged Billy ahead, one of them the front door. He saw a two-by-four joining it to its frame, just above the lock. He was listening hard now, trying to focus past the noise in his inner ear.

Thumpa-thumpa-thumpa-thumpa-thumpa-thumpa-thumpa

If the secret party was to rush in now, would he even make it to one of the front rooms?

You're trapped, Reynolds. Your thick Irish hide is trapped and you did it to yourself. You'll earn all that's coming when the cops get you.

I have to try! he swore inside. *At least if I get caught cowering behind a stinking, piss-stained sofa, I can say I tried.*

But will Mom, Raina and the rest of your family appreciate that?

Noise... A footstep behind him! Whoever they were, they were standing in the back hallway just off from the kitchen for sure now!

Billy gazed at the floor ahead of him one last time before his thumb lifted up off the cig lighter pump and the burning stopped. The edges, right by the skirting boards told him to step there. He obeyed in one, two, three huge strides, pulling his weight up into his thighs.

Sound travels easily here; if they hear a creak, you're finito, pal.

He made it as far as the door on the right when he heard the whining of wood. He froze with his hand around the handle, listening for all he was worth.

Had that been his foot doing that? No. He hadn't felt the give in the floor that he knew would have had to accompany the creaking sound.

Back there in the kitchen, then?

Billy could feel his heartbeat trying to rip through his throat now. He turned the lever handle downward and pushed gently.

No give. The door was locked.

Thumpa-thumpa-thumpa-thumpa-thumpa-thumpa-thumpa-thumpa

He reached over fast and hard at the other door's handle then... The door to the room with the gap between the window and the cover board.

Billy could feel more vibrations in the floor now. As he pushed down the lever handle he could see everything play out in his mind's eye: the two cops, two flashlight beams blinding him, and then the yelled commands. If that was Nash, it would end in a fistfight.

And if it was the old woman whose house this was - the witch?

The door gave as soon as Billy put his weight to it. He hadn't expected it to be so light. Before he could co-ordinate himself, he fell sideways – the beginning of an unwanted, awful cartwheel.

The air rushed colder at him than it already was on his way down to the...

His face was suddenly half-buried in stinking, powder-caked dry fabric. His elbow banged the floor, uncaring if the sound had been enough to draw attention.

Billy spat out a mouthful of the fungus dust and shot to his feet, feeling for the edge of the door, pulling up and round on it when he found it.

When he got it closed, he felt for his lighter and failed to find it. He had just a couple of seconds to hide before whoever it was came through the door and...

I'm dead, then. Or jailed for a felony.

Sweeping his arms in arcs before him as he trod, it took Billy just a few seconds to find the sofa back, two more to move in behind it after he had pulled back the overlay, which was...

Carpeting?... Rolled up carpets, rugs or bedclothes. He jerked the section of fabric up higher over his head as he crouched then let it flop down to cover him.

Then came the listening... Five seconds later, Billy heard the creak again and felt his muscles seize up.

The sound was there in the room with him.

-41-
20<u>th</u> April, San Diego, California

'Where's he going?' Hank Jarvis asked Nathan when Fenton closed the door.

'You got me there, pal,' Nathan replied sarcastically. 'Business.'

Dave Reynolds was over by Kenny Piper now, his knuckles pressed hard against the work bench.

Had he said too much? Had Jarvis provoked him to sacrifice their usefulness?

He looked down the bench at Jarvis. Jarvis was sitting calmer now, but his face was all furrowed in worry creases, like a scared school kid. *Wuss,* Reynolds thought. *If you've cost me my contract, I'll smash you.*

'Reynolds, are you *sure* there's no remedying the hard drive of a system once it's been green-lined by the super-virus?'

'Sure I am,' he told Nathan. 'You can't access the "D" drive if there's nothing in the computer to sense that it's there. Using that restore disk was just a fluke and we caught it early.'

Nathan frowned, nodded. 'Yeah, okay - I see the logic there. So there's no way round that at all?'

'Not unless you've got a systems engineer with some savvy of the paranormal and its relation to the problem.' Reynolds rubbed his eyes. 'But then, it might be along the same lines as pre-green line knockouts and we just haven't found the *method* yet.'

'I think we could use a coffee break,' Lippmann said, rising from her seat. Reynolds nodded, became second in her entourage behind Nathan.

They were back in the lab only two minutes when Fenton returned with some printed sheets. He gave them straight to Nathan before sitting himself down in silence.

'What's that?' Reynolds asked after a full minute had been obliterated by quiet.

'Could be something; it could just be something.'

'You mean you got something fresh on the super-virus?'

Nathan looked up at him from his papers then turned to face the other Anliners. 'You guys are being contracted to work on fighting the virus only,' he said. 'Now that you've proved to me this thing's virtually unstoppable, I can't say I see the point in releasing classified intelligence to you.'

'I never said it was "unstoppable"; just *difficult at this present moment*,' Reynolds heard himself say in a harsher tone than he'd meant.

'I don't know on this one,' Nathan replied.

'You said yourself "it could be something", Nathan. If we can help with it, then-'

'Alright, Reynolds. Here it is. You all understand you're still bound by secrecy here.'

After nodding, Reynolds took the sheets, started scanning down the top one. 'A criminal profile?'

'Correct. Jurgen Hiram Ganz.'

'You think this guy's behind the virus?'

'See for yourself… Page two, about halfway down, I believe.'

Reynolds flipped a leaf, ran his eye down the paragraphs. They all read like specifications for a machine: Ganz's education, his places of residence.

'Computer skills… No formal training. "Rudimentary?"?'

'I know. But a lot of people are self trained these days.'

Reynolds squinted, read the paragraph beneath the one he'd read aloud. 'Known hobbies… Let's see here: reading, occult, alternative life styling?'

'Ganz was… is a self-professed occult expert,' Nathan said. 'He's wanted for the arson of his Cultural Anthropology professor's office and a few others' at North Dakota College, two years ago.'

'The Sumerian words,' Hank Jarvis said. 'That's tied in with that stuff, right?'

'Have any of you ever heard of a book called *The Liber Fati*?' Lippmann asked. 'It was a text of occult symbols that surfaced recently, supposedly after centuries of disuse.'

Reynolds looked up from the sheets. 'That's fairytale nonsense.'

'Is it?' Lippmann asked. 'How do you know that?'

'Horror film crap,' he replied. 'I've heard of it from that.'

'So how can you just go out and pick it up from any bookstore, then.'

'You serious?'

'We think this Jurgen Ganz took it very seriously. Serious enough for him to want to bring down the Internet and knock the world back a couple hundred generations in evolution.'

Reynolds went back to the first page of the fax. 'But if this guy's some kind of religious maniac,' he said, pausing for effect, 'How could he have cooked up such a far-out pseudo-virus?'

'Pseudo-virus?'

'I thought I already explained that. Remember when I said I thought it just *looked like* this guy wanted to give people a scare?'

'That's why we're sure there's a link here,' Nathan said. 'Fear is his key.'

'And yet,' Reynolds continued, 'To conceive of a program that could do what it does... trigger a wipe-out procedure with the user only being *initially* close to a conventional virus danger situation; reversing the logic of formatting the hard drive; making that crap appear on your screen, never mind the fact there's a spiritualist's message showing up there?!' He scratched his chin. 'And yet, if we can somehow get it so an afflicted computer can be made to take a command from that restore disk...'

'He could be an associate of the virus author,' Lippmann offered calmly. 'If that's true then this could be a whole cyber-terrorist outfit we're after.'

'Think, Reynolds,' Nathan joined. 'An angry, smart guy like Ganz. He's got a beef with the Establishment and he's an Internet user.'

'Anline. Was he with us?'

'Yes. But he had a Forserver account, too. That's on the back page.'

'God,' Reynolds said. 'That complicates it... We can't plug him in.'

'On the contrary, it shows he was working in a group. I was saying he's an angry young man, knows a few other angry young men he's met through chat lines on hate sites. This Satanist stuff always sells well there.'

'You think he struck up a friendship with a hacker?' Reynolds asked.

'Could be,' Nathan replied; 'Or several hackers.'

'But a virus author *that* good would've had to have surfaced before somewhere. Look at the intricacies of what we're dealing with in this,

Nathan; look at how *impossible* it would be for most experts to even work out the theory behind it all.'

'That's the academic bit, Reynolds. 'Til we get him, we'll have to focus on pragmatics.'

'But, in this case, the academics are telling us it's this way above anything that -'

'We have nothing else to go on here. You were talking about the M.O. of this virus being impossible, but you said its purpose was straightforward. *Fear*, yes?'

Reynolds nodded, trying not to think of a point to argue with yet.

'This agent 104 chemical that's been turning up. Now, supposing Ganz, his friend or friends, see that...see that science can't grapple with it. And then they look at the other problems in the world. That war in India which nearly went to nukes, China's collapse, the African blow-up of bubonic plague that can't be treated.

'Now these people are hurting, mad - they're unhappy campers and they see something they can tap into as a resource: *confusion*.'

'And cook up a computer virus that's fifty years ahead of its time?' Reynolds queried.

'Never mind that yet.'

'Sorry, Nathan but this is nuts. How can you conclude it's a small group of amateurs seizing an opportunity to scare the world and coming up with this? We're talking about something that's way over the top for most virus authors to even *try* dreaming about!'

'Or would you call it supernatural?'

'I'm at a loss for calling it anything right now.'

'Reynolds, do you believe in God and the Devil?'

'Oh, now wait a minute; come on!'

'Just indulge me here... *please*.'

Reynolds noticed Hank Jarvis biting his nails beside Kenny Piper. Kenny Piper had his head hung low over his coffee cup, looking like he'd just had a hundred IQ points removed with the aid of a pair of pliers.

'I believe there's a force, yes. Whether it's a guy in sandals with a white beard, I don't-'

'And psychics. What's your view of them?'

'They have their uses, provided you have the cash for dialing the premium number.'

'Well, let me tell you that psychics have played no small part in the solving of quite a few cases that would otherwise be left *un*solved.'

Nathan narrowed his eyes, as if in warning. 'Now, this is a little beyond F.B.I. territory. That's my line, Reynolds.'

'I thought you *were* F.B.I..'

'Well, yes *and* no. As I was saying about the psychics that we use: I've been in the trade since 1989, Reynolds. You'd only have been in grade school then.'

'You could tell me anything now, Nathan and I'd just have to listen, wouldn't I?'

Nathan grinned nastily. 'My very first big case was the Car Trunk Ripper. Yeah; you know what the unofficial story behind our nailing him was? Psychics. Five people from very diverse backgrounds, never meeting each other and never meeting him. They were able to net the bastard in days, just from using this.'

Nathan ran his palm across his receded hairline. Reynolds could feel his guts knotting now. His parents had never poured the brand of Christianity they had received over him or his kid brother. Hocus pocus… He tried thinking of a magic show, of a funfair, but couldn't get that far because his heart was in his stomach. That *this* was their last resort!

'Now let's figure that in this happy bunch Ganz either formed or joined, there's an individual or individuals with psychic powers. These guys have already cooked up this idea for a virus. Ganz has already attacked his professor for massacring his thesis and he gets thinking he's safe after a suicide cover-up in Israel.'

'Do you know where this is going?' Reynolds asked. 'Can you actually hear yourself?'

'Son, I'm not one who's usually given to this belief but, like I said before, there's gonna be nothing but a big dead end for us if we don't start looking for alternatives.'

'So now it's a psychic sitting down with the virus creator, touching it up with-'

Nathan touched Reynolds' shoulder. 'I've seen stuff that would boil your analytical little mind into nothing.' Nathan turned to face the two lower

FBIs, waited until Fenton nodded his head with his eyes on the floor. 'You people heard of the Tierney assassination?'

'Yes,' Hank Jarvis said faintly. 'Awful.'

'Yeah.' Nathan looked straight into Reynolds' eyes. 'A Cardinal from Ireland comes over to do a tour of Massachusetts, urging the ethnics there not to go sending money to the "struggle back home." Only problem is, Cardinal Tierney doesn't get to go very far with that because, the same day he arrives in Boston, he gets his head blown off by an unknown assailant. Everybody frisked in the aftermath, hundreds of officers poured in to do a dragnet tighter than a weasel's ass, and they turn up empty.'

'Your psychics never kicked in on that one?' Reynolds asked.

'We've still got them on it. The only thing about this case was the killer decides to leave his signature behind on the surveillance tape.'

Reynolds' upper stomach had risen with his heart up to his gullet now. 'I don't get you on that... *what* tape?'

'We found an image smaller than a sugar granule on it there. Only lasted a single frame - one thirtieth of a second or so - but it was there. So we run this tape back again and again in the lab, me and some C.I.A. guys. Hours we spend on it, trying to find the source. The only problem was in the way the good cardinal's skull came apart from the blast meant that the trajectory would've had to have come from directly above.'

Reynolds tried to ask how that was possible and found he couldn't work his jaw.

'An impossible shot... The first exit wound straight down in behind his chin. We were baffled, spent the first number of hours trying to zoom in on everything. First we figured it might have been a ricochet,' Nathan continued. 'Then we noticed that Cardinal Tierney was stood more than ten feet in front of the podium roof. So we tried another direction, just as you did with that formatting disk. We went over every frame until we found that one with the black spot on it, zoomed in.... one hell of a long shot, even for the sharpest mind. We beefed up the magnification until that tiny sugar granule was the size of a finger nail, then on and on until we saw.....'

Reynolds saw Nathan rub his eyes, heard him exhale a deep bit of breath. 'A face, Reynolds; a face lurking in that dark patch. The face of Jurgen Hiram Ganz!'

'You mean he was...something had *projected* his likeness?'

'Yes - directly onto the tape. The camera couldn't have recorded that. Some power....a psychic force of some kind put his likeness... *recorded* it over the tape.'

'You know what most analysts would say if you-'

'If we *what*, Reynolds? No-one can ever know about this. I'm only telling you because you are, by proxy, *committed* to this investigation now.'

Reynolds picked up the fax printout, tried to reread and found he couldn't digest.

'This man and his accomplices are responsible, we believe, for the deaths of Cardinal Tierney plus a number of other international incidents that have happened in the time since Jurgen Ganz vanished.'

Nathan reached for the fax, flipped up the papers until Reynolds was looking at the next-to-last page. 'Here; see for yourself. Twenty names or more, every single one of them either a public figure, an official of an international agency or someone who had adverse ties with Ganz.'

Reynolds ran his eye down the list until he reached the second last name. 'This one... Who is he?' he asked.

Nathan leant over, looking until he found the words above Reynolds' nail. 'Bartholomew Nash. That was Ganz's roommate at ND College.'

'What happened to him?' Reynolds' heart rate was going haywire. 'Barry Nash?'

Nathan ran his fingertip over the line until he found the incident location. 'Yes; Barry Nash. You know what spontaneous human combustion is? How it's an urban myth?'

'Jesus Christ. I better call home.'

'Well, that's what happened to young Nash. Here in San Diego, in fact; just last month.'

-42-

21ˢᵗ April, San Diego, California

Billy Reynolds' stomach was fully heaving now. His breathing was coming faster and faster. He knew he was starting to hyperventilate. If there was more air under his cover it would have been easier, but as it was it was making it worse.

The other sound he could hear was changing with every moment. The moments were starting to get long and agonizing for him now.

Movements... Whether they were made by shoeless feet or hands and knees was beyond his caring. The movements would start, continue for a second then cease.

The way an animal would move as it might sniff in one place and then trot over to another. Billy's jaw was quivering. He wanted to call out, announce himself, just to get it over with, this torment, but he couldn't follow through.

The door hadn't opened for anyone to have been able to come in. That much he was sure about. He'd closed it. He'd *felt* the run of it end at the frame, had *heard* the latch engage so that door and doorway were united.

His heart was hurting him, punishing him for endangering himself in this way.

Not cops. That could not be cops, he told himself.

He'd forgotten about the sounds of movement beyond the corridor door earlier.

It couldn't be Nash, either. In a calmer state, he'd be able to *convince* himself of that. But...

The noises started up again then stopped within a second or two. Billy had felt the vibrations through his shoes, his kneecaps, his knuckles. Even the back lining of the sofa had reverberated from it.

The room was how big? Ten feet by ten?

During that lull, his memory kicked in, played him back the view he'd had of the gap when the darkness had come and blotted out the mold on the wallpaper, back when he'd been safely on the outside of the house.

His mind's eye was picturing thick black curtains when the rustling started again, the vibrations nearly twice as strong as before.

Billy had had enough. He reached for his Cruzman, drew it out under the covers.

Something was spilling onto his shoes and the floor – his ball bearings.

The fingers of his left hand were trembling so badly he could hear and was sickened by the tap-tap-tapping sound they made against the plastic run of the barrel. They finally touched the top, found where the ammunition level flag had snagged on a hole in the sofa lining.

'Wh....who...who's there?!' he yelled.

How many shots did he have? His fingers slapped against the marker flag, compared its position to the top of the slit in the barrel.

About halfway. Nine...maybe ten rounds, if he was lucky.

'Mmm...Ma'am...if that's you, say so *now!*'

The vibrations started again. Billy could feel the sofa lining moving on his cheek, could not help but think of...

Pulling the cover back from his body, he shot to his feet, raised his gun arm so it was pointing forty-five degrees leftward and shot the first ball bearing, then the next.

Billy heard the wood in the wall splinter. He swung his arm down to the end of the sofa where he'd entered, fired round number three straight into the blackness.

The hissing started then and Billy felt the air current on his fingers and face.

An animal's hiss: a serpent's or a lizard's, coming from another direction.

Straight ahead! For God's sake, shoot at twelve o'clock!

He had aimed, fingertip over the trigger, ready to fire when something hit his hand hard.

Billy's arm flew with it, the skin on his wrist crackling numbness from the contact as he heard his Cruzman smash into the wall or the inside of the window board covering.

He tried to run. He had his right leg out but his left refused to work, its ankle caught up in the sofa coverings...

Billy fell, nicking his forehead against the wood of a table or the windowsill.

The hissing hissed louder when he rolled to face it, his good foot lashing round, trying to contact the source at the ankles, to take it down.

Billy felt the force of a foot ram him in the chest. He coughed out dry air before he was even able to try to grab the offending leg.

Another blow smashed into his shoulder, but this time he had caught the leg.

Jeans; denim rasped against Billy's palms. He jerked it hard to the right, prayed his offender would topple so he could...

His cheek screamed at him suddenly from a punch. Billy lost his grip, fell back, knocking the back of his head against a table leg.

The blackness above him was loaded with threat. Billy's arms flailed through it for contact, for something to latch onto for a moment before he heard the hissing get even stronger.

'*Nash! I'll kill you!*' he screamed, trying to roll over.

Pressure came to his shoulders and ribs then. Billy tried to bring his arms up, found the barriers of his imprisonment in the form of two jeaned legs, the smell of rotting-onion seat sweat wafting onto his face.

'Get off me! Get *off* me, *you*-'

When the blade came to his shoulder, Billy screamed. When it came down again he'd managed to pry his right arm up from under the legs and this time the serrations of the edge merely nicked him. He screamed harder that time, not because the pain was starting to sink in or the fear of death was spiraling up now, but because he could see how much he'd let his loved ones down on a stupid risk. He screamed because the hot drips and drops he could feel on his face were the tears his mother was going to cry at his funeral, which he was already dressed for... the tears they would all cry at the cane table with the glass surface as they tried to drink tea in the conservatory that overlooked his back lawn. They were also the tears Raina would cry for months and, years down the road when she was asked about the boy in the picture who looked like Grandpa, she'd cry them all over again.

Billy punched up with that hand, although he already knew the pins and needles from the nerve damage meant it couldn't carry the force he needed. He had it reeled back and ready for a second hit when the hissing noise started again and the blade came down once more.

The tool that was to take his life from his world missed this time, though, because Billy's panic had forced him to jerk his head to the left a little.

The fist from the unknown's other arm slammed into the side of his head then - the soft part. Billy clenched his teeth in protest and felt the blow a thousand times worse, felt the pain of his own nullification amplify as he opened his eyes and saw up through the stars and fizz the same meaninglessness in the dark – and surely that dark was the same as death.

He owed it to four people to survive this.

And he shrieked, hoping that the sound would be strong enough to cancel out the hissing. Billy tried to force the killer forward by raising his knee, picturing its knife tip slamming into the top of the low table nearby instead of into him.

But it was useless. He felt consumed by pain now. He'd managed to free his left arm which now was parrying the knifed or unknifed forearm of his assassin, but the nerve endings in his right side were screaming too loudly to hear his commands.

Suddenly, somehow, he had that bad arm up and clutching the killer's, gaining power in his grip from realizing how his prayer mightn't have put his agony on hold but it had put the *uselessness* of that agony on hold.

He hadn't noticed the new sound over the hissing, though, because the hissing was too intense, too anti-him for Billy to listen past it.

'I'm going to kill you!' he screamed into the figure above and spat, spat back what little spittle he had in his mouth plus the steely taste of his own life fluid.

Spat back the tears that he refused to let be cried over his death.

His stamina gained as he brought his shoulder blades up from the floor. Both his hands were gripping the freezing cold wrists of the attacker, its hissing growing worse, more pained as he shook, shook and shook harder.

Something came to his mind then. A gamble: another risk, but one he hoped wouldn't go out of its way to drop him into his death.

When he felt he had enough of his top half out from under the crotch and the thighs of the hisser, Billy shot forward and up, felt the skin just behind his hairline rupture against the top teeth of the one who sought his destruction.

Quick as a flash, he brought his left hand over to aid the bloody, bleeding, ever-weakening one on his right, and seized the wrist of the killer's knife hand. Billy hurled his own weight over and round so that the knifeman was now pinned beneath him, the spittle of the hissing against Billy's collar wetting through the fine fibers of his white shirt.

The air seemed to get colder to his left even before Billy heard the whooshing sound. As he forced his attacker back down with his shins on the bucking, frantic shoulders, Billy caught the weird light in his side-vision.

He turned for an instant and wanted to scream. Wanted to scream so much that even the force of the unseen attacker's collapse passed by him then.

Eyes...two azure eyes devouring him, threatening, mocking him for the amount of blood he knew he was losing. An ally of the attacker he was trying to subdue beneath him.

'I hate you!' Billy screamed then turned back down to face the silhouette that was his original attacker. He shook the knife hand so hard that it fell to the floor with a plop as he smashed a hating, fearful fist into the face beneath.

Cold liquid squirted into his face. He deduced that he must have just crushed the attacker's nose, that it might be Barry Nash that he had just killed.

The eyes glowed brighter as Billy gibbered, casting a benumbed set of fingers at the floor beside him to find the stilled attacker's knife. He could feel himself running out of strength, losing it through his shoulder like a ruptured oil tanker out in the ocean sea.

When he looked up again, he noticed that the light coming off the eyes of the new threat was powerful enough now to show him the outline of their owner.

Billy saw the hunched form, the stick, the long skirt and the scraggy hair.

He rose to a weak stand, transfixed, hypnotized as an idea came.

His air pistol... *where was it?*

'No!' the old, phlegm-seeded voice crackled. 'You're done with that weapon!'

'Wh....what are.....what are you talking about?!'

The lights flicked on then and Billy had to close his eyes, was forced to hear the laughter begin without his sight.

When he could bear to look, the first thing he saw was the blood on the floor.

And then he saw the old woman at the door, her eyes glowing still but not with their old luminescence.

Billy put his hand to his shoulder again, could feel the stream of warm still coming: not oozing but pumping out in tune with his heartbeat.

On the floor, by a battered, calf-height coffee table, he could see the jeaned legs of his original assailant, its face an unrecognizable morass of blood, mostly obscured by the bent forearm of one of the murderous arms, now also charred and bloody.

From one of the rotten sofa cushions, the knife taunted Billy, double daring him. The knife was the one Billy had seen before – the one he had picked up in the kitchen. He started to feel himself retch. As he looked up and over at the figure in the doorway, he suddenly dreaded that it was a million times worse than an old woman.

His foot tapped against something as he moved back: the handle of his gun.

Blinking, Billy's eyes shot down to the floor, found the gray barrel of his air gun protruding from the bundle of green and brown, mold-stained chair covers.

The figure's laughter was getting stronger. Billy knew he was going to cry. He didn't... he *couldn't* even care that he had been stabbed and was losing precious spurts of blood.

'Iyur Setot!' the owner of the laughter hailed. Billy looked at the face, the home of the two blued-over eyes and felt the paralysis numbing his body.

'You have just killed yourself,' the figure said. 'It is *over!*'

-43-

21ˢᵗ April, San Diego California

Dave Reynolds ran straight for the front door of his parents' house, leaving his car door open. That had been nine times he'd tried calling them, five since he'd left Nathan in the Anline offices, and the results had amounted to many dud voicemail attempts. Voicemail was an iffy commodity now, thanks to Agent 104.

It was starting to rain. A thousand droplets glinted at him from the mosquito screen over the door, made him think of his mother's teary face.

She was going to cry hard when she heard this. Reynolds stabbed the doorbell with his thumb, allowed ten seconds then stepped back to examine the window at the front. His parents were always in at night, but it was too early for bed for those night owls. Billy's music in the basement invariably kept them from heading up until midnight... at the earliest.

Reynolds went right up to the family room windows and found the heavy curtains drawn tight with no lines of light at the top the way he knew they happened.

Nobody in?

But Dad's Cherokee was in front of the garage... That was all wrong, too, because he knew damn well his dad put it away every night. But that left his own wife and Raina. They just had to be in the guest bedroom, waiting and wondering, probably.

He'd tried Helen twice from his car - no reply.

No lights on upstairs. Reynolds broke into a full sprint to get to the back of the house. When his dress shoes smacked the flagstones, he found the first thoughts had verbalized in his head.

Billy. Whatever this was, Billy had caused it. Billy caused everything bad that had ever happened to him, Mom and Dad. Billy was the wildcard in the family, the one that had never and would never fit in.

Predictable, though, he thought. *Give the little shit that much credit.*

Dave Reynolds poked his way around the round table, parasol and white chairs that sat in front of the slide doors and started to rap at the lifeless glass, daring to hope against hope.

The buzz of his cell phone shocked Reynolds' thigh just when he found his lips were starting to curse his brother in whispers. 'Hello?'

'*Fzzzt*-vid! Oh my God!'

'Mom? What is it? What's the matter?'

The crackles in the line were abysmal, *inexcusable* at that shortness of range.

'David, are you - *Fzzzt* -ack door?'

'Y-yeah, Mom. Back door. What the hell's going-'

'*Fzzzt* - there! *Fzzzt* - right there; *Fzzzt* - dad's coming - *Fzzzt* -et the door.'

'Mom, I don't get this; what's wr-'

Light. The net curtains warmed instantly as far as a dull ochre and Reynolds saw the outline of his dad approaching him. 'Dad?! What's going on?'

'Billy's in trouble.' His dad pulled the slide door over the rest of the way. 'Here, get in and get down to his room. Your mother and I have been down there since the police came at six. We... we couldn't reach you!'

Reynolds' guts went down thirty stories in an elevator shaft as he moved through. 'Dad?!'

'He's miss- he's disappeared, Dave. We haven't seen him since the day before last and God knows where he's at now. Helen said he'd told her he was out with friends yesterday. You know what his *"with friends"* means, don't you.'

When Reynolds got to the bottom of the basement stairs, his mom rushed up, crying, and hugged him harder than she'd ever done in the past. 'Oh my Lord, David! We've been so worried! So worr-'

'Easy, Mom. Don't talk now.' Reynolds squeezed her shoulders hard then shot a look at his father. 'What did the cops say?'

'Usual garbage. They know diddly squat when it comes to doing their jobs. Saying he can't be listed missing because Helen saw him yesterday. I mean, Billy could be de-'

'No! Don't go there!' Dave gripped him by the wrist with his free hand and shook his father hard. 'He's *not* dead!'

But Barry Nash was. Dave Reynolds cast the least-wounded portion of his mind back to the last conversation he'd had with Billy.

'The police asked us a lot of questions, David!'

'Nash. Barry Nash, right?'

His mother balked. 'Oh my God! What do you know about him?!'

Reynolds nestled his chin into his mother's crown and hugged her hard. 'I wish I knew. Oh Christ, I wish I knew!'

'David, they - they went away then came back and told us that this friend of Billy's has been *dead* for some time. *Dead!*'

'So the kid lied! Jesus, Dad; when have you known Billy *not* to!'

'No. There's something about this that's different this time. Your brother wouldn't just take off like that for over a day and not say anything to us! Not nowadays with all this going wrong in the world…'

The ring of the kitchen phone caught Dave Reynolds straight through the heart. 'I'll get it!' he said, releasing his mother.

'Hello? *Hello?!!*'

Click

'Jesus!' Reynolds hissed then he hit the magic numbers on the handset and waited. He bit his lip when he found the caller was untraceable. Hanging up, he moved back, hoping, trying not to picture his sorry-assed brother in a payphone on the outskirts of town, or...

What if he'd been tied up and they were torturing him?

'David? Who was that?!'

'Hung up, Mom.'

'For God's sake, trace the number back and call whoever it w-'

'Tried that. No go. *Number could not be traced.*' Reynolds looked back at the phone and thought hard about his own family. 'I better get upstairs.'

'No,' his mother said. 'Not yet. I'm sure Raina's asleep now. Please, David, let's just keep this tight among *us* for now. Helen's already told the Police all she-'

'Mom, you know Billy was lying about this Barry Nash character, don't you?'

'That's what the police told us. But why would Billy lie about something like-'

'He's quit that drugs lark for good; he'd promised us two years ago he had.'

'I don't think it's that, Dad. There's just something about all this that I don't get. Jeez, I've got to go the can.'

Reynolds felt the throb of his cell phone on his thigh as he was urinating. If that was Billy, he would fly off the handle with him, maximum volume…Maximum everything.

Two seconds later, he clenched, stopping his stream and yanked the phone out of his pants. 'Yeah?!'

The silence was clean, crisp, crackleless. It allowed him no time to recall the other phone call on his folks' line… or indeed the quality of *any* phone call of late.

'H-hello? Who is th-'

'Iyur Setot. You're dead.'

-44-
21ˢᵗ April, Bremen, Germany

Becker didn't recognize his surroundings.

Worse, he didn't recognize the reason why he felt so cold now. He groaned in the bed, shifted himself to lie on his side and heard the door open on his other side.

'Carl, you awake?'

Kurt. The digital display read seven forty-five. 'Yeah....but I feel awful.'

His brother came up to his bedside, looked down at him with a hard gaze.

'What's wrong?'

'You remember any of last night, Carl?'

'No. Wait.....that old woman in the parking lot....she...*God.*'

'Easy. You were upset. You passed out you were so stressed.'

Carl Becker shot bolt upright, grabbing his brother by the sleeve of his work parka jacket. 'Don't say that, Kurt! I saw that old bitch! The same one who did that to Dad... I - I *saw* her out there, outside this block, *staring right at me!*

Kurt bowed his head. 'Carl, I'm sorry, but I didn't see that. *You* only did bec-'

'Because *what*?! You think I'm lying or I'm crazy then?'

Kurt shook his head so hard a shock of gelled back fringe swung down into his eye as his brother sighed.

'Kurt - do you think if it'd been just an old woman passing in the street...you think I would've *leapt down your stairs* then run the hell outside into that lot beside here?!'

'I don't.... I don't know what to make of this! I mean, one second you're in here trying to calm me down, saying we should head out for beer... Then you fly off the handle without warning!'

'Look, she was down there, looking right up at me with a curse in her eyes like she'd been listening to everything we'd said in here!'

'That's nuts, Carl.'

'You reckon? In all the years we've known each other, have you *ever* seen me erupt like that?'

'Dad. Dad being put in hospital did that to you, Carl. We've had a nasty-'

'*Shock?* Is that it?! Is *that* what you think made me see her?!'

'Don't yell at me! Please...you saw what state I was in last night. With Dad the way he is and you out there last night, I don't need this!'

Becker let go of Kurt's retracting sleeve and folded his arms.

'Okay, let's say she was staring up at you from the street, Carl. How could you tell it was her if you've never even seen her in your life before?'

'Because of the look in her eyes! That look was just *loaded with hatred*, like she was cursing me for seeing her down there...and her hair; that white hair all over her! Like no other kind of hair I've ever seen... Like a witch!'

'But how would she know where I lived if she-'

'Because she hates us, Kurt. She has something against our family. I know it sounds crazy but after seeing that goddamn ship, I'm open to believing *anything* now!'

'Jesus...it just doesn't scan, I mean-'

'Does Dad - fit and all as we both knew he was - does him having a stroke fucking scan at all?!'

'Uhm...Listen, I'm gonna call in sick... I just can't take this...'

'Don't. Please; go in as usual. Don't let this-'

Kurt sighed, rubbing his eyes. 'Al...Alright then. But I'll try to get out early. Sure you'll be okay here today?'

'I'll be alright, Kurt. Thanks for putting me up.'

'You going to visit Dad later?'

'Yeah. I better. When's the operation scheduled for?'

'Twenty-seventh.'

Becker eased back on the pillow, noticed the pain in his shoulders. 'Kurt? What exactly happened to me last night?'

'You passed out in the lot of the Mittendorf apartments next door.'

'Who found me? You?'

'Yeah, I got you. Just in time, too. We were lucky. The guy who has the pickup truck you took that wrench out of...'

'What...what about him?'

'Called the Polizei. I was at the top of the alleyway when I heard the clunk of the spanner and you shrieking. Pulled you right out of there; got you in barely a minute before the car came and the cops started poking about out there. Lucky the guy who called didn't know me, but Christ, that was close.

'And you were cold, Carl. From the feel of your skin when I was carrying you, I thought you'd gone into major shock until I got you on the sofa, checked you over.' Kurt sounded worried as he said that, his earlier anger conquered.

'Hey; only one Becker in hospital at a time. Those are the rules.'

'What's happening to us, Carl?'

'Beats me; it really does. Blame it all on the world - I bet everybody else does. That was a witch down there... I know it was...'

The silence was delicate until Kurt shrugged. 'Hey, I was *this* close from getting an ambulance round here. Don't do that again, okay?'

'I'll try. You just get on to work, Kurt. Put this out of your mind.'

'Well, try real hard. Looks like I'm the strong man of the family right now.'

'See you later, Kurt. Take care out there.'

Becker's brother turned at the doorway and fixed him with a cautious look. 'I've got the keys to Dad's boat if you feel the need to go out on the water, get some air.'

'Thanks, Kurt, but I'll take a pass on that.'

'You sure?'

'Sure I'm sure. Dry land for me for a long time to come.'

'Okay, well they're on the coffee table. See you around six tonight, then. I'll try for earlier though.'

Carl Becker left the hospital at eleven o'clock with a bad taste in his mouth. Seeing the desolation in his mother had put that there, trying to talk it out of her.

He got off the bus at his parents' waterside house, stuck his hand in his pocket. He'd taken the boathouse keys after all and was now trying to fight the regret in his heart.

Yeah, he hated the water, but he had to get out on it, face his fear.

Face it and then destroy it.

His father's boat had an ancient Yamaha outboard. After undoing the gate, he stepped into it, checked the fuel level then pulled the ripcord.

The sea was calm, so unlike his feelings. As he made his way out onto it, he thought how wrong this had all gone for him. That old woman; so she was trying to kill him *slowly*. But why?

He was also somehow certain that she couldn't leave land, that he'd be safe out here.

He stopped dead in the water once he saw he was nearing the last set of buoys and stood, gazing at the expanse around him.

How could Kurt bear to live amid the menace of that scenery day in, day out?

But Kurt was different from him in so many respects. Where Kurt loved the wide expanses of water, he couldn't stand them – his own love for the sea needing to be satisfied by communing with the underwater kingdom. Kurt would never dive. Kurt, his only sibling now.

There'd been another – Maria… But Maria had died slowly, painfully of leukemia when he was just ten years old and she seven. Her red tresses had always been wavy – just like the sea. She would have grown to be a water lover, too.

The shine coming off the darkness in the water taunted Becker as he stood staring at it, threatening to remind him of the same dark gleam that had shone off his sister's coffin that day, all those years back.

Becker kept standing in his semi-trance for close to a minute before he saw the glow in a stretch of sea, just a hundred yards from him.

Was that a buoy? Same color...but brighter, almost incandescent ...fiery.

Things can't burn underwater, idiot.

A fish...maybe it was a dead sunfish. They happened in these waters.

Becker took the outboard, started it up and steered for the anomaly, his eyes peeled, drinking up every detail of the approaching, enlarging glow.

No; this was unnatural. Nothing looked like that....not in the water.

Fifty feet ... forty ... thirty. He got the boat hook at his feet ready to tug.

The smell was beginning to hit him now - not the saltiness or the stench of seaweed he had been expecting, but something.....

He couldn't place it. The smell was more like a total absence of the sea air he'd grown up with in his early life. This pocket of it was too noticeable after so much time out on the water today.

Becker killed the engine at fifteen feet, found he had to squint to see the object. It wasn't round at all - more rectangular, but with rounded corners.

He let his boat drift on residual for a few feet more then extended his windcheatered arms all the way with the boat hook, prodding the thing with its tip.

It was hard and plasticky. He'd heard the tapping sound. Now he was starting to think it might be a parcel — something wrapped in waxed paper that had just fallen in from a passing boat.

The noise from his second prod told him it wasn't saturated. He caught the underside with his hook, found a groove on the surface and pulled it in.

When he had it on the deck, he kicked it first, only then realizing the danger.

No. Explosives don't look like that. Even dynamite has to be lit first, anyway.

And nitroglycerin would have detonated already, you fool.

His fingertips touched the surface and Becker allowed himself a half-smile. It *was* waxed parcel paper. He tore at the corners until he was able to rip back a huge triangle of it.

White inside. He touched it...Styrofoam. Ripping the rest of the paper off, he examined the interior and felt a chill come to his innards.

A Styrofoam case, taped with insulation adhesive.

Someone had intended this to float...someone had intended it to be *found.*

By him.

No. Don't think like that. The witch couldn't have done this...surely?

Becker set the package on the bow seat plank and hunted for his father's tool kit. When he had the Swiss Army knife he pulled out the longer blade and dug into the white tape at the join that ran all the way around the middle of the parcel's depth.

His fingers froze when he heard the tinny, hollow sound come a second after he'd cut his way round.

Could still be a bomb. You were meant to find this, remember?

Becker raised the foam box to his ear and shook it gently.

Nothing rattling… It might be plastique, though.

You found this out in the middle of nowhere, Becker… Too random for that.

But weren't you meant to find it?

Don't be stupid! Life doesn't happen that way… It can't.

Then last night shouldn't have happened at all, yes?

Becker gave an inner scream to make his mind stop, but it was too late. He had pulled the top casing off and chucked it.

'God Almighty,' he whispered then dug his fingers in among the bunched cellophane wrapping that covered...

Photos. Thick, ancient-looking photographs. He sat by the outboard and started to undo the bag. When he reached inside, he found there was only one card, so thick and its sides and edges so frayed it had separated into gills so it had looked like there were more in there.

Becker lifted the card out and turned it right-side up.

What....who.....where was that?

A set of red shacks lying at the base of a huge sandstone hill. The people in there were mostly children, looking up and away to the left side, some pointing rifles to the air, wholly indifferent to the photographer. The top right corner was strewn with white, stringy fibers.

Becker touched the surface of the photo, expecting to feel the gooey waterlogged gloss where the finish had reacted.

It was as dry as a bone, like it had been pre-wetted then allowed to dry in there. He turned the card over to the other face, ran his fingertips over it, found it curiously rough, like those ancient photos he'd seen in a collection back in America, just before his college days.

Junk, he thought. *Got enough to think about without picking up other people's shit out of the sea.* Shaking a little, Becker took one last look at the photo then chucked it overboard with its package. He reached into his pocket, took out the tin of beans he'd got on the way to the hospital and pulled up the tab.

He was just three plastic fork loads into it when he felt the shaking again. He put the can down, put his hands on his thighs.

It happened again, only this time he was sure it wasn't him. He was *sure* he had seen the join in the boards between his feet move a little in relation to them.

Becker stood up, surveyed the water around the edges of his father's boat.

It was calm, murky, quiet, dead: no boats, ships, barges or skiffs, except for a fishing trawler far, far away and a stationary commercial goliath far round in the waters just off the business district.

This was Bremen, a busy port town. Why the lack of water life today?

But your folks live away up around the river mouth, Becker. You've come a long way out on the water today.

'Lordy!' Becker cried when the force knocked him forward. When he got up from the bow end he felt the third, fourth and fifth spasms in the water beneath.

He raced for the outboard cord, tugged it and took the lever in shaking hands. The boat surged forward... painfully.

What the hell was that under him? Nothing that big ever swam round here, unless... Maybe it was a basking shark.

Becker pulled the throttle all the way, stopped and relented a little only when he heard the bearings strain in the motor.

Not enough oil. God…what would he do if…

Forget that, you're okay - the thrusting has stopped. You'll make it okay.

He glowered back at the water, where the white foam lids were bobbing now, where he'd discarded the photograph that hadn't looked like a photograph.

Nothing. He could not see even one ripple there, over a hundred feet away and the water had smoothed over quickly in his wake. His eyes narrowed, squeezing every bit of light and surface glare from the water, but still found nothing.

Becker traced the water back to his engine, his gaze penetrating as deeply as the white-edged murk would permit.

Still nothing… Nothing but the constant, eternal purple-black blanket of void.

Turning back, he saw the second set of buoys he'd passed on his way out. He let the throttle handle back a little so he was at fifteen knots or so.

He had to get back. It was no good. He'd tried coming out here today to exorcize a little of the pain, to meet face to face with that other great devil inside him – his sudden disenchantment with water.

And he had failed.

Becker kept on at that speed until he saw the shore buoys getting level with his nose. He felt bad now, not because of the water but because he knew he'd lost against it… how he'd go on feeling that way no matter what happened from here on out.

No, you don't do that to me! he thought when he saw the figure on the shore a few seconds later. It was a figure with a white, wiry mane and dressed in a black maxi frock.

His blood gelled right then. He tried to stand up, tried to think about looking about in the storage locker in the bow's compartments when the shaking came back harder: much, much harder than before.

He had the grip of the flare gun in his palm, loaded and ready when he saw the huge strand of flotsam-entangled seaweed ensnaring the tank on the outboard.

He dived for the throttle lever just as the tilt came and the bow raised up behind him. He dropped the flare gun. Panicking, he reached for the ripcord, burning his palm against the fibers as his grip slipped.

Thrusting back, Becker dug his heel into the mess of weed at the stern. The water was sluicing over the lip and the cleats. If it was a basking shark or a whale joined up to that and his foot got snagged in the kelp, it would be over for him.

Kddammm.....Kddammm. He could feel the old bitch on the shore's laughter biting into his chest… her guffaws at his fate if he was to be dragged under now by something so large as a behemoth of the Deep.

'*Nnnooooo!*'

He let the ripcord travel back into the hole all the way before he yanked again.

The boat was rocking hard again but laterally this time. Becker felt the malice under the boards, could sense the smile of the hag on the shore…the lips dampening with relish.

Not daring to look at her, he reached down with his left hand, seized the flare gun and yanked the ripcord a third time.

The engine engaged, held for a few revolutions then sputtered dead.

Becker waited, waltzing his feet on the hull boards to counterweigh the jerks.

In the tiny part of his mind that was still unfrenzied, he realized that the shock waves were too rhythmical to be an animal under there. He could feel the *intent* of his unseen assailant coming up into his shoe soles.

'*Why me?!*' he screamed to both sides of the boat.

Bubbles. Tiny, white bubbles were billowing up, breaking the surface in droves.

Becker turned to look at the shore then scanned for other vessels….for help.

The flare gun's grip was oily in his hand now.

There was nobody about. A few cars heading toward Bremen on the coastal 'B' road glinted their paintwork dimly to his eyes.

But that would be futile: by the time they saw him, they-

Becker lurched to his left, away from shore and plunged into the water, shrieking. The hideousness of the cold and the sliminess of the murk made him open his mouth before he resurfaced.

The taste of the water was like well-rotted eggs.

He was trying to pull himself back up over the side when he felt the pressure on his ankle…taking bone and ball joint like a vice. His heart skipped several times as he strained to look down at it.

In the dimness, he saw his jeaned leg vanish into murk just below the knee and, below that, what could only be white fingers.

Screaming, he kicked once, twice with that leg before he back-swiped with the other, a stuttered prayer trying to form on his lips.

His arms were jerking on the side of the boat. He had his elbows on the rim, trying with every ounce to raise his torso above their level.

The grip on his ankle released when he back-kicked a third time.

Out! Get out of there!

Becker had his ribs against the rim, his affected leg fully out when he felt the grip on his other ankle.

'No! No! No! Leave me*! Leeeeeave meee!*'

It yanked him back. Becker saw the boat begin to dip, threatening to capsize.

If it did, he knew he'd be done for. He thrashed his leg in the water, not looking...not being *able to* look down at it and its jailor.

The rim gouged his ribs as he slid back toward the water. No sooner had his other leg fallen back in when he felt the fingers close round it at the calf.

His own fingers were now glued to the flare gun. He thought about trying it. Five seconds, maybe less passed before the hands from below jerked hard enough to pull him in all the way, his weapon dropped, useless.

Becker held his breath, but his head didn't go under. From the surface, he was able to see the white bones of the hands down there between the white splashes he was making as he flailed his arms.

They were jerking downward on him again. For those few moments he had before he went under fully, Becker saw the uselessness of it all, saw the uselessness of his purpose in having come out there today, saw the pointlessness in his drowning.

Underwater, he reached down and started punching at where his legs were. Once, he felt his numbing knuckles strike the double-bones of the skeletal arm.

He kept swiping that way for a few seconds.

The vices on his legs were holding, the one on his left squeezing him tighter the harder he lashed, wrenching a prayer to a higher power out of his soul.

Pins and needles were starting to come to his brain. Becker opened his eyes and saw the huge bubbles of life air that were escaping back up to a world he knew he would not be returning to.

Every muscle in him was thrashing, contorting or distorting under his chilled skin.

Then, with one kick, he saw the whiteness lift off from his calf.

Becker raised his leg high up behind him: so high his tennis shoe hit the hull. He reached for the remaining hand and pried up on its digits.

I've got you! an unaffected part of his brain rejoiced for him. *Got You!*

Through the stinging in his eyes, he saw the digits release all of a sudden. Becker swung his arms back up to make a breaststroke and kicked for his life.

A death's head came face to face with him at the surface, opened its mouth, spitting saltwater into his face. Becker saw the seaweed in its eye orbit glisten like it was its blood.

Get Out! Get Out!

Gibbering, he turned for the side of the boat and thrust upward with the remainder of his might, coughing seawater, phlegm and his spent hope into it.

His elbows ached but they were working. Becker put every last bit of himself into levering himself over on them, pushing through the suffocating mask of fear.

When he heard his foot slap against the floorboards, the adrenalin surged even harder all through his body.

The flare gun was lying away in at the port side.

No! No - restart the engine first!

Becker's fingers closed round the ripcord and tugged. It came halfway out before his hand slipped from all the slime on its surface and he tumbled back toward the bow, dazed.

When he got up again, he caught the skulls and the bare ribcages in his side-vision…a mini-sea of boned bodies clustered about his boat, ready to board.

Before he could tell himself what to do, he had the cord back in his hands.

The shaking was starting again, only now it was coming from the starboard side only.

One jerk, two jerks, three jerks on the ripcord and the starter didn't engage.

Becker turned, caught the arm of the nearest skeleton reaching in at the seat plank of the bow. He crouched, took up the boat hook, raised it high in the air then smashed it into the grayed shoulder blade.

The skeleton turned, hissed at him, hissed at its comrade to leap into the boat.

Becker brought the hook down a second time. He caught the arm just above the elbow, shattered it into a dozen shards and the skeleton fell back.

Its comrade had nearly got fully into the boat. Becker turned with the hook, dug the shaft just below the metal into its cheekbone. It plummeted through the air behind it.

Becker dropped his weapon when he stood erect and looked down at the water. Half-a-dozen, perhaps eight more human skeletons were rising from the murk.

Start the engine!

He pulled once, feeling the vibrations on his right, hearing the sickening *clack clack* sound going with it. Without turning, he pulled a second time and thought of his father, how he could still keep him alive by not dying himself now.

The *clack-clack*ing was getting louder. He turned partway, kicked one of the three new skeletons that had made it into his boat with all the might he'd recovered, sending its skull flying from the neck like an oversized golf ball from a tee.

The third ripcord pull was his hardest, so hard that Becker overbalanced, landed bang beside one of the monstrosities.

'Get out! Get out of my boat! *Get out of my damn boat!*' he yelled as he unclasped its fingers from his throat. His damaged mind was trying to console that this should be easier to do in the air than the water...but the way the kelp-weighted skeleton was lying crossways on top of him forced Becker to feel that this was the doom to end all doom.

He hadn't heard the thudding of the engine at first. Becker had to mash the skull of his new assailant against the boards before he was able to stand, run at a crouch for the lever of the Yamaha.

The skeleton nearest it latched onto his ankle just as he twisted the throttle, tearing its upper half away from its lower as the boat burst forward a precious few yards before…

The dragging started underneath the boat and Becker's heart sank lower still. He kicked the head of another grasping skeleton and sent it back into the water, excluding its hand.

As if triggered by that, the last skeleton on the rim suddenly lurched forward, sank its teeth into the jean fibers at his thigh. Becker punched its cheekbone, yelled at the gash that made in his knuckles then reached down for the boat hook.

As he rammed the point through its face, he felt the tug at the other end of the shaft, turned round and found another two sets of arms and heads coming up from the other side.

No! he prayed; *no! Don't let it end like this! I'll never go back in the water!!!*

The pole started jerking violently back and forth. Becker saw his chance and let go. The skeletons on his left fell forward from the boat rim, spearing one of their number on the starboard side.

Now! Do it now!

Becker's foot contacted the tailbone of the nearest skeleton, sending it hurtling into the back of its companion and the duo shot overboard on the other side.

He seized the outboard lever and pulled for full power. He could feel the engine expend its best effort, could nearly enjoy the scraping of the bones under the keel…

Scraping so hard it sounded like they were burrowing into the hull. Wheeling round, he saw the skull emerge from behind the outboard, its arms locking around the shaft that fed the blades.

*My God…*they're trying to kill the propeller.

Becker looked for his hook, found it floating in the slick three, four boat lengths away, ignorant of their - his - cause.

The skull behind the Yamaha began to chatter its teeth as Becker lifted his flare gun from the boards. When he moved back to the stern, he could hear them all at it, was able to see a dozen death's heads now up and risen at shoulder height in the murk, ready to board him.

'Go, *you bastards!*' he shouted, aimed at the group congregated at the back near their leader then fired.

The flare seared into the core of a skeleton in the second row from his boat. Becker saw that before the extreme heat and light forced him to fall back.

From the boards, he watched the volley of bone fragments fly past... he heard the faint screams of their owners ebb after the last splinters fell back into the drink.

Becker's eyes stang when he shot back up, grabbed hold of the outboard lever and tugged it forward full throttle.

He made it back to his parents' boathouse a little over ten minutes later. He felt for the bunch of keys in his jeans pocket, located them through a mess of slime and spoiled Euro bills.

As he climbed out of the boat, battered and benumbed, gazing back out at the tiny stretch of sea for signs of movement, Becker could just feel his eyes oozing from the exertion.

He had to get to a phone. Army...cops...he wasn't sure which. *Jesus Christ!'*

He was at the door of the boathouse when a thought hit him. He froze, his jaw dropping. The hag. He'd forgotten all about her. She had *puppeteered* this.

She's old - can't travel too far. Where was she standing?

She was on the shoreline, about a mile to the west of him, where the grass ran straight over the rocks... no sand dunes or beach.

Quick! You can get her if you race out now.

Becker willed his hand to turn the doorknob, but the blood in his arm had frozen.

From where he stood with his head turned, frozen like that, he could see something in the boat, about halfway down lying beside the discharged, blackened nozzle of the flare pistol.

A cap - not peaked like a skipper's, but ribboned at the back, like a beret - an ordinary seaman's, from a bygone age.

Becker's eyes were now as frozen as the rest of his body. They told him the cap bore the name 'SS BERNICE'.

Another dead ship.

'Sweet Jesus. *No.'*

-45-
21ˢᵗ April, Western Siberia, Loyalist Zone

Olentiev landed ahead of the other Fulcrums on the airstrip. Behind him, Gorov was silent and had been that way all the way home.

Olentiev disengaged the canopy, pushed up on it and looked down at the field, trying to take his mind past the fizz of anguish and wonder why the men rushing for his plane weren't bringing a ladder.

For a moment, he thought how merciful the Afterlife would be compared to this. That had been Askenskaya and an ancient crone in that cockpit back there.

The first couple of privates to reach him stopped well shy of him, pointed their AK-74s upward, barking.

'Under arrest?!' he gasped. "What have I done, though?"

How could he be *under arrest*? Arrest in the Russian military entailed detention in a cement chickenhouse and a single court martial appearance to answer for *crimes*.

The ladder came a minute later. Olentiev looked behind him, counted the MiGs that had landed: eight.

Askenskaya was still airborne.

'Get down out of there!' another soldier he couldn't recognize grunted.

'Gorov... *Gorov!*' Olentiev shouted when he reached away in behind him to shake his co-pilot.

'Never mind him!' an approaching sergeant yelled. 'Get out, *now!*'

Olentiev swung his legs out and onto the ladder rungs. Now, in the shinier parts of his fuselage, he could see every wrinkle in his face. The terror of what he'd seen was coursing through him like electric current. When his feet hit the asphalt and he raised his arms, he saw the same menace in the faces before him as in what he'd seen up there, many kilometers back now.

'What's going on?' the pilot of the plane behind him asked.

'Never mind, you!' the sergeant growled then: 'Major Olentiev, you're under arrest for the subversion of a government mission.'

'But you heard our transmissions up there!'

The privates nearest him jerked their rifles, motioned him to move forward.

Olentiev walked past five buildings before he saw the detention hut – a metal shack - by the outhouses. He turned, found the sergeant a few paces behind him.

'Please, I don't understand what's going on!'

'Marshal Bucharin will be speaking with you shortly,' the sergeant said. 'Until then, find yourself a seat in your new quarters.'

One of the privates pulled back the bolt, opened the door on a four meter by four meter dirt floor, a steel chair and a galvanized pail.

Olentiev waited on that chair until he saw the sky darken between the corrugated iron slats in the window. Then he began pacing, wishing to death he had to a smoke to help him think now.

Askenskaya. No, he wasn't insane: that *had been* Askenskaya. Before his plane had vanished into ether and its presence from the radar, Olentiev had seen the markings above his helmet - the badly chafed insignia, the markings on the shoulder.

That had been Askenskaya.

But could he tell that to Bucharin? Bucharin who would be sending guards at any moment now to come, yank him out of there and fix him for interrogation.

Or worse...

Had he been suspected of mission subversion by neglect or deliberate sabotage?

Treason...military treason was still firing-squads, after abrupt, farcical trials.

Olentiev moved back to his seat and collapsed onto it. What were they going on to trump up these charges? The front man had maintained base contact until the static had become too harsh...surely Bucharin knew about the old woman and the children with the semi-automatics. Surely he'd found out about the exploding ground surface and the destruction of some of their strike force?

Bucharin had to have known by now. The static had not been complete, not like over Lake Baykal.

Olentiev replayed his memory, hoping that something might start to make sense. But this time he just couldn't understand it. He had rolled the channel selector all the way round to base frequency before he had sent the Mayday.

But they hadn't responded. It didn't matter; hadn't he kept doing that all the way back? Except for those bad moments when he'd seen...

He buried his face in his hands, found he could see his family through his eyelids, their faces sullen, their heads hung low.

Daddy was a traitor, his son and his daughter would have drummed into them. He could imagine the firing squad's bullets tearing through his body, destroying his family.

It was getting cold now. His flight suit was freezing. He hadn't realized how much he'd sweated until he moved his feet in the silence and felt the squelching in his boots.

There was just a little bit of shadowed floor left against the wall when he opened his eyes. He leant towards it, pressed his palm against the grit-sullied paint.

Cold. *You're cold when you're dead. Blackness - the blackness of the Great Atheistic Afterlife they taught you about in your little country school will be absolutely freezing.*

Olentiev looked down at the dirt between his feet. If he had a stick and enough time, he'd draw a map. His right foot was here and his left could be Britain or America.

No. Don't hope; hope will only make it hurt all the more now.

Noise. A door grating....a set of footsteps....no, two.

'Alright, Major; Marshal Bucharin will hear you now,' said the guard. 'Come.'

'Have a seat, Olentiev,' Bucharin said when Olentiev entered the portacabin. 'You can leave us,' he said to the privates.

'Marshal, please,' Olentiev opened. 'I don't understand any of this. Why is this happening? I did nothing wrong!'

'Cognac, Major?' Bucharin's smile was wolf like.

'No, thanks.'

'You were wondering about this misfortune that has befallen you and us, no?'

'You mean the way the mission had to be aborted, sir?'

'Aborted! Why, Olentiev, I'm sure you're unused to hearing that word.'

'But the transmissions you received here...they would have told you what-'

'No.'

'I'm also talking about *my* transmissions here! You heard them. I know you d-'

'Unfortunately, Commander Kukolev's messages terminated after the explosions began.'

'Then you know of the rebel strike force on the ground, sir?!'

'Yes. We also know that the numbers described to us failed to match the intelligence we briefed you people with. Even so, don't you see your fault here, Olentiev? When you broke off and turned tail, your seniority placed *you* in full, acting command.'

'What are you saying here, Marshal? I was supposed to lead the remainder of the force further into rebel airspace?'

Bucharin clicked his fingers. 'Correct,' he said. 'Your force stumbled upon a group of rebels that should not have been there.'

'Did Kukolev tell you about the bodies we saw lying in those encampments?'

'What bodies, Olentiev?'

'Siberian rebels. I counted about twenty or so lying about their foxholes, stone dead. By the looks of it, I wouldn't say they were hit by rockets.'

'And how might you account for their deaths?'

'Gunfire, I would think. If I'd had time to evaluate it properly, I'd end up believing that our own infantry might have been responsible.'

Bucharin frowned. 'Impossible. You knew our troops were miles from there.'

'Irregulars then. Rival, anti-independence group might have done it.'

Bucharin leant forward. 'We don't have friends here, Olentiev. But what interests me is the group you encountered after these alleged bodies of yours. If indeed a force friendly to ours had cleaned out the threat, why then were there hostiles left over? Why, Olentiev, would an old peasant woman and children attack MiGs?'

'They did anyway, sir. You can check the undercarriages for evidence. Our attackers weren't even wearing protective radsuits… no gear!'

'The only evidence I'm interested in here is how a force that small would have had super-high explosive capabilities. A suicide detonation, obviously.'

'No. It happened *after* we rocketed them, Marshal.'

'So, a land surface the size of this base and more just *exploded*, did it?'

'Yes. I can't explain how. Some kind of chain reaction. Massive fires.'

'Olentiev, we're talking about a wasteland: arid soils. There is no way, short of underground hi-ex dumps that that could happen. And let me assure you that these vermin are not that sophisticated, Olentiev.'

Olentiev could see his future disintegrating, melting in Bucharin's pupils. 'If you don't believe me, sir, do a recon run of the area and let me fly in it. If there's no trace of a massive fire, you can shoot me on the spot.'

'We already have arranged a reconnaissance, Olentiev. Soon there will be a complete examination of the rebel outpost. But the thing that concerns me is that your judgment was swayed by the losses you sustained. Some of our planes were destroyed outright by the detonations. Am I correct?'

Olentiev nodded, found a little piece of hope shimmering in Bucharin's corpse-like eyes.

'Which left you as one of nine, still under the command of Kukolev. Now, Kukolev – still alive and in command at that point, let me assure you - was instructed not to return to base until a full sweep of the region had been conducted. I assume he passed that message on to you and the other pilots, some of whom, I should warn you, have been interviewed.'

Olentiev balked. 'Kukolev never passed that on, Marshal. His plane was destroyed… maybe even at the strike site.'

'And yet the others, Olentiev - men with solid service records - told me he did, some of them voicing that grievance as they flew back under your command.'

'But the fact that Kukolev was leading us out of there should tell you that-'

'We deduced that Kukolev's Fulcrum was too damaged to take the lead and no, Major, he didn't crash or explode at the strike site or just a few kilos away. Our radar showed his path as having made it as far as the Khurgus border... presumably giving chase to you for attempted desertion.'

Olentiev took the pain in his chest with a poorly silenced whine.

'Try to see it from our point of view, Major. Your front man – the commander at the time - issues a direct order under fire... and there are not sufficient communications difficulties to constitute despondence on your or any of the others' parts. Your plane was equipped to handle a larger rebel force further in and, in spite of the mishap at that first, unmarked outpost, that was the *directive*. Please stop me talking when you think it's appropriate, Major; I don't want to bring up "cowardice", unless I am backed into it.'

Olentiev's eyes fell to the bottom of the desk. He saw the three power leads going up from the floor: one for the desk lamp, one for comms and one for Bucharin's computer, whose voice recorder was soaking all of this up.

He couldn't tell about Askenskaya. Did he even dare considering it anymore?

'Nine blips on the radar, Major. You were at the lead, burning back here. Now, I have to contact General Kvashnin in Moscow in less than twenty minutes from now. I want you to tell me what I'm to tell him.' Bucharin pulled a cigarillo from the box behind his lamp, lit it and sat back, eyes on the far wall. 'And yet you panicked your squad with words of a rogue flier.'

Olentiev's heart was pounding now. The reconnaissance planes would find Kukolev's wreckage way back there - the truth could be sustained, his name cleared of this travesty. Maybe if he was to play Bucharin at his own game for the moment, it might work out best for him.

'Very well, Marshal; there were *nine* blips on your radar, but the ninth - the one who came in from the back whom...whom you took to be Kukolev - wasn't.' Olentiev saw the eyes widening, the cigarillo dipping in unborn mockery.

'That was not Kukolev, sir. On all my honor, I *know* it was not him. And I can prove it.'

-46-

21ˢᵗ April, San Diego, California

'The densitometer confirms it, Rick. This image is not a photograph,' Kelso the film tech told Coleman as he pointed over at the bench.

'Makes sense as far as the way it looks,' Coleman replied. 'But if not a photo then *what* exactly?'

'That's something we have to work on. It looks like a photo in that it's a print of light on paper, but the emulsions aren't there... wrong chemicals entirely.'

Coleman nodded. 'Do you think there's a chance it *had been* a photo but got tampered with so badly that we can't-'

'That was *never* a true photograph, Rick. Nothing – not even any silver-halide content anywhere.'

'Then how might you go about explaining it?'

Kelso frowned. 'To be honest, I can't. For an hour I've been trying to strip that thing through its layers, work back the color-separation process and I couldn't find either. As far as I can tell, it's just an extremely thin layer of gelatin overlying a single layer where the light has been recorded.'

'But doesn't color film need three layers?'

'Yeah: cyan, magenta, yellow. But here, there's just a single strip minus halides, minus anything that a conventional emulsion would have.'

'A lot of the colors in that picture look really weird, Bob.'

Kelso nodded. 'Yeah, I know. Never seen anything like it, to tell you the truth. It's as if whoever came up with that print, I dunno, just *willed* an image onto the card.'

Coleman started scratching his head. 'That mark on it; what you think made-'

'That doesn't seem to be a break in the film itself.'

'Looking at it, though, would you say it was?'

239

'Rick, we're talking about a discoloration that was recorded into the image.'

'So how come when I first saw it, the black mark wasn't there?'

Kelso's frown rejuvenated. 'It *must* have been. That's under the gel film.'

'It *wasn't*, Bob. When I got that, there was no black "burn" mark or anything on it like that. And now it looks like we've got another front to cover on this case.'

'Rick, have you ever heard of remote viewing?'

'Sure, lotsa times. *In Search of* with Mr. Spock; what about it?'

'It's just that this is so far beyond my expertise...I mean, I been in film for fifteen years. I analyzed suspect residues on bogus images, hoaxes, the lot, but this...'

Coleman bit his lip. Sure, Kelso knew about the war they were waging, but that didn't include Ganz. No, he wouldn't want to enlist Kelso's help or advice outside of imaging topics. 'You'd have to call it paranormal?'

Kelso nodded, began twiddling his moustache hairs. 'Look, I know you're whacked out, but I think you'd better come over and see this.'

'See what?' Coleman asked as he followed him into the imaging lab darkroom.

'I only noticed it a couple of minutes before you came down here.' Kelso lifted the card onto the scope plate, wiggled his red-tinted finger at Coleman.

'Yes. Yes, it's a little bigger now in the longitudinal diameter. See this?'

Coleman pressed his eyes against the scope, took a few seconds to find the dark spot among the black heads of the African soccer delegates.

'Jesus...Christ; it's...' he whispered, stopping just in time.

'That there's a miniaturized face of a young Caucasian man fused into the print beneath the veneer isn't the thing that disturbs me the most about this picture, though. You have to look at the *lighting*. That's supposed to be natural light coming out on an overcast day and yet just look at how different everybody in here is being illuminated. But then that would be the case only if it had been a *real* photograph we were dealing with here.'

'I can't buy this,' Coleman issued. 'No, this goes too far.'

'Rick, what we have here has to be a hoax. I know that, you know that, every tech I know and would ever read would say that. But we don't have the stuff to work this back from.'

'Yet.'

'If somebody made this in some darkroom then they'd have had to know splicing, exposing and overlaying techniques that just don't happen in photography.'

'But couldn't they try and still come up with something like that? With the right resources, some joker somewhere goes way in over his head with progressive photoplay...maybe gets the black dot to appear when it hits a certain temperature?'

Kelso hit a switch on the control bar of the image amp, pulled some tweezers from a tray by it. 'Let's just put this into an equation,' he said as he scraped some fuzz from the top right corner of the photo. 'Say it's a, I dunno, an eleven *million*, eleven thousand and eleven times negative somebody used in a sentence of speech. You know: "I ain't never done nothing never"... and we're being left to run a tally and see if the sonofabitch means "yes" or "no". Are you with me?'

Coleman watched a minute tuft of card fuzz slip from the tweezer head and spiral into a test-tube. 'But the properties involved are finite, right?'

'Yes,' Kelso answered. 'But, unluckily for us, there are a few more wildcards stuck in this mess. Now, working for you guys has opened up a lot of weird stuff for my eyes, but this...this is-'

'This shouldn't be happening is what you're saying; hoax or not.'

Kelso raised the test-tube to the red-bulbed ceiling, shook it about then stoppered the top. 'Rick, you see the card in it? Do you know how long it's been since anyone has been using this material to make a photograph?'

Coleman screwed up his face. 'That was the first thing I noticed about it. I just thought it was card that'd got really wet.'

'No; at least, I wouldn't say so. Listen, we don't know enough just yet but when I get this back fr-'

'What do you think, but? Just tell me off the top of your head what-'

'No, Rick; it's too way out. No way on Earth anyone could do this.'

'Try me.'

'Then I say it's a Daguerreotype-era or just after material. We're talking the 1840s or 1850s here. But d'you have any idea how hard, how all-out *impossible* a trick that would be?'

'Yeah. Unless someone took the top half - the picture half of the image and grafted it onto the card.'

'Not that simple. I've analyzed the depth of the veneer and it just doesn't scan. Rick, call me crazy but a lot of that picture is actually fused on the card itself. That's not transposition or anything at work on there. It's just nuts.'

'Then that means the world's favorite sport is about to take a big kick.'

'How'd you mean?'

'Soccer. That's the Friendship Cup delegation these terrorists are after now.'

-47-
<u>21st April, Bremen, Germany</u>

Becker winced when the black jet of instant coffee scalded his tonsils. Pain was good, he thought; at least pain was real. The cap was in his hands now as he leaned against the cherry wood sideboard in his parents' house. He was wearing his father's clothes... He was dry but still shivering.

He examined the Luger pistol in his right hand. The peak of the scrunched up cap covered the rustiness of the bolt. He pulled it up then ran his fingers over the top section of his grandfather's gun. His father had kept it in the liquor cabinet, under the radar of the law.

The ammunition clip had been in there since the spring of 1945. Sure, there was a little rust, brownness on the top by the bolt, but it would still...

Fire.

Could gunfire destroy skeletons?

He squeezed the sailor's cap with his left fingers and dared to peel his gaze from the back windows to the wall phone through the open hatch of the kitchen.

What're you going to do? Call the cops and tell them that...

A bead of sweat bled out from his eyebrow and stung his gaze.

Every single search engine he knew of he'd used on the Internet and, of the ones that had hit the target on the first page of results, he'd been given the same confirmation. The SS Bernice *disappeared in the Indian Ocean in 1926.*

'God, why me?' he whispered for the umpteenth time. Beyond the slide door that led out to the back deck, the clouds were dark, anvil shaped above the water.

Becker shivered, squinted at the gray-purple murk of the sea.

Fifty wave crests glinted back white death - fifty skulls about to rise from the depths and close on the house.

Idiot! Those are stretches of sea out there. Nothing's in them. Not now.

Becker's arm extended toward the old sofa with the sunflower-print throw. He had to test out the Luger, just to be *sure...* Just in case those things *did* try to come for him.

That was his mom and dad's sofa. It would be their neighbors who'd hear.

His dad would never be coming back here, though, would he?

'Damn you!' Becker spat. He hauled in his gun arm, jabbing himself in the ribs.

Outside, the slight surf was getting whiter now.

His mind wandered. The SS Bernice was a freighter bound for Bombay. Those dead men were English down there under the waves.

Dead men stayed dead. Becker tightened his grip on the Luger. His Granddad had died and stayed dead, even with all the restlessness that had been pumped into his head from being in a world war. It wasn't fair that others got to...

Alta Vista, Yahoo, MSN, Infoseek, Mamma, Dogpile, Google, Excite, Lycos... he'd tried and tried and tried and all he'd got in return was this...

Becker raised the cap to his nose and sniffed, just to ensure he wasn't asleep. He found it to be all-too real.

How about being insane or dead, as well?

The froth on the closest breakers wasn't moving the way crest froth did. No. Becker had played at the sea frontiers too long not to pick up on that.

The froth was never like *this*, though. It always curved or swirled like a serpent then dipped back into the murk to allow another the chance to rise up.

But not this. The white disturbances looked more like they were staying put, holding themselves in the drink like....

And they were too small: way, way, *way* too small to be wave crests.

Try a shot now, you fool.

No. Run for the damn phone and get the Police out here, now!

Try your damned gun... Eight shots minus one will still damage th-

Six. You'll need the last for yourself, his mind's voice jabbed at him.

Becker moved all the way up to the window. Each step felt like what he might feel in a vertigo attack, like the kind he always used to dream about when he was walking by the side of a deep canyon and the winds were nothing short of being gale force.

'You bastards,' he muttered when he failed to notice a change in the breaker pattern on the water. He leaned so his face froze against the huge window of the slide door.

He jerked back and shot his head to the left when his dad's computer screen went into star rush screensaver mode.

Once he'd got himself together as best he could, Becker made for the kitchen door; he was thirsty, but, more importantly, it had a better view of the seafront.

-48-

21<u>st</u> April, San Diego, California

The skin over Billy Reynolds' heart had crawled several inches over his ribcage by the time he realized that he couldn't leave the room. Somehow… just somehow, he had stopped bleeding now.

The figure lying still before his dress shoes was his size, only blacked-out now, like a charred husk.

'Wha- what are you?!' Billy's voice demanded from atop legs of jelly.

The form of the old woman that had entered the room retained its smile. It also retained its upraised palm in the air.

'You think you can flee destiny, young one?' the lips spoke, curling upward at the sides, reveling in his agony.

'No - no I don't know who you are,' Billy stammered with his hands straight up. 'Plee- Please; I'll just get out and that'll be…that'll be the end of it… I *swear* it!'

The form advanced. Under the jaundiced haze of the forty watter above his face, Billy found he could discern no more in the old lady's face.

'The end of what?' the elder asked. '*What* end do you seek to what *beginning?*'

'Pl- Please don't hurt me. I'll get out and I won't te….. *I won't tell if you just-*'

The form raised both of its hands now. Billy saw that the stick in its right fist bore the worn-down image of an old man's face on its handle. 'Just do what shall I? Tell *who*, shall you?'

The first drop of urine warmed the inside of Billy's boxers just when he felt his right leg beginning to return to him. His breathing quickened horribly when he took his first step away from the stinking, burnt body lying by the sofa.

Looking up at the old woman through the smoke from the scorched flesh on the ground, Billy found himself gazing straight into her eyes.

The blue was harsh, blind-person-eye turquoise.

'You do not see, young one. *You* are the end.'

'What are you talking about?!'

The form shuffled closer. 'You are the end to this. Don't you see?'

'H-h-how am I the end?!'

Oh Jesus, he thought as he remembered Barry Nash and the reason for it all. He backed up as far as the wall. 'Please don't...'

'What, do I not bring comfort to you, young one?'

Billy tried to think as he raised his palms higher still and let his jaw start quivering. 'Just leave me...just leave me al-'

Alone, the thought flashed to him. Alone after all this would draw madness. Which kind of madness would it be? What color of pill would he receive on the tray by his plastic cup in the hospital refectory, and would he get it every day including those days Mom and Dad would visit with the remainder of his sorry, defeated family?

'Why?!! Why are you doing this to me?'

The old lady was pointing at the floor by his left shoe. Billy lowered his eyes to find the dark patch on the threadbare beige industrial cord, recognized it as the place where the knife maniac had fallen. The person he had murdered in self defence.

Where had he gone... Where had that *body* gone?!

'Have you not done this to yourself?' the voice of the old one asked but not through her lips.

'No!!! No!!!! I'm not *doing* anything!' Billy gibbered.

The lips were parting now, showing him jagged, yellowed teeth. 'You poor fool.'

-49-

21st April, Western Siberia, Loyalist Zone

'Major Alexei Olentiev, you have been charged with deliberately subverting the course of a military operation. The War Measures' Act gives us immediate emergency sentencing powers on evidence. Because of your actions, the presence of Russian forces in the rebellious zones has been compromised. Have you anything to say before this court passes sentence?'

Olentiev stood. 'Only that I acted in full awareness of the mission's directive and that unforeseen circumstances prompted me to adapt our strategy.'

'Your testimony did not seem to be corroborated by the other pilots in your command. However, in view of your immaculate service record, this court has decided to allow for leniency. Two years' imprisonment, but you may have an honorable discharge... Further to their completion.'

Prison life. Olentiev said it out loud as he was led from behind the desk. Irkutsk, where he'd been flown to stand immediate, kangaroo trial was like a prison itself, he thought. The notion of an honorable discharge didn't reach him all at once. When it did, he allowed himself half a smile. At least his family would be okay.

The stench hit him as he turned into the stairwell, and then the pictures...

He knew how it was these days - ten men to a two-man cell. Rusty bed irons, piss-stained walls, crumbling mortar and fights in the corners.

He hated Irkutsk more than he did any man now, and that included Bucharin.

'This is just for starters,' the red-mustachioed guard said as the turnkey opened up the cell. 'Don't get too friendly with these two. You won't be in here long.'

'What are you in for, *brass*?' the younger, spiky haired one in greasy sweat pants asked him as soon as the door closed.

Olentiev bit his lip, shook his head and made for the window. He gripped the coarseness of the middle bar in front of it and clenched his eyelids.

'It's all right, soldier; don't pay the lad any heed.'

'And just who are *you*?' Olentiev asked, grimacing.

'I know. Don't worry about it. I'm doing eighteen months for stealing mopeds out in Bratsk. I was lucky it got commuted 'cause they'd tried to get me down for three years' hard labor.'

The kid in the sweat pants was spitting over the bars, mumbling gibberish. '*He* got one year for credit card larceny,' the old man continued.

'I'm in here because of a botched army job.' A pang of worry hit Olentiev's chest for a second before he counted the words he'd said.

They still shoot you if you blab classified stuff these days.

The old man's eyebrows arched at that. 'They run a lot of those here, due to the war…court martials, I mean.'

'I don't want to talk about it.'

'Well maybe *I* wanna hear about it,' the youth larcenist drilled.

'Shut your face, Fill!'

'Fuck you, old man.'

Olentiev made for the lower bunk nearest him, sat down next to a massive sepia-toned blotch. 'God, I wish I'd never gone out East.'

'You from Omsk?' the old man asked. 'Your accent isn-'

'No.'

The older prisoner sat down on the sepia blotch, smiling. 'I'm sorry about the accommodation. I try to make the best of things,' he said and outstretched his hand.

'Olentiev. Major Olentiev.'

'Ganz.'

'You're not Russian?'

'Swiss-German. You won't run into many of us here.'

-50-
21ˢᵗ April, San Diego, California

Nathan poured Coleman a strong coffee in Carmichael's office and took his seat by the cabinets. 'Looks like it's a new ballgame again.'

'Ganz isn't a constant for us to weave stuff around.' Coleman was amazed at just how deflated and crestfallen his own reply to Nathan sounded. 'He's a variable we can't rely on.'

'Bingo,' Carmichael agreed. 'We take it from here, but in a different way.'

Coleman grimaced. 'Christ, though - why is he going after *soccer?*'

Nathan drummed his fingertips. 'Because it's an international language? Because this maniac is just playing around a little before he *really* slams us hard with something like nukes.'

'You don't call cutting the guts out of the Internet really *hard?*'

Carmichael smirked into his glass at Coleman's question. 'Rick, I want you assigned on something you'll be able to work your best at.'

'Which would be *what?*'

'Well, you're a good brain. Good brains aren't just born; they have shit happen to them. In your case it's been quite a bit of shit... You with me?'

'You mean the way *I'm* the one Ganz seems to have the hots for right now?'

'Big time.' Carmichael eased himself back into his seat and grinned benignly. 'You know, if I hadn't been at the center of this with you and seen what I have, I'd be a mental case by now. We're dealing with a field of national security work that even our psychic friends can't crack with Plan A.'

Coleman bit the plastic rim of his cup. 'Red Dove's off *completely?*'

'For you, yes. We had a volunteer and the decision was made above the Fifth Floor. Operation Red Dove is... well, it's not *your* concern now.'

'Allinson?'

'Maybe. *Someone* is going with the majority of the psychic squad.'

'So what d'you have in mind for me?'

'It's not me, Rick. Once again, this is from above HQ's Fifth Floor. Now, Ganz is on to you...something, *something's* been watching you for days now, according to three of our top psychics. If you go on the team and do Red Dove, there's a chance you'll lure him – Ganz - to the strike base and then everything'll go ape shit.'

'Spare me the justif-'

'You know the Internet crisis this Agent 104 crap has brought about.'

'Who the hell doesn't know about it by now?'

'Alright, this is me getting on the war horse now. Agent Nathan here has been updating me on developments at the Anline Building. Looks like our boy Ganz is up to more tricks than just turning up on pictures.'

Coleman's eyebrows raised. 'You think this internet block virus's his direct doing?'

'We *know* it. We know it because there's too much evidence that's got his marks on it. *Your* home system hasn't been hit yet, has it?'

'I've hardly logged on since I first heard about the virus. If it wasn't for the pager, we'd be doing smoke signals. Why - what've those guys found?'

'You know that green line?'

'You've got something in that?'

'Seems it's a message, and not a very nice one, let me tell you.'

'What's the code base?'

'Sumerian or Akkadian,' Nathan cut in. 'They're still trying to verify one or the other.'

'And me? I don't know anything about that sort of -'

'Coleman. Rick, please, just hear me out. They've got crack people working on it over at Anline; virus-experts. Now, the idea is this - these people give you the names and addresses and you follow up with the third degree.' Carmichael shrugged as he finished, smiling.

'That's FBI territory, Carmichael.'

'Not in this case. And I think you'd better be getting back to the Anline team now, Nathan. There's nothing else to tell you at the moment. I'll call if we dig up anything.'

Coleman was warmed a little by one of Nathan's more intense pissed-off looks. What right did Nathan, an FBI'er have to be here, listening to a domestic-based CIA conversation, anyhow?

He waited until Nathan left before speaking. 'Why are you guys doing this to me?'

'For the simple reason that you're a magnet for Ganz. He's on to you, Rick. And if he's on to you, we need you as a decoy.'

'Well that's mighty smart. He's watching me and now you've spilled the beans out loud. Just how in Hell d'you hope to keep him off your backs now?'

Carmichael grinned so hard his face inset itself. 'Because we know this guy is making mistakes, Rick. He's fallible. He's got limitations on what he can do. That virus is flawed. As effective as it is, the gist of it is that it's relying on making people afraid.'

'Fear.' Coleman blinked hard. 'You mean this jerk's feeding off of *fear*?'

'That's what the psychics say...and that's what the virus guys are saying. Ganz is relying on the entire world losing it over him.'

'But that message you get from the virus. How could it do any damage fear-wise if all it is is a jumped-up ECG? I mean-'

'One that plays on your monitor when the power's cut off?'

'But why did he go to all that trouble? Isn't a virus that radical sweeping that fast going to scare the hell out of the world, anyway?'

'We were *meant* to decode that green line, Rick. Ganz knew we would. It's his calling card. The fact that it comes on whether your PC's on or off is enough of a worrier for home users. But for us to get so far as to work out *what* he's saying underneath that is what he wants. Different types of fear for him to taste. He's playful about doing this to us. He sent you that photo and that anthrax scare, I'll bet.'

'And that means he's set himself up for one Hell of a fall.'

Carmichael reached into his top drawer, produced a black folder. 'Now this is one of the first places Ganz struck with the virus. Naturally, he aimed for a big cookie - the International General Assembly of Spiritualists in Norfolk. That's in Virginia. '

'A bit far flung, though, isn't it?'

'I hate to bring it to you like this, Rick, but you either work at this or you don't work at all. Okay?'

Coleman pictured himself heavily stubbled on the basement sofa with his gun at hand watching static-scrambled re-runs of 'Quincy', his wife starting to lose it with him as the days would become weeks.

'I take you can appreciate how sitting at home would be likely to bring you grief, too. Ganz has you pegged as a target, Rick. If we can make it so you're-'

'A decoy's better than being bait, at least.'

'Come on. We're just putting you somewhere you can't get hurt. The I.G.A.S. people have been hit already; they're duds. If Ganz wants to follow you there and mess up things then we think it won't be anywhere near as catastrophic as staying here.'

A wry smile warmed Coleman's lips. 'So the Red Dove team's all ready to roll and they won't have Ganz to worry about?'

'*Wrong.* The Red Dove mission is going to be so secret that none of the team know where they're going yet.' Carmichael rose from his chair, picked a bend in the blinds and shook his head like he was about to sentence the midnight streets of San Diego to death. 'Look at them. Handful of people still coming and going as if there was nothing going on. I tell you, Rick, on one side of the coin that's good because it gives Ganz less fear to harvest. Not that I'm saying people aren't *scared* down there, but you have to wonder how much they have to put into looking tough, making it look like they're getting on with their lives.'

'What can we *do*? Get every TV and radio station to keep telling them not to be afraid every half hour?'

Carmichael released the blinds. 'You're right. Look, you're made of strong stuff. It's bad enough for me to hear about you getting a photo like that with Ganz's face on it, but-'

Coleman picked up on Carmichael's tone. 'What? That burn mark?'
Carmichael couldn't have been talking to Kelso.
There was no way he'd have had time to, let alone find out that he'd seen him.

Carmichael turned to face him. 'Sorry. You know what I'm talking about. If *his* face is on there...'

Coleman checked a squint just then. He had caught enough of Carmichael's expression in that moment to begin to understand something else now. 'Sure... Well, I think I'd better stay here in San Diego now, sir.'

-51-
21ˢᵗ April, San Diego, California

'The one who brought you to this place was an instrument of the Beast.'

'B-Barry? No.' Billy Reynolds could actually feel a trickle of surprise coming through from saying that. 'Barry Nash's - was - a friend from sch-'

'No, young one. You were brought here to be consumed by your own fear.' The crone bade Billy to take a seat on the middle sofa cushion while she squatted. 'If you believe that was your friend who brought you here then he is dead and his likeness is being used.'

'Oh - why *me?!* What have *I* done?!'

'Connected with the persecution of the Beast are you. Your father...or -'

'D-dad's retired. Je-Jesus; did you say the Beast?! You mean, like, the Devil?'

The crone's face shriveled even more. 'You look at me as if I was not real. That is natural, young one; this world has more in it than you could ever dare to hope knowing.'

Billy could feel his gullet heave up to spark off a sobbing attack. He clenched his throat, stared down at the outline on the carpet. 'P-please...I still don't understand.'

The crone's eyes had followed his. 'Assailed were you by your own fear. It is fear the Beast wants, but you are one of those few from whom he wants to extract *total dread.* You had to go through that so you could be cleansed from his influence. You were attacked by the embodiment of your own fear!'

'But that thing tried to *kill me!*'

'True; what you say is true. But what the Beast sends are illusions.

Here, look at your wounds now.'

Trembling, Billy patted above the damp lapel of his suit.

No stinging. No cut. 'H-How?'

'Only *belief* will make them and their weapons real. I believed in the beginning… but that was because the Beast had planned me to.'

'The beginning? What – *who are* you?'

'Cards and crystal balls were my trade, they were. Many came from all over this world to learn what they had ahead of them. Until one evening the cards lied.' The old lady stared so deeply into Billy's eyes that he could feel his spirit being squeezed like a sponge. 'The cards never lie. Never lie, must they; not the way they did that first night; and then the one afterwards, and then the one after that one.'

'You mean…you mean the Devil did that?'

'Young one, in the world I know there is one Devil and there is one God. The Devil, try as he might to rise up, will always keep his place and never equal God's power. This Beast I speak to you of is not the Beast of the Bible.' She outstretched her arms, turned her palms up to his face. 'Sixty-six years of age have I, yet now I look twice that. It is the work of the new Beast.'

Billy felt a shudder take his backbone just then.

Wait… What was that moving to his left?

'Quick, young one, give me your hands!'

Billy turned his head, dropping his jaw. 'Holy sh-'

'*Away*, Dark One; leave this hearth and draw thee not from this child of purity. Away! Abandon our sight and be ridden of this place! Thine being is formless! Thine spirit torn asunder!'

Billy watched the knife fall to the carpet and the dark space of air that had been forming over where his attacker had fallen dissipate.

He felt the fingernail scratches from the battle easing into nothing on his wrists and forearms now. 'That was-'

'That was your *fear* resuming its form, young one. You must leave this place very soon. It's too early for you to have the strength you need for what you must do.'

Billy sensed himself trembling again. 'What are you talking about?'

'Go home; go to your family, but take this.' The old lady reached into her blouse and produced a small, sun-shaped medallion on a necklace cord. 'When you feel fear, touch this as soon as you can. Also, you must find a passage, some words you can say to yourself to block out the thoughts that fear will try to put into your soul.'

'You mean you're staying here?'

'I cannot move. No. The Beast knows that I can't so he thinks himself safe. Much strength has he in the assumption that my going outside will only hurt me.'

Billy could see a tear forming in her left eye. 'Please,' he said. 'If you've got the answers to all this then you have to help us!'

'I can't, young one. Your brother: the *one* I meant. He is one of the *few* who can *really* destroy the Beast's grip. But me? I am a prisoner here!'

'But what about-'

'Go now. The longer you stay here, the greater the fear of ones who love you. Remember that fear is the Beast's food.'

-52-

21ˢᵗ April, Bremen, Germany

The Swiss clock in the kitchen chimed twice, the first one driving an ice pick point into Becker's heart, the second telling him how agonizing the wait was to be.

No. It couldn't be two o'clock already: he was sure of that.

He checked his Quartz: 13:00... *lunch time.*

His guts were churning now, but he couldn't eat. Not after...not *during this.*

Outside the slide window, the blotches of whiteness were still there, holding, foaming, threatening to disgorge death. Becker was leaning so hard on the edge of the countertop by the hatch he could feel the pumping of his heart raise then drop his chest.

The Luger's grip was sweat laden as hell. He reached for some kitchen roll, wiped it hard then resumed training it on the slide door. He'd laid both the house's fire extinguishers and three full jerry cans of gasoline in front of it. The kitchen was safe - it had less glass in it and it had the side door that led straight out to the street.

But was there any hope of escape from demons such as *these?*

Bubbling, bubbling... bubbling. After five minutes, Becker thought the faux breaker crests were getting more violent. He turned to check the clock - yes, five minutes *had* passed - then dropped his gaze to the counter space by the sink. He needed coffee; he would need coffee for quite some time to come and he knew it.

The telephone caught his eye just then, started him thinking with the tiny bit of brain that was capable of doing that. The *what ifs* were mercifully easy to deal with:

If you call the cops, you'll go to an institution; if you shoot the Luger, you'll go there, too. If you make a break for it, you may as well call the fucking institution yourself and ask them to send you an application for self-committal.

What if you tell the neighbors, though? No. Hear me out. What if you tell 'em you found a body and that...

And one of them might have seen the old hag; where she'd gone, also.

No; no neighbors. This is a matter of life and death. You have to call that kind of thing in yourself. It'd be too suspicious otherwise.

Becker bit his lip, reached round for the telephone but could only get his palm to hover over the handset.

He looked back at the water outside. Twenty, perhaps more circles of foam were spurting spray high into the air less than a hundred yards out.

Higher than last time? He trained his stare hard at the closest of them again, caught the petroleum stains on the carpet. The cops would be in here; they'd be asking about that.

Screw it; it's only three tiny patches. You can damn well Febreze 'em all.

Kurt will find out, but maybe that'll help because when they dredge the surf and find those bones I can prove to him that I wasn't...

Crazy.   But then you'll go crazy keeping this up like this.   Share a problem, halve a problem?

Becker searched for the cuts in his ankle and failed.   His eyes scanned the kitchen until they found the ship's hat.   He reached, lifted it off the counter top then looked at the phone on the wall again.

He only noticed that the cap's fabric was disintegrating fully after he'd turned to look at the breaker crests and found that the strange frothy areas had vanished.

-53-
21ˢᵗ April, San Diego, California

'Billy! Oh Lord! Billy!'

Billy had caught the glistening and the redness in his mom's eyes from the doorway.   'I'm sorry, Mom. Oh…I'm sorry.'

Dave Reynolds emerged from the living room doorway, closed the door to block out Billy's view of Helen and Raina on the sofa with a small slam and moved toward his brother at the double.   'You owe us a big explanation and we want it now.'

'And it better be good, Billy,' his father joined.   'This is the last time you ever take off like this and don't call home.'

'And what's with the lies, Billy?!' Dave asked.   'Barry Nash is *dead!* No!* Don't start crying, 'cause it *won't* work!'

'I know he's dead!'   Billy grabbed his elder brother's shoulders hard for the first time in his life.   'Dave! The thing that's been wrecking *everything* is after us now! *Us!'*

'What in Hell could *you* know about it?!'   Dave fixed his gaze on Billy's pupils and saw the awful truth, that this was *not* a lie.   After shooting a glance at his mom's covered mouth, he shook him back. 'I said *how* do you know anything about any of it?!'

'Ther-ther-there's an old woman who lives east of Gaslamp. I-I was driven there yesterday by someone who looked like-'

'I don't need this crap from you, Billy,' Dave said, shaking him again. 'You're talking about big things here so you better stop the lying now or I'm going to get really *upset* with you! Now tell me *who* drove you!'

'The old woman tol-told me it was one of the Beast's followers! Dave, this is not lies! The thing that's doing all this made it up to look like B-Barry Nash!'

'That's enough,' their father said. Billy turned, noticed him hugging his mom, fully unaware that his brother had unclenched his fists.

'Alright, big guy,' Dave said. He started leading Billy down the stairs to his room. 'Alright, you and me are going to have a talk down here and you're going to *tell* me *everything* and I'm not going to say *anything*. Get me?'

'Jasmine Street was where I went.'

'And the night before you stayed at Nash's?'

'Yeah. Yeah.'

'Then whatever the hell that was must have got ahold of the vehicle that Nash died in and then conned Nash's folks into pretending he never died!'

'I never saw them there.'

Dave Reynolds slapped himself in the forehead. 'Billy, we have to find that old woman, but I don't know what I'm going to do about you. This is classified, you know. If I even leaked the teensiest little thing to you about what I'm doing, I'd go totally in the shitter. Given the way things are with the world right now, I'm talking firing squads here!'

'You- you're fighting this Beast of hers, aren't you? That's why you're working at Anline still when there's no Internet left?'

Dave answered with his eyes then said: 'When did Nash first get in touch with you?'

'A few days ago. He'd...he'd just got back from NDC.'

'He actually *died* last *month*, Billy.'

'Holy shi-'

'And what did you guys do last night?'

'Listen, I can't -'

Reynolds grabbed Billy's shoulder and squeezed until Billy started whining again. 'This thing told me he wanted to get even with this old lady so we went out to scare her a bit.'

'You idiot.' Dave shook him again. 'You are a fucking stupid dick.'

'No. I couldn't go through with it. Please; this guy just knew about my bad old days. He threatened to tell everybody if I didn't-'

'Okay...okay, so how come you wound up there tonight talking to her?'

'Nash...that *thing* drove me back there tonight. Please, Dave; it was the only way or he would've deep sixed my ass.'

'And this thing that looked like Nash left you there?' Dave watched him nod.

'This old woman said she's a fortune teller...cards. She told me one day the cards turned up all wrong and she wound up looking like she's over a hundred.' Billy grimaced. '*It's that weird.*'

'Jesus...I think I understand this stuff a whole lot better now.'

'So what do we do now?'

'*I* call back to base,' the elder Reynolds replied.

-54-

21ˢᵗ April, Western Siberia, Loyalist Zone

Olentiev's stomach complained to his tray with a growl. He downed the potato mash, sausage circles and black bread so slowly that the older inmate came over to sit by him again when he was halfway through.

'You'll want to eat up. No sense in ending up looking like one of those withered old banshees you find beyond the Urals.' The old man stole a corner of Olentiev's bread. 'I saw one once in Tashkent, maybe ten years ago. You find strange things sometimes. But there are legends.'

Olentiev's joints froze. 'What kind of legends have you heard?'

'Pied Piper of Hamelin kind of thing, if you know that yarn. Well, apparently there are some old, old women out that way who are like witches. They steal the local children and take them into the wilderness.'

'How do you know this?'

'Before I turned to harvesting property here, I cut tobacco out in the east. I spoke to many locals. The herdsmen, the carpet weavers, the children themselves all talk about them. Their word for them is like our *witches*.'

Olentiev slid his tray closer to the man called Ganz, offering. 'And this practice is still going on?'

'As far as I know, yes. The old women are usually albinos or have some other physical thing that gets them outcast. The revenge tactic they all seem to use is to child steal. *Uhmm*, this bread is good. Sure you don't want any more of this?'

'No. It's yours and the boy's, if he wants it.'

'Are you sure you're not ill, sir?' the older inmate said then put on a cautious smile. 'You look like you've seen one of the things I talk about.'

'No. No, I'm fine. Thanks. I'm just tired.'

'Maybe you're looking forward to a couple of days from now.'

'You know how soon I'll be moved?'

'I'm sure it won't be any more than that. They always shift brass — sorry, army cases fast. And then you won't have to put up with old farts like me carrying on with stories, true as they are, though.' Ganz turned to the youngster, still gazing out the window.

'Hey boy - here's some bread for you!'

-55-
21<u>st</u> April, Bremen, Germany

The boathouse was colder than the last time. Becker unwound both mooring lines, surprised he'd taken the trouble to tie both, and tossed them over the cleats while trying to cover the jerry cans with a tarp. He took the Luger, placed it alongside the flare gun in the bow locker and then reached for an axe and another boat hook from the back of the boat house.

'I'm not letting you mix my goddamn bones with yours,' he promised when his jaw was rigid enough for speech. After checking everything looked concealed from the jetty, he jumped in and yanked the ripcord. He was adamant... The only way forward was to go back out there.

Idiot, he thought. *You should be more worried about that Luger working, just in case it comes to it.*

The water was choppy, but the strange waves had so far yielded nothing on the way. When he felt he was nearing where he'd been before, Becker shut off the gas and sat on the stern plank, Luger in one, hand-axe in the other. 'Come on...come on... Where are you? *Show* yourselves...'

All about, the whites on the wave crests lapped normally, the way he'd seen them do for so many years before he'd been taken to the States. 'I'm here! I'm right here! Take me! Take me now!'

The old hag. It dawned on him he hadn't been checking the shoreline. His eyes panned the green banks and peeled them raw: trees, bushes, litter, gulls. Maybe he should have gone looking for her back there, when he'd been in the house... too late.

Leaving down the gun and the axe, he got his feet and turned back to face the open water. 'I'm *here* if you want me! *See?!* I can't hurt you!'

The waves carried on around him. Becker hadn't noticed the whiter foam when he'd been seated. Now he could feel the mocking hisses from all the frothy wave crests around him. 'Come on! I'm daring you! An unarmed man!'

Unarmed. Becker thought he could feel a stronger surge come up under him and crouched back down, taking up his axe. He rose again but only went halfway up on his knees.

Father would want him to be a man; men took things head on.

Your dad took death head on and he's losing, isn't he, Becker?

'Damn you all down there! Why don't you just come up and take me if you were ever there at all! You cowards! *You pricks!*'

The surge came to the underside of his boat a few seconds later. From his semi-crouch, Becker didn't feel it as well as he had the first time. He stood up for a second, just to see if it would come again.

When it did, he nearly went overboard, squeezing the hatred into his axe.

'Alright, you want to fight, fight fair, then!' he shouted. He shot his hand for the Yamaha ripcord and jerked it. When it turned over, Becker allowed himself a smile.

'Yeaawwwwhh! That's it, *you pricks!*'

The fourth jolt broke the boards about the keel. The space of the join enlarged to a millimeter on both sides, inviting a geyser of white-lined bilge to break through.

Becker crumpled back, banging his head hard on the Yamaha. '*Bastards!*'

The boards were droning loudly from the strain beneath them. He could feel the scraping now. Kicking his feet about on the slick of seawater, Becker saw the fiberglass spiderwebbing out in formations from points by the keel and screeched himself hoarse.

Surges numbers five, six, seven and eight sent half of the contents of his boat bounding up and out to starboard. Through peeled, crazy eyes, Becker gazed at the maelstrom all around his dad's boat. '*God in Heaven, what do you want?!!!*' he yelled, realizing how deadly a mistake his returning had been.

Frenzied eyes told him all that was left on board was one jerry can, the flare gun, the axe, the other boat hook and the Luger. Becker seized the Luger, *tried* to keep it steady.

He dipped its barrel over the starboard side and pulled the trigger. The sound was weak… awful, but the recoil and the resultant *splosh* in the water lent him…

Hope?

'I'll kill you down there! I'll kill the whole goddamn bunch of you!' Becker squeezed again, again, again while moving the gun about in an arc.

He didn't notice that the scraping underneath his vessel had now given over to a deep, whirring grind. The water level lapped at his ankles, even though the fountain effect had subsided.

He dared listen for a moment before he tossed his grandfather's pistol onto the seat board at the bow. The whining made him think of the noise of trying to free a big saw jammed halfway through a tree trunk.

Metal, that was. But it wasn't smooth.

Before his fingertips found the knob of the ripcord, Becker thought of the barnacle-encrusted hull of the SS Bernice shredding his craft to pieces, after the remains of its crew had risen up to carry him down to Davy Jones's locker.

The Yamaha roared into life then. Becker kept clinging to the cord for a few seconds after the engine told him that it wanted to live just as much as he. He grabbed the power bar and ground it round all the way, trying to ignore the lack of wake behind him.

'Move, you *bastard! For Frig's sake, will you damn well move!*

The vibrations under him were excruciating. Only when Becker detected the stench of bearings starting to burn out did he ease.

You redline the engine and you're screwed.

You screw the engine and you're dead.

Fishing the boat hook shaft up from under the bilge, Becker got to his feet, stooped over to the port side and jabbed into the sea surface with its business end.

It took him several seconds to discern the edges of the greener water immediately about him. His boat hook couldn't get down deep enough to touch, but he could see it.

The new smell was unholier than any stretch of water he'd ever had to jump into in his life. 'Hell…'

That was the bow end of a ship's deck. No question at all about that. '*Whole ship's not just after me, it's under me, too!*

Wheeling round, Becker expected to find a rusted, seaweed-clad control bridge, funnels and masts. All were absent. '*You! Where's the rest of you?*'

Something else; the grinding had stopped entirely now. Taking his hook, Becker prodded the water just off the stern of his boat that was a darker shade of green.

A depression that ran at least as deep as he could get the hook's shaft. After all that, there was still room for his propeller to work in!

Moving around the sides of the boat, he struck at other spaces of water and found the same.

'I'm outta here!' he cried when he dived for the ripcord one more time. He yanked once - '*Please!*'... twice - 'Don't do this to me!'; three times - 'A *charm* - you *must* work now!'

The droning came back then. He waited for it to pass, easing the cord back on its runner then counted to three.

'Please give me a sign now,' he whispered then pulled again. The Yamaha sputtered into life. He seized the power bar with his left hand and took it just a third of the way round while his other fingertips felt for the hook.

The boat surged forward ten meters then beached with a shrill scrape.

Becker twisted the power bar fifty degrees to port and prayed as he rotated the accelerator first down then up but couldn't stop the stall. 'Come on. Lord, get me out of this for my dad's sake if not me...please.'

Ten seconds passed:

One   ...the boat eased back with the waves.

Two   ...Becker felt the grinding vanish.

Three   ...he waited.

Four   ...he waited until he could see the bow turn in a little port-ward.

Five   ...he finished his prayer.

Six to eight   ...he yanked the ripcord as hard as he could.

Nine   ...the engine kicked into life.

Ten.

'Get me forty kmph, baby. Please get me up to forty.' He kept talking to himself, trying to add it to the noise from the Yamaha so he could drown out the newer anthems of horror now surging up from the Deep.

'No. *Oh, no!*' His boat was flooded well over halfway now.

Becker saw the shoreline in a new way when he realized how far he'd get before full sinkage. Oh, *why* had he come out on the water a second time?!

He also saw the frothing, spitting bits of water. The closest breaker top smacked the side of his boat hard enough to tell him it wasn't water.

'God!' Becker repaid then surveyed the twin crests of froth that were just ten feet off his sinking bow.

The impact was immense. Before he had braced and tried steering to avoid, Becker had managed to grab the Luger.

A solid white ellipse thrust up from the center of the foam as he passed by and saw it was a skull. Speed: about 5 or 6 kmph and sinking *fast*.

Becker surprised himself with his agility. He had chucked the jerry can into the feeble wake behind the Yamaha and had the Luger aimed before he caught on that a few feet's distance would have to do if it came to it. There were demons in the waves all around him now!

'Come on, bastard...come on. Three...two...*one.*'

Becker thought he could see the path of the ancient bullet as it veered off into the spray.

Moron! Aim, damn you... Stop quaking!

He released the power bar then went for a two-hand aim while kneeling in the bilge.

The skeletal eye holes of the new attacker now were staring up through the spray of the breaker crests, just ten, twelve feet back there.

Becker fired. As the explosion lashed his face, his hot, narrowing eyes caught the core of fire throwing white, steamy spray up before the black mushroom cloud sprouted. Turning to face the shoreline, he tried to get the Yamaha back into action.

Forget it. Only place this tub is going is Davy Jones's locker.

Three pulls was still no good. Becker let go of the ripcord and sloshed through the water in frustration. The axe, flare gun and boat hook shimmered in the murk. Squinting, he tried making sense of the way ahead.

Five breakers lay ahead of him. None were behaving normally. In fact, they were rolling *away* from the shore, *towards him!*

Becker selected the axe and tore back the locker doors to get the lifejacket. Just as he stepped over the side of his father's boat and began to swim, he caught sight of the flames behind him and dared to hope for a rescue.

After ten strokes, he was sure the axe was too heavy to carry.

But you need it. There'll be more of those things inside the foamy wave crests.

You were a fool to come back.

But I had to know, damn you! Shut the Hell up!

Becker took a tiring, wide berth of the five crests he would have rammed in the boat and kicked like a madman. His guts were cramping from the cold now, his arms and legs losing precious calories to the icy water.

Two hundred meters more to shore, he estimated and tried to start hoping.

It was a minute later when he let go of the axe handle. The tiredness that had taken him was starting to make his muscles relax with that dangerous restfulness of energy loss.

He couldn't see any more of the strange wave crests between himself and the shore.

The shore…

Becker couldn't believe his eyes when they came to rest on the hag's form, now standing closer to his parents' house than before.

Even at that distance, he could read the *evil* in her smile.

'No! Let me be!' He tried to front crawl it toward the boathouse but the life preserver wouldn't allow him any more than a few splashes with his arms.

…A hundred meters to go. A little ahead, he could see the beginnings of white crested waves beginning to bubble up.

The hag's grin made him wish he'd kept the Luger and had another ammunition clip to go with it.

Becker tried kicking again to avoid a cluster of froth crests. He lasted only a few seconds before he passed out, exhausted.

-56-
<u>21st April, San Diego, California</u>

'I can't go with you, Billy.'

'Dave, you *have* to. She's in just as much danger as us. And she can help.'

'That's not the point. I'm working under secrecy; even if we turn up good with this person and bring her to the Feds, I'd still be toast.'

Billy frowned. 'So, *what* then?'

'I take what you've told me to them instead.'

'Why don't you take *me* instead? I'm in this just as much as you, Dave! If I stay here, this thing will know I'm here. That means Mom, Dad and Helen and *Raina* could get hit, too!'

His brother's face paled. 'Okay. Okay. I'm gonna call base, gonna bring you back there. You okay without sleep tonight?'

'Yeah.'

'Well get some coffee or something, anyhow. Don't change outta that suit, either. Understand?'

It was two-thirty that morning before Nathan put down his voice recorder and nodded to Fenton. Fenton produced a cell phone and vanished into the corridor. 'I've tried to fax this to Washington fifty-plus times since you left, Reynolds. No go. Now if what this young man has just said pans out then we've got something big. But I'm prepared to take a risk on you, Billy, so we're going to talk about things the way they are.'

'Ganz knows about what I'm up to here for sure now,' Dave said. 'That's why I had to bring my brother here.'

'Don't stress over it. Reynolds, I want you, Jarvis and Piper to go back up and attempt an anti-virus program. And I want *you* to remain here, young man,' Nathan commanded.

'Be good to him,' Dave Reynolds warned Nathan. 'See you later, Billy, okay?'

'Remember - I said you *won't* be able to get her out of her house. You *won't*.'

Nathan smiled. 'Right now, we're just doing research, son. Just research.'

The two were alone for just over two minutes when Nathan's cell phone went. Billy listened over his second cup of straight espresso and felt no joy when he heard him ring off.

'Jasmine Street. You said the house this person drove you to was on a street called that. Only trouble is, Jasmine Street's name was changed in *nineteen fifty-two* to *Farragut* Street. You knew that, did you, Billy?'

'No. No way.'

'Well, all I can say is it's lucky we found that out, otherwise we and you would be in at the deep end of a pool of crap by now.'

'Mister Nathan, are you going to go into that house?'

Nathan leant forward, grinning. 'It's FBI territory now, son. But don't worry your little head about it: I can see that it gets treated properly.'

Dave Reynolds was finding he could work in peace alongside Hank Jarvis and Kenny Piper. While he'd been away, the whiz kid had begun modifying an antiviral disk and was gung-ho about sticking that into transplanted, infected HDUs.

Reynolds had noticed Jarvis was quieter. The armpit stains on his shirt had dried to leave white tide marks. It looked like stress had worn him down to zombie land. But he'd managed to discuss a few things with him and they'd been through it all: Agent one-oh-four versus dealing with Ganz directly; the new susceptibility of fiber optics lines; the seeming irreversibility of the virus, but how the right kind of boot drive might solve it.

'Guys,' Reynolds began, 'We need to cook up a program that'll introduce the Restore Disk effect to the recipient without them being able to download it.'

'Nice theory, sir,' Kenny Piper said, looking up from his own work. 'The only trouble is the time factor. So much of the country's been knocked out for ages now. Point of no return.'

'So plan "A" stays a theory. Okay, if we can't restore the 'Net, the next best thing is to attack the virus source.'

Hank Jarvis shook his head. 'How can we even start to hit at Ganz? Number one, no account address; number two, he doesn't even ex-'

'Hank, we've got to try this. We know what we're dealing with shouldn't have happened, so that kind of takes the ludicrousness of anything we do out of it, I think.'

'I'm afraid the antivirus disk's not working,' Kenny Piper piped over from the side bench. 'This disk is well wrecked but the sweep doesn't recognize anything's wrong...and...*there!* Green line!'

'Okay, she's kaput,' Hank noted. 'So where does that leave us, Dave?'

'It leaves us with a countervirus strategy. We know Ganz was on Anline so we try all the Ganz's we have. Forget Hotmail, CompuServe, Yahoo and the others for now. The only secondary account we could use is whatever email setup North Dakota College has or had at that time.'

'You mean try *address permutations?*' asked Kenny.

'That's right. Ganz is a pretty unique name. Unless he was smart enough to use a nickname or something, it shouldn't be impossible.'

'You're assuming his account's still active, though, Dave.'

'It's either this or it's nothing, okay? This stuff's too intense for us to get canned right now. *Ganz* is an impossibility with what he did; it's slightly less of an impossibility that we should still be able to reach him. Fuck it all...if we don't try, we'll never know. So let's do it.'

Fenton and Lippmann entered Parker's office just after three o'clock. Billy had been allowed to doze by Nathan, who'd remained at the desk, perusing printouts and making calls to Carmichael, the primary role he had to play as CIA liaison agent for the FBI. Lippmann handed Nathan a page and the latter started reading aloud.

'Irene Jungerwitt; age sixty-seven years; entertainer; height, weight and all that crap that our young friend here says doesn't count for squat anymore because she's *changed* into some magical being.'

Billy perked up in his seat, scowling at Nathan. 'Wait! You said you wouldn't *need to* take her in!'

'She's alright,' Lippmann said, touching Billy's shoulder. 'She came voluntarily and we have her somewhere safe. If you want to know what's going to happen to her, I can tell you she has to give us a statement just so we can verify things. Billy, we think she could be a *really* important asset for what we're doing against...'

Lippmann shot Nathan a look for permission to name names and got it. 'Ganz.'

The door swung inward after two hasty raps. It was a breathless Kenny Piper.

'What? You guys get something?' Nathan asked.

'It's easier if you come...come up and see.'

-57-

<u>22nd April, Western Siberia, Loyalist Zone</u>

Olentiev plonked down on his new bed the instant the key turned to lock him in. His new cell was warm and it didn't stink. But the mattress was newer and harder. He could feel the fear in his guts turning over and over.

Why had they moved him after just one night at the first place?

He actually wished the old German inmate was with him now. There was something calming about the way he seemed to know so much and stress so little.

His cell was about the same size as the other one, only this far out in Irkutsk allowed for a little more extravagance, hence the wash basin and the double panes.

Why had they dragged him all the way back *here?* he wondered.

He got up, moved over to the window. The view from the third floor allowed him to catch some of the city: road overpasses, grotty warehouses, a power plant, innumerable billboards and cranes in the far distance.

The foreground caught his eye… A small park with a concrete play area near the gates. Olentiev counted eighteen little children before he slid his palm against his stubble, thinking about time off for good behavior.

When would Valentina be allowed to bring their kids to visit him?

What were they to know about why he was in here?

He stayed that way for close to a minute, just enough time to abort the idea of writing a book from jail, before a coolness on his face and wrists knocked him out of his reverie.

The sun had fallen in behind low clouds. In the subdued light of the afternoon, he could see the children were all sitting cross-legged in a semicircle now.

When he picked out what was standing at the center of them, Olentiev pushed back from the window bars, gibbered for a few moments then he…

And then he *screamed.*

-58-
22ⁿᵈ April, San Diego, California

3:32 a.m.

'Coleman. Rick?'

Carmichael's voice came down the phone like a lover desiring a tryst. Leah grunted upstairs. 'Yeah?' Coleman replied.

'Red Dove 21.'

Click

The windows in the warehouses out by the docks looked like skulls' eyes when Coleman moved through the estate. He was nearly at the meeting place but, with every step, he could feel Ganz watching, plotting.

Once inside the chosen building, he found Carmichael, one unknown FBI agent and a briefcase-carrying, black-suited official.

The déjà-vu was getting painful very quickly now.

'Okay,' Carmichael said. 'That's us.'

'Straight down to business, then,' the black suit said, taking a seat. 'My name is Blanks. I'm a liaison officer between the Pentagon and Washington's various intelligence agencies.'

He paused for effect. 'Gentlemen, we have to examine the possibility that there may be *no* way to counteract the hold this force has on us all now. I have to tell you now that Operation Red Dove has unfortunately *failed*. Because of the extreme secrecy of it, you will not hear this from any other source.

'Eleven nations were involved: the US, France, Germany, Japan, China, Russia, the UK, Italy, Canada, Brazil and Australia. Over one hundred of the world's top psychics were taken to the French sub-Antarctic island of Kerguelen late yesterday, plus experts in astronomy, physics, telecommunications, meteorology, religion, the occult sciences, historians, archaeologists, linguists, *et cetera*.

'Members of the crew of the ship which serves the island usually only once every four months claim they saw huge forks of lightning hit Port Aux Francais, the island's only settlement and staging point of the operation. They knew nothing of the meeting.'

Coleman flashed Carmichael a glance during the lull that followed. Carmichael's face was vapid, but not seemingly from shock. It was like he'd already sat through the first telling.

'Of the seven hundred and twenty-four members of the project, *none* survived. From the information we have so far, it looks like massive heart infarctions all across the board with the exception of the psychics.'

Blanks undid the clasps of his briefcase and produced a wad of digital color and black and white proofs.

'One hundred and eight psychics were operating in three groups in three different buildings in Port Aux Francais.' Blanks passed the wad to the unknown FBI. 'All three teams were over a hundred yards from each other.'

The FBI man shook his head, handed Carmichael the pile.

'As you can see, the wounds are identical. Massive loss of cranial matter above the brow but brain intact, pretty much unmarked.'

Coleman leaned over, stared hard at each A4-sized image, searching.

'I already looked, Coleman,' Carmichael said when he was about halfway through the stack. 'Ganz didn't leave any autographs this time. He didn't have to.'

-59-

22<u>nd</u> April, San Diego, California

By 4 a.m., Dave Reynolds began to feel the depression dissolving his guts. Twenty-four straight hours they'd now sunk into the project without sleep.

No. He also had to be strong for Billy. Nathan had let him out half-an-hour ago and he had dozed on the couch by the water dispenser outside the lab.

Rubbing his eyes, Reynolds turned to address his team. 'Okay, guys, let's try this out now that we think we've got something.'

Kenny Piper took an uninfected hard drive unit and slid it into the test bed while Jarvis readied the email on the master base unit. 'Ready. Set. Go.'

One minute passed. In that minute, Dave Reynolds gnawed a fingernail down to the bloody quick.

His eyes had been captured by the recipient's Anline welcome screen for a lot of that time.

The virus he'd created was of the companion variety. Taking the name of Ganz's virus, when sent it would replace the operations of Ganz's.

He was amazed no-one had thought to try that already, but also terrified that it was so obvious that it had been tried at the very start of the whole mess, had failed and no-one had dignified it with a mention after that.

But he could only send it to Ganz's account, assuming that still existed. Lippmann and Fenton had uncovered his North Dakota College one the same time Billy had come back from the eighteenth floor.

They had told Jarvis it had been inactive for too long to be hopeful.

Bullshit, thought Reynolds. Ganz would have been smart enough to hide his tracks, but then Ganz was also an angry young man who might screw up all too easily... very hard to predict him.

'Dave! Look!'

Fenton abandoned his cheese and mayo sandwich and came over to look, also.

'I see it....I see it.' Reynolds reached over Jarvis's shoulder for the mouse then he clicked the 'unread email' icon once. 'Don't touch anything. Same with you, Kenny. That's right... just let it execute.'

A hundred seconds after the receiver screen had changed, Kenny Piper gasped. 'That's the Lord's Prayer on the cover text.'

'Why that, Dave?' Jarvis said straight after. 'What will that do for -'

'It's partly a stall, partly a warning to Ganz; and if there are any unhit servers left, it'll turn his virus into this.' He heard the door open behind and Billy groan mildly as Lippmann entered with a coffee.

Fenton couldn't understand. 'Why that and what does it do?'

'Nothing much – it's just a harmless substitute virus with text and a small preemptive operation. We know Ganz makes mistakes. This'll distract him, but it's better than a simple stalling method.' Reynolds replied.

'So *this* virus replaces his because it's got the same name?' Lippmann sounded astonished at its simplicity.

'Yes; so that if it was to be launched to every single email address Ganz managed to kick this off with, the program would be this instead of his virus. Same size file... It'll also negate the boot destroying files on the latent original for all the *unhit* accounts,' Reynolds said. 'The properties are close enough to fool anyone or anything. We hope.'

'Wishful thinking.' Lippmann now sounded like she resented that this was not her idea.

'Well there's nothing remedial we can do with it to those he hit, but our agenda's different now, isn't it?'

'Shit,' Jarvis whined to his screen. 'Mailer Daemon's returned it. That account's defunct.'

Dave Reynolds inserted the disk they'd prepared. 'Okay...okay; now comes the hard option. On this, we have that address plus over four hundred fifty others. They're all based on Ganz's name, either initialed, full or combination, then "at" sign, then as many provider companies that there are. There's a strong chance he had multiple addresses, I think now.'

'It's a good plan,' Kenny Piper said. 'We're bound to hit something with all these addresses.'

Reynolds pasted the first batch of twenty into the group send field and hit 'SEND'. 'That's going to be some minutes before Mailer Daemon gets back to us with hopefully all but one of 'em. Right...next group.'

Billy emerged in the lab by the time his brother was sending the second-last lot. He was about to talk when he saw everybody's expression.

'No good,' Lippmann said when they checked the returned email list. That's four thirty-five for four thirty-five.'

'I don't get it,' Jarvis moaned. 'What in Hell is his address?!'

'Can it, Hank. We're not through yet.'

'But his university one was our best shot!'

'Maybe the address was something totally away from names.'

'Then we're screwed here,' Jarvis repaid.

'We should ask the old psychic,' Fenton mused to Lippmann in a tired whisper. 'If she's so smart, she has to know it. '

At four twenty-five, Dave Reynolds bowed his head in his palms and got it out in words. 'That's it. We can't reach Ganz. We need help.'

-60-

22<u>nd</u> April, San Diego, California

4:53 a.m.

When Billy made eye contact with the old lady, his heart froze in shame. Lippmann and Fenton moved her past him like she was bound for the slammer.

Nathan had shown up ten minutes before the wagon had deposited her at the service entrance of the Anline building. His calmness Dave Reynolds found annoying as well as his faked genteelness toward the poor creature Billy had found.

'I hope you can help us, Irene. As you can imagine, this force is-'

'Getting too strong for you is he? Tell me, sir, do you believe in God?'

'Now listen - I'm not on the payroll for *this*,' Fenton hissed.

'That's enough of that!' Nathan snapped.

Billy Reynolds rose from the lab bench and pulled her up a swivel chair. 'I'm so sorry. I didn't mean to tell them!'

'Fret not, young one,' she smiled. 'Fret not. Their approach was destined. I was ready to go…and I've had a little more time to plan things.'

'Okay, now…*Irene*; if you don't mind, we have to ask you to work your mind a little on our subject.' Nathan opened a green folder and passed her a stapled set of papers. 'I hope I'm not patronizing you by asking if you're a remote viewer as well.'

Irene glanced over the top lines of the first sheet then handed Nathan the pages. 'You can't catch water with fingers.'

'You can't do this?' Lippmann asked. 'Is that it?'

'You still don't understand what you're dealing with, do you? You think you've got a puzzle based on your one little word and that that's the whole of it.'

'Yes,' Nathan replied. 'As a matter of fact, we do happen to believe that.'

'And that's why you've failed.'

'Why? What do you know?'

'Tell me, Mister Nathan, sir; if a bottle of that whiskey you used to enjoy so readily was to break and you wanted to deal with the problem, would you only deal with the bottle's shards to clean up?'

'What are you talking about?'

'Answer the question.'

'Both. Bottle, mess. Both; both, okay!'

'And what is the bottle and what is the whiskey here?'

'Ganz is the bottle and all the shit that's happened is the juice.'

'Wrong.'

'You can't sit there and say that,' Nathan said. He had broken a sweat on his forehead so beady that Dave Reynolds found solace in seeing it. 'You can't tell me that global disasters, insoluble assassinations and three billion damn television sets only picking up fizz isn't because of what Gan-'

'Ganz. Again with this Ganz character.' She pulled a fierce grin. 'He was the bottle, all right, Mr. Nathan; but the state of the Lord's Green Earth is only a *second-hand* effect of our beloved Jurgen Hiram *Ganz.*'

Nathan signed angrily at Fenton to start recording. He waited for the click of the mouse before he tried to continue. 'Alright, Miss Jungerwitt; why don't you just start telling us all about what you're getting at.'

Billy smiled when she looked past Nathan at him and smiled. 'William...*Billy.* Those are the same clothes you wore when you visited me, I take it. Please come here.'

Dave Reynolds watched Nathan's face wrinkle as his brother knelt in front of Irene and she put her hands on his shoulders. He'd been ready to deck Nathan in case he'd tried to block Billy.

A minute passed before Irene let go and opened her eyes.

Billy was the first to see the extreme bloodshot effect. 'Are you all right?'

'What is it?' Nathan jabbed. 'What have you seen?!'

'Let her breathe!' Billy snapped. 'She's sick from it!'

At length, Irene spoke. 'You can't get them.'

'Get who? Get Ganz?'

'It...it isn't Ganz any longer, Mister Nathan. You have all been deceived by your notions. Jurgen Ganz is departed from this world and any other world, too.'

Billy watched Nathan shoot a look at Fenton first then at Lippmann that carried more mortification than fear. 'But it *has* to be Ganz! His face on those pictures...the virus he put on the....Christ, he's left his mark everywhere! How can it not b-'

'Because that is what they want you to follow, Mister Nathan, and you all.'

'Wait, wait, wait! Who the hell is *they*?'

Irene closed her eyes for a few seconds as she exhaled. "'They", Mister Nathan, are the Ones whom that poor young fool Ganz invited to cross over.'

-61-

22ⁿᵈ April, San Diego, California

Coleman followed Carmichael's Taurus over the freeway to the Anline building, holding it at seventy-five. He was trying, failing, to take his mind off thinking about how lucky he should have felt for not going to Norfolk and leaving Leah to Ganz. Operation Red Dove was kaput, like the world it had so cleverly tried to save.

7:25 a.m.

The freeway was close to empty. Weekday freeways never used to be *this* clear, even with the crisis dragging on the way it was now.

The glasswork in the Anline building flashed fire at his eyes from the sun. A warning to him to stop his involvement now, while he had a chance?

He failed to obey the omen more because of Carmichael than

himself. If the fat bastard was going to try and lead him to his death, he wanted to be there to see it... be *ready* for him.

Blanks had vanished at the warehouse compound just after dawn. He'd returned to esoterica, along with his enigmatic props.

Coleman bit his lip so hard a flap of chapped skin came up as he pulled into the drive. He hated being Rick Coleman now and would have loved to sell the franchise to his identity.

'It's a whole new ballgame, once again,' Nathan told Carmichael as soon as the elevator doors opened on the lab floor. 'This is *really* getting out of our territory now.'

'You told me already,' Carmichael said. 'Let's just ask this old bitch who her informant is and get it over with.'

Coleman kept his stare on Carmichael's triple nape as they made their way halfway down the corridor. 'God damn it; the cream of the crop of psychics spends a million damn man hours working this all through and we get some hag from a caravan telling us we've been wrong from Day One!'

'I'm not sure about her,' Nathan offered. 'But it looks like-'

'Don't give me *it looks like!* And what's with that counter-virus team?'

Dave Reynolds stood up glowering as Carmichael entered. 'We're re-evaluating. Why?'

'Sure of yourself, aren't you, sonny?' Carmichael sneered.

Irene finished her bottle of mineral water and laugh-coughed. '*Sure?*... Where has your sureness got you, Mister Carmichael?'

'Let's have the tape of her,' Carmichael parried, indicating to Fenton to begin playback of her conversations.

Carmichael stopped the Mp3 files after a minute, shaking his head.

'So you say you can see things? Alright, lady, what do you see in the latest effort that we've put into nailing this hostile force?'

'Always you believe yourself over what truly is.'

'Don't give me riddles and poems, please. You may not realize it yet, but you've been made privy to information that's classified. National Interest, National Security. Now you're playing with serious charges if you don't-'

'Do you believe a lost spirit can ruin a world?'

'What?' Carmichael turned to Fenton. 'What is this trash?'

'Call you my knowing of a hundred and eight mediums with melted heads on an island far away *trash*?'

'God help us,' Coleman allowed in the silence that followed.

'Yes, Mister Coleman,' Irene said. '*Our God* is going to have to do just that.'

Carmichael dropped his stare to the floor. 'What else do you know?'

'I know that before we can expend any efforts of our own, there is one more whom we need. From another land.'

'Yeah? And just *who*'s that?'

Irene closed her eyes and shook her head gently. 'He is a worker with water.'

-62-
22<u>nd</u> April, Bremen, Germany

'Can I see him now?' Kurt Becker asked the ward clerk. 'I'm his brother.'

'I'm sorry, but that patient is under restriction until further notice,' she replied.

'Please; please, you can't send me away! He's my *brother*. Please.'

'Doctor Schenker. Doctor Schenker! This is Patient Becker's brother. He wants to see him now. I told him about the res-'

'No. It is possible to visit. Please, this way.'

'How is he?' Kurt Becker asked.

'He has been sedated heavily. You must understand that what happened to your brother is technically impossible.'

Kurt Becker stopped, waited for Dr. Schenker to follow suit. 'My brother is not a psychopath, Doctor. He's just had a major shock.'

'No; but you have to admit that what happened once he was rescued does defy the parameters of human stamina. And to be found in water *that* cold... Hypothermia?'

Schenker slid his key card down the swipe slot and treated Kurt Becker to a view of white that made him ill. 'Stay back until I awaken him fully,' Schenker said before he moved over to wave his fingers in front of Carl Becker's eyes. 'Herr Beck-'

'Uhhhh! Uhhhh! Get away from me! *Killers! White* is killer!'

Schenker moved back and shook his head at the doorway. 'I am sorry, he's-'

'Kurt! Kurt! Get away from here, Kurt! They're after us both. *White death!*

Schenker's thumb tip slammed home into the room call button before he motioned to Kurt to back up. 'I'm sorry, but that's it.'

'Don't let the white death take you!' Carl Becker screamed at their backs. 'It's not him anymore! It's *not him!* There's more than one!'

-63-

22<u>nd</u> April, San Diego, California

'What do you suggest?' Nathan asked Carmichael. '*Hypnosis?* The full nine yards?'

'Yeah; a lot of good that did any of the Red Dove team.'

Billy was looking at Irene. She shook her head but seemed to him to be deep in thought.

'What, does that mean you *disagree?*' Carmichael jabbed.

'That art is manmade. The adversaries we have are as good as deities.'

'So we're screwed, then. Is that what you're saying?'

'Hypnosis failed the men and women who sailed to Kerguelen

simply because they had placed their lives in their faith of it. All who went were trying so hard not to have their feelings discovered that the effort showed itself to the Ones who watched as if they were trying the opposite.' Irene nodded after saying that.

'Absolute values,' Kenny Piper sounded quietly in the corner to himself.

'Then what can we do to safeguard ourselves?' Dave Reynolds asked.

'No. This is too much,' Carmichael interjected. 'I can't buy this. No way can we be the only ones on the entire planet who're trying to do this.'

'Mister Carmichael, as a department head of the Central Intelligence Agency, do you not think that the ability of weaker nations to marshal themselves against these Demons will be smaller than ours?

'How many of the greater cities have been afflicted by disaster when San Diego has thus far suffered *pittance*?' Irene continued asking the silence around her. She understood the problems that this man and other men would have in understanding the Ancient Kings that Ganz had summoned.

Carmichael reached for his cell phone and dialed, spoke, dialed, spoke and dialed then spoke once more before he said: 'One...seven...seven...five...Dove...White. I want the President on the line.'

'Billy, let's get coffee,' Dave Reynolds said.

'No you don't,' Carmichael said calmly. 'No-one goes anywhere except in this room until I say otherwise.

'Hello? Yes, sir: further to the fax we've...uh, *yes*. We have assembled a team but apparently for it to be of effect, we still need one head. A foreigner. Yes, sir; ASAP... ASAP and thank you. We'll do everything we can on this. Understood. Over and out.'

It's a cover up, Dave Reynolds thought. That had to be an *aide*. Nobody higher.

'Their brains need caffeine, Mister Carmichael,' Irene said. 'You don't need to hold them back at all.'

'You can't work my brain round your fingers; let's get that straight right now.'

'Mister Carmichael, all of our brains are about to be wrapped around the fingers of the Ancient Kings. All they need is the type of outburst you have just given.'

'What are you talking about?' Nathan interjected. 'You mean we have to convince *ourselves* everything's *ay okay* all of a sudden?!'

'If we are to represent the hope of anyone in this world now, the first thing we must overcome is fear... Fear is the killer and it will kill you, Mister Carmichael, you also, Mister Nathan, and the rest of us if you dare to exhibit it anymore in that way.'

Coleman watched Carmichael lean against the lab bench closest to the door and allow the Reynolds boys to pass. 'Okay,' he said when they'd gone. 'If you're so sure of yourself then tell us: what *do* we do?'

'We focus; we channel our energies upon the reality of our foes.'

'Oh Christ, will you stop speaking that Double Dutch sh-'

'Ease up! I won't let you get the rest of us killed, Carmichael.' That was Coleman. He almost enjoyed watching Carmichael's pudgy lips contort in outrage.

'Damn you, Coleman,' the lips vented. 'I'll see you never work again. Never!'

'Gentlemen, this will bring only death.' Irene lowered her hands. 'Please. Now, the first order of business. I trust either the gentlemen or the lady has in their possession a copy of the *Liber Fati*.'

Fenton hesitated before he made for his briefcase at the other end of the lab bench, undid the pop clasps, rummaged and produced a paperback.

'And just what can we do with that?' Nathan asked, moving nearer Carmichael.

Irene took the paperback and flipped through the leaves with her eyes closed until Coleman saw her stop about mid-way.

'Here is the book of banishings... the rites that will shut the entrance they are trying to use.'

'Wait, wait,' Carmichael said. 'What do you mean "*trying* to use"? Didn't you say these things are the ones who're *already doing* all this?'

Irene seemed to ignore him for a minute. At length, she lowered the spine on her lap and smiled wryly. 'If these demons had already crossed fully, Mister Carmichael, you would have been destroyed long ago.'

-64-

22ⁿᵈ April, San Diego, California

8:03 a.m.

'Sudden onset – symptoms of paranoid schizophrenia. Full name's Carl Heinrich Becker. Seems he was asking for Irene here by name. And: "witch".'

Carmichael smirked hard, jerked a thumb at his temple. 'Great - we dig for help and we wind up with a wacko.'

Lippmann flicked through the fax printout. Coleman, sitting in a huff over by Kenny Piper, saw her incur a disdainful look from Irene. 'I'd be careful,' he said.

'Mr. Coleman, you're C.I.A.; I'm F.B.I.: let's remember that,' she replied.

'To the Ancient Kings, there will be but one type of person soon if we don't keep our emotions in check: the *dead* kind.'

Carmichael screwed up his face at Irene, looked like he was going to come out with more backchat. Coleman felt relieved when the Reynolds brothers came in from their second coffee run. He'd been ready to deck Carmichael, to hell with consequences. 'We've got the profile of our helper,' he told Dave Reynolds.

'Really? Who?'

'A German-American by the name of Becker.'

'That's not your info to pass out, Coleman,' Carmichael hissed.

'Our task force consists of *all* present here, Carmichael. And don't tell me the President told you otherwise because I know it's a lie.'

'Stop this,' Irene said. 'We need that man brought over here. Whatever the trouble there will be for getting him here, we *need* him.'

'Agreed,' Carmichael said. 'The top people are working on the transfer with the German Government right now.'

Coleman's eyes shot up from the floor. 'What top people?'

'*Top* people, Coleman. Understand what *top* means? Top.'

The wall phone rang then. Fenton went for it. Ten seconds later, he called to Carmichael: 'Sir, you're wanted at base.'

'This *is* my base.'

'Sir, it's pretty urgent. Military-'

'Give me that! Hello?! Yes. I'm on assignment. No; that's not possible. *Talk* to the President then. Go over my head. Fine. No problem!'

Irene waited for Carmichael to hang up then pursed her lips. 'We need to concentrate now on stratagem.'

'You mean your exorcism hocus-pocus, right?' Carmichael said.

'Leave her alone!' Billy Reynolds spat. 'She knows what she's talk-'

'No, young one. Hold your angst. They feed from it. As regards your question, Mister Carmichael, yes. We get the rituals prepared as is prescribed in the text.'

'And this German recovery diver?' Nathan asked. 'Why do we need him?'

'We just do.'

'Well done,' Carmichael jabbed. 'Great. "We just do" - You really know your stuff!'

'This man – *Becker* - came to my mind for no small reason. They are after him, the Ancient Kings. They have already sent fear feeders to destroy him.'

'Fear feeders?' Fenton asked.

'Puppets of the Ancient Kings on Earth. They are here to reap our dread. By building up what scares us to the maximum so that their dread masters can nourish themselves on the negative spiritual energy. The fear of those who threaten them the most gives them the best power boosts they can ever hope to receive.'

'But you said *destroy* as well,' Carmichael said. 'Correct?'

Irene shook her head gently. 'These agents destroy their targets by increasing their fear, Mister Carmichael. All the calamities in the world have brought the Ancient Kings a general type of "fear food", but they are now concentrating a more intense power on those few whom they deem have the power to harm their entry into the World.'

'This is nuts,' Nathan said. 'I'm sorry, but this is.'

'Wrong,' Dave Reynolds bit. 'This would have been nuts a *year ago*.'

'So the upshot is we get this Becker fella here and then either you or he will know what to do?' Nathan asked when the silence started to drag.

'No; we pave the way for his arrival with these protective rituals and pray that the German gentleman will survive his journey here.'

'"Survive"? They'll try to kill him?' Billy Reynolds asked. The picture of his own Fear Feeder and the darkness that had shielded it from him at the time, back in Irene's house, was starting to return.

'Young one, there could be fear feeders all around us. The Ancient Kings are powerful enough to ensure that. I can tell from their auras who they are. They have *no* auras – there's a total absence of it with them, whereas people always have *some* kind of field. But it is something I cannot do immediately.'

'And if Becker gets hurt *en route* here, what then?' his brother asked.

Irene shrugged. 'We can only pray that he won't.'

-65-

22<u>nd</u> April, Western Siberia, Loyalist Zone

'Suicide by a pair of trousers, Olentiev? Not a very distinguished means for such a man of alleged honor!'

It was Kvashnin. Olentiev tried to raise his back from the bed and failed.

'Don't look so alarmed, Major; please, be at ease. You are no longer in peril.'

'Where am I?' Olentiev's eyes panned the ceiling and curtains of his private room. His neck was sore but a lot less sore than it should have been from the noose he had improvised.

His eyes stared and panned. The room was too clean to be a...

Hospital?

'You are in a private clinic, Major.' Kvashnin pulled up a chair. 'Tell me; what incited you to try to destroy yourself?'

'What...what incited *you* to save me and bring me here?'

'I asked first, Major. Please, do not return a gift from fate with sarcasm.'

'I...I was extremely upset; disturbed.'

Kvashnin's face produced fake worry. 'By what, Olentiev?'

'My imprisonment. It only just occurred to me... the shame.'

'Doctor!'

The door opened and in came a goateed, middle-aged, Turkic-looking man in a white coat. 'Yes General?'

'The Major is in need of a friendly discussion.'

'I'm telling you the truth!'

'I think the Major is concealing the trigger for his mania,' the doctor said as if he were talking to a group of first-year students.

'I agree. Olentiev, while you were being revived you made references to an old woman you had seen from your cell window. Now just what could *she* have meant to you to make you want to die?'

'So you know. Alright then, I'll tell you. I *did* see an old woman in the park outside my window. She looked identical to the one I encountered when we ran the air strike...same features and she had children around her...the same way the other one had.'

Kvashnin grimaced. 'This is insane. Surely, you must know how *crazy* it all sounds?'

'She looked up at my window, General; she *saw* me!'

Kvashnin turned, gestured for the doctor to leave them be.

'Olentiev, you may find this strange, our having brought you here. Do you know *why* you're out of prison?'

Olentiev's lips froze just as his heart rose into his gullet. Had he ruined his chance for ever tasting sweet freedom again?

'We have a task for you to complete,' Kvashnin continued. 'You'll get to fly again and, if you succeed, your conviction will be quashed. A free man again; if you can bear being free.'

'Where do you want me to go?'

'South-eastern Tunguska. Same region you struck.' Kvashnin frowned. 'You might know better than to ask why, Major.'

'But I'd be leading another surgical strike?'

'Yes. But you'll only be leading yourself.'

'What's going on out there, General?'

Kvashnin rose from his seat and walked up to him, producing an envelope from his inside pocket. 'Read this.'

'I can't believe that,' Olentiev said when he was done. Prison would have been better. How could he fly ever again, now that he knew?

'Major, the Kremlin would not give authorization for your release to go on this mission unless there had been a development of this kind.'

Olentiev reread the shaking page. 'No. Askenskaya is *dead*,' he said. 'He is *dead and you know it!* …This is just a ghost… a phantom..'

'No. Lieutenant Askenskaya was never *found*…until now, Olentiev.'

'But he's been calling for *me*?'

Kvashnin frowned. 'Initially, no. The Lieutenant's aircraft was discovered during a reconnaissance run over the Tunguska heartland ten hours ago. Piecemeal radio contact was established with him, but the first pilot to do that was killed…blown out of the sky. Now that's a SukHoi destroying a MiG-29; think about that. Other sightings have also resulted in conflict.' He leaned closer to Olentiev. 'How does a SukHoi with no fuel outrun and outfight four Fulcrums?'

'Askenskaya…'

'Has defected to the rebels' side, Olentiev. I don't know where your lieutenant acquired his flying skill, but he is putting that to very good use against us now.'

'And he wants to fight me in the sky?'

Kvashnin nodded. 'Listen now, as this will be your briefing. Nearby, we have a MiG waiting for you. Your mission is to take it up, find Askenskaya and obliterate him.'

Olentiev felt his insides grow really cold past the pain in his neck. 'Where - where am I?'

'Still in Irkutsk. You were unconscious for just a couple of hours, Major. You're lucky the only thing you broke was a few blood vessels.'

Kvashnin rose solemnly. 'Hopefully, you have not broken your nerve.'

'There's something else; you're not telling me something, General!'

Kvashnin stopped at the door. 'You have your orders, Major. Knowing things for sure is nobody's luxury while these calamities continue. Remember that when you fly.'

-66-

22ⁿᵈ April, San Diego, California

'This reception is *crap*,' Carmichael spat at the portable TV he'd pilfered from Parker's office. 'It was never this bad before!'

'So at least we know the Friendship Cup's officially canceled now,' Nathan offered from the chair behind him. 'And Ganz never struck.'

'Their strength lies in our belief that they will strike,' Irene said from her seat on the floor.

Carmichael shook his head when he looked round at her. 'Lady, I hope that whatever you're doing down there will make us laugh at least.'

'Lay off her, Carmichael,' Dave Reynolds snapped. 'No more... *do you understand?*'

Carmichael sneered. '*Tech*, just what do you think you can do with your Internet skills seeing as how most of it's wrecked now?'

Irene stopped the first verse of her chants halfway through and looked at Billy.

'What is it?' he asked.

'I...I have just seen something that I.... It is...*someone in here!*'

Coleman had his .357 out just as he saw Carmichael hiss and reach for the bulge within his lapel. *'Damn you!'* the pudgy lips spat.

'Carmichael, I'll blow you aw-'

Bla-Blam

Coleman saw the flash rip through Carmichael's jacket the instant he pulled his own trigger. He heard Fenton scream before he saw him topple, clutching his thigh, fountaining red in front of Carmichael's fleeting form.

Coleman let off another round. This time, he saw its path plow straight into Carmichael's right shoulder blade, sending a spray of white shirt fibers high into the air and leaving them to spiral downward, feather fashion as their owner vanished.

'Watch out!' Billy Reynolds yelled when he saw Agent Fenton pull out his weapon and train it on Coleman's back. '*Watch-*'

Blam.

Fenton collapsed with his thorax blown open very wetly.

'You want to go the same way then try to take me out, too,' Coleman said coolly to Lippmann and Nathan. He could sense no remorse as he watched her grimace at her colleague's bloodied form.

'You *all* saw Carmichael pull on me first!'

'Okay,' Nathan replied then gestured to Lippmann to join him in the tossing of his .38 onto the floor and kicking it up the room.

'Holy God,' Kenny Piper gasped from the far bench. 'Holy, holy -'

'Don't follow it!' Irene called. 'Carmichael is a feeder of fear.'

'Right, no more of this,' Coleman said, looking at Irene and finding her eyes totally blank. 'Listen, I'm taking control of this situation now.'

'If you go out there, you will destroy *yourself.*'

'Jesus,' Hank Jarvis said. 'That guy just went craz-'

'Carmichael's one of them,' Dave Reynolds said then checked Irene for confirmation. 'He's one of them.'

'What happened to make him do that now, though?' Billy conjoined.

'Me,' Irene replied. 'When it became agitated, it let down its field and it could sense what I saw.'

Nathan squinted, shaking his head. 'What *field?*'

Irene replied simply: 'Carmichael is another apostate, Mister Nathan.'

Coleman frowned, lowering his weapon. 'But I plugged that bastard twice and no blood. How?'

'*The real* Carmichael was destroyed *long ago.* No aura on him; or blood within him.'

Coleman's eyes narrowed in understanding. 'So that was a fear-feeder that these Ancient Kings are using?'

'Yes. It was here to thwart our attempts.'

'Agent Fenton wasn't, though. See *his* blood all over the damn floor?!' Nathan demanded.

'I didn't know that, and he couldn't have understood what Carmichael was.' Coleman gritted his teeth then. 'Does that make *sense?*'

'So what do we do now?' Lippmann asked as she draped her jacket over Fenton's top half.

'We listen to Irene.' Coleman picked the two pistols from the floor and handed both to the Reynolds brothers then went back for the one by Fenton's corpse. 'And we think about how to beat these things once and for all.'

'Mister Coleman,' Irene said shakily. 'There is one more thing: while the apostate was amongst us, I was being *blocked.* But I have seen it now. There is another force we need if we're to stand a chance.'

'What are you talking about?'

'The one called Becker isn't enough; there is someone *else* we must contact...must win over.'

'Who? Can you see a *face?*'

'I.....I.....far away from here....I- I see...open air...clouds.'

-67-

22nd April, San Diego, California

Becker awoke from the plane touchdown. His brain was wounded but it did let him recall how tough it was flying these days because of the comms difficulties.

Agent 104, the automatically assured terrorist supreme, sky jacker *extraordinaire* had mercifully not shown itself to him.

He did not feel privileged to have flown so far in such a special airplane.

'So we're awake,' the official he was handcuffed to said. 'How do we feel?'

'I'm...I'm fine,' Becker managed before he wanted to bite his tongue off. Of course he wasn't fine. Kurt hadn't been *fine* when he'd been allowed to speak with him on the phone from Frankfurt International. Even with their dad stabilizing, things weren't going to be fine again, *ever*.

Once he and the goon entourage got through the red tape, the San Diego sunlight burned into Becker's jetlagged eyes.

The last time he'd felt sunlight like that seemed like more than a year ago now.

Two black BMW's awaited them outside. Becker was ushered into the front one. He felt a cold surge take his circulation suddenly.

'Where are we going?' he asked as the door slammed.

'To the C.I.A.,' the leader of the goons beside him replied.

'Nie av rhitak; suh tesh ashfure.'

Billy Reynolds turned from the monitor and caught Irene's expression. 'What's wrong?'

'Nie av rhitak; suh tesh ashfure. Don't go!'

'Who is it?'

Irene looked up in tears from the floor. 'Young one, I cannot explain...'

*   *   *   *   *

When Becker saw they were past the third freeway turnoff for central San Diego, he felt his intestines pull in tightly. 'Where are you taking me?'

The silence was excruciating. 'I said where are you-'

'Iyur setot, Becker.'

Jesus.'

Becker had his fingertips in the door latch before the C.I.A. goon next to him had his knuckles curled into a full fist.

The door jammed. 'You son of a - *no!*' Becker cried. He saw the pistoled hand of the goon in the front swing backward just as he kneed the one beside him in the face. *'No, you bastard!'*

Becker squeezed the wrist, tried wrenching it round to train the aim of its payload on the other, recovering goon.

Something was wrong. Becker's fingers were too tired now. The gunman's punch came hard, knocking his head against the strut by the window, sending a cascade of stars over Becker's eyes.

The borehole of the Beretta was about to train on his forehead when Becker found that he could see straight. Sliding down the door, he brought his velcro-trainered foot up to engage the goon's nose and mouth.

He had the wrist of the front-seat goon in his hands again. Half using the chain of his own handcuffs, Becker jerked it upward so the gun barrel cracked the plastic casing of the ceiling light.

Blam

Becker yelled when his elbow caught the armed goon in the teeth.

Pressure. The other goon's hands were round his neck. Becker tried turning the barrel, but the front-seat goon had his fingers spidered around it.

Blam-blam

The windshield fell like a sea of sugar.

Becker had his eyes closed when the next shot rang out and ripped splittingly into the driver's cranium. He also had them closed when he felt the shockwave from his skull bashing straight into the face of the goon in the front seat.

But he did have them open just in time to see the strangler careen past the shot driver and smash against the concrete shoulder guard of the road like a sack of lima beans.

Bleeding. The taste in his mouth was as strong as train rails. As he clambered over to the door, Becker looked back at the remains of the front-seated goon's face and found them to include the lack of a nose.

No blood there, though. Becker wiped his nose and scanned his surroundings. He saw a tiny key by his foot and undid his handcuffs with it.

All the spilt red belonged to him and him alone.

As soon as he had both feet on the asphalt, he turned to find the other BMW emptying of its personnel.

In his bloodied, numbed palm, the Beretta swore it had enough bullets to take all four of the black suits. Becker lunged behind the front of the smashed car. He pulled the trigger twice and the nearest goon screamed into oblivion, clutching his throat.

Becker saw the others reaching for their inside pockets and felt his guts churn.

He judged the concrete wall beside him would be an easy jump. Yet, it'd be too risky turning his back and exposing his side as he made his way over it.

Beside him, the stream of traffic was furiously rapid. He ran out in front of a Cougar, waving his arms and gun and jumped to the other side of it when he saw it would not stop.

He heard the glass on the Cougar's back driver's side window shatter from the rippling gunfire. Hunching, Becker ran two lanes over and waved his piece in front of a Daytona Laser.

The driver, a woman maybe in her early twenties, screamed then started to nod, jumping out.

Still ducking, Becker leapt in, wrenched the shift to 'D' when he heard the surviving BMW's tires squealing, screaming for his blood.

He was close to a hundred yards from it when he noticed it beginning to weave in his rear-view. The Beretta was still hot in his hand, its heat now realer than the blood in his mouth.

The back window spat two times, the second hole shattering the whole glass.

'You're not taking me! *You're not taking me!*' he hissed.

Before Becker looked over his shoulder to consider returning fire, he caught sight of the traffic's slowness a few hundred feet ahead.

The road was close to gridlocked. Five seconds later, Becker found he could make out the army truck far ahead through the lines.

A checkpoint... They'd had checkpoints all over America for weeks now, he had heard. How could he have been so dumb as to hope for an escape?

More shots rang out. One cut through the headrest by his ear and smacked a spider web into the windshield.

Frozen veined, Becker checked the rearview and found the BMW but precious feet off his tail.

He could see the arm and the gun pointed right at his back.

They were on a flyover now. As he heard the shot shred into the vinyl dashboard covering, Becker checked his speed - twenty-eight.

You're dead if you -

He tore his gaze sideways and fostered the mad idea that had sparked just then. It had to be twenty feet straight down onto the road below but only about eight onto the valley wall.

You won't take me alive! his mind's voice shrieked.

After the sound and the shock came and went, Becker saw the guardrail flap back from its post and sail downward with him and his getaway Laser.

Kerrrrrrrrrrrrrrrrrrrrrrrrrrrrrrrasssssssssssssssssssshhhh

He fought past the pains all over his torso and exhaled hard, trying to take in the new view and trying to consider what might be going on back up on the road.

No; they couldn't follow just like that. He'd virtually turned eighty degrees there – a new direction onto a new road, surrounded by staring, bemused, swerving motorists.

The Daytona's suspension was wrecked. Becker cut in front of the screeching of tires and the honking of horns on the underpass, feeling every hum and bump of debris sear through the floor.

Ten seconds later, a glance in the rearview made him scream.

-68-
<u>Demon Vortex</u>

The portal was shimmering now. The gods and their servants gathered by its rim and cast their gaze into the azure ether. Some leant forward to lap at the stream flowing up from the center of the disc.

The fear tasted sweet. The agents they had dispersed on the surface of the faraway yet familiar orb had done well. Soon they would be strong enough to break through and take the land back.

The New Kingdom.

-69-
22<u>nd</u> April, San Diego, California

'S.E.T.I.?'

'It is the strongest transmission point in the world, is it not?'

Dave Reynolds didn't like Irene's tone; it was like she'd just deemed all that he, Jarvis and Piper had done with the virus to be useless.

'That's right,' Kenny Piper said. 'But it's been scaled down a lot because of Agent 104.'

'And what are we attempting to hit with our message? The message you yourselves created?' Irene asked Dave Reynolds.

'Well, if not Ganz then these Ancient Kings of yours?'

'Who are now hovering above the upper atmosphere of this world. The weakest section of it, that is.'

'The hole. The Russian hole in the sky?' Billy Reynolds offered. 'God. I'd never have figured that out. That- that's how they're going to get in, isn't it?'

'Not if we adapt our strategy, young one. Your brother's computer code mechanism should be enough to stall them, provided we adapt it.'

'Don't go out there!'

Coleman trained his gun on Nathan's fleeing back and squeezed the trigger.

His shot skimmed past the doorway, came dangerously close to lacerating the hull of the fire extinguisher.

'*Jesus Christ!* What made him do that?'

'Ignore him,' Irene said softly. 'We have no need of him; the Ancient Kings have put little or no currency on his life.'

Lippmann raised her arms to implore them all to focus, just as Coleman poked his head around the doorway. 'No. I've gotta get after him;

if Carmichael catches him there's no telling what he could do. Could turn him into one of them: *one more* to worry about!'

'Mister Coleman, why must you understand so little when you care so much? You look at the small picture all the time,' Irene said and motioned him to come back with her cupped hands.

'Because that's my job! A lot of small pictures can add up to one big one and then that's the case solved, okay?'

'Not in this instance. Remember our enemies.'

Billy Reynolds put down the paperback copy of the *Liber Fati*, shivering a little. 'Why did they pick Siberia?'

'Because it's unpopulated, right?' Hank Jarvis cut in. 'They'll meet with next to nothing in the way of resistance if they come down there.'

Irene shook her head and reopened her eyes. 'The Ancient Kings have chosen that point of entry because it has been breached before.'

'You mean the 1908 meteorite crash,' Kenny Piper dared declare. 'I knew it all along.'

'Yes. But also there is much energy that had been trapped in the earth over there which is being robbed by these demons.'

Lippmann frowned. 'Gas. They're taking natural gas deposits.'

'Not taking them for themselves,' Irene said. 'The Ancients are *building* a corridor to enter by. The abandonment of the Soviet system and the rot caused by the new way has ensured the loss of its mining. All the more for these devils to use now.'

'So what's the point in this book, then?' Billy asked. 'Ganz had tried summoning them on his own!'

'Summoning by incantation is all very well for contacting and using the spirits, young one. But you forget one other thing: very few texts on occult summoning have ever been found *complete*.'

Coleman came back from the doorway rubbing his forehead. 'Which means Ganz only *thought* he was going all the way with it when he-'

'The Ancient Kings are not interested in that. They wanted to clear the land about their entrance point because they wanted minimum interference so potential threats could not get close to them. The letting in of all that deadly ultraviolet would have achieved most of that. I sense they have placed a Fear Feeder to act as a sentinel for the Gateway, also'

'But we can still get them with radio; S.E.T.I. transmitters, right?' Dave Reynolds asked, barely able to believe what he was saying.

'That will stall them, not destroy them. Only spiritual means can do that.'

'So why the gas being taken from the ground?' Coleman asked Irene. 'I don't get it.'

'These beings are summoned in the spirit of fire. This is why Ganz immolated himself after the invocations. The gas is a catalyst for an explosion. That is how they can enter physically upon this world.'

'And they feed off our fear,' Coleman said. 'Destroying millions with disease, war and then cutting off communications between the rest of the world... That helped them, too, didn't it?'

'True. They know who is a threat to them. Why you, Billy and his brother here have been singled out. *Your* fear is their strongest fuel.'

'But if these things are so powerful and godlike then how come they're locked out above the sky?!'

Irene shook her head at Coleman. 'I do not hold every answer. I believe that the Ancient Kings caused those things to happen here so they could propel themselves from their place of sleeping. They are made animate through respect: and the kind of fear they can generate is the ultimate form of respect. Do you know where *Sumeria* was, Mister Coleman?'

'Sanatolia. And Sanatolia was getting bombed a hell of a lot around the same time our friend Ganz decided to do his stuff.'

'My God,' Lippmann said. 'It all started with that star in Aries.'

'That was *after* Ganz had summoned them,' Irene said. 'That constellation is their point of origin.'

'And the disease, strife here on Earth...they were able to do all that just like that, from way out there?' Dave Reynolds asked.

'It was all their design, yes,' Irene replied. 'But remember that we and two others have been selected by the Ancient Kings to experience the *worst* fears of all.'

'Where is this man Becker?' Billy asked. 'Is he safe?'

'Becker is near; I have been trying to guide him as I have been speaking to you all. It is difficult: the demons...They... They are getting far more powerful now.'

Dave Reynolds tapped Hank Jarvis on the shoulder. 'That's it - we *must* contact S.E.T.I. base now; get them to turn everything full strength on the sky above Tunguska.'

'I can get you clearance for that,' Lippmann said, reaching for her cell phone. 'That agency will more than listen to us, no fear.'

Coleman trained his weapon on her kneecap, his eyes peeling at her face for the slightest hint of a deception, glimmering a dull note to him that the lower half of her face was the same as Leah's.

Coleman lowered his gun then, just as a new fear tightened around his spirit. Leah, all alone in the house.

The voice that came to him then was through his ears, not his mind. He knew that because the others had registered it, too. 'Oh my God. That's her – Leah's *here!*' He waited out the five-second pause before the voice came again. Yes, she was out there in the corridor.

His mind spun crazily as he ran back to the doorway, thinking in stabbing flashes of the dangers. Carmichael would have had just enough time to find her, abduct her, bring her back here as bait. She'd be dead for sure then.

Coleman wiped the sweat from his brow, ignoring the warnings the others were calling to him from behind.

No. That was her, all right. Muffled, like she was only one wall away. 'Leah?!'

'*Help me! Rick?!*'

'Leah?!!!'

'*Don't go out there!*' Irene screamed when she saw Coleman vanish around the corner. 'That's what they want! It's just an illusion! They'll *kill you!*'

-70-
22ⁿᵈ April, Eastern Siberia, Hostile Zone

Olentiev took the Fulcrum to four thousand meters and read the scanner for blips. His neck dressing had been off for only one hour when they'd bundled him into the cockpit.

He felt as weak as a kitten. How more unlikely a hero did they want?

Kvashnin would have been next on his hit list. This was a suicide mission for sure that he'd been put on. If they wanted him dead, why not just shoot him and be done with it?

Far across the clouds to his portside, Olentiev thought he could make out a squadron of MiG Fulcrums on the prowl for Siberian rebels.

That was a joke. The rebels had fewer aircraft in their control than he had fingers and toes. Kvashnin could have popped Askenskaya like a ripe pimple if he'd seen fit to call in the cream of the crop.

Plip

Olentiev dropped his stare to the centermost instrument panel, cursed himself for trying to think about his family. His heart was thudding hard against the base plate of his air hose as he waited…waited…waited for the signal to come back.

Plip

The signal was weak. At that range, Olentiev had expected a fiercer LED flash but this was like a…

Ghost.

The ghost was holding now at eighteen kilometers from him at an 11 o'clock aspect, plus or minus a few seconds. Olentiev locked on via the mainframe, found his padded fingers hesitating above the comms link.

Communications with base were out of the question now that he was under the ozone hole. He hadn't needed Kvashnin to tell *him* that in the briefing.

Cut off, helpless… Up against something not even *human* anymore.

Olentiev dared to desire that the combination of extreme UV and the presence of Agent 104 in the air would be lethal enough to burn through his canopy and end it all for him right there. The soreness in his neck returned in a pang at that thought.

The way it should have ended in his cell after seeing that hag with her children.

He couldn't face Askenskaya. Not after all of *this*. *She'd* reappear alongside him or pull something equally nightmarish.

The blip was holding solidly now, emigrating toward the center of the scanner in a way that made Olentiev think of a killer walking after the running prey, himself the latter.

He could feel the sweat pooling in his boots now, trailing down his frozen shins. He climbed two thousand meters. The higher clouds offered no comfort other than giving him hope the confrontation could happen sooner in the thinner air.

Olentiev primed his weapons, heat-seekers first. Before he could lower his hand, he tried the radio and spun through the frequencies on the fine tuner switches.

I have to know... For sure. Damn you, Kvashnin.

Fizz, fizz and more fizz cackled at him in his helmet loudspeakers. By the time he'd finished with the dial, Olentiev took two seconds to realize that the scanner blip was getting weaker... yes, considerably weaker now.

Seconds later, he had to blink. The blip was gone; the skies it should have inhabited were turning up vacant except for the odd low cirrus cloud and the deathly gleam of the Tungus sun.

He was almost knocked out by the loudspeaker when it crackled 'Dead Voyager' into his ears at a deadly volume.

-71-
22ⁿᵈ April, San Diego, California

Becker figured he could keep the Daytona at eighty-five all the way to the city center, less ten for any turns sharper than the fear he could feel skewering his soul.

He'd shaken the other BMW, only managing that by the maddest weaving he'd ever done. And now the rearview was being good to him. If he was able to avoid military checkpoints, he'd be okay. He'd passed eleven cars since the leap.

He knew there was one shot left in the Beretta. He didn't shudder at that revelation. It was for him; they would not take him alive.

How, his mind was finally asking him, had they followed him so easily over the edge of that overpass road?

The skyline of the business district loomed. He could already see the huge, broken horseshoe form of the Marriott and the huge marina that had once been his playground. The C.I.A. building was just over a mile from there.

The *real* C.I.A., that was.

He froze for a moment but maintained his speed. Phony CIA men trying to knock him off; this whole deal about flying him out from Bremen after....

After *that*.

Something in the rearview caught his side-vision and he clenched the pistol.

Mists were forming, parting, reforming in the silver glass.

Fear not. I am not she whom They have frightened you with. Do not go to the place the others have told you. Come to the Anline Building after you have made good your escape. Come...come...

Becker swallowed his scream when the crone's face faded to leave him with one white pickup, a gray Corvette and as much emptyish road right behind him as in front.

Something on the overpass a couple of hundred yards ahead made him look up.

'No!'

Against the jet black of the BMW's paint, the flash of gunfire was cruelly bright.

Sprak

Leaving one hand on the lowest part of the steering wheel, Becker flung himself over the handbrake and began counting silently.

Five, six seconds should clear it, he hoped.

How in Hell did they get up there?

Becker raised his head the instant he felt the coolness of the bridge's shadow hit him.

A clanking sound behind him made him look round.

Plop-plop went the grenade on the cloth backseats before it came to rest somewhere in the pile of T-shirts, lipstick, compact disks and potato chip fragments on the floor.

-72-

<u>22nd April, San Diego, California</u>

The lights in the corridor were off… busted, too. Coleman's sweat was oiling the diamond patterned grip of his .357, making its barrel dip in the darkness.

'Rick! Rick! Oh my God, Rick!'

It's not Leah, he decided. *It's a trap; Carmichael's doing that …or maybe Ganz, or….*

You can't know that; not for sure.

Coleman drew himself in tight against the wall and surveyed the lightless area.

'Rick?'

Leah's voice was muffled but not far away. Could she be behind the elevator doors?

Coleman caught movement from up the other way, turned his head to find Lippmann's faraway form hugging the lab doorway, monitoring him. He gestured that he was okay then reached into his pocket for a Kleenex to wipe down the sweat.

The second the elevator doors opened and lit up the gloom, Coleman cocked his gun. He hadn't got as far as pressing the button to summon it.

'What the hell?'

'Rick.'

Biting his tongue, he crouched and peeled his eardrums past his heartbeat. Leah's voice sounded again, this time way clearer.

The doors were shutting when Coleman finished his scan and leaped inside. Once they clapped together behind him, he checked his inside pocket: four speed-loader rings of revolver ammo.

The floor below was bathed in total blackness. Of course; they'd boarded up all the windows, hadn't they, the quitters! He took four paces into the dark then froze.

His name was being called from far ahead in the black. This floor was far different from the one with the lab. It was an open plan concourse. Past the first two rows of seat backs and powerless monitors, Coleman could see zilch.

The flash came to his eyes just before he heard the shot and the scream.

Coleman ran into the blacker black of the central causeway. 'Leah?!'

He'd seen two silhouettes, one of them Carmichael's.

Blam - blam

Coleman raised his piece high and let one round go. He watched it spark off the ceiling far ahead of where he knew....

'It's okay! Coleman... that you?'

Nathan. No. Nathan would have to be *dead*.

'Drop it!' Coleman yelled. 'I mean it; I'll blow you away!' In the matt darkness, he could barely make out the outline of the figure not ten feet from his face.

'Coleman, it's me; Nathan,' Nathan's voice gasped. 'I got that bastard.'

Click

'Coleman...hang on...let's get some light on in here.'

'How did you find Carmichael?' Coleman jabbed in disbelief.

That had definitely been a woman's form he'd seen just a moment ago. Leah had that shape…*and* he had heard her voice earlier. *'Where's my wife?!'*

Enough seconds passed without the addition of light to nearly freak Coleman out of his grief for her safety. 'Tell me, *damn you*, Nathan! *Where the hell are you!?*

The air on his nose was too calm - like a warning that something was about to…

'Christ, that's better,' Nathan admitted to the stainless steel Zippo lighter he now held in his left hand. 'See, Coleman? I got that bastard square.'

Coleman's eyes cast a desperate inspection of Nathan's form before they fell to scrutinize the heap of black cloth, flesh and leaking red on the floor. So he had bled, after all!

Carmichael looked like he'd been hit by a jeep doing 80 mph.

'How did you track him here, Nathan?'

Nathan's face screwed up. 'I heard him. I heard Carmichael calling.'

'*I* didn't hear him.'

'No; he was making voices. Women's voices.'

Coleman lowered his barrel to cover Nathan's kneecap. 'Another gun? Let's have it.'

'Hey. What is this?'

'Just do it.'

Nathan produced a .38 snubnose from his right ankle. 'This is my reserve. I didn't give-'

Coleman snatched it. 'If this did that to Carmichael then I'm a Rabbi's pet pig.'

'You got him when he escaped from the lab, remember?'

'Carmichael took a shot at you?'

'No. Coleman, I'm telling you, he just jumped out of the dark at me.'

Coleman motioned for Nathan to move past him. 'Alright; you and me are going to do some searching around here. And the slightest wrong move and I'll shoot, Nathan. I'll really do it. Okay? Now let's go check out the rest of this floor. There's something not right here.'

After a fruitless eternity of a search, they went to the floor below.

Coleman made Nathan get out first. After a two-minute scour in near darkness, they abandoned the effort and repeated the procedure one level below.

Coleman found this to be a floor marked 'Restricted Access 1: Admin' on the stainless steel plate that was screwed to the sealed fire doors as soon as they left the elevator.

His guts were leaden by the time they managed to get the fire doors reopened. He had tried his cell phone twice since finding Nathan. No good. The crackling from the poisoned air about them had thrown the line almost as badly as he knew land lines were affected. He'd texted Leah ten times already, too, but no reply.

He had to make sure that....that Leah hadn't been here.

'I think we should get back to the lab soon, Coleman,' Nathan said, moving through the doorway first, his hands raised.

'I don't care *what* you think. We'll do this my way.'

'Okay, okay. But I won't forget this. You see if I don't.'

After stepping back to wedge the elevator doors open with a mop handle, Coleman moved past Nathan to flick the light switches by the double doors on.

Dead. No power. 'Why are these even off? Wasn't this the other floor where...Jeez!'

He picked up the extension phone by the fire alarm, dialed for security and maintenance, all the while keeping Nathan's figure in view by the light coming out of the elevator car.

Nothing. Not a sound on that line. 'Christ. Is that that shit in the air or where *are* those guys down there?'

'Iyur Setot, Coleman. Ha-ha-ha...'

Before he raised his .357 and fired twice between the closing elevator doors, Coleman felt a shiver take him in the heart.

It was then he realized that he'd seen Carmichael's carcass bleeding upstairs in the manner of shred wounds and not silenced gunshots. 'Jesus Christ.'

The laughter that came from behind him in the concourse was getting much louder now; the breath he could feel at his nape so much hotter.

And the stink....

-73-
<u>22nd April, San Diego, California</u>

'It's no good,' Hank Jarvis said for the fifth time. 'We can't upload.'

Dave Reynolds ignored him, tapped Kenny Piper's shoulder. 'C'mon, one last shot. This time, don't use an FTP.'

'That's crazy,' Jarvis interjected. 'Without a firewall, it won't-'

'Everything's *won't* or can't with you, Hank.'

'Let's try and chill, shall we?' Lippmann said. 'Remember what the lady said about stress and these things.'

Billy Reynolds was kneeling by Irene, ready to pour water between her desiccated, moving lips when he saw her eyes open gradually. 'Young one, we need to begin the incantations once again. Bring...bring me the text please.'

'Hey! We've got something!' Dave called to his brother. 'It's going through!'

'Be careful,' Irene said, taking up the paperback. 'They home on extremes of emotion; remember...remember that.'

Lippmann approached the bench. 'SETI command base received the program?'

'Without a firewall,' Kenny Piper declared. 'That's just a regular attachment.'

'So now they convert that to radio signals?'

'Yep,' Dave said. 'In English, Sumerian, French, binary code. It's going out.'

'Hey,' Billy called softly. 'I think I heard something. Shouting.'

Dave Reynolds gestured for quiet and waited. 'That's Nathan.' Gripping his weapon, he passed Irene's cross-legged form and readied himself at the doorway.

Ten seconds later, Nathan appeared. Reynolds cringed at how much blood was plastered over Nathan's face. 'What's happened?'

'Car....Carmichael. He's got...he's got Coleman down there. I think he killed-'

'Whoa- wait a second,' Reynolds replied. 'Where's *there*?'

Lippmann moved up to Nathan. Reynolds saw her eyes searching his with sincerity. 'Sir? What's going on?' she asked.

'Carmichael; he-uh. I found him and he did this to me.' Nathan pulled back his jacket to reveal a dagger-shaped stain of blood on his shirt and a large wound above his right bicep. 'If Coleman hadn't made it to that floor in time, I'd've been smoked.

'Listen; we have to get out of here *now!*' Nathan pleaded then.

'Out of the question,' Dave Reynolds snapped. 'We don't move from here.' He focused on Nathan's eyes, now scrutinizing Irene.

Reynolds had his weapon trained on the space between Nathan's eyes in a flash. 'What's up with you, Nathan? I thought you were wounded...why're you so worried about *her* all of a sudden?'

'Easy, Reynolds,' Lippmann said. 'Don't cause more trouble.'

'They've... eh, acknowledged,' Kenny Piper called nervously. 'They say they're converting.'

'Do you hear that?' Billy Reynolds whispered when he noticed Irene lower the book and still her lips. 'That'll give them something to think about, those devils.'

The frown she pulled chilled him. 'What is it? What's wr-'

'There's something wrong with this, young one. There is a presence that is...that is....I cannot tell yet.'

-74-
<u>22nd April, Eastern Siberia, Hostile Zone</u>

The blip was intermittent, erratic now.

The clouds were all wrong, Olentiev was thinking when he was done circumnavigating the signal's last location from twenty-odd seconds ago. Askenskaya was in here somewhere, spiraling, double-backing or utilizing some unknown technique of evasive action.

Clouds *always* told an experienced pilot what cargo they held.

But not these ones...somehow.

Olentiev kept blinking to assure himself over and over that there was not a second blip on the grid.

No. Askenskaya could not have deployed chaff.

He *was* that blip and that blip meant an aircraft almost as deadly as Olentiev's was moving within a lateral parameter of only a couple of hundred meters...wait, not really moving...more like...

Hovering? Impossible. No plane could hold that vector without stalling.

Olentiev noticed his airspeed falling and tugged the flight stick hard left. He had to sweep back round to evaluate from a distance.

He was only a kilometer out when the blip vanished again from the grid line adjacent to the circular center of the scanner.

'Where are you, Askenskaya?!'

Twenty seconds of empty scanner passed... Thirty.

Around the canopy, Olentiev caught a break in the clouds.

No. That had been a flash of *light*.

Instinctively, Olentiev swung his MiG round then initiated a nosedive, praying that the heat-seeker Askenskaya had just launched would not take him.

He couldn't perish yet.... He had to *know*.

He straightened when his altimeter read a lethally close four hundred meters from the desert rock, just in time to catch his ex-lieutenant's maniacal cries of triumph coursing through his helmet.

On his ascent away, Olentiev noticed that the second, smaller blip had not vanished. His fingertip jammed the chaff pod switch on the console, powered by the rawest kind of hope known to him.

All Askenskaya needed now was to lob another heat-seeker.

Three...two...one... *Please explode in the chaff...*

The second blip remained. Olentiev felt its nose cone tailgating him when he pressed the other chaff pod switch, hoping against hope that the voice in his mind was on his side.

Dead Voyager, Olentiev? Huh, the Voyager is you...

...And a death trip, this voyage of yours shall be.

Three...two...one

Olentiev felt the shock wave from the explosion judder in his chin pad. When his eyelids parted, he caught the absence of the second signal.

The joy had no time to warm him as Olentiev was made to stare upward to take in the silhouette a few hundred meters above him.

'Catch me if you can, Olentiev!'

Askenskaya's SukHoi shot into an impossibly near-vertical climb, its engine spewing fire and vibration onto Olentiev like he was sitting under a lava fall in Hell.

Crazily, Olentiev started a conical ascent, sharper than any he had ever attempted or seen attempted. Up...up...up he went, teeth pressed back into his headrest, his head squashed into the seatback as he waited to engage his targeting system.

When he had Askenskaya locked and centered on the smaller screen, Olentiev released his first missile.

His guts sank deeply when it vanished into the purple ether.

'Must do better than that, Major Moron!' Askenskaya cackled.

Olentiev waited to re-zero in on the blip on the targeting scanner then pressed for a heat-seeker. 'Die, Askenskaya! Just die!'

The plume of exhaust spiraled crazily upward. Olentiev could feel his heart ripping out of his chest, as if it, too, was on that warhead. He held his breath, eyes peeled, a silent prayer for the anticipated ball of black and yellow destruction playing out in his mind.

One...two... ...three... ... ...four... ... ...five

His eyes fell to the targeting scanner first then switched to the main scanner to make sure that the impossibility the first had shown was real.

It couldn't be real; a malfunction. It *had* to be a malfunction... No *way* that he could have missed that lock on Askenskaya's plane!

'*Where are you?!*'

The altimeter suddenly begged his attention with a flashing LED. Nine kilometers up; at this angle and at this speed, the G-force could only do more harm.

Olentiev eased the flight stick forward. He had leveled out to an inclination of just under thirty degrees when he caught three blips on his main scanner: two of them fainter than the third.

'By Gregory's shroud. *No!*'

There was no time to think, no chaff to deploy to soak up the lethal payload Askenskaya's SukHoi had sent his way.

Olentiev had barely yawed to face the twin rockets when he realized his gamble.

And how the heat-seekers' paths might converge to send him a doubly deadly shockwave if he had managed to outrun them, at any rate.

Trembling, he locked onto one with two minor missiles and pressed the button through sweat-drenched gloves.

-75-
22ⁿᵈ April, San Diego, California

'No! *No!*'

Billy Reynolds seized Irene's forearms and tried to steady her. 'What?! What?!'

Her eyes flicked open to reveal iris-sized pupils. 'The other one of us: a Russian! Oh my God! He is in...he is in...'

'She's hysterical,' Nathan said, shaking his head. He stared Dave Reynolds straight in the eye and grimaced. 'Look, we better get our asses out of here now while we still can!'

'I don't trust you.'

'Carmichael's dead, all right? But something came out of him, some kind of demon. Okay? That's what happened down there. I couldn't see any more – I had to run.'

'You're bullshitting.'

'*Am I*, Reynolds? Tell me, what have I to gain by feeding you a crock now, eh? Coleman's in big trouble down there!'

'And you ran out on him.'

'He told me to get out and get you all *out of* here!'

'Dave,' Billy called. 'Dave! I think she's having a heart attack!'

Dave Reynolds surveyed the wreckage on the floor by his brother. He lowered his pistol slightly, gestured to Lippmann to move closer to the bench. 'Okay, we get ourselves together first and then we-'

'*Get that one!*' Irene screamed, pointing at Nathan. 'Destroy it!'

Dave Reynolds had raised his barrel only a few degrees when he felt a buzzing sensation go through his body.

Had the shock left him conscious, Dave Reynolds might have suspected that he'd been Tazered by Nathan.

Billy saw his chance and threw the nearest laptop at Nathan, only to see it bounce off him like a sponge.

Billy already had his hands on the grip of his forgotten firearm when he felt the buzzing take him from the chest outwards.

'Now I have you prepared for the Gods as planned,' Nathan hissed, beaming at the remainder of the room.

Shuddering, Irene began to recite a banishing from the dreaded text. As she spoke, she caught sight of the blue sparks leaking from Nathan's fingertips.

When the death stream came at her, she was ready. Although her eyes were closed, she could see its path bounce off her protective power bubble and sear into Hank Jarvis's form, crackling it.

-76-

22ⁿᵈ April, Freeway, San Diego, California

Becker hobbled down, down through the dirt to the waterfront. His pants flapped at his shins and thighs as he moved, warning him that the explosion he had fled could have just as easily resulted in flaps of skin and flesh bouncing off charred bones. His hearing was shot, too. Even the ringing he had expected was absent. Without sound, all he could do was imagine the carload of fake C.I.A. agents already taking potshots at his fleeing form.

Have to know for sure, he promised himself. *Can't die unless I-*

Stopping to catch his breath, Becker turned to check the gentle slope behind him.

His throat felt him scream when he saw the parked BMW barely a hundred yards back up there, its doors opening, disgorging black-suited death.

A group of tiny divots of dirt puffed near his feet from the guns of the two passenger-side goons.

Becker turned, broke into a full sprint, praying with toddler grimaces and whimpers over his shrapnel-shredded pains.

At the bottom of the slope, he could see a concrete service promenade through some trees – a small waterfront utility quay.

As soon as his feet hit the harder surface, he felt a stabbing, electric-like ripple take the side of his arm.

Shot....but...NO!

They won't take me, no! I have to live, if only for the sake of Dad.

A few seconds before he dived, Becker noticed the tiny, pipe-fed cabin at the base of the steps which sat over a low wooden jetty and the likelihood of its having a hiding place where he could.....

You're just prolonging it, he told himself when the water hit his hands. *Get it over with now, for pity's sake!*

When he came up, Becker had been certain that he was underneath the cabin. From the shadows, he judged there was no way he could have screwed up and missed it.

But this air pocket was gray. Becker urinated when he turned his head and read the engraved lettering on two rusted plates by the light of the single, caged wall lamp.

And, when he caught sight of the glow in the water below him, he screamed.

-77-

22nd April, San Diego, California

Running in the dark.

Coleman slammed into the wall and whined from the pain in his cheekbone.

He heard Nathan's .38 clunk on the ground somewhere to his left, dropped...useless to him.

There was no time to look for it. Not *now*.

The beast was near now - much nearer than when he'd first heard it.

Coleman started retreating by sliding his right side backwards along the wall, his gun hand raised so his trigger finger was inches from his temple, shaking Parkinsonsesquely.

Solid obstruction at his buttock – a steel cabinet. It clanked on its feet as he fumbled around it.

Twin jets of flame shot forth from the darkness to his left. Coleman yelled when one skimmed past his kneecap.

By the time he had his .357 up and shooting, he could just make out the silhouette of the beast.

Firing in succession like that, he counted two hits dead center.

His third shot coincided with the force that knocked his gun out of his hand.

Whimpering, Coleman scuttled away from the stench of the thing's lower half.

You're defenseless… dead, his mind stabbed. *How's it feel?*

Coleman felt the damage in his arm when he started to run through the black space behind the creature. He was using his other arm as a feeler now; it would have to do.

A glimmer of colored light beckoned from far ahead: a fire exit light. The breathing was intensifying behind him. Coleman pictured the slavering thing behind him chasing on all fours, its talons primed to dig into his flesh, jaws to his carotid and jugular.

He was closing on the light when his hip glanced off the corner of a work station and made him shriek.

Turning sideways, he saw one of the streams of fire fly past him while he felt the heat of the other singe his shirt.

If you hadn't have turned, you would be dead and this would be over.

Thank God.

One of the double doors immediately under the illuminated sign was unlocked. Coleman was through it and had the bottom bolt in the floor hole two seconds before the huge slamming sound sent a shockwave through his core.

The light coming from the open elevator screamed at him to enter. Coleman leapt into the car and punched the 'CLOSE DOOR' button before he dared breathe again.

'Oh my…oh my God!' he cried when nothing happened.

The slamming at the double-doors was getting harder. He could hear the whines of pressure on the top half of them as they were battered forward.

Coleman prized himself up from the floor of the elevator car. He pressed button after button on the panel before he wrenched the emergency backup phone from the recess at the bottom, not having time to notice or to care that his wounded arm was, at least, unbroken.

The line was quite dead.

He was just out of the car when he heard the crash and had traveled a few paces in the other direction when the first spray of bolts and wood plinked onto the floor.

Coleman saw the yellow eyes of the demon reflected in the metal elevator doors as he threw himself forward through the space before him, just in time to miss the dual streaks of flame.

The fireballs seared the floor where he had been. Skimming past the beast's swinging arm, Coleman was already sprinting when he saw the next pair of fireballs slam into a pillar somewhere in the middle of the workstation concourse far ahead. By the light they made against it, he found he could see a glimmered wealth of hiding places in and around the desks.

Coleman's guts froze when it cemented in his mind that the fire stairs were back in the other direction.

-78-
Void From Our Time - Demon Vortex

'Dave? Are we dead?'

'I don't know.' Dave Reynolds reached for the image of his brother and grabbed its wrist. 'No... No. I don't think we are.'

'Don't let go!'

They both looked down at the maelstrom beneath their floating forms. Billy thought of a huge bath of lava swirling down a plughole and shuddered. 'Jesus!'

'This isn't real!' Dave said, squeezing him. 'Say *"This isn't real"*! Say it!!'

'But...but where are w-'

'Billy, this is *an illusion!* We should be burning up by now *and we're not!*'

Dave Reynolds took his brother's other wrist to make a skydivers' ring. 'Close your damn eyes and say it isn't real, Billy! *Deny* that this is this!'

Billy almost had his eyes shut when he caught sight of the fleck of black flitting about far below them, its distance impossible to compute against the perspectivelessness of its surroundings.

He shook a wrist free and pointed down through the substance. 'Down there!' he yelled.

Dave let go as his brother began thrashing away from him, doing a frantic parody of a breaststroke.

When the elder Reynolds gazed at the thing below him, he found he could block it from view with his foot.

When Billy had gone beyond his striking distance, Dave could see that the black thing's spread had grown to the size of a car wheel right beneath his shoes.

A demon on wings, amid this sea of heatless fire.

'Come on!' Billy yelled to him. *'It's gonna get us!'*

Dave kicked hard to propel himself so he could reach Billy. 'God no! *No!'*

The moaning winds were parting to let the growls through now. Billy could feel the roar in the balls of his feet as he kicked harder, harder to escape.

But where to?

Dave summoned the courage to look behind and below them several seconds later. He was not surprised that he couldn't scream.

He was surprised, however, that he could maintain his kicking motion.

The thing's gaping, razor-toothed jaws were widening barely ten of their body lengths behind them.

-79-
22ⁿᵈ April, San Diego, California

Lighter.

Some pressure was lifting from Irene's lap. She was sensing it now in her skirt fibers, even though she was all but paralyzed. She had to watch as the copy of the *Liber Fati* vanished from the only one of Nathan's blue blasts to have penetrated her shield so far. She could hear nothing inside the force field, except the danger of the fizzy, erratic crackling of her power as it tried sustaining the field.

Outside, to her left, she found the FBI lady and the young whiz kid taking cover beneath the lab bench, the fried carcass of the Internet specialist called Jarvis lying within arm's length of them both.

BOOM

She turned back and found Nathan standing right in front of her bubble, grinning, his hands gouging at its surface, trying to push through in order to widen the tiny breach he had somehow made.

The incantation of banishing was still fresh on her lips from earlier, though. As she began it, she saw him withdraw his arms and cover his ears, convulsing, the spittle flying from his mouth like a disturbed cobra's greeting.

Her eyes closed and she saw the skies parting.

The Ancient Kings were above the rupture, waiting to enter and freefall to commence their reign on the planet of hated inferiors.

And there, just below them, the Russian…flying in combat.

Irene's mind sounded louder than she ever could have screamed then.

No. No! Don't follow the apostate! It's what they want you to do!

-80-
22nd April, Eastern Siberia, Hostile Zone

Olentiev's MiG plowed up through the thinning air at an angle nearly as acute as his initial climb. On the console, a dozen red and yellow LEDs were flashing, telling of damage ranging from fuselage skin gouges to comms faults.

His targetter was functioning, though. It had allowed him to survive the launching of twin heat-seeker missiles and destroy them; it would allow him anything else after that, surely...

On the main scanner, Askenskaya's SukHoi was entering the central circle. When Olentiev switched to his targeting scanner, he found the blip still some way off the cross-haired area required for a lock.

A weapons check showed him he had three heat-seekers left, six needle rockets, and the gun. When he read the inscriptions next to the closest LED, his heart sank. The closeness of the explosion from his shooting the heat-seekers from Askenskaya had knocked out one of his own and two needle rockets.

Another LED was beginning to flash higher up on the console.

Undercarriage damaged: the landing gear was down.

'Dead Voyager! Dead Mir! Space belongs to our Masters now, Olentiev!'

Olentiev winced at the lizard-like raspiness of the voice in his helmet speakers. Taking another look at the scanner, he eased the flight stick back and leftward a little.

His angle of ascent was approaching seventy degrees: he was as good as being a cosmonaut with that. Logic demanded he go no higher...yet, he had to!

The deep purple air about him was blackening horrendously now. Through the veil caused by the last of the highest clouds, he could see the yellow streaks caused by Askenskaya's afterburners.

Thirty-five thousand meters.

Olentiev could almost feel the sheer power of the lethal, cold air outside his canopy. He had Askenskaya targeted at a distance of one thousand, five hundred meters and closing.

The blip on the targeting scanner was an inch away from the

necessary zone.

Ten seconds later, when it was inside it, Olentiev locked on and pressed the button to send off his next-to-last heat-seeker.

The 'Device Failure' LED flashed on the console.

'No...' Olentiev switched to the needle rockets and, when he was certain that the blip had not been allowed to leave the targeting core, he fired.

A small ball of yellow erupted ahead of him, although the streamer of the other rocket continued past it.

Olentiev took a moment to increase his airspeed then he began the bullet salvo.

In three seconds, he had emptied one of the six drums. Askenskaya's plane was still going up, wounded, in flames but intact.

'Time to die!' Olentiev cried in the near vacuum. He lowered his nose by a couple of seconds then re-engaged the gun.

Pataka-pataka-pataka-pataka-pataka-pataka-pataka-pataka-ka

The ball of fire dazzled Olentiev, even through his visor.

Wait... Something was *different* about this explosion. At nine hundred meters from his target, its shockwave was far too great.

The residual waves ensured the MiG's tailspin and nosedive.

When he finally managed to recover his stalled Fulcrum from its falling spiral, Olentiev found that the sky around him was too deep a shade of purple to match the time of day, or even to be the highest stretches of stratosphere.

He pulled back on his flight stick to survey the break in the clouds through which he'd dropped.

Through them, he could just make out the jet black forms of huge, humanoid beings stepping down through the sky as if they were on a flight of glass stairs.

Once the static cleared in his speakers, Olentiev found himself listening to the words they were issuing:

'Thank you, fool.'

-81-

<u>Void From Our Time - Demon vortex</u>

The glow had vanished below Becker. Now he could barely see the first two or three inches of himself below the shoulders in the water. The caged lamp flickered, seeming to intensify like it was warning him to dive back down and seek an escape route before some mammoth explosion came.

The water was cold: the kind of cold he knew was born of depth rather than simply a chilled current. He could feel it robbing his body of calories, soothing it with tiredness at the same time.

'I can't be aboard the *Graf Spee* again....no way.'

But you can. Nothing is normal - not now; especially not for you.

Seeing the remains of a series of hand rungs behind him, Becker reached for one and pulled himself up from the black water. His hand darted to feel for the wounds the bogus CIA men had pumped into him.

It froze when it patted over the smooth, unbroken, shirted and panted skin for the second time. He was unhurt but deaf. 'This is crazy.'

He dropped back into the water. He was in for a few seconds when the surface smoothed out to reveal a dim, dim yellow square somewhere in the depths below his right arm.

'What the hell....what the hell is that?' he gasped. He thought that he knew every story there *was* to tell from a body of water... every kind of consistency or quality or temperature... but this was different.

...Visibility near zero. He suddenly felt compelled to investigate the dull, yellow shape in the water below him. Submerging, he thought about which way might be the least agonizing to die.

I always said no-one would ever bury me.

He reckoned he was about twenty feet under when he saw that the yellow object – a pair of aqualungs - was attached to....

A dead diver. But then death always went with the territory, didn't it?

Becker's lungs were already beginning to burst when he unstrapped the harness and tested the mouthpiece. The first breath he took was deep, trusting, risky....

.....Suicidal?

The dead diver was lying across either a platform or the real floor of a vessel. Becker felt about for the all-essential flashlight, found it lashed to the left wrist. After he removed the man's facemask, he ascended back to the dappled amber oval above to see if the gear could be used.

The air tanks were half full... the man's mouthpiece must have seized up. From the state of their casing, Becker surmised they'd been under for barely a day or two. He donned them and the mask quickly, thought about a prayer then allowed himself a grimace.

At least the flashlight's beam was strong enough to penetrate the first few feet of murk. The water was stirred up and debris infested, as if some huge beast or machine had been doing its rounds in the passageways, gyrating itself to disturb all the surfaces.

He didn't recognize any of this section. In fact, the layout was too small in scale to even be vaguely like the *Graf Spee*.

He'd been under for just over two minutes when he found the torpedo room and it told him all.

A submarine.

German markings.....over well-rusted surfaces.

This was a U-boat.

This was the third anomaly he'd encountered since the End of the World (as the mass media had been terming it to *no* end for months) had pulled him into investigating its nature.

He did not know what had become of the *Graf Spee* or the *SS Bernice*.

He did not care anymore.

Becker was breathing quickly enough to court hyperventilation when he rubbed his fingers over the handles and grips of the torpedo tubes.

As his flashlight revealed square inch after square inch of rusted chamber interior, he figured that, at this pressure, he had much less than half an hour's oxygen left now.

And to do what? To escape? And go where in this nightmare?

Just then, he sensed a change in the water flow. Turning at lightning speed, his guts churned, made him expect to find a blockage in the passage behind him.

No; there was light *shimmering* through the doorway. Becker kicked toward it. When he reached the bunk room, two chambers down, he paused, took hold of a railing and surveyed the way ahead.

Particles of light-colored murk swam about like plankton, trying hard to conceal the big secret behind the source. Becker killed his own light and instantly the foreground cleared of blinding flecks and meaningless bubbles.

He soon picked out the huge, gaping blast hole in the hull of the adjoining submarine chamber. It pulsated irregularly, the shadows it created nonsensical and macabre.

You have nothing to lose. Investigate. To Hell with the world.
It's already sent you there.

-82-

<u>Void From Our Time - Demon Vortex</u>

Twenty-two…twenty-three…twenty-four.

Coleman tried to wipe the sweat from his brow and cursed when his shaking fingers tapped the underside of the desk he was under. He hadn't made himself count that way since the time…

He couldn't remember since when. Not that it mattered now. What *did* matter was the breathing he could hear getting fainter and fainter outside.

It'll double back in a minute. You better get away while you can. Get back to the others by way of the stairs – if you can find them.

That old lady is the only hope anymore.

Through the gap beneath the panel between the desk legs, he could make out the dark landscape and the only route to a chance for freedom. The thing's breathing was at its faintest now. Coleman reckoned it was at the far end of the concourse.

He could not bear to have his life ripped from him by a dumb animal… no, not dumb – it *knew* things… *evil* things! It was truly evil. An animal would be knocking metal trash cans and chairs over all the way since it had first seen him.

This thing wants to kill you… for you to die and be dead…not to give it simple sustenance.

He had his foot outside the safety of the desk for barely a second when it hit him.

Of course... ...diversion. He needed a *decoy*.

Coleman reached up to the desk's surface, gently closing his fingers around what felt like a fax machine and pulled it closer a few inches by its cords. As he crouched round to study it in the near blackness, he thought of Leah and sensed a sudden urge to....

Die?

No. That wasn't her. That was *not* her whom he'd seen. *They* were doing this just to screw him up, to make him fearful. They were Fear Feeders, that's what they were.

When he'd undone the input jacks and power cable, Coleman waited, wound up with all his stamina then hurled the machine into the silent void ahead and spun round to sprint back for the elevator lobby. He heard it transform the visage of a neighboring monitor into a thousand shards as he ran, ran, ran.

Something was wrong. No, he *had* fine-tuned his hearing to detect anything above his panting and panic sounds... And he could hear nothing now over his footfalls.

He was in the elevator area before he could bear to look into the black expanse behind.

Nothing back there: no yellow eyes, no growling, nor...

He wheeled round, anticipating twin sets of claws raking his neck before the liquid fire melted his eyes.

Nothing that way, either.

Coleman hadn't noticed the alcove door before. As he tiptoed toward it through the matchwood and scratched fragments from the other double doors, he thought about the chances of retrieving his gun from further in there for a crazy second.

No. It's a trap. Bullets did shit all anyway, didn't they?

You have to try, though.

Why bother? The world has given up already.

His fingertips ran over the finish of the door, probing for vibrations, heat - anything that could betray the terrible presence. Opening it, Coleman drew back from the gap and held his breath.

The pressure in his chest was agonizing.

Please let it end now; forget you're CIA - you're a man and no man can live with this kind of fear.

Before he stepped inside the stairwell, Coleman took one last look behind him, hoping that anything that could pass for a weapon lay within reach.

Not a hope in Hell. You're on your own... On your own.

Entering the blackness, he ran his hand over the light switch plate and bit his lip.

Dead.

Like YOU!

In the dark, as he made his way up the first few steps, he thought he could actually see the silhouette of Jurgen Ganz's head somewhere ahead: somehow a deeper, deadlier shade than even the jet black all about him.

Coleman reached into his pockets when he made it to the first landing. He cursed when his fingers confirmed the uselessness of their task.

His cigarettes and lighter were not there.

Demons can see in the dark. You're dead.

'Iyur Setot' his mind spat at him as he stepped, each step very nearly a stumble. *'Iyur Setot.'*

-83-

Void From Our Time - San Diego, California

Irene knew her convulsions were soon going to culminate in a heart attack. Her bubble's walls had smoked over now; there could be no telling where the thing once called Nathan was.

She was hardly aware she was screaming until she felt the trembles on the floor with her fingers.

She could see that the Ancient Kings were starting to get through from the Outside. In one sequence, she saw their accursed bodies drop through the sky's upper limits; in the following, demons trying to push through from flames; in another, demons trying to break through the sea-bed to emerge.

It took her many moments to think beyond them; to try to cast that last bit of her brain that was undamaged back to a different era, to a time when she was stronger.

Her tarot deck was in the pouch she kept under her skirt. Reaching for it, she could feel the repulsion between fingertips and cards. Checking the walls of her force field for interference from her assailant, she found herself quivering hard.

'I'm going to read you your cards,' she whispered to them as she shuffled. 'We'll see how much of a future you'll have now.'

She was five cards into the spread when the crackling sound came from behind. Turning, Irene saw Nathan's grinning face and hands protruding through the wall of her energy bubble.

They held there for a matter of seconds before…before…

Nathan's face melted, running like wax down over the beast's head beneath it before sizzling away in flames. The flesh of Nathan's fingers fell away from their bones to show talons like a bear's.

Irene had the incantation halfway read as the beast pushed more of its top half through the field. She could see the intent in its eyeless sockets now, the despise and the wrath.

No. The banishing was no good. The text it had come from was gone, useless now. Even if she could recall all the words, this creature – a lesser demon sent by its masters from afar - was somehow now immune.

She dropped her gaze to the tarot cards and continued to deal them out, hoping against hope that her old skills could save them now.

-84-
<u>Void From Our Time - Demon Vortex</u>

Billy Reynolds took one last look into the whirlpool now so far below them before he turned to join his brother in their last battle. 'Oh my God, our guns?!'

'Forget that, Billy!'

Dave Reynolds undid his belt, shut his eyes for a moment and pressed his thumb tip against the prong before he gathered enough of himself to find the eyes on the form that was flitting up from below on gargantuan, bat-like wings. 'I'm going to murder this thing.'

Of course he was; Helen and Raina were not going to be deprived of him so cheaply. Dave could somehow now feel them and their love being compressed between himself and the body of that thing as it thundered upward to destroy them.

He grabbed his brother by the shoulder and pulled him closer, noticing how Billy's feet were moving.

Solid. Somehow, they weren't floating any longer... like an invisible ledge had manifested itself underfoot in only the previous few moments. 'Billy, take off your belt and get ready.'

'Oh Jesus!'

'Billy!'

Billy began to cry. 'I can't die... I can't *watch you die.....oh no! Noooo!*'

Dave decked him at medium force. *'Do it! Take that belt off and get re-'*

Billy flew backwards from the impact. When he picked himself up, he saw his brother gripped in a death struggle. He screamed and charged at the exposed side of the demon.

Its structure reminded him of a creature he'd seen years before in a movie about aliens.

Its stench nearly knocked him out when he made full contact and began to pound away at the cold exoskeleton, hammering hopelessly.

-85-
Void From Our time - Demon Vortex

Airspeed: 1347 kilometers per hour. Altitude: forty-two thousand meters, rising.

Olentiev shook his head and pounded his fists against the console. This could not be happening. All around him in the pillar of fire he saw them dropping, falling to Earth: giant, man-shaped life-forms, many with scaled skin, some with hard, insect-like body parts.

They seemed to be ignoring him, their faces blurred mostly by the speed at which he was soaring by them. In spite of the destruction of Askenskaya's aircraft many precious seconds ago now, crazy flames were burning up the skies, all the way up to a very dark object, high above him.

A trap, he figured as he tried to slow the Fulcrum.

His forehead was sweating heavily, stinging his plum-sized eyes as he gazed and gazed.

The canopy would melt soon if this heat kept up.

After five seconds of toggling, Olentiev killed his afterburners and fell back to 600 kilometers an hour.

The nose of the MiG dipped and presented him with a *sea* of falling demonic bodies. Yanking the plane hard to the right, Olentiev hazarded a hope then engaged the machine gun to cut a swathe.

The heat was making his head sway now. Outside on the nose cone, he could see the skin of his craft starting to buckle in curling, blackened platelets.

When he straightened up and released the trigger, he counted them....

Three, four, five, six, seven of the falling creatures jerking their heads to face him, hissing, some raising claws to threaten him with a serrated-edged, bloody death.

One of the last beings he had hit had wings. He zipped past it once more, noting its flaps intensifying so it could catch him up for combat.

Finding the edge of the vertical fire-stream, Olentiev prepared himself to loop back and attack the abomination with....

The LEDs that had forbidden his accessing control of the needle missiles and the heat-seekers were unlit. Olentiev had his fingers on the heat-seeker's priming switch when he felt a force keep them from flicking it.

He closed on the creature at just under six hundred kph. The targeting scanner was not giving him a blip to lock on to.

Olentiev counted down until he could feel the straightness of the missile's path to be.

He could see the flower-like design on the creature's chest when he pressed the first missile free and raised his nose by several degrees.

'Eat death,' he muttered when he saw the explosion below detach the being into triple-figure sections. The uppermost components rained against the Fulcrum's canopy and hull when he passed through and out towards the far side of the fire-stream.

Somehow, he knew what had to be done now.

Yet somehow, too, the fire-stream trapping him seemed to be getting much darker with demons…

Or is that something far worse up there? his heart jabbed to his mind as his eyes drifted up.

-86-
<u>Void From Our Time - Demon Vortex</u>

Steam. Beneath the columns of gray bubbles, Becker found he was watching lava flow between the cracks in the seabed just outside the submarine's hull.

But wait, what's th-

Claws.

Get out of here.

No; I can't move my legs.

Get out of here now!

He remained frozen to the jagged blast hole in the hull, his eyes and heart exchanging pulses in insane, stroke-provoking conversations.

The first tentacles were starting to rip through the sand on the seafloor. Becker spent a couple more moments transfixed, observing them as they lashed out over the bed, uprooting the odd rock from its hitherto eternal rest.

Get back! his mind screamed. *Now!*

The light was getting brighter. Before he scurried back into the sub, Becker wrenched his stare to take in the vista above him.

Bubbles; the steam bubbles and smoke had made a pillar that went upward for what looked like miles.

Another fear flashed in his mind… the pressures at this depth. He was back in the torpedo room now, his hands raking the surfaces of the torpedo tubes, his feet kicking up dirt and bones as he stumbled beneath the weight of the dark blue water.

Bones. His grandfather had gone down in his sub: could this be…

Becker could already feel the pressure change long before the tentacle burrowed through the passageway and into his chamber. Taking refuge against the wall, he let the wish to be dead and blessedly free of this vanish into the back of what was left of his mind.

He had to fight.

-87-
Void From Our Time - Demon Vortex

'What the Hell?!'

Dave Reynolds clutched his bloodied throat and fell by his brother's feet.

Billy had seen the beast bend back in pain when the object had struck.

That object had been Kenny Piper.

Before he could kick the creature in the groin, Billy saw it turn on Piper, now a dazed heap on the invisible ledge floor, his eyeglasses cracked.

The spines on the demon's back bit into Billy when he leaped onto it and began a series of half-nelson jerks.

On the fourth tug, he felt the demon quake.

Billy could only watch as the huge streak of fire flew out and smashed into Piper's hapless form, blast frying it like a rack of ribs.

Snorting brimstone, the demon swiveled on its hooves to hunt out supplementary prey. Rotating with it, Billy caught sight of his brother rising from the surface, shaking his head like a downed boxer and screamed.

It was then when Billy remembered the medallion Irene had given him. Ripping it from his neck, he curled his fist over it then smashed down on the thing's head, raining blow after blow after blow.

-88-

Void From Our Time - Demon Vortex

Coleman believed that he was on the landing of the nineteenth floor now. Somehow, the dark was going from jet black to a blue, hazy texture as he ascended step by agonizing step.

Too slow: you're way too slow!

Screw yourself. I'm trying here.

His ears were tired from listening for anything beyond the slapping of his soles on the vinyled-over concrete. But there had been nothing, yet… no signs of the hunter.

He went up another floor before he noticed the humming. He'd heard that before somewhere…in some movie, a long time ago. Poking his head over the railing, he looked up and found the blue haze had given way to blue flashes a little further up.

It was like lightning coming under the gap in the door on that landing above.

That landing. Using the brighter flashes for illumination, Coleman started to run up towards it. If he could just get to the others and help them now…

He barely had time to wheel round on the third last step when he heard the other sound. In fact, Rick Coleman found he had no time to even yell when he managed to turn and face the hated predator from below… the thing he had dared to forget for just a few seconds.

-89-
<u>Void From Our Time - San Diego</u>

Irene closed her eyes and braced herself for the invading demon's death blow. She'd seen that most of it had torn through the bubble with her high peripheral vision.

Its breath was raging, warm, hissing at her whilst uttering words either from another dimension or words not heard since the time of the Sumerians.

She froze long before she would have completed the tarot card spread on the tiny patch of floor before her.

There was no time now. The demons' servitor would be through in a matter of seconds. Her side channel of energy that had been staving off the demons' mind attacks was ebbing.

No. She could actually feel that bit of her mind *dying* now.

You've come to the end, old duck. You've tried and you have failed. There is no way to combat these things.

Let the Lord take you in His loving arms now and be finished with it.

She had just unclenched her eyes and pictured her long dead mother when...

No. Still impossible... But wait, *maybe* she could! Why hadn't she thought of that *before*? The cards were more than a weapon or a tool. They were knowledge beyond all things knowable.

Claws as sharp as dockers' hooks raked at her cheek, plowing dragging, stinging furrows.

The pain galvanized Irene. Of course; *of course!* It might just work. It would have to be a ramshackle Celtic Cross card spread, but...

The demon's eyes were scanning her deck worriedly. With one hand, Irene snatched the loose cards back onto the pile; with the other, she dug deep into her necklace bunch.

The crucifix was tarnished, small but...but...

The thing shrieked when she waved it before its face. 'Avaunt. Avaunt. Stay at your place. Stay at your place!'

The abomination froze. She took a last glance at it in the bubble wall before she pulled the crucifix up to her chin and clenched its chain in her mouth.

Please Lord; please keep it there in Thine prison.

She was reading her *own* Tarot future now. Cups...so many cups.

Then, the six of swords... Stress or pressure.

Death came up; a change....

Seven of swords... Treachery or deceit.

Irene proceeded until she turned up the eight of Cups.

Hang in there... don't be disillusioned, she demanded.

Crackle

Irene was two cards shy of the spread's completion when she looked up to find the demon leering anew, jaws slavering over the death it had designed for her.

'Avaunt. *Avaunt!*'

No. Don't exclaim. Your fear lends it strength.

Her eyes force fed her the sight of its chest and some of its abdomen protruding through her bubble wall. The smoky texture was light, milky around the outline.

Irene was not aware whether her fingers had turned over the last card or last card but one as the slime-coated, hot claws closed about her face.

She screamed once and prepared herself for the End.

-90-
Void From Our Time - Demon Vortex

Becker was drawing his breaths slowly. His military training was playing out like a renegade bit of software, triggered by a failure in the situation.

He had himself pressed motionless against the wall beside the rust-peaked torpedo breech, confused.

Not afraid. No....he wasn't sure the strength for that existed in him now.

Fear taketh power from the Fearer to bestoweth it to the Fearee.

Fucker, he thought, *YOU WON'T HAVE ANY MORE OF ME!*

Time and again, the tentacle brushed over his waist and arms. A hundred tiny hooks scraped him, robbing yet more energy from his dying body.

Dying… It wasn't the same as Death.

The idea of dy*ing* chilled Carl Becker. He couldn't....just could not let go.

Forget it. This feeling is just a silly spark: you have no hope.

Where there's life, there's hope...

You could blow this thing back to Outer Hell that way, he thought as he touched the torpedo tube's breech lever. *If this thing still has live ammunition...*

Becker's lips moved gently about his mouthpiece as he opened the breech and began to wonder how he might invite the tentacle tip to a nice new torpedo tube home.

Please, he dared to hope... *Please....*

-91-
Void Form Our Time - Demon Vortex

Olentiev closed on the ship above him. The flames about him were dying now, permitting huge stretches of matt blackness - the color that truly *did* exist at that absurd altitude - to wash over his plane.

He locked onto it with his targeting scanner.

Just over three kilometers away - *up* from him now.

UP - Into the Heavens, a piece of HELL, he thought...praying to the old, once-forbidden deity his parents had had to renounce.

The structure was huge and rectangular. Olentiev's wounded brain reported that it could be close to a kilometer from end to end.

'I have you!' he muttered. 'I have you!'

He lifted his shade visor to examine the underside of the ship.

There - close to dead center, a half-globe protrusion.

He locked on, waited then engaged his last needle missile, then he watched...watched its path wobble, soon overshooting to vanish into a tiny ochre speck against the distant craft underbelly.

'No!'

Before he thumbed the console to engage the last heat-seeker, Olentiev allowed the rest of the prayer he'd begun to spin out.

Target - one and a half kilometers away and closing... Airspeed *critical* now.

At this speed, half of that distance now spelt the point of no return to pull a perpendicular yaw and avert collision or destruction from a residual heat-seeker detonation.

To survive through this...

Olentiev punched the launch button once then twice then once again.

To survive through this....

-92-

Void From Our time - Demon Vortex

Billy bit his lip and jerked the demon's neck to the side once more.

Dave was up and crawling off to the left, barely three body-lengths away. Billy felt his vocal chords tensing again, about to bawl a warning when he traversed with the head while it tried locking onto his brother.

Remember what Irene told you: don't let them feed from you. No fear.

No fear.

'No fear,' he gasped. 'No fear. No fear. Help me now then,' he whimpered as the thing's head stopped rotating and its mouth roared.

-93-

Void From Our Time - Demon Vortex

The copper taste in Coleman's mouth was gushing. Now he was reaching for the large cylinder that had nearly snapped his back in two vertically when the beast had tossed him.

Gunless. In the dark, as his good arm took the weight of the fire extinguisher, Coleman felt truly naked.

When the vibrations of the approaching footsteps thudded their hardest at him, he heard the *click* of the catch.

Carmichael's sneering countenance appeared in his mind.

'You're not taking me alive, you...are...*not!*' Coleman spat when he saw the eyelids part to reveal twin ovals of fire staring at him confidently. 'Not alive.'

Coleman had the nozzle aimed at the flame-edged eyes when the *last plan* hit him.

The creature's jaws opened wide just then.

Please, please let this work, he prayed as he flung the tank into its gaping maw.

-94-

Void From Our Time - San Diego, California

'Avaunt...avaunt... ...avaunt,' Irene gasped.

Suddenly, the fingers lightened about her throat, allowing her to hear the sizzling sound.

The demon screamed and flew back on its haunches, a ruby cross smoldering on its vermilion breast.

Irene tore at her necklace and pushed the crucifix right up to the side of its face. She leant over the completed tarot spread so far that her shins covered half the cards.

'Avaunt...avaunt...avaunt...'

The last she saw before the images came to her was the orange smoke rising in a pillar before her.

Now she saw fear in the sky from a pilot, fear in the flames from two brothers, fear in a building from a lover and fear beneath the waves from a warrior.

Air, Fire, Earth, and Water.

'Banish them,' she heard the voice of her Tarot cards say. 'Banish them back to *Hell!*'

-95-
<u>23rd April, San Diego, California, New Earth</u>

'Who...who...My God.'

'This is who we owe it all to,' Billy Reynolds gasped as he pointed Irene out to the water-drenched, pale man with the slightly Teutonic accent.

There were five men and one woman around her when Irene awoke. The inside fingers of her right hand were sore, some nicked by the card edges she found herself gripping. Somehow, they hurt more than her gouged cheek and her crushed psyche.

She raised her eyes to find two of the men were backing away from her. The helmeted one – the Russian - was gibbering, crossing himself while the wet one turned, started to hobble for the doorway, a belt line of blood etched onto his pants, thin streams of red threading down from his ear lobes to his shoulders.

'Fear nothing, my friends. It....it-'

'It's over, isn't it?' Billy Reynolds gasped. He was sitting in a ball, hugging his legs close to his chest, next to his silent, battered brother. Dave Reynolds was moaning now, lamenting the destruction of his hapless work colleagues.

'I think it is, young one. You foreign gentlemen have seen my likeness on others, no? Let me assure you now that those were under the control of the demons. Their agents had done their best to send you the most fearful kinds of abominations... perhaps even the ones controlling you – giving you orders.'

Olentiev nodded. His smattering of English allowed it to finally latch in his damaged mind. Becker nodded also, although his understanding keyed solely off the acceptance that these calm-looking faces around him meant that the time of doom was done.

'We destroyed them,' Coleman said, nodding. 'I got that bastard to chew on that extinguisher so hard his head blew-'

'Locked out,' she corrected. 'Just... only locked out. You can't *destroy* the Ancient Kings.'

'Then they'll...they'll come back one day, won't they?' Coleman ventured. 'If another one like Ganz works the voodoo, we'll have to go through this *all over* again.'

'I don't think so,' said a second female voice behind him. Coleman turned his neck until it hurt to find Lippmann rising up from a crouch.

'You are crazy!' Becker yelled without being able to hear his voice. 'I had to lock one of those thing's arms inside a submarine. If that breech hadn't been loaded and the force on the torp strong enough, I would have never made it bleed and die!'

Lippmann's vapid expression survived. 'All I'm saying is I figure that, after all this, they likely won't try to *get through* the Earth's defenses again.'

She walked slowly over to the middle of the office concourse that had once been a laboratory to near where the benign old lady sat in front of a strange layout of Tarot cards.

Lippmann touched her own burnt blouse. 'They won't come back *from wherever they came from* now,' she said, rubbing her fingers over the stinging but intriguing cross-shaped mark between her upper breasts. 'It's time for *us* to live now.'

-96-

Transcript from CNN Headline News, 19ᵗʰ August

'Congress has approved a motion to ban sales of copies of the New Age title, the *Liber Fati*. President Failey has called for an unprecedented nation-wide outlawing of ownership of the text, which is suspected in connection with the onset of disasters last year that culminated in the destruction of the entire Tungus region of Russia.

(Show Senator James Dealey (D) Delaware)

"Collecting all copies of the book from private collections and individuals will prove next to impossible, even if amnesty drop-offs at police stations are facilitated. We don't even have a figure for how many copies there *are* in America and even if their being in America or not will make any real difference. Also, the type of individual likely to have purchased the *Liber Fati* is not the type of individual who is likely to participate in an operation in the National Interest. Catch Twenty-Two."

-97-

Transcripts from BBC News 24, 23<u>rd</u> September

'Authorities in America are on full alert for a second wave of terrorist strikes on FBI buildings. At least twenty-seven major American cities have been struck by blasts, each target an FBI headquarters or building where forensic work for the Federal Bureau of Investigation is conducted.

President Failey has invoked a clause which gives him the power to institute martial law throughout the USA.'

-98-

October 30th

The woman pulled her shawl tightly about her face as she staggered from the bus stop. The ancient town was greeting the onset of night with tired, dusty haze rising from the winds.

Her words, none of them in Arabic, began to run in a litany of 'must do this' and 'must go on'.

She was clutching her Xeroxes beneath her long, flowing robes as if they were a dying infant now. On, on through the dirt she paced, every now and then stopping to imbibe from her flask.

After an hour of trouncing over the desert plains, she found she could just make out the edges of the crater by the ebbing rays of the fallen sky disk. A streak of joy, or what she might have once understood as joy warmed her chest. She started running towards it.

The sky bore the sacred Seven Stars overhead, as appointed - *as demanded* by the rite. She pulled her ream of pages through the gap at the front of her robes and knelt by the rim of the crater, taking up the knife. Before she began the incantations, she rubbed the mark at her breast and cracked a smile.

'*Iyur Setot*, fools,' she mused gleefully then turned her head to look away to the western skies, up at the triangle of stars that made up the

Constellation of the Ram.

The Hamal star was cool now. 'Back to normal' they'd said Stateside. The same was true of that Siberian air hole now...or so *they* thought.

That hole had been punched *twice* before.......

The Gate would swing again this night. The world of men would not be ready to take a second dose of what had struck so soon.

A smile came to the woman's lips when she reckoned that the ancient crone would be too drained to fight again... and as for the shattered husks that had acted as her allies, well...

The smile cracked into the beginnings of cackling above the cursed, ancient pages of summoning.

'Tyur Setot!' its voice began when it deemed the laughter to be done.